THE WOMAN AT
1,000 DEGREES

THE WOMAN AT 1,000 DEGREES

HALLGRÍMUR HELGASON

TRANSLATED BY
BRIAN FITZGIBBON

ONEWORLD

A Oneworld Book

First published in Great Britain and Australia by Oneworld Publications, 2018

Originally published in Icelandic as *Konan við 1000°* by JPV útgáfa, 2011

Hardback ISBN 978-1-78607-169-9
Trade paperback (export) ISBN 978-1-78607-170-5
eBook ISBN 978-1-78607-168-2

This book has been translated with financial support from

 ICELANDIC LITERATURE CENTER

The line from Halldór Laxness's poem *Í landsýn* is taken from the collection *Kvæðakver*.
Reprinted with the permission of Forlagið.

Typeset by Fakenham Prepress Solutions, Fakenham, Norfolk NR21 8NN
Printed and bound in Great Britain by Clays Ltd, St Ives plc

Oneworld Publications
10 Bloomsbury Street
London WC1B 3SR
England

Stay up to date with the latest books,
special offers, and exclusive content from
Oneworld with our monthly newsletter

Sign up on our website
oneworld-publications.com

MIX
Paper from
responsible sources
FSC® C018072

AUTHOR'S NOTE

The Woman at 1,000 Degrees is a novel. It is partly based on events that actually occurred and people who lived and died, but it should be emphasised that the story is a work of fiction. Hans Henrik, Gudrún Marsibil and Herbjörg María are fictional characters. The author would therefore like to ask readers to show consideration for the models they may be based on and not confuse their real stories with the fates he has invented for them in this book.

History is factual, novels are fictional.

– HH

THE WOMAN AT
1,000 DEGREES

1

1929 Model

2009

I live here alone in a garage, together with a laptop and an old hand grenade. It's pretty cosy. My bed is a hospital bed and I don't need any other furniture except for the toilet, which is a real pain to use. It's such a long way to travel, all along the bed and then the same distance again over to the corner. I call it my Via Dolorosa and I have to totter across it three times a day, like any other rheumatic ghost. My dream is to be hooked up to a catheter and a bedpan, but my application got stuck in the system. There's constipation everywhere.

There aren't many windows here, but the world appears to me through my computer screen. E-mails come and go, and good old Facebook just keeps on going, like life itself. Glaciers melt, presidents darken and people lament the loss of cars and houses. But the future awaits at the end of the baggage reclaim carousel, slant-eyed and smirking. Oh yes, I follow it all from my old white bed, where I languish like a useless corpse, waiting to die or to be given a life-prolonging injection. They look in on me twice a day, the girls from the Reykjavík Home Care Services. The morning shift is a real darling, but the afternoon hag has cold hands and bad breath and empties the ashtray with a vacant stare.

But if I shut my eyes to the world, switch off the lamp above me, and allow the autumn darkness to fill the garage, I can make out the famous Imagine Peace Tower through a narrow window high up on the wall. Because the late John Lennon has now been turned into a pillar of light up here in Iceland, lighting up the black strait on long nights. His widow was kind enough to place him vertically in my line of vision. Yes, it's good to doze off to an old flame.

Of course, you could say I'm just vegetating in this garage like any other old vintage clunker that has run its course. I mentioned this to Gudjón one day. He and Dóra are the couple who rent me the garage at 65,000 kronur a month. Dear Gudjón laughed and declared I was an Oldsmobile. I surfed the net and found a photo of an Oldsmobile Viking, 1929 model. To be honest, I hadn't realised I'd grown so darn old. It looked like a glorified horse carriage.

I've been lying alone in this garage for eight years now, bedridden because of the emphysema that's plagued me for three times that long. The slightest movement cuts my breath away until I'm on the point of choking – not a pleasant feeling, *the discomfort of the unburied*, they used to call it in the old days. The result of decades of smoking. I've been sucking on cigarettes since the spring of 1945, when a warty Swede first introduced me to these wonders. And their glow still makes me glow. They offered me a mask with nasal tubes that was supposed to make it easier for me to breathe, but to get the oxygen cylinder they told me I'd have to give up smoking 'because of the fire hazard.' So I was forced to choose between two gentlemen: Nicotine, the Russian Count and Oxygen, the British Lord. It was an easy choice. Consequently, I draw my breath like a steam engine, and my voyages to the toilet remain my daily penance. But little Lóa likes going in there and I enjoy the tinkling music of her maiden's piddle. She's my help.

Oh, I'm rambling. When you've lived through a whole Internet of events, a whole shipload of days, it's hard to distinguish one thing from another. It all flows into one big muddle of time. Either

I suddenly remember everything at once or I remember nothing at all.

Oh yeah, and then our nation collapsed, been a year now. But it's all relative, of course. Dóra and the nurses assure me that the city is still standing. There are no visible signs of the crash in Reykjavík, unlike in Berlin when I roamed through it as a silly young lass, after its fall at the end of the war. And I don't know which is better – an overt crash or a covert one.

Personally, I revelled in the crash. Throughout the boom years I'd lain bedridden while the greed around me was devouring all my savings, so it didn't upset me to see them disappear into the bonfire, since by then I'd developed a slight indifference to money. We spend our entire lives trying to put something away for old age, but then old age arrives with no dreams of luxury beyond the ambition of being able to pee lying down. I won't deny that it would have been nice to shop around for some German toy boy and have him stand here, half-naked in the candlelight, declaiming Schiller to his old pillow hag, but apparently they've banned the flesh trade in our country now, so there's no point in bemoaning that. I've nothing left except a few weeks of life, two cartons of Pall Malls, a laptop and a hand grenade, and I've never felt better.

2

Feu de Cologne

2009

The hand grenade is an old Hitler's egg that I acquired in the last war. It's accompanied me over the rivers and fjords of my life, through all my marriages, thick and thin. And now, at last, would be the time to use it, had the seal not broken off many years ago, on a bad day in my life. But it's an uncomfortable way to die, of course, to embrace a firestorm like that and allow it to blow your head off. And to tell the truth, I've grown quite fond of my blessed little bomb after all these years. It would be sad if my grandchildren weren't able to enjoy it, in a silver bowl inside an heirloom cabinet.

Meine geliebte Handgranate is beautiful in its deceit, fits nicely in one's hand, and cools a sweaty palm with its cold iron shell crammed with peace. That's the really remarkable thing about weapons: although they can be unpleasant for those who get in their way, they provide their holders with a great deal of comfort. Once, many cities ago, I left my golden egg in a taxi and couldn't put my mind to rest until I'd recovered it, after countless frantic calls to the minicab office. The cabby hovered awkwardly on the stairs, trying to work it out.

'That's an old hand grenade, isn't it?'

'No, it's a piece of jewellery. Have you never heard of the Imperial Fabergé eggs?'

4

At any rate, for a long time I kept it in my jewellery box.

'What's that?' my charming sea bear Bæring once asked me, as we were about to set off for a ball.

'Perfume: *Feu de Cologne.*'

'Really?' the old sailor gasped in astonishment.

Men have their uses, but quick-witted they sure ain't.

And it never hurt to know that the hand grenade was there in my handbag when the night was over and some jerk wanted to take me home.

Now I keep it either in my bedside table or between my rotting legs, lying on the German steel egg like some post-war hen, in the hope of hatching some fire – something that is so sorely missed in this dreary thing that society has become, totally devoid of violence. It can only do people good to lose the roof over their head or to see their loved ones shot in the back. I've always had problems with people who've never had to clamber over dead bodies.

Maybe if I throw it on the floor it'll go off? Hand grenades love stone floors, I once heard. Yes, of course, it would be wonderful to exit with a bang and leave them to pick through the dust and debris in the hope of finding some morsels of my flesh. But before I explode, permit me to review my life.

3

Herra Björnsson

1929

I was born in the autumn of 1929, in a tin can of a house in Ísafjördur. And got saddled with the peculiar name Herbjörg María, which never suited me, nor itself for that matter. A blend of pagan and Christian strands that mixed like oil and water, and those sister elements still wrestle inside me.

Mum wanted to name me Verbjörg, after her mother, but Grandma wouldn't hear of it. It was too close to *verbúd*, the Icelandic word for 'fisherman's hut,' where she claimed people led wet, cold and miserable lives, and she cursed her own mother for naming her after such a shameful thing. Grandma Vera rowed seventeen fishing seasons between the little islands of Bjarneyjar and Oddbjarnarsker, winter, spring and autumn, 'in the rat-pissing rain they've invented in that briny hell of theirs, and it was even worse on land.'

My father suggested Herbjörg instead, and apparently my mother didn't hate him enough to disagree. Personally, I would have chosen the name of my maternal great-grandmother, the great Blómey Efemía Bergsveinsdóttir. She was the only woman to bear that name in the history of Iceland until the twentieth century, when, after lying in the island's soil for fifty years, she finally acquired two namesakes. One was a textile artist who lived in a dilapidated shack,

6

while the other Blómey, my little Blómey, who departed
a very young age but still lives on in the dearest realms o
and appears to me now and then in that strip of grass that ᴄeparates
dream from reality.

We should be baptised for death, just as we're baptised for life, and
allowed to choose the name that will appear on our gravestones for
all eternity. I can see it now: *Blómey Hansdóttir (1929–2009)*.

In those days no one had two first names. But just before I was
born, my dear and gifted mother had a vision: the Virgin Mary
appeared to her in a valley on the other side of the fjord and sat there
on a rock, about four hundred feet tall. For this reason her name was
added to mine, and of course, it must have brought some blessings
with it. At any rate, I have endured all the way to this peak of my
now-bedridden existence.

'María' softens the harshness of 'Herbjörg,' but I doubt that two
more different women have ever shared the same life. One sacrificed
her snatch to God, while the other devoted hers to a whole army of
men.

I was not permitted to be called *dóttir*, even though it is the right
and privilege of all Icelandic women to be known as 'daughter.'
Instead, I became a 'son.' My father's kin, sprinkled fore and aft
with ministers and ambassadors, had made their careers abroad,
where no one uses anything but surnames. And so the entire family
was nailed to the head of one man, forced to carry the surname of
Grandad Sveinn Björnsson (who later became Iceland's ambassador
to Denmark and eventually our first president). No other member
of the family was able to make a name for himself, and that was why
we failed to produce any more ministers or presidents. Grandfather
had reached the summit, and the role of his children and grandchildren was to go slithering down the slope. It's hard to preserve any
ambition when one is constantly on the way down. But naturally, at
some point, we'll reach the bottom, and then the only way forward
for the Björnsson tribe will be back up again.

At home I was always called Hera, but when, at the age of seven, I visited my father's family in Copenhagen with my parents, their maid had trouble pronouncing 'Hera' and called me either *Herre* (the Danish word for 'Mister') or *Den Lille Herre* ('The Little Gentleman'). My cousin Puti found this highly amusing and from then on never called me anything but Herra, the Icelandic word for 'Mister.' At first this teasing hurt me because I really did look a bit like a boy, but the nickname stuck, and I gradually became used to it. So that's how a miss became a mister.

In small-town Reykjavík I received considerable attention when I arrived back in the 1950s after a long stay abroad, a radiant young lady with lipstick and worldly ways, and the sobriquet was almost akin to a stage name: 'Other guests included Miss Herra Björnsson, granddaughter of Iceland's president, who draws attention wherever she goes on account of her open and cosmopolitan demeanour. Herra has just returned home to Iceland after a long stay in New York and South America.' So the unfortunate name produced some good fortune.

4

Hotel Iceland

1928

My father, Hans Henrik, was the firstborn of Sveinn Björnsson and his Danish wife, Georgía. He was born in 1908 and was therefore four years younger than my mother. She was the daughter of the aforementioned Verbjörg Jónsdóttir and a one-night stand named Salómon, who died in the storm of 1927.

Mum was always called Massa, although her name was actually Gudrún Marsibil Salbjörg Salómonsdóttir. She had been given the names of the three women who had helped Grandma the most. As Grandma liked to say, 'Since I'd been such a miser with my eggs, I had to give all the names to my Massa.' And it paid off. The three women had obviously fused in Mum to produce one good one. A triply good one. If Grandma Vera had been 'good and good,' as she would often say about things, then Mum was good and good and good. Then I came along and I wasn't even plain good. Somehow, I was totally devoid of that gentle, tireless spirit, kindness and innate sense of sacrifice associated with the Svefneyjar islands of Breidafjördur, where I spent my first seven years. I was a rotten mother and an even worse granny.

Mum and Dad met in Reykjavík, at a ball in the Hotel Iceland, or so the story goes. Maybe they'd met dead drunk up some blind alley and ripped each other's clothes off behind a rubbish bin. What do we know of our conception? Barely more than 'God' about the creation of the universe.

Massa was a lively girl from the West Fjords, who lodged at Mrs Höpfner's at Hafnarstræti 5. Dad had yet to finish high school, a pale, intelligent boy with timid eyes, a privileged child who lived south of the Reykjavík Lake, in the second-nicest house in town. Grandad Sveinn and Grandma Georgía had become an ambassadorial couple in Copenhagen by then, so Dad lived alone in the big house with the cook and a paternal aunt who was entrusted with the care of the boy and later blamed herself for how things turned out. Dad's best friend was Benni Thors, who lived next door in the finest house in the country. Benni's father was the wealthiest man in the land, and his brother Ólafur later became prime minister.

How could a boy with a background like my father's have fallen for a maid from the west who'd been conceived in a rowing boat under a glacier and, worse still, came with a past and was a whole four years older than he was? It was obviously no small feat to bring me into this world. But the Almighty Farmer Above, as my grandma used to call the Creator, had cast His nets and hooks over the town and lured my future father into a drinking binge with the Thors brothers that night, and they dragged him to the Hotel Iceland, chucking pebbles at the ducks on the way and chanting the latest hit song at the cops they passed – 'I scream for ice cream!' – while Mum was doing up her face in her Hafnarstræti loft and giggling herself into the mood with her friend Berta, the broad-faced daughter of a teacher.

As soon as they got into the place, Dad, of course, had to pee and got delayed in the toilets, cornered by a dead-drunk employee of the Icelandic Steamship Company, who immediately had something to say about Dad's father, who had founded the company: 'A great man, your father – great man. But how's it going? Doesn't he get bored there in the embassy?'

It unfolded as follows: when Dad finally stumbled out of the gents, the first thing he saw was a girl who had just sat down at a table with her friend – a thick-armed beauty from the Svefneyjar islands with bushy eyebrows, three men under her belt, and one at the bar.

Through the hubbub of the dance a blond cupid whispered her destiny into her ears, and she turned her head as Dad walked by. Her dark red lipstick singed itself into his soul, along with her black eyebrows and sea-pebble blue eyes. Her skin white, all so evenly white, like a calm white sea between those enchanted islands. He was clueless when it came to girls and always remained so, but he felt a comforting security as a kind of paralysis took hold of his heart, and a heavy blow from that Breidafjördur gaze struck his forehead.

Mum rolled her eyes at her friend, and they smirked: a typical Reykjavík lad.

Two glasses later he came staggering across the dance floor, like a small salmon elbowing its way through a shoal of herring, and stopped in front of her table. He planted himself there swaying slightly, and started acting stupid: pressing his arms against his sides and gesticulating with his right hand as he lifted his right leg and cackled, as if he were trying to mimic a goose trying to piss like a dog. He repeated this act at least three times, Mum endured my father's idiocy with that uniquely Icelandic forbearance and rewarded him three out of five possible smiles. (No woman can resist a man who is willing to make a fool out of himself for her. It's an unequivocal declaration of love.) She shifted back one seat just before an invisible hand struck the back of my father's neck and pushed him down on the chair she had just vacated.

'What's your name?' he asked, licking his lips.

'Huh?' The band was playing a lively polka.

'What's your name?' he repeated.

'Gudrún Marsibil.'

Mum exchanged a glance with Berta, who sat at the other end of the table, with her broad face and curly black hair.

'What?'

'Gudrún Marsibil.'

Mum cast another glance at Berta, who seemed amused, with her big chin and small, wide-set eyes.

'Gudrún Marsibil . . .' he parroted, releasing a drink-laden gasp, like a marathon runner who has finally crossed the finish line and hears his time, which he repeats to himself, before collapsing from fatigue: 'Gudrún Marsibil . . .'

'And you?'

'Huh?'

'What's your name?' There was a smirk in her voice.

'Me? I'm Jan Flemming. Jan Flemming Pedersen Havtroj.'

'Huh? Are you Danish?'

'Yes, I've got bloody Danish skin and I can't get rid of it!'

He pulled on the skin of his right wrist with the fingers of his left hand and let go of it, watching it snap back like elastic. He repeated this and then clawed at his arm and skull and finally slapped himself across the cheek: 'Just can't! Oh! Damned, damned Dane.'

'But you speak very good Icelandic.'

'Are you with someone?'

'Yeah.'

'And where is he?'

'Over there.'

'Where?'

'There.'

She pointed to a short man with a big head who was approaching the table with a bottle of wine and three glasses and a deadly serious expression.

'That guy with the forehead?'

'Yeah.' She laughed.

'What's his name?'

'Alli.'

'Alli?'

'Yeah, Adalsteinn.'

'Adalsteinn?'

'Yeah. Or just Steinn.'

'Or just Steinn? Can't he make his mind up? If I were your boyfriend . . . Your eyes are like stones. Two stones.'

'Oh yeah?'

'Can I have them?'

Everything that came out of him was unclear. He was totally hammered, with his fringe toppling over his forehead and shaking incessantly.

'Have them?'

'Yeah. Can I have them?'

And then something odd happened, something that can only be explained as a keystroke in the weaving of destiny.

'Well then.'

The short man with the big head had reached the table, where he put down the three glasses and bottle of wine. He muttered something that no one heard and sat in front of Mum. The stern eyes under his swollen forehead were like two fishermen's huts under a steep cliff. He filled the glasses clumsily, as if he had never offered anyone else a drink before.

'Alli, this is . . . Jan . . . er . . . Flemming, didn't you say? Is your name really Jan? Your name isn't Jan. You're Icelandic.'

'That's Björnsson. A bourgeois bastard,' said the forehead man in a voice that was strangely strong and deep. It flowed out of his frail body like a tow rope from a dinghy.

'Huh? Do you know him?' Mum asked.

'I thought you ducklings weren't allowed to drink.'

It was like the voice of a mountain piercing through a colony of screeching birds.

'Huh?' Dad exclaimed in his alcoholic haze, smiling internally at the two sea stones that Mum had just given him. Adalsteinn ignored him and raised his glass: 'Cheers!' Mum and Berta crashed glasses with him.

'Ah, there you are, man!' Benni Thors and his brother had reached the table and stood over them looking smug. 'You obviously don't know how to drink, man. You've got to drink yourself UP, not DOWN, as my brother says. C'mon. We're leaving.'

'I didn't know that the Danish princes of the fishing industry were allowed out of the palace gardens,' Adalsteinn quipped.

Benni Thors made to punch the man with the forehead, but his brother managed to halt his fist. Adalsteinn turned to Dad and proclaimed in his thunderous voice, 'A plague on both your houses!'

It was a curse we would long have to contend with, placed as it was by Steinn Steinarr, who would become the greatest Icelandic poet of the twentieth century, and who, if I remember correctly, was quoting Mercutio's dying words from Shakespeare's *Romeo and Juliet*.

The Thors brothers hoisted Dad from his chair and dragged him away. On the floor the dance was still in full swing; the tables were bustling with chatter and flirtations. Men hung at the bar, cheap paintings on the walls. Everything bore the marks of the present, from the décor to the fashions – October 1928 was a time like no other, and no one knew what awaited them outside those walls: sunny times, depression or war.

Dad followed his companions through the streets. Someone had mentioned a late-night party in Bergstadastræti, which turned out to be in a loft apartment that was obviously very small because the line stretched down the stairway and out onto the street. A snake of hat-clad boys loitered on the veranda on top of the steps, gulping down the night, as men are wont to do. It was a still and mild autumn night and their voices echoed across the treeless gardens. The Thors brothers joined in the medley, but Dad hung out on the street with his hands in his pockets, drunk as a skunk and as awkward as any Reykjavík kid throughout the ages, pondering on the Breidafjördur lass who had given him the two beautiful sea pebbles of her eyes.

The die had been cast. Yes, that much was sure. Mum preferred Dad to Steinn Steinarr, and chose the ambassador's son instead of a *Voyage without Promise*, a choice she was severely punished for, thus proving the old saying that he who forsakes a poet brings bad luck.

5

The Braces of Iceland

1929

For the Christmas of 1928, Hans went to Copenhagen, to stay with his parents and siblings. Granted a welcome break from the Reykjavík night life, which was no less wild back then than it was to become and will remain for centuries, the firstborn could fall asleep at midnight undisturbed and wake up at noon to the smell of hot chocolate, which Helle, good Helle, the Danish cook for the Icelandic ambassador and his wife, had the pleasure of making for the Björnsson boys. Dad's younger brothers, Puti and Henni, still lived with their parents and went to a Danish high school. They whiled away the time playing endless pranks on each other, but the carefree spirit in the gaze of the eldest had been glazed by the first autumn of his careless youth. A woman's pregnancy weighs heavily on a man.

In addition to the Christmas food sent from Iceland, Dad had received a letter written from an attic at Hafnarstræti 5. And after New Year, the twenty-year-old blond with the dark eyebrows walked into his father's office (in those days all men of stature also kept offices at home, though they looked more like small panelled chapels, where numbers and phone calls were venerated) to inform him of a certain incident that had occurred in Iceland earlier that winter, a certain incident, yes, mishap even, a certain thing that carried a certain weight, which could only grow heavier with time. He muttered the girl's name and then ended his speech by making a vague rotating gesture with the index finger of his right hand, presumably to symbolise the future course of events. Grandad Sveinn removed his glasses and slipped his thumb behind his braces, just above the waistline of his trousers. These were Iceland's braces on foreign soil.

'I see. And who is her family?'

Damn it, although this was the first question that all Icelandic fathers had asked their offspring about their children-in-law since the First Settlement, it caught Dad completely off guard. In fact he'd never thought about it. And it proved the classic aphorism that a young man never thinks further than the jet of his sperm. He just about remembered that the girl was some Salómon's daughter and that her mother was some old woman from some island somewhere. He wasn't even sure she was altogether human; she could have been the offspring of some obscure tribe that dwelled on a remote Icelandic skerry, a cross between elves, seals and flatfish.

'Erm . . . I don't know.'

'You don't know?'

'Er . . . no.'

And now the ambassador was silent. Silent long enough for his son to realise what he'd done; it was as if he'd invited his father to a wild Charleston dance in his very own office, in broad daylight, just like the wild one that he himself had danced with that bloody island girl on the night I was conceived, a girl who, on top of everything, was called Massa. She might just as well have been called Massive! So low class! God forbid that the old man should ever find out her name. And to think his father had gone all the way to Copenhagen to find a wife, who bore the dignified name of Georgía, and now he was sitting here as the country's primary representative in a sumptuous residence under a twelve-foot ceiling, with an extra six feet in case the ambassador of Iceland suddenly needed to jump higher than his own height, like Gunnar of the Sagas. The sordid island girl had obviously been raised in a pathetic single-room, chimneyed tussock that could probably have fitted into their front dining room without even having to raise the crystal chandelier. No. Yes. No. This was disgraceful. My father burst into a sweat as he sat in front of his father, who was still silent. Except for a sigh, a solemn snort. The ambassador remained silent for a whole seven seconds until he said, 'Well, my dear son . . .'

No, my good father. Just forget it. This is just . . . It's nothing, this is just a child, just one little life . . . no one needs to know about that.

Dad stood up and walked through the wrong door into his father's wardrobe, only to be confronted by pressed shirts with stiff collars, Iceland white, and behind them the famous uniform, the gold-lined jacket that my aunt had designed for Grandad Sveinn so that he could stroll past the king of England. Hans Henrik turned crimson and said agitatedly, 'No, it's . . . it's nothing,' before he found the right door.

'It's nothing.' That's how I was ushered into this world.

This was followed by difficult months in the young man's life. He headed back to Reykjavík, where he lived a double life, peppered with small lies, until the moment of farewells came in the spring, the *moment of betrayal*, when it was Dad's turn to be silent until Mum understood.

She boarded the mail boat with a drooping head, while Dad travelled south across the moorlands into the straits. The evening sun shone on the young man's tears as he followed the coast from the Raudará River back to town. Across the sun-bathed bay he spotted the slowly shrinking boat, and beyond the mountain range a few clouds hovered, like smoke signals from the islands that slept beyond them.

Mum never spoke of her nervous breakdown, not to me at any rate, but as the five-month-old tenant inside her womb, I wasn't spared the consequences and have been in therapy ever since as a result. No, I'm lying now; what a cow I am.

Shortly afterwards she appeared like all her foremothers before her, pregnant on the home pier, and carried me under her apron for the whole of that summer until she was packed off on a boat to the west to give birth to me. But I'm not lying when I say that I came enraged into this world in the house of her father's parents, screeching at all the misery I had caused and announcing a world depression, a prophecy that proved accurate twenty days later, when the famous crash occurred on Wall Street. That same autumn my father was admitted to the law faculty of the university like any other incurable love hen. The summer after that, he was dispatched to Vejle, Denmark, for further healing, to Grandma Georgía's paternal uncle, who owned a small pharmacy there with thousands of tiny drawers, and was supposed to teach Dad Danish bookkeeping and the art of courting well-bred girls.

6

Lóa

2009

Well then. Here she comes, Lóa, my little dung flower. Like a white rose out of the morning darkness.

'Good morning, Herra, dear. How are you today?'

'Oh, spare me the niceties.'

The grey light of day has only just begun to break. And a grey day it'll be, like all its brethren. *Daggry*, the Danes call it.

'Have you been awake for long? Had a look at the news?'

'Oh yes. It's still tumbling, the rubble of the crash . . .'

She takes off her coat, shawl and hat. And sighs. If I were a randy lad with a sparkling soul, I'd do myself the favour of marrying this girl. For she's goodness and gentleness personified. And her cheeks are a heavenly red. The red-cheeked ones never deceive us. I, on the other hand, was pale with deceit from the very start, and now I sit here, yellow as a corpse in a coffin-white nightshirt.

'Aren't you hungry?' Lóa asks me as she turns on the light in the kitchen alcove, pecking her beak into the shelves and cupboards. They are visible on the starboard side of my bed-wide ship. 'Porridge as usual, I suppose?' She says this every morning when she bends down to the small refrigerator that Dóra gave me, which sometimes keeps me awake with its chilling murmur. It's got to be said, she does have a bit of a big ass, little Lóa, and legs like forty-year-old birch trunks. That's probably why she never gets laid, poor little thing, and still lives with her mother, childless. Who can fathom men? Letting all that goodness and beauty pass them by? And all that soft, smooth skin.

'Well, what have you got to say for yourself? What did you do over the weekend? Any "how's-your-father" to report?' I ask, as I fumble on the laptop's keyboard and take a deep breath. That's a lot of words for an emphysema patient.

'Huh?' she asks, a blue-and-white milk carton in her hand, with that idiotic expression she so often has.

'Yes, did you go out anywhere? To cheer yourself up?' I ask without raising my eyes. I could swear I'm developing a death rattle in my voice.

'Out on the town, you mean? No. I was just helping my mother. She's changing the curtains in the living room. And then on Sunday – yesterday, that is – we went to visit Grandma.'

'You've got to think of yourself, too, Lóa.' I pause for breath before continuing. 'You mustn't waste your youth on an old hag like me. The breeding season will be over before you know it.'

I'm so fond of her that I inflict this torture on my speech organs, throat and lungs. The dizziness that follows is like a swarm of flies behind my eyes before they all kamikaze on my optic nerves, crashing against them with their leaden wings. Oh, heavens above.

'Breeding season?'

'Yes. No, Jesus, has he answered me?'

'Who?'

'My Aldon from Australia.'

'Aldon?'

'Yes, that's his name. Ah, now I've really got him going.'

'You've got so many friends,' she says as she starts to do the washing.

'Yes, well over seven hundred.'

'Huh? Seven hundred?'

'Yes. On Facebook.'

'Are you on Facebook? I didn't know. Can I see?'

She leans over me with all her fragrance as I summon up my page from the magic world of the net.

'Wow. Nice picture of you. Where was it taken?'

'In Baires. At a ball.'

'Baires?'

'Yes, Buenos Aires.'

'It says here that you've got a hundred and forty-three friends. You said seven hundred.'

'Yeah, that's just me. I've got all kinds of identities.'

In my mischief I've borrowed names, including that of Linda Pétursdóttir, who was Miss World in 1988. Bóas, my male nurse, who has gone abroad to study, created the e-mail address for me: lindapmissworld88@gmail.com. That one brings me plenty of good stories that shorten my long, dark autumn nights.

'Lots of identities on Facebook? Is that allowed?'

'Nothing in this world isn't allowed, in my opinion.'

'Huh?' she chirps before returning to the kitchen alcove. It's funny how good it feels to be near people who are working. It brings out the aristocrat in me. Half of me came from the sea and half from a palace, and because of that I soon became a leg spreader. My aristocratic Danish paternal grandmother was a first-class slave master, although she was also pretty hardworking. Before every gala dinner she would dance around the banqueting hall from noon to night, with one cigarillo in her mouth and another in her hand, trying to remember everything and get the seating arrangements right. Nothing could be missing, nothing out of place. Otherwise our land and people might have faced ruin. A fishbone getting stuck in the American ambassador's throat would have thrown the Marshall Plan into jeopardy. She knew perfectly well that the negotiations meant next to nothing. '*Det hele ligger på gaffelen!*' she'd say in Danish – it all hangs on the end of the fork!

Had it not been for Grandma Georgía, Grandad would never have become president – and someone should have told him that. She was the perfect lady: gave everyone, prince or pauper, a sense of well-being in her presence and treated all men equally, from the local bum to Eisenhower himself.

Three cheers for the political wisdom of those days, which chose that couple to represent the newborn republic in 1944, he an Icelander, she a Dane. It was a courteous gesture towards the old master race. Although we'd divorced the Danes, we still wore the ring.

7

Svefneyjar

1929

As I mentioned, I was born in Ísafjördur, on 9 September 1929. Mum
had been sent away, out of public view, to give birth to the one whom
nobody wanted to see and who should never have existed: me. There
was a minimum time delay set on entering my father's respectable
family, so Mum and I spent the first seven years alone together in
the Svefneyjar islands, where Mum worked as a maid in the home of
Eysteinn, a farmer, and his wife, Lína.

Lína was the sweetest of women, sturdily built and buxom, always
with some verse on her lips, but with a rather high-pitched voice. She
had a soft heart but incredibly strong arms, as women did in those
days, and over time she developed wooden legs from arthritis. She
helmed the large house like a sea captain, with one eye on the waves
and the other on the stove. To Mum, she was like a mother because,
although Grandma possessed many good qualities, maternal warmth
wasn't one of them. By the will and whim of the Creator, Grandma
had ended her life's voyage in Svefneyjar, although she didn't live in
the house, but in an old boat shed along with three other women.
Mum and I, on the other hand, dwelt in Lína's fiefdom.

Eysteinn had clear-cut features, a downy beard, sea-red cheeks
and eyes as calm as a tranquil bay. He had bulky hands and broad

shoulders and, with the passing of the years and the swelling of his belly, he used a walking stick. He was chirpy in the mornings but pigheaded in the evenings; amiable at home but mulish when it came to contracts or anything to do with 'foreign affairs.' He was renowned for having kicked some Danish land surveyors off the island when they tried to move the southernmost skerry on his land three yards to the south.

He was a 'good and good man,' Grandma used to say. She was of Breidafjördur stock on both sides and had made hay on more than a hundred islands. She always repeated her compliments twice. 'Oh, that one's fine and fine,' she would say of a boiled sweet or a labourer. Grandma was a hundred years old when I was born and a hundred years old when she died. A hundred years old for an entire century. Baptised by the sea and hardened by trawling, no man's daughter, and married to Iceland, mother of my mother and eternal heroine of my thoughts. Verbjörg Jónsdóttir. Soon I will meet her, in age and rage, and knock at her door. 'Oh, is that you, my darling little dung cake?'

Well, I'll be darned if I haven't started looking forward to dying.

Yes, I enjoyed seven blissful years in Breidafjördur until my father recovered from his amnesia and remembered he had a daughter and wife in this part of the Icelandic coast. My childhood was sprinkled with islands. Islands full of rowdy sailors and seaweed-eating cattle. Sun-bright, grass-yellow islands, sea-beaten by the gales on all sides, though in my memory it is always dead calm.

They say that he who has visited all the islands of Breidafjördur is a dead man because many of those islands are buried underwater. And it can probably be said that, even though they seem innumerable at high tide, they're even more innumerable at low tide. This applies to so many things in life that are hard to count. How many men did I have? How many times did I fall in love? Every remembered moment is an island in the depths of time, a poet once wrote, and if

Breidafjördur is my life, then these islands are the days I remember now, as I go chugging between them on my boat of a bed, with this trendy new outboard motor they call a laptop.

Chug-a-chug-a-chug.

8

A Thousand Fathoms

2009

But I'm no sailor, I'm no captain, and now I sink into the depths of my quilt, the downy-soft, ice-cold depths, deathly blue and breathless, where drowned sailors, women and the great poet go about their business on the flatfish-covered bottom. Dear bottom dwellers, look, I'm sinking now with all my load, sails and oars. With all my lies.

I squint my eyes and can hear bubbles of air coming out of me. The wig slides off my small head and turns into an unusually solid jellyfish, waving its tentacles in front of the cod and haddock, while the lanugo on my head flutters like famished plankton and the hospital pyjama bottoms swell up to my groin, exposing the horror of fleshless legs: the skin on them flutters like fish gills, and the heels are convex like ancient electrical sockets attached to my calves by cable-thin tendons, but there's no electricity in them any more, they don't dance the tango the way they did in Baires of old. And the sail-stiff pyjama top clings to the tubular frame that was once modelled with firm white flesh and desired by muscular seamen all over the globe. From the long, open neckline flows a condom-shaped sack of skin called a breast . . . Oh dear, oh dear.

Here sinks a skew-backed shadow of itself, a sinking garage

goddess, a marble mummy that deserves no tombstone, deserves no anything, nothing but the shovel.

Yes, see what a wretch I am, and hear me sing as I sink:

Sea, sea
See, my sea,
I sink into the depths of me.

But what do I see as I float about in the darkness of the deep? Yes, I see the depths of life, I see my ice-cold salty life, all my eternal cursed confusion. Below me I can make out glowing cities, islands, countries. Men grin like sea wolves, sharks glide by overhead, marked with the German Luftwaffe cross, and in the distance the air-raid sirens of whales can be heard.

And out of the green twilight my relatives come sailing, like a shoal of tuna fish. Grandad, Grandma and her entire upper-class Danish pharmacist family, and Grandma Verbjörg in sodden Breidafjördur woollens; Eysteinn and Lína, happily exhausted as ever, and Great-Grandma Blómey like an old sea-beaten sailing-boat mast, but not at all mouldy; then come Mum . . . and Dad . . . they swim together, in evening dress, followed by Dad's siblings, all sombre . . . and right at the back comes a little girl . . . my little, little girl . . . with her blond hair fluttering around her ears like gently flapping fins. Oh dear, my soul. See the expression on her face, so pretty, so peaceful, and yet she caused more damage than a night of bombing on Berlin . . .

They float past, all with the same wonderfully shoal-like air. And they leave me sinking, alone.

Down into those thousand fathoms that make up a human life. And now below me I see a city engulfed in war, everything in black and white, but glowing red in the flames. I take a ride on a bomb, a falling bomb. I'm a Norn on a crater, a witch on a broomstick transformed by sorcery into rain . . . yes, I'm being dissolved into thousands of drops, I'm falling, falling . . .

Now I'm falling on Thingvellir. Dissipating all over Thingvellir. On 17 June 1944, the day of the inauguration of the Icelandic Republic, a day of heavy rainfall. I drench the flags, wet the spears, drip down the shields and swords, the railings, hats, brims and backs of chairs, and yes, I also drip on the document that my grandfather is signing. He wipes away those shimmering tears from Iceland's future, thinking they're rain, but tastes the salt and looks out over the wet fields, sees that he is taking over a nation under water.

And on I trickle, through the grass and further down, far below Grandad's signature, down into the earth and a chasm through a crevice, into the quick of the land, the flowing lava, where Hitler thunders on a rostrum, spewing the fire that cast its flames on my life . . .

'Do you want your porridge now?'

'Huh?'

'Do you want to have your porridge now?'

'No one eats in hell.'

'Huh?'

'No one needs to eat in hell!'

'Herra, dear.'

'I'm no Herra.'

'Herbjörg . . .'

'My name is Blómey!'

'Blómey, dear, here's your porridge. Would you like me to help you?'

'No one can help me.'

'Do you want to eat it by yourself, then? You have to eat.'

'Says who?'

'We all need to eat.'

'You're only shoving that into me to make me shit. To give you something to do. To wipe me. That's what you want and want. I don't want to need to shit. I've shat enough!'

I'm gasping breathlessly by the end of my speech.

'Herra, dear . . .'

'Blómey! *Blumeninsel! Das Blumeninsel im breiten Fjord. Das bin ich.*'

'I don't understand German, you know that.'

'You don't understand anything.'

She stares at me, at this hissing cat of a woman, this queen of wrinklehood in a ludicrous wig, and stands there in silence for a while, with the bowl of porridge in her hands, like stupidity itself with eyebrows. I deserve better than this, goddamn it. I deserve so much better. I thought I would at least be allowed to die in my own bed, even with my so-called family by my side. But the boys don't seem to know whether I'm being dressed or dissected. They don't seem to realise that a mother was needed to bring them into this world, that they would never have reached here on their own. No, a splay-legged, hairy-crotched mother was required to push their piglet asses through the tunnel out into the light. *Honour your father and mother*, it's written somewhere, but who remembers Scripture in the computer age? It's been three whole years since I last heard from them and their saggy-titted wives, although I actually have my ways of keeping an eye on them now.

'Maybe you're not hungry?'

'*No tengo cinco años.*'

'Huh?'

'I'm not five years old.'

'Shall I maybe take the computer away so that you can eat by yourself on the overbed?'

'Over dead?'

'No, overbed. They call it an overbed at the hospital.'

'Don't talk about hospitals. I'm not in hospital.'

'No, no, I know,' she says, raising the headboard for me, totally unsolicited, and then she adjusts my pillow, pulls up the quilt, and spots the war egg. Careless of me; I forgot to put it away. She picks it up from under the quilt. Were I still able to blush, I would.

'What's that?' she asks.

'That? That's . . . that's a so-called cooling ball that I used in hospitals in the olden days.'

'Oh yeah?'

She swallows it, the gullible child, and puts the object away in the bedside table drawer, like the humblest of property masters. I regain my composure.

'You've got to have some sex. You don't want to become a mouldy virgin, do you?'

'I know, you've already told me.'

'Your mother won't knock you up.'

'No, ha-ha, I know.'

'I can fix you up with a boy. How do you like my Australian?'

'I think I'd rather have an Icelander.'

'Nonsense. They're just wooden fish. It's all about mixing the blood. A little golden plover like you ought to be mating with a pelican; that'll start something new.'

'The golden plover waits for the spring and the right mate, too.'

'Yes, you're a smart girl. You know it all better than I do; I squandered my virginity on rocks and ditches. Right, then, you cheeky thing, give me the porridge.'

9

'Your Cab Is Here'

1959

The feet of Jón the First, or the Pre-Jón, as I would later call him, were always a turn-off. He would frequently plonk them down in front of me in the evening and order me to take off his socks and rub his toes, soles, heels and calves. There was no way I could love those Icelandic men's feet, shaped as they were like birch stumps, hard and chunky, as screaming white as wood when the bark is peeled off. Yeah, and about as cold and damp, too. The toes had horny nails that looked like dead buds in a frosty spring. Nor can I forget the stench, because smelly feet were very common in the post-war years when men wore nylon socks and virtually slept in their shoes.

How was it possible to love these Icelandic men who belched at the table and farted relentlessly? After four Icelandic husbands and a whole string of plump paramours, I'd become a real connoisseur of flatulence and could describe its varieties with the same confidence as an enologist describing wines. *Howling blaster, loaded stinker, gas bomb, coffee belch, silencer* and *Luftwaffe* were among the terms I most used.

Icelandic men just don't know how to behave, never have and never will, but are good fun, on the whole. Or so Icelandic women think, at any rate. They seem to come with this internal emergency box, crammed with humour and irony, which they always carry around with them and can open if things get too rough. It must be a hereditary gift wired into their genes. Anyone who gets lost up a mountain, is snowed in or has to spend a whole weekend stuck in a lift can always open this special Icelandic emergency box and wriggle out of the situation with a good story. After wandering around the world and living on the Continent, I'd long grown weary of polite, fart-free gentlemen, who opened doors and paid the bills but never had a story to tell and were either completely asexual or insisted on fucking till the crack of dawn. Swiss watch salesmen who could never fit a quickie into their schedule, or hairy French apes who always required twelve rounds of screwing at the end of a five-course meal.

I guess I liked German men the best. They were a decent combination of the belching northerner and cultured southerner, of western order and eastern folly, although in the post-war years they were, of course, shattered men. There wasn't much you could do with them except try to straighten them out first. And who had the time for that? Londoners are positive and jolly, but their famous irony struck me as mechanical and tiresome in the long run. That irony machine seemed to have eaten away their true essence. The French machine, on the other hand, is driven by unadulterated seriousness, and the Frogs can drive you around the bend once they slip into their philosophical jargon. Italians worship every woman like a queen until they get her home and she suddenly turns into a whore. The Yank is a swell guy who thinks big and always wants to take you to the moon. At the same time, though, he can be as smug and petty as the meanest seamstress and goes berserk if someone eats his peanut butter sandwich on the spaceship. I found Russians quite interesting. In fact they were the most Icelandic of them all: drank every glass to the last drop and hurled themselves into any merriment, knew countless stories, and never talked seriously until they had reached the bottom of the bottle, when they started to weep for their mothers, who lived a thousand miles away but came on foot to bring them their clean laundry once a month. They were totally nuts and better athletes in bed than my dear countrymen, but in the end I had enough of all their bedroom acrobatics.

Nordic men are as tactless as Icelanders. They get drunk over dinner, laugh loudly and belch, and finally start to 'sing,' even in public restaurants, where people have paid good money to get away from the racket of the world. But their wallets always waited dead sober in the cloakroom, while the Icelandic purse lay open for everyone in the middle of the table. Our men were the greater Vikings in this regard. 'Reputation is king, the rest is crap!' my Bæring used to say. Every evening had to be legendary, anything less would have been failure. But the morning after, they turned into putty weaklings. Icelandic women don't shy away from managing their marriages: some run them like businesses, and they can be unlucky with their staff, of course. I frequently had to fire my personnel and didn't always find satisfactory replacements.

Still, though, I did manage to love them, those Icelandic oafs, at least down as far as their knees. Below that, things didn't go as well. And when the feet of Pre-Jón junior popped out of me in the maternity ward, I'd had enough. The resemblance was minute and striking: Jón's feet in bonsai form. I immediately developed a physical repulsion for the father and prohibited him from coming in to see the baby. All I heard was the note of surprise in his bass voice from the corridor when the midwife told him she had ordered him a taxi. From that day on, I made it a rule: I dismissed my men by calling them a cab.

'Your cab is here' became my favourite line.

10

The Jónic Order

1959–1969

In the years following the war and preceding the endless Cod Wars, every second man in Iceland was called Jón, our version of John. You literally couldn't go anywhere without bumping into a Jón. You only had to step onto the dance floor to be sure of conceiving a little Jón. In the space of ten years I had three baby boys with three different Jóns, and some people nicknamed me the Jónic Queen.

Jón Haraldsson was the first in line, a Brilliantined wholesale merchant with a double chin and black-peppered cheeks. With him I had Harald Fairhair. Then there was Jón B. Ólafsson, a ginger-haired hack who wrote for the newspaper, hard in bed but limp outside it. With him I had the Smorgasbord King, Ólafur, who lives in Bergen in Norway these days, where he gets along best with bread, but few things irk him as much as visits from his Mum.

Finally, there was Jón Magnússon, the solicitor and genealogical genius, the soft, wobbly one, who had cultivated the art of carpe diem, which he practised on a daily basis, with a bottle and bravura. With him I had my Magnús, 'the Lawmender.' For the sake of convenience I call my Jóns Pre-Jón, Mid-Jón and Post-Jón.

11

Große Freiheit

1960

And then there was Peace-Jón.

After ordering the cab for Pre-Jón, I left my newborn son with my mother and Fridrik Johnson, her second husband, and travelled to Hamburg, where I stayed for two years, as I recall. I was still too young to settle into the humdrum of Icelandic existence and needed to savour more of life before surrendering to 'infant mortality' – because women know that as soon as their children are born, they themselves die. I'd actually had a child before and refused to die for it and instead went on living, which was the biggest mistake of my life. I hadn't planned on repeating it, but after six months of ploughing against the gales of northern sleet, I'd had enough. I wasn't made for greyness.

This was my last attempt at making something of myself. I was almost thirty and had learned nothing from life, apart from how to handle a hand grenade and dance the tango. In Hamburg I'd intended to study photography. I'd always enjoyed drawing, and in New York, Bob, who was my boyfriend at the time, had introduced me to this new art form. His father owned an original picture by Man Ray and books on the work of Cartier-Bresson and Brassaï, which caught my eye like ink-black claws. Back home in Iceland, there wasn't much worth seeing, so I did my best to keep up and sometimes bought *Vogue* and *Life* when they were available. Few Icelandic women had made careers as photographers back then, and my father said that if I had a talent for anything, it had to be 'the art of the moment.'

I had stayed in the Hanseatic city back during the war. In those days it lay in ruins, but now it had all been cleaned up and rebuilt. Always quick to pick themselves up, those Germans. But there was a housing shortage and I soon found myself sharing a room in the Schanzenviertel, the District of Chance, in an apartment with a German girl and her French girlfriend Joséphine. They were a lot younger than I was, pleasure-seeking girls, who lived fast at night and slow during the day. Nevertheless I got sucked into the bright lights with them, and my memory of my time in that city is pretty hazy, as I roamed between the nightlife and the darkroom.

Josie was one of those city girls who knew only the 'people who mattered.' And Astrid Kirchherr had by then become something of a star among the young people in the clubs, a short-haired blond of delicate beauty who, like me, was smitten with photography. In those days the main venues were the Kaiserkeller and the Top Ten Club, and one night we popped into the former and saw the boy band from Liverpool playing their electrifying numbers. There was no explosion in the cellar – that came later – but you could see how this music was ushering in a new sensibility. They played American rock music in a European way. The youth of Hamburg, who had been brought up on Bach and beer jazz, had never heard anything like it. I didn't know much about pop music, of course, but I fell for these long-haired lads' innocence and joy in playing. They radiated a kind of newly won freedom: finally we had put the war behind us.

Große Freiheit – Great Freedom – the street was called. They played the Kaiserkeller eight days a week. And I read somewhere that this was how they honed their craft. They were kept in constant training because there was plenty of competition. Entry was free and people were quick to leave if they got bored. There was a strip club next door, so it was probably a rivalry with sex that brought all those tunes into the world. That's the secret of the Beatles. You could probably say the same about Shakespeare and the tons of genius he left for us to enjoy. While he didn't have striptease to compete with, there were all those bear and dog fights in the next building. And to think people say that sex and violence are the enemies of art.

12

Beatles Party in Hamburg

1960

It was through this company of Astrid and my fellow lodgers that by a stroke of luck I tagged along to a party with these conquerors of the age. It was an extraordinary moment for an Icelandic girl, of course, though it could all have ended differently.

Astrid had started going out with the extra Beatle, Stuart Sutcliffe, his name was, a shy and sensitive art student whom John, the rascal, bullied, always making fun of his clothes and stage appearance. After one of the concerts, Astrid invited us all back to her place. In those days the Fab Four were five in number, and of course it was a real adventure to stroll along the Reeperbahn with them, the famous haunt of prick-teasing hookers, adorned with windmills and red lights. John was clearly the leader of the group. He did all the talking, asking the hookers if they were tired and wanted to come to a party, he would pay them the same as they'd get for the other thing. On the way there, John also made fun of Astrid's German accent and the street names we saw, but we girls just laughed as we were expected to in those years, and I probably laughed the loudest: he gave me the glad eye.

Astrid was a Twiggy clone. She had painted her room black, white and silver and hung twigs with no leaves from the ceiling. It was on the verge of what I could tolerate by way of pretentiousness. But there were drinks and music. Old Platters records, I remember, and Nat King Cole. Lennon asked our hostess if she had inherited her record collection from her grandfather. I detected a certain tension between him and Astrid, and most probably his teasing of Stuart, whom he sometimes called Shutcliff or Stuffclit, was inspired by jealousy. As the Beatle stooped, sputtering over the record collection, I saw my chance and told them I'd been to the States. I asked him if he knew Buddy Holly, because with all that Brilliantine, that was who he reminded me of. 'Buddy Holly' turned out to be the magic words, because now John began to ply me with questions about the singer, of whom I knew nothing except that he was dead. But the ice was broken, and soon John and I were dancing together, although they said he never danced. Someone turned the lights out, the Platters sang as we danced cheek to cheek, and before long a Breidafjördur girl received a Beatles kiss.

It was only later that I realised this was a momentous event in Icelandic history, albeit of the kind that wasn't supposed to be mentioned. I could picture it in our tabloids: BRITISH BEATLE KISSED IN HAMBURG. At the same time it was such a trivial one that it was hardly worth reporting. One dance, one kiss. I guess I felt like the girl who kissed Jesus before he had his first big breakthrough and who bore her fate in silence, even after her relatives began to worship him as a god. My last husband, Bæring, wanted me to tell the local rag or some other tabloid about this kiss, thought it was pretty remarkable, but I refused to, even after John's death. I found it too 'glitzy,' as Mum would have said.

But I do keep him in my collection of Jóns, as the Peace-Jón, though I later read that he was no angel of peace. He himself admitted that all his great efforts for peace were due to inner conflicts and even confessed that he had assaulted women. That's what they're like, those visionaries: always got something simmering on the stove back home.

But even though he was young, he already had a sailor's salty humour radiating self-confidence and, of course, that magic charm. Was a wonderful kisser, asked me if the British would beat the Germans in a kissing war, and was amazed when I told him I was Icelandic.

'Oh? So that's why I'm so cold.'

'Are you cold?'

'No.' He grinned. 'I'm from Iceland, too.'

'Huh? From Iceland?'

'Yeah, that's what Mimi calls my bedroom, Iceland.'

'Why?'

'Because it's always so cold. The windows are always open.'

'Why?'

'Smoke gets in your eyes,' he answered, singing the Platters song we'd just danced to. 'Mimi doesn't want me to smoke.'

'Who's Mimi?'

'My aunt. Or my mum. Mum died in a car accident. Got run over by a drunk.'

'Oh? How awful.'

'Yeah. I've yet to kill him.'

To my surprise, this sentence imploded like a bomb in my soul. Everything went dark, my eyes filled with tears, and I excused myself, went out to the balcony, gripped the ice-cold railing, and looked out over the buildings and river. I wasn't going to start crying in front of those youngsters. He cautiously poked his head out to the narrow balcony.

'What happened? Did I say something . . . ?'

I turned towards him.

'No, no, I . . . it's . . . I also lost . . . in the same kind of . . .'

'Your mum?'

'No, little . . . little . . .'

'Sister?'

I couldn't answer. Just shook my head. It was still so incredibly painful. It is still so incredibly painful. I thought that, bit by bit, I would have got over losing my daughter to that car, but there I was, seven years later, and I still couldn't even hear a car accident mentioned. And here I lie, fifty-six years later, dabbing a solitary tear on my wrinkled cheek. But what a stroke of bad luck, getting a lump in my throat in front of that boy, precisely on that night. He behaved well, but our 'exchange' was obviously over. Young men don't go to bed with old problems.

'You mean . . . a child?'

I nodded, swallowed, and tried to smile away the tears. Through the music you could hear the screech of a train in the darkness of the night. The Beatle grinned back, finally stepped onto the balcony, lit a cigarette, and, as he was exhaling the smoke, said, 'You're a lot older than me, aren't you? How old are you?'

To my surprise I found his brashness refreshing. I asked for a cigarette and recovered my speech.

'You . . . you don't ask a lady her age. Aren't you a gentleman?'

'No, I'm from Woolton, how old are you?'

'Thirty-one; and you?'

'Twenty.' He smiled. 'I'll be thirty later this year.'

There was a lot of truth in that, since that was the start of a decade that flew by faster than any other decade of the twentieth century. I watched him open the balcony door, which was really just a large window, return to the cheerful atmosphere of the party, and then grow into the long-haired world-famous ex-Beatle who had rewritten the musical history of the age and taken half the world with him into hippiedom, in a bed in Amsterdam.

I remained alone and turned towards the city again, my miserable past. Somewhere out there was the station where in the middle of the war I had 'lost' both my father and my mother on the same day. And somewhere inside me there was a little blond girl playing on the pavement in another city. I could still hear Blómey laughing as I entered the bar and heard *the thud*, which hit me like a brick in the back of my head, the most horrific sound life can produce, one that changed me into the most terrible woman who has ever lived. I heard that *thud* (the impact of a two-year-old skull meeting the steel bumper of an American car at twenty miles an hour on a narrow street in the capital of Argentina) inside my head every month, sometimes every day, all my life. He who loses a child loses half his reason.

And yet I had had another child, but left him with Mum so that I could run out here to kiss some other women's boys. Now he slept in Grandma's house, the one-year-old Haraldur I felt no connection to. Far away from both children, I missed the one who was dead more than the one who still lived. Maybe I was the one who was dying slowly. Had I abandoned the little boy out of a fear of losing another child under a car?

I pulled myself together, wiped my tears, and noticed that I was still holding an unsmoked cigarette, the one the Buddy Holly boy had given me. I rummaged through my coat pockets for matches, without result, but didn't feel like going back inside right away, so I let the cigarette fall down to the street.

I can see, as I lie here bedridden, warming myself on that ice-cold Imagine Peace Tower, that I should have kept that cigarette from Lennon's pack, an unsmoked reminder of what might have been. I could have sold it on eBay, along with a wet Beatles kiss, and done up the garage nicely with the proceeds, put in some furniture and wallpaper, and bought a flat-screen TV that would show nothing but films based on my life.

13

My Own Herra

2009

As a woman I was terribly lonely in my generation. While my peers sat in secondary school, I had a whole world war to contend with. I graduated from that war at fifteen, but with the life experience of a thirty-year-old woman. I was twenty by 1949 and, according to the spirit of the times, was expected to apply to finishing school in Denmark and pursue marriage plans back in Iceland, a well-bred girl from the president's family grooming her hair for balls in the Independence Party headquarters. An up-and-coming politician would have invited me, and together we would have ended up in the presidential residence at Bessastadir (he would have won with me at his side) surrounded by children and reporters. Instead I threw myself into yet more adventures, dancing on ship decks south of the Equator, never waiting for men to ask me out but going after them myself.

To compound it all, back in those days Iceland lagged a good sixteen years behind the trends of the day, so I always found it hard to cope with the small-town life of Reykjavík. I was a war child, but not in the sense that I'd been reared in the war: the war had reared me. I was a woman of the world before I ever became a woman. I was a party girl and drank all the men under the table. I had become a practising feminist before the word had been so much as printed in an Icelandic newspaper. I had been practising 'free love' years before the term was invented. And, of course, I had kissed John Lennon long before 'Beatlemania' struck our frosty shores.

And then I was expected to behave like a 'normal person.'

I was independent, had few scruples, and didn't let anything hold me back – dogma, men or gossip. I travelled around and took casual jobs, looked after my own interests, had children and lost one, but didn't let the other ones tie me down, took them with me or left them behind, just kept moving and refused to allow myself to be drawn into marriage and *to be bored to death*, although that was the toughest part, of course. Long before the hippie girls appeared on the scene and began to hand their children over to their mothers so they could continue their debauched lives, I had devised the concept of the long-distance mother. 'You can't let the fruit of your previous sex life spoil the next,' one of the heroines of the sixties once said, or was that me? Of course, you could say I led a kind of hippie existence, but I made it up all by myself, without following the latest trends from Paris.

I suspect the uninhibited lifestyle I enjoyed has become more commonplace among Icelandic women only in recent years. I recently came across an article about Iceland in a Spanish magazine in which young Ice Ladies praised the flexibility of life in a small country where anyone can have children with anyone, since everyone already has multiple spouses, children and foster children. If the article is to be believed, Iceland is one big orgy of divorces and relationships in which children are able to choose their homes and families for themselves.

I'm still waiting for a call from these modern women and for the bouquet of flowers they'll present me with for being their pioneer, at a short ceremony here in the garage. Just so long as they don't bring our first woman president, Vigdís Finnbogadóttir, star of my generation, with them. She's always made me feel like shit.

14

Blitz Cancer

2009

Grandma ended up in a boathouse, I in a garage. That was what fate had in store for us two old women. But at least she had company, oh yes. Even though my laptop knows about everything and is very warm, I still haven't managed to teach it the art of laughing. But of course, I'm quite happy to be free of other people's snoring, farting and chit-chat, so for me it is absolutely fantastic living here in the garage. And here come the drugs. Here come the wonderful drugs. Oh dear, all those things they've invented for us.

'Right, then, shall we start with the Sorbitol?' says the girl in the short-sleeved uniform, pouring the sugary goo onto the spoon. To lubricate my bowels.

The taste reminds me of Grandma Georgía. She was really into sweet liqueurs. Then came my mother's generation: they loved port. My generation just went for vodka. Then came other groups with shots of their own. Poor Lóa says she drinks beer only on those few occasions when she bares her beaver. That's probably beer fat I see shimmering before me.

'Right. And then there's the Femara, isn't that next?'

'Oh, I don't remember.'

'Yes, two of those with a drop of water . . . that's it, yes.'

'Can I touch it?'

'Touch what?'

'Your arm. It looks so soft . . .'

'Ha-ha. Yeah? Sure. It's just way too chubby, ha-ha.'

Now I'm the dribbling witch groping Hansel and Gretel's arms. Come now, Lóa, dear, and let this dried-up old fish of a woman feel your soft maiden flesh. With her last real tooth. Oh how soft and soft it is.

'I'm sure it tastes really good,' I say. The kind of thing I say.

'I hope you're not going to eat me!'

'Just you wait and see.'

These are obviously the long-term side effects: the drugs seep into me like toxins into the soil. But poison must be fought with poison, the doctors say, to establish a lifelong ceasefire in the intestines. Apart from that, I've no interest in this *toma de medicamentos*. I do it only for Lóa's sake. She enjoys poisoning me with this stuff, she does.

It was in 1991 that I got the diagnosis that I wouldn't survive the spring. I'd been gasping with emphysema for seven years and fuelling it unremittingly with nicotine, which almost triggered a full-scale demonstration in the health care system. But then the cancer suddenly decided to invade the hollow of my chest like a German army. 'It's blitz cancer,' I explained to the doctors as soon as they admitted me.

They would give me the spring, but then I would be pushing daisies under the green of summer. I wouldn't be seeing the new century and was only sixty-two years old. I just couldn't get my head around it, as young people say. But with treatment after treatment, injections, speculations, drugs and more drugs, it was as if a Russian winter settled over me, forcing the German army to retreat. For a while. It always came back, the bastard, and still does.

In hospital I also caught some abominable virus, and it was only by a miracle that I scraped out of there alive. I haven't set foot in a hospital ever since. I don't have the health for it.

For eighteen years now I've been carrying my Cancer Boy under my belt, though he is neither born nor dead yet. Canker Björnsson is an eighteen-year-old lad with stubble and acne, who could take his driving test if he wanted to. He will obviously only come crawling out when he is a fully qualified doctor, just to pronounce me dead. Some people think I'm the Icelander who has lived with this disease the longest. But the president hasn't yet invited me to Bessastadir to pin a medal to the ruins of my departed breast.

World War II therefore still rages in my body; it's an eternal struggle. The Germans marched into my liver and kidneys just before Christmas last year with their ruthless malignance and still occupy the area, although the Allies pushed them into retreat from the stomach and colon the previous spring. (The battle for the breasts ended long ago, and one of them is now a member of the Breast Assembly in a better world.) The Russians, however, continue their assault on the breast cavity and are rapidly heading towards my heart, where sooner or later the red flag will be planted. And that'll be the end of me; peace will reign in this part of the world until Stalin shows up with his scalpel to dissect my body in two.

Then I'll be burned. I'm dead set on that.

So eighteen years have passed since I was given three months to live. I survived it and continue to do so. When I'm bored being Linda Pétursdóttir, I sometimes appear under my own name on dating sites: 'Single-breasted woman with cancer in her lungs, kidneys, liver and elsewhere seeks healthy male. Port-wine stains not a problem.'

15

Flames of Purgatory

2009

Lóa lent me her mobile phone yesterday while she went out to the 7-Eleven to buy me a lightbulb. I grabbed the chance to call the crematorium and get some information about the procedure. They tell me they cremate seven to ten bodies a day, each of which produces four to seven pounds of ash (depending on their weight, I presume), and the temperature of the furnace goes up to a thousand degrees Celsius. One probably needs to stay in it for an hour. 'Or possibly an hour and a half, I would say,' a young girl told me in a dreary tone. She seemed to be a whole lifetime away from ash and fire, despite the fact that she was standing there right in the centre of death's smelter. I'd imagined it would take less than that, but I suppose I won't be in any great hurry when the time comes. The girl seemed incredibly dim-witted.

'I'd like to book an appointment with you for a cremation.'

'Book an appointment?'

'Yes.'

'Right, okay . . . could I . . . have your name, please?'

'Herbjörg María Björnsson.'

There was a slight rustling of papers.

'Right, I can't find it in our register. Have you sent in an application?'

'Yes; no, I'm making a booking for me, for myself.'

'For yourself?'

'Yes.'

'But . . . you see . . . we need to get the form first, you understand.'

'And how do I do that?'

'You can just fill it in online and send it to us, but we won't actually process it until . . . well, yes.'

'Until what?'

'Yes, well, we don't actually, you know . . . until people are, you know, deceased, you see.'

'Yes, yes, I'll be dead when the time comes, you can be sure of that.'

'Yes? Erm . . .'

'Yes, if the worst comes to the worst I'll come over and you can just shove me into the furnace alive.'

'Alive? No-o, that's . . . not allowed, you see.'

'Right, well, I'll try to come dead then, when do you have a slot?'

'Yes, well, er . . . when would you like to . . .'

'When would I like to die? I was thinking of dying before Christmas, during Advent, around mid-December.'

'Yes, we have vacancies . . . Yes, it's all blank, I think.'

'Right, so can you book me a place?'

'Er . . . yes, sure. When, then?'

'Let's say the fourteenth of December. What day of the week is that?'

'Erm . . . that's . . . that's a Monday.'

'Yes, that's perfect, perfect way to start the week by having yourself cremated. What times do you have?'

'Erm . . . the very first slot is free as it happens, nine o'clock. You can also come after lunch, you know.'

'Yeah, I . . . I guess it would be safer to have it in the afternoon. Then I can take my time.'

'To . . . to come here, you mean?'

'No. I might have to slash my wrists and I'm not going to do that on a Sunday evening. I mean, the blood could take some time to flow out of me . . .'

'Uh-huh . . . I'll just write that down . . . but you . . .'

'What?'

'Are you absolutely . . . I mean . . . are you absolutely sure that you want . . . ?'

'Yes, yes, I just want the furnace to be really hot, I don't want to be half-cooked. A thousand degrees, you say?'

'Yes, yes, don't worry, we can heat it up well in advance before . . .'

'Yes, and I go in headfirst, right?'

I prefer the incinerator to the grave, although I could easily afford a coffin and wreaths. Of course, the boys might be drawn to the idea of carrying their mother down the church steps, but I don't really know whether I feel like letting them do that. On the other hand, there's no guarantee that they will even attend their mother's funeral. They're busy men, so they might not even listen to all the death announcements on the radio.

Yes, I'm determined to depart at Advent. I couldn't stomach another Christmas stuck in this garage. We had such a lonely Christmas in here last year, the laptop and I, and a cold one, too, even though dear Dóra had some roast meat and gravy delivered to me. Actually, I'm surprised the council hasn't thought of some way of recycling people like us who would like to donate their organic waste to the planet. They could grind us up for fertiliser to give the flowers, instead of killing them in our honour. But I probably wouldn't be eligible, with all these toxins in my body. Yes. The more I think about it, the more I like the idea of those thousand degrees. The flames of purgatory could hardly be any hotter and ought to remove some of the blemishes on my wretched soul, which I've been unable to erase myself.

16

Gudjón and Dóra

2009

Simplicity is number one in this garage. Everything I need is here because I don't need anything. Just drugs, food and the net.

Yeah, and cigarettes: seven a day.

My bed is an old but good hospital bed that got wheeled down the road from the clinic, all the way here, thanks to the initiative of some good women. I can adjust my back and neck, which I normally keep quite high. My pillow is propped up against a sturdy, windowless wall that faces southwest and shields me from all of life's showers, like the man I never found. The wall opposite me faces northeast and contains a door with a glowing knob and, to the left of it, three small windows, high up. The one furthest to the left offers me a view of Lennon's light pillar on dark autumn nights.

Then, on the left side, is a thin, non-soundproof partition, concealing the garage and Gudjón's junk. To the right, along the eastern wall, is a kitchen unit with a sink, a refrigerator and hot plates, and my daily ordeal sits in the corner by the door: the toilet cubicle. It's a strange society that we live in that forces its elderly to walk. I've repeatedly tried to point this paradox out to the girls – in the olden days, even the poorest of the poor had the right to defecate in bed! – but always in vain.

'Sorry, we can only assist people with ILS.'

'What's ILS?'

'Independent life skills.'

'But I don't have them, never had!'

I forgot to mention the bedside table, a four-legged antique from Grandad Sveinn and Grandma Georgía, carved out of the Danish family tree. On top of it I keep an ashtray, an heirloom from Dad, made out of German brass. Oh yes, and then there's the antique desk chair by my bedside, which leans inexplicably forward. Awaiting visitors with infinite patience. I sometimes use it as a walking frame to help me along the Via Dolorosa.

All the fixtures are the fruit of Gudjón's labours. Where would I be without him? In addition to the toilet, he set up the kitchen unit and partitioned off the garage, varnished the floor, and adjusted the lights. He's a craftsman by nature, like every other Icelandic male. We've always been such a keen DIY nation. People are either knocking down walls, building verandas or fixing the wiring, all for the sake of patching up their marriages. But everyone knows that modern difficulties all stem from what I call male inertia. Marital problems didn't exist until men stopped working at sea and started pottering about at home on weekends. Men have finally understood this themselves and try to fill all that unfortunate free time on their hands with imaginary urgent tasks. 'I promised Gummi I'd help with the summerhouse,' I heard him say on the other side of the partition the other week. Yeah. There's obviously no marital hell in Iceland you can't build a veranda over.

17

Behind the Seven Summers

1929

He who has no memories of his mother had a good mother. I can't remember anything of my mother from our years in the islands of Svefneyjar, seven summers and seven winters. And yet for most of that time we slept in the same bed. One never notices the most evident things and yet they are the best of all.

In the isolation of that remote part of the ocean, I enjoyed what the big cities of Europe were later to deny me: safety and warmth. My childhood was like an extension of the pregnancy: Mum was always around me and I in her, although I never got to see her face. For seven years we never went anywhere. I would later be torn up by the roots but was consoled by the fact that no one's went deeper. They were so deep, in fact, that I managed to cling on to them for a whole world war.

Mum and I lost each other at the beginning of the war, and I blamed her for it. After the war, we were kept apart by the grand dame named Georgía. Most women are forever trying to flee their mothers, but I was constantly searching for mine. I longed for her company but at the same time wanted to *spare her mine.* By then I was no longer Mum's child but rather Dad's little woman; the war had thrown us together, and finally I followed him to South America.

That was the seed of what was to become my basic feeling towards that woman: guilt. Mum was a *better* person than me, a more *decent* person than me, she was *reliable*. What's more I'd failed to 'make something of myself.'

For centuries her people had slaved away on the islands, far from all schools and office lifestyles, not to mention opportunities for women. I was the first in that thousand-year-old family to be offered the chance of an education, but instead I drifted through life without fulfilling the dreams that Mum had denied herself to preserve for me. On three occasions she asked me to think about it. Maybe the Commercial College would suit me best, maybe domestic sciences. 'Look at how well that Vigdís Finnbogadóttir is doing,' she'd say, 'gone to France, to university.' In the end I gave in, took a secretarial course for three weeks, and learned how to type, a skill that has served me well all my life, all the way into the garage, thanks to that good woman.

I sometimes try to imagine what it must have been like for Mum to travel back west again. A stunning twenty-five-year-old woman who was forced to squander the flower of her youth with a toddler girl, stuck on an island, toiling away in the cold and singlehood. Spring after spring, Christmas after Christmas. What was she thinking?

But things were even worse for Dad, since there's always the other side of the coin. Every action conceals its opposite. Although it may be painful to be betrayed, it's even worse to betray. When a bond of trust is broken, it leaves a gush of pain at first, but then a sense of freedom. The person who breaks that bond, however, has it tied around his neck and thinks he's free until he senses it tightening. Slowly and slowly. That much I know.

Sometimes good fortune gives you only one chance, and woe to whoever botches it. No matter how hard Dad tried, he couldn't get anything right. He bungled his law studies, crumbled at the pharmacy counter, fiddled with his violin, but could no longer find the right tune. He who gets lost in a wood tries to find his path again, but he who loses himself has no use for a path at all.

His indecision finally ushered him into a business he should never have got into: German clothes pegs (I'm still embarrassed to talk about it). In the end it was he who was hung out to dry for having confused stocks and stockings at a crucial moment. Dad could just as well have been stored in a wardrobe for seven years. He lost a whole chapter of his life. We waited for him on the other side of the sea, Mum and I, patient women in the age of man.

Because those tie wearers could do this: steep their love in vinegar and pull it out again seven years later, totally intact, just slightly bitter. Not that Mum didn't dance with some of those sea dogs at the Flatey balls and smile at their desire behind the building, but hardly more than that. I don't remember anyone showing up on the island to kiss her, but then again I've no recollection of anything about her in those years.

But I do remember Dad, of course, when he reappeared like a water-combed angel from the ocean.

18

The Haymaker

1936

It was the summer of '36. On a beautiful, silvery mid-August day –
when the season has reached its crest, clouds hang puffed up with
heat over a viscous sea, and the mountains acquire slightly more
European colours, milder and deeper – a blond man came sailing
into the strait.

'I stood for the entire crossing on the boat from Flatey. I just
couldn't sit down,' Dad later told me.

And he stepped ashore. Without noticing her, he walked past a
seven-year-old girl who had idled down to the shore to see what
was happening, and found his Massa out in the field where she was
raking hay: as dark haired as before, dreamy eyed as before, beautiful
as before.

'Hi.'

She looked up, and the rake froze momentarily in her hands
before she continued, as if nothing were happening. The toothed
crossbar of the implement shook as it struck the short, dry grass, and
although the sun was hidden, her bare upper arms clearly bore the
hallmarks of summer, brown from labour on top and a shimmering
white below, which reminded him of a beautiful trout. He longed
(this is something I'm sure of, I know my men, having lived with a

whole army of them, though the teeth of their sexual beasts may vary in size) . . . he longed to kiss the brown part and bite the white.

'Hi,' Dad repeated. 'Do you . . . do you remember me?'

She carried on raking vigorously.

'No. Who are you?'

'Hans. Hansi. You . . .'

'Hans Henrik Björnsson? I thought that man had died. Giving birth.'

'Massa . . . I . . . I've come.'

Once more the fork froze in her hands and she looked him in the eye.

'I was expecting rain, but not you.'

Then she started raking again.

'Massa . . . forgive me.'

'Have you come here to moan?' she said coldly, continuing her work with even more zeal than before. She was wearing a sleeveless steel-grey shirt with blotches of sweat under her armpits: dark half-moons that looked as if they had been embroidered into the material. Pearls of perspiration were about to fuse on her forehead. 'What do you want?'

'You.'

'Me?'

At this point, Mum stopped raking and started to laugh.

'Yes, Massa, I . . . I've been . . .'

He hesitated yet again, and Mum poked the pile of hay that lay between them and stretched along the field like a yellowing frontier between love and hate. Further down the way, other labourers were hard at work, Sveinki the Romantic and Buxom Rósa, both armed with rakes. The latter positioned herself behind a haystack to observe the newcomer.

'It's also been difficult for . . . but now I . . .' Dad continued to stutter around his thoughts. Mum looked at the man, waiting for the rest. He tried again.

'Now I know . . .'

But when nothing more came out of him, the woman gave up and said decisively, 'I'd have more use for your hands right now. Go and get a rake from the shed.'

Dad later told me that he never worked so hard in all his life. Not even in the war, when he was digging trenches east of the Don and Dniester. He laboured like a hundred men that day and that whole week and almost finished the haymaking for the Svefneyjar farmer single-handedly. I remember admiring him as he tossed the bales into the barn, the muscles of his pale arms glistening in the sun. This half-Danish pharmacy cashier had revealed a secret talent for haymaking and concealed the blisters on his hands at mealtimes, although his daughter had spotted them and worshipped them just as the first Christians venerated Christ's sacrificial wounds.

Naturally, there was something exotic about him. My dad Hansi cut a handsome figure with a particularly striking profile, like a well-bred bird with a straight nose and high chest. Unlike the locals, he always walked with an upright back. Back then he had a pale face, as white as a sheet in the midst of all those weather-beaten faces that sat around the kitchen table at Lína's, gobbling down smoked seal meat and singed fins. It was only later that his face turned burgundy red. Mum had told me that this man was my father, but he paid little attention to me in those first days and had few more words for my mother. The future president's son first had to complete his mission in a classic tale. He was the son of the peasant who had to overcome seven challenges before he could win the princess's hand. Finally she invited him on a boat trip, and together they found their love island, which was invisible to the naked eye.

We sailed south in September, Dad, Mum and I, who stared at the man in the hat for the entire journey. I remember nothing of that first winter in Reykjavík, except that I started school and attracted attention for my stubbornness and precocious manners. 'Can you read?' they asked me.

'Only tern's eggs.'

In the spring we headed for Germany. Dad had found not only love but himself, too. He closed his law books to open others, starting a course in Old Norse studies at the University of Lübeck.

Contrary to what Mum had imagined, her parents-in-law gave her a warm welcome. The first ambassador of Iceland and his Danish wife had probably harboured greater expectations for their firstborn, in view of their position, but they were basically decent people. The reason my father had denied himself the country girl had not exactly been a categorical order from his father. He had *assumed* that Grandad Sveinn was opposed to the match purely on the basis of seven seconds of silence.

19

The Icelandic Tradition of Silence

2009

In those days, silence was one of the pillars of Icelandic culture. People didn't resolve their arguments through dialogue, and they were more skilled at interpreting silences than asking questions. They believed it was possible to erase a person's entire existence through the sheer power of silence. But that was understandable, of course: we were crawling out of the millennium of muteness that had reigned over land and sea, when our strife required no words, so that they were best stored in a book in the communal living room. This is the reason why the Icelandic language didn't change in a thousand years – we virtually never used it.

For centuries on end, very little was said in Iceland. Because people so rarely met. And when they did meet, they systematically avoided conversation. In our living quarters, people listened to readings, in churches to sermons, at big birthdays to whole speeches; and when the population started to grow, in the twentieth century, we developed the perfect way to preserve our silence: whist. Icelandic was much more a written language than a spoken one. It wasn't until we started to learn other languages that we realised we could use language for other things than poetry, writing and reading.

I've heard it said that the great Icelandic silence came from a pact that was made with the Nordic countries: they would leave us in peace, provided we preserve the language for them, since they were rapidly losing it from sucking up to the French and German courts. And one shouldn't touch the things one is keeping for others. They, however, didn't hesitate to break the pact, since before we realised it, we'd been turned into their colony. Now they expect us to speak their watered-down variation of the golden treasure we stored, the *Latin of the North*, no less.

We Icelanders therefore walk around with gold in our mouths, a fact that has shaped us more than anything else. At least we don't squander words unnecessarily. The problem with Icelandic, however, is that it's far too big a language for such a small nation. I read on the web that it contains 600,000 words and over 5 million word formations. Our tongue is therefore considerably bigger than the nation.

I did get to know other languages pretty well, but few are as solemn, because they're designed for daily use. German strikes me as the least pretentious language, and its people use it the way a carpenter uses a hammer, to build a house for thought, although it can hardly be considered attractive. Apart from Russian, Italian is the most beautiful language in the world and turns every man into an emperor. French is a tasty sauce that the French want to savour in their mouths for as long as possible, which is why they talk in circles and want to ruminate on their words, which often causes the sauce to dribble out of the corners of their mouths. Danish is a language the Danes are ashamed of. They want to be freed of it as soon as possible, which is why they spit out their words. Dutch is a guttural language that gulped down two others. Swedish thinks it's the French of the north, and the Swedes do their utmost to relish it by smacking their lips. Norwegian is what you get when a whole nation does its best not to speak Danish. English is no longer a language but a universal phenomenon like oxygen and sunlight. Then Spanish is a peculiar perversion of Latin that came into being when a nation tried to adapt to a king's speech impediment, and yet it is the language I learned the best.

Few of these nations, however, have mastered the art of silence. The Finns are Icelanders' greatest competitors when it comes to silence, since they are the only nation in the world that can be silent in two languages, as Brecht said. We Icelanders, on the other hand, are the only country in the world that venerated its language so much that we decided to use it as little as possible. This is why Icelandic is a chaste old maiden in her sixties who has developed a late sex drive and desires nothing more than to allow herself to be ravished by words before she dies. And that is what she will do. After my latest incursions into the blog world, I am convinced that the coming generations can be trusted to extract the gold from the bullshit and jettison the former to preserve the latter.

The Icelandic tradition of silence is therefore intertwined with the tradition of the Icelandic Sagas. And in line with that, my father pretended that my mother and I didn't exist for a whole seven years. He shut up for seven years because his father shut up for seven seconds. But a heart is best heard in silence. And after seven years of its knocking on his chest, my father finally went to the door and opened up what he had locked inside. And thought that by doing so he was performing a heroic deed: triumphing over the so-called patriarchy, as modern women say. And he was allowed to entertain that illusion, because even though Grandad and Grandma had never opposed their firstborn's choice of a wife and welcomed the fact that he had finally manned himself up to marry the mother of his child, they too remained silent about that.

20

From Lass to Lady

1937

Instead of being allowed to grow accustomed to high heels and reading menus in the crystal tea salons of tramway cities, Mum had spent seven formative years filleting fish and slaughtering seals. Nevertheless, she was quick to adopt the posture of a lady when it came to strolling on the steamers' decks, despite her initial difficulties with high heels.

'I'll be damned if I didn't look like a cow on stilettos when your father led me across the glistening floor of Ocean House.'

Ocean House was the name of the family residence in Skagen, on the tip of the Jutland Peninsula. And it must have been the summer of '37. I can still hear the clatter of massive Massa's high heels and see how they looked her up and down, Grandma Georgía and her elegant friends, like some bitchy fashion reporters. But I never had to feel ashamed of my mother. She soon mastered those heels; she wasn't a total country bumpkin and she had, after all, been the muse of a poet.

But it was a brutal change for her.

'The worst thing for me was going to bed without having milked the cows and having no chores to wake up to in the morning. I had pains in my hands from the lack of labour for many weeks afterwards.

And I always found it difficult to enjoy the summer days without *using* them. The sun might shine there for days on end without my being able to get my hands on a rake. I was so relieved when your granny allowed me to paint the outhouse.'

The old woman took to her kindly but could never bring herself to call her Massa, preferring instead to shout 'Massebill!' down the corridors. I was never anything more than *Den Lille Hveps* – the Little Wasp.

And if my mother inherited anything from her mother-in-law Georgía, it was her generosity of spirit and the way she treated everyone with the same respect, whether it was an Icelandic pauper or a German aristocrat.

It didn't escape me as a child that my parents were more in love than ever before. The flames of love that hadn't extinguished themselves in seven years were bound to last seven times seven years. And I allowed myself to envy them for that, because my heart has always been a fugitive.

21

Lone Bang

1937

It was at Ocean House in Skagen that I saw the famous Lone Bang for the first time. She was a relative on my father's side and by then already world famous in Denmark and Iceland; a folk singer who had performed in most European cities. She'd enjoyed a particularly good run in Germany, but after very nobly refusing to sing at a gathering for the Führer in person, all further concerts there were cancelled for her.

Lone was connected to us in every way. She was the daughter of Grandma Georgía's sister and had, moreover, been born in Iceland. Her father, Mogens Bang, had been a doctor in Reykjavík at the turn of the century and Lone was reared in Reykjavík until the age of twelve, when her family moved to Nykøbing on the island of Falster. She therefore always spoke impeccable Icelandic, although her vocabulary was occasionally slightly infantile. When Grandad Sveinn was appointed ambassador to Copenhagen in 1920, she was invited to live with him and Grandma while she studied singing at the Royal Academy of Music. A twenty-year-old woman entered the home of a forty-year-old couple, her maternal aunt and her husband, and immediately gained the affection of her children. She later studied in Paris and dedicated herself to the folk songs of all countries and could eventually sing in seventeen languages and speak seven. She was a constant guest of the family's, right up to Grandad's death. He never called her anything else but his Songbird, and her visits were greeted like the joyful arrival of spring.

Lone was no classic beauty, but possessed an unusually striking air. Her face was as alluring as her voice, her cheekbones as high-set as her hair, a majestic nose that was often considered 'Jewish,' although I'd often heard her regret the fact that there was not a single drop of Jewish blood had been traced in her family. She had passionately embraced Judaic culture, sang their folk songs both in Yiddish and Hebrew and was never able to forgive my father for having joined the National Socialists.

One hot summer evening in July 1937 a party was thrown at Ocean House. The guests included the famous actor Poul Reumert and his Icelandic wife, Anna Borg, who owned a summer house in the area and were acquaintances of my grandparents. I recall very little of that night, apart from the clatter of Mum's heels and the concert after dinner. Her accompanist was Reuter, who sat at the grand piano, and my cousin Lone stood erect in a simple black dress with her hair and chin up. She introduced the songs in Danish, with their history and the stories they told. In my memory her voice is just as peculiar as her face: not exactly beautiful, but clear and enchantingly quirky. The final song was in Icelandic:

Little children playing,
Lying in the moor,
Lying in the gullies and laughing ho ho ho . . .

Grandad stood up in the middle of the applause and walked over to her, radiating with joy. He took her hand and made her bow once more, as he exclaimed out loud in Icelandic: 'The Songbird of Spring has arrived!' At that moment the whole family, inebriated by the wine and the sun, was united in joy; apple-red faces in white shirts with rolled-up sleeves. It was the first time I sat in their midst and the last time I saw us whole.

22

Leader-Induced Paralysis

1937

My father caught the military bug early on, as Grandma Vera used to say. She saw something in his working methods in the haymaking back home on the island that others didn't see: a kind of relentlessness mixed with the premonition of his own defeat. 'He had the same blind zeal I'd all too often seen out in Oddbjarnarsker, which pushed many men to drown at sea.'

Dad embraced Nazism, was one of the very few Icelanders who fought with the Germans in the Second World War, and was the only one to cross into Russia with a gun. I think it was the uniform that seduced him more than anything. His grandfather had been the second Minister of Iceland and his father the first ambassador of the country; they both had gold-embroidered uniforms in their wardrobes and hard hats with feathers. Dad, on the other hand, had none of that garb; even if he'd managed to run an important company in Copenhagen for fourteen months, the adventure came to an abrupt end in a shady bar in Kiel. An unscrupulous colleague in the whorehouse had run off with his receipts, bills of lading and wallet, leaving my father hostage to the pimps for two days until the ambassador of Iceland intervened and settled the bill for his nocturnal escapade and seventeen thousand steel clothes pegs for industrial laundries.

A few weeks later he showed up for the haymaking in Breidafjördur, and then he headed to Germany the following spring to pick his university. By some unfortunate coincidence, having barely reached the age of thirty, he happened to be standing on a pier in Hamburg on 5 May 1937, when for the first time he saw 'Hjalti,' who was officiating over the launch of the gigantic cruise liner *Wilhelm Gustloff* in a grand ceremony in front of a vast crowd. (Before the war, Dad and other Icelanders used to call Hitler by the Icelandic name Hjalti, and a few years later, after the famous series of Hjalti children's books came out, I started calling him 'little Hjalti,' much to my father's horror.) Dad often spoke about that event. Beholding the Führer seemed to have branded his soul. Already by then the Nordic Studies faculty in Lübeck had changed into some kind of Nazism-justification department: its roots were steeped in Old Norse mythology and the Icelandic Sagas; its ideology stemmed from those glorious blonds who inhabited the Great North. Dad was therefore a weak man in the wrong place, a blond Viking who spoke German with an Aryan accent and, what's more, came from a high-ranking family. Twenty minutes before the war, Himmler's bloodhounds sniffed him out and discovered that Herr Björnsson was not just a super Aryan but also the son of the highest official in the land, a formidable catch. They offered him a gilded grey uniform. With runic letters: *SS*.

Hans Henrik suffered severely from what some people call leader-induced paralysis, or starstruckness. The symptoms are clear: In the presence of a leader or film star, the subject loses his faculties of speech and free will. The ability to reason diminishes and the face moulds itself into a canine smile, coupled with a hanging-tongue syndrome. This is a paralysing condition that can afflict the most unlikely people and transform noble gentlemen into drooling puppies.

People who suffer from leader-induced paralysis (LIP) always feel a compulsion to follow strong men. In that sense my father was representative of the German nation: an upright man bent by humiliation, a man of great heritage but no future. But he was far from being a Nazi by nature. He was kind to everyone, and his only friend in Argentina after the war was a Jew. He didn't subscribe to the Nazi heresy because he agreed with their extreme views, but simply because of his vulnerability to the dazzling glow of power. He mistook his weakness for strength and his uniform for proof that he was a man among men.

Instead of being a son of the new Iceland, he joined up with the murderers of Europe. That was the real tragedy of his life, a fact he could never flee from. Like a stray dog he roamed from one country to the next, without ever being able to remove that SS collar. Not even Mum could get it off him when, freshly widowed, she took him back into the house. And death didn't manage to remove it either. His memory will always be soiled by the mistakes he made at the age of thirty.

How would the great Freud have interpreted my father's error? Most sons kill their fathers sooner or later. The lucky ones do it with their own hands, others hire someone else to do it for them, but Dad would settle for no less than the entire German army to avenge himself for his defeat in the battles of Reykjavík, Vejle and Kiel.

There is nothing more risible than the vengeance of a coward, and nothing more tragic.

23

Aldon Heath

2009

There is a man named Aldon Heath and he lives in Australia. I've
never been there. But he writes to me enthusiastically at the end
of his day, which is the morning mail for me. I skim through it,
along with the obituaries, and answer if I feel like it. It's mostly
tedious abdominal measurements, really. In the olden days it was
said that the people down under walked upside down. In the case
of Aldon, this might be true. His mind never stretches higher than
his waist, and his waist seems to dominate his whole existence. But
I doubt he's any more gifted down there, even though his entire
intellect is stored right there in that small skin pouch split into two
compartments.

He works as a muscle inspector in some gym in downtown
Melbourne and updates me on the status of his torso the way
Icelanders do about the weather.

'*Just got home from a three-hour power session with Bod. It sure takes its
toll, working out this hard after a day's work. But of course, we intend to do
even better after your e-mail last week.*'

What a bitch I can be.

*We really went for it tonight. Sixty minutes on the mill and then bench
presses and weights. Bod did 295 lbs on the bench, which doesn't happen every*

71

day. We were the last out, after Jeff gave up on the bench. As I was telling you, he got first prize two years ago and second last year when Héctor won. But Bod is way better than them now. Makes all the difference having Miss World behind you! He's increased his muscle mass. This evening's measurements are: weight 196, muscle mass percentage 44, arms 18, torso 48, waist 33, thighs 26. Promise better readings tomorrow. Might cut eggs down to six.

'*Love, yours, Aldon.*'

I'd like to point out that the brute writes in a lingo that's too modern for a woman who learned her English in Greenwich Village bars in the fifties. Lóa has been polite enough to translate some of it for me and discreet enough not to ask any questions.

I allow 'Linda' to torment this macho wonder mercilessly. He has absolutely no brain, this guy, and refers to his own body in the third person, as if it were his pet dog. Linda plays along with the game and sends her regards to Bod, saying that she can't wait to meet him and hopes he'll be 'in shape' when the moment comes. But the beauty queen sets clear demands on results; she only mixes with winners. The Melbourne bodybuilding tournament is imminent, and our man is throwing heart and soul into it. He comes home boiling hot at the end of the day and fries his eggs on his flat belly and bacon on his forehead. Then he downs some steroids, bless him, and something called a protein drink, which Lóa tells me people drink in all the gyms of the world.

It occurs to me that I could try to build up my 'muscle mass' with those steroids, but Lóa tells me I'm aggressive enough as it is, without having to top myself off with that stuff. Some body-obsessed relative of hers had a bad experience on that front, showed up at a family do with a puffed-up chest and winged arms, threw himself on the table and started biting it, and got involved in some rape case, which was all fist and fury, however, since one of the unfortunate side effects of steroids is that they shrink a man's tool to the size of a pea.

No doubt this is also the case with Aldon, the Aussie. The guy's raving mad.

'*Bod starts his tanning sessions tomorrow. Three weeks to go and everything on full steam. We want to keep the engines going full throttle after the victory because Bod wants to be in top form when he meets you in London. And the pussy ban is still in force, of course. You can trust me on that. The Linda muscle is still a restricted area.*'

Miss Pétursdóttir has promised to meet him at the May Fair Hotel in London right after the competition. I'm playing with fire. Because I've got a fire organ, too, somewhere, rusty and sooty as it may be.

24

Fire Organ

1953

She called it 'the fire organ,' my German friend in Argentina, while others call it 'twat' or 'snatch,' but Mum always called it 'the date.' This was in the days when dates were never seen in Iceland.

Sex was never a taboo subject here in Iceland; we just never spoke about it. But we've never been prudes, we women of ice and vice, fish workers and fancy queens.

I was slow to awaken to my body, not for the lack of cock-a-doodle-doos, but it took me a long time to master my instrument. It wasn't until seven years after my first rape that I finally reached carnal nirvana, after lengthy fumbling. It was in Buenos Aires after the war. I lived there for a while with a German girl from a major Nazi family, who taught me a lot, but in particular one invaluable thing.

I can still hear her cries of feminist liberation in that zealous, exuberant Bavarian Nazi tone of hers. Hildegard was her name, although she called herself Heidi, pretended to be Swiss, and wore a cross instead of a swastika around her neck.

'The spark lives in every woman. Who doesn't want to kindle it into a flame? That's why we've got *die Werkzeuge*. And this is something we can do on our own; men don't know how to handle our fire organs,' said the curly blonde carnal creature, adjusting her breasts in the high, narrow kitchen of our boulevard apartment in Baires, where we sat at length in front of the oven, our only source of heat, smoking like chimneys and baring our secrets. Then she lifted her middle finger and asked what it was called in Icelandic.

'We call it *langatöng,* which literally means "long poker,"' I answered, explaining it to her in German.

'Long poker! You see! Fire organ!' she exclaimed, screwing up her eyes as she burst into a joyous laugh that reshuffled the freckles on her face. She had beautiful golden-brown skin, which almost seemed artificial it was so perfect. She had chosen far too banal an alias. For a girl like her, Heidi was just a joke like everything else. And we could certainly joke and laugh, God, how we laughed, two blond girls in their prime.

Outside the tall kitchen windows our male contemporaries sounded their horns and yelled from their cars, the impatient and badly shaven sons of the twentieth century who never learned the art of unlocking a woman.

Heidi possessed this knowledge. And passed it on to other women. She'd acquired her bed skills from a Colombian cowgirl in a ranch at the foot of the Andes, a true finger master with a clitoris the size of a nipple. She herself had most probably learned it at a young age from a half-Dutch mulatto girl on a river ferry. Heidi taught me the science, and I in turn taught it to others. I remember two students at least, a Norwegian nun on the ship back from my American exile, and then Lilja, my Bæring's daughter, a colossal hulk from Bolungarvík who later converted to lesbianism.

Bob, the Yank, was the only male I managed to some extent to guide along the tortuous path of feminine pleasure. My Icelandic Jóns were more interested in male genealogy than in female sexuality. The Kansas man was also the only man in my life who knew and wanted more than I did. He opened up new frontiers of pleasure that an Icelandic maiden had hardly even read about. He gave me a vibrator, a wondrous tool, and then wanted to photograph me in full action, but I told him that Icelandic presidential protocol prevented me from doing so.

The Americas therefore provided my schooling in eroticism, so to speak, north and south. Up until then I'd lain under men without thinking of my own needs and assumed those physical exertions had more to do with vanity than with pleasure. Although there was little satisfaction to be drawn from it, one could pride oneself on having done it. For me it was just an interlude of tedious pumping or a 'boink,' as Bæring used to call it much later in that unbearable way of his. I've always said it takes the average woman twenty years to fully master her bed tools. That's why I'm so insistent on my Lóa getting started as soon as possible; she's over twenty now and her face is starting to show signs of LDP: lust deficiency paralysis. A person's facial muscles are a clear indicator of how active they've been on the mattress and how much electro-cock treatment they're getting. That woman who reads the news on TV looks pretty frigid.

Heidi's parents were famous Nazis who had managed to flee and had lived on the banks of the Silver River, Río de la Plata, where they are now buried in Catholic soil under Swiss names. Of course, I could have denounced them since I had once seen the couple's address on the back of a letter addressed to Heidi, but I was a miserable coward and, what's more, grateful for the gift she'd given me: with all the intransigence of her father, the commander of a concentration camp, she spurred me on towards achieving the megaorgasm, *Großorgasmus*.

'You can never give up! Never!' she yelled at me after I'd been slaving away at it in my room for days.

But after several arduous training sessions, a triumphant cheer echoed down the corridor as she heard me hit the target. Up until then I'd only felt a hint of satisfaction produced by friction against door frames, saddles and broom handles, but with her dictatorial powers Heidi had opened up a bottomless drilling hole to me, which is somewhat lime-encrusted today. Finally I understood sex.

But this demonstrates the peculiar meanness of the Almighty Farmer Above towards us women: the fact that we have to rub ourselves to the bone to reach the core of rapture, while all a man has to do is touch his wand with a stick. To be a woman, one has to be a Nazi.

25

The Cogwheel of Time

2009

I don't know what happened to my Heidi, any more than those seven thousand other people whose paths I've crossed in my days. I see on the net that every day the equivalent of half the population of Iceland dies. That's 100 people a minute, 1.6 people a second. I guess we could call that the speed of human history.

The cogwheel of time keeps on turning, and a hundred ants are crushed with each rotation. While the rest of us try to climb that gigantic wheel to escape the relentless onslaught of the cog, those who dwell 'above' can *enjoy life*. But they're barely halfway through their champagne glasses when they suddenly find themselves 'below' again and have to rush if they don't want to be squashed as time meets space.

Seven billion ants form a glistening black 'tyre' around the toothed wheel, which flattens as it rolls against the ground, like the punctured tyre of an old lorry.

That's the life that some genius created for us people of the earth, setting those famous parameters called the cradle and the grave. Life never allows anyone to relax, no one except me, lying here in my sorry old state, waiting for the cogwheel to drag me down to my end.

26

On the Fifth Floor in Lübeck

1940

Well, well. Lübeck is a beautiful city with all its marzipan and its Thomas Mann and all those pavements he once strolled upon, but the main drawback is that a petty salesman lurks on every corner. Everything revolves around small change there, that eternal pocket jingle. People spend the whole day giving you back the right change. I was an eleven-year-old girl who'd never seen cash before except when Grandad Sveinn bought us ice cream, but I was quick to realise that coins were as precious to those Schleswig people as words were to Icelanders.

The German word for small change is *pfennig*, a word that is impossible to pronounce without the greatest respect. The face of an Icelander acquires the cold and empty expression of a cash register as he spurts out his insignificant words for something even more insignificant. Money savers never enjoyed any respect in Iceland, while squanderers were always admired.

But there we were, a newly reunited family of three in a new country and a new city, with a new future. After Grandad had liberated Dad from German custody and cash duty, the young man would accept no more support, least of all financial, so we lived in a cold cubbyhole on the top floor of a tall, narrow brick building where I counted 133 steps up and 132 steps down. 'Always longer up than down,' Dad would say. The view from the kitchen window was memorable: crow-stepped gables and mediaeval towers, the whole of Europe stretching beyond the horizon. Dad enrolled at the Nazi faculty and specialised in Hitlerian concepts and Aryan mythology. As already mentioned, the runic SS letters held him firmly by the balls, but he was careful not to mention this unruly mistress in front of his wife. Mum had been brought up in Breidafjördur, where no nonsense had washed ashore since Christianity had been dispatched to the island of Flatey in 1002.

She possessed an uncontaminated mind.

When the first spring of the war came, the issue could no longer be ignored. I remember the conversation in that tiny attic kitchen in May 1940. Mum stood by the open window, Dad on the threshold, and I between them at a minuscule table where I was busy colouring an Icelandic flag that flapped majestically like an unmanned magic carpet over an abandoned turf farmhouse.

'The army?' said Mum. 'Why? Who ... who are you going to fight for?'

Dad shrugged. 'I'll fight with my friends.'

'For God's sake, Hansi. What has an Icelander got to do with a war? Has an Icelander ever fought in a war?'

'No, up until now we haven't been manly enough.'

'Manly enough? Thank God, I say.'

'Massa. Iceland was occupied this morning.'

'What are you saying?'

'I heard the news on the wireless today, at Peter's. He can listen to the British news on the BBC.'

'Isn't that forbidden?'

'Yes. But he's in the party, so no one suspects him. They took Iceland this morning. Not a single shot was heard.'

'Thank God.'

'Thank God? That just shows you what cowards we are, we Icelanders.'

'Hans Henrik, what's got into you? The Danes put up no resistance either.'

'No. Naturally they saw that surrender was their best defence.'

'What do you mean?'

'They landed on the right side and don't have to fear a war in their country. They can sleep soundly while the missiles fly over the skies of Denmark. Like snow buntings in a snowstorm, that's the Danes for you. Because they're not the target, Germany is.'

'Don't you think the English will try to liberate the Danes?'

'Why should they do that? Who gives a damn about Denmark? A few pig farms and two breweries . . .'

'How can you talk like that about . . . about your motherland? And the Danes, who've treated your father so well . . .'

'Father has no illusions about them, even if he has a Danish wife. He knows nations never do other nations any favours. It's each man for himself.'

'Didn't the English go to war because of Poland?'

'The English only think of London,' said Dad. 'Their only fear is seeing Germany from Dover.'

'Hansi. What I don't understand is this . . . this need for aggression. Why do the Germans need to conquer all those countries? What can they do with all these countries? . . . Aren't they happy just living at home?'

Dad lowered his voice: 'Massa, watch your tongue!'

'As if they understood this tongue.'

'Wilfried downstairs is a fellow student. He's fluent in Icelandic.'

Mum hissed: 'How many countries does this man have to rule over? I say what Mum says, why can't he hop on a train if he wants to visit places? This is as if . . . as if Eysteinn in Svefneyjar suddenly wanted to rule over all the islands in Breidafjördur. Then he wouldn't be able to do any of his farming work. All his time would just go into holding on to those lands. He who has everything can't enjoy anything, Mum says.'

'Mum … Mum … and what if … if the islands of Grasey and Lyngey had been taken from him? Wouldn't he have the right to reclaim them? Germany was humiliated in the last war. We have the right to—'

'For God's sake, Hansi, don't say "we."'

'What about the Sudetenland, Prussia, Alsace? . . . That's all German land.'

'Yes, and Norway, Denmark, and Iceland as well. Hansi, can't you see, this is nothing more than … than megalomania.'

'Iceland?'

'Yes, didn't you say that Iceland was occupied this morning?'

'Yes, but not by the Germans.'

'No? By whom, then?'

'Iceland was occupied by the English. We've turned into an English colony.'

'The English?'

And now there was a pause in the conversation. I continued colouring the Icelandic flag, but the blue lead was getting all used up, starting to smudge on the sheet. But I didn't dare lean over to grab the pencil sharpener on the kitchen sideboard beside the dustbin. When super powers are battling, little people should sit still. The news clearly came as a shock to my mother.

'Do you understand what I'm saying now?' said Dad.

Mum was silent. She turned to the sink, slowly turned on the tap, and stared at the water a good while.

Dad admonished her. 'Don't let it run like that. They say there might be a water shortage this summer.'

She stretched out for a pot, filled it up halfway, shut off the tap, and placed the pot on the stove without turning the gas on. Then she turned back to Dad, who was still standing in the doorway in a white shirt with rolled-up sleeves, one elbow propped against the frame. He brushed his hair back from his forehead with his hand.

'And did they take . . . has the whole of Iceland been occupied?' Mum wanted to know.

'Yes.'

'The islands, too?'

'Breidafjördur? I expect so.'

'But . . . there are so many . . .'

I pictured two thousand soldiers capturing two thousand islands. And standing their watch, one on each skerry, straight as arrows, with rifles slung over their shoulders. And the seals on the surrounding foreshore, like a navy of fat, unknown enemies.

We'd lived there in a place that was a world unto itself and not always a part of Iceland. One of the farmers on the islands had commented that it was good to live there but a shame to be surrounded by Danish mountains. And when the country was finally granted independence in 1944, Grandma is reputed to have said, 'Now maybe we can start trading with those good people.' By then she'd lived a long life under the Danish flag, as a Danish subject, but her soul never yielded to them.

'And what does that mean, then,' Mum asked, 'the fact that we've been occupied by the British?'

'It means that Iceland, which is ruled by Denmark, which is now ruled by Germany, is under the British.'

'Can't we get any more nations to rule over us?'

Dad bowed his head and watched himself gently kick the base of the door frame with his pointy shoe. That is the scene as I picture it now, but back then I had my back turned to him at the kitchen table facing an open window, stooped over my drawing.

'We're just small change in the world's pocket, sullied by thousands of dirty fingers. Danish yesterday, German today, British tomorrow. We own nothing, are nothing, and can do nothing. *Für immer und ewig kaputt.*'

'But we always have the spring,' said Mum dreamily. 'That'll always be Icelandic.' That's the way people sometimes spoke in Iceland before the war, and one never knew whether they'd borrowed it from a book by Halldór Laxness or whether he had stolen it from

Mum spent the entire first evening crying in Helle's arms while Grandma, who because of her position couldn't embrace people, sat opposite them and shook her head at her son's incomprehensible decision. How could he have joined the army that daily humiliated his mother's native land? Yes, here we sat: four disenchanted women who had found some respite from the infernal clutches of time to sigh a little about the stupidity of men.

All the jollity had vanished from the streets of Copenhagen. This great 'redbrick Paris' was but a shadow of its former self; German long coats were on every corner and the streets were smothered by a Sunday-like silence. Restaurants were closed, lights were out in most windows, and even the spiral towers seemed terrified. Virtually no one had been killed and not a single building had been blown up, but the people's eyes reflected a nation in ruins.

Icelanders, on the other hand, were happy to be invaded. Anyone who lives on a forsaken cold crag an hour's journey by boat away from the nearest post office will gladly welcome any guest, even if he is bearing a gun.

I sensed, though, that the German occupation of Denmark went down worse with the men than with the women. They took the humiliation more personally and muttered into their breast pockets that they would have happily died trying to delay the Germans' march into their flat country. 'Even by just half an hour.' And that's men down to a T. They choose death over wounded pride. Women deal with it better because they're used to lying under strangers.

Still though, I'm not sure the Glistrup approach to defence (abolishing the army and buying an answering machine with a 'we surrender' recorded message on it) is the best solution for the wretched nations of the north. It would be more suitable to put together a Nordic army made up of only women. That way there would never be any danger of an invasion. Men never shoot women unless they're unarmed.

Like the city itself, the embassy had acquired a funereal air. Grandma had aged by a whole decade and was never without a cigarillo. We later realised her marriage was in shreds. In the preceding years Grandad had travelled a great deal, attending meetings in Malmö and Madrid and Icelandic promotions in Brussels and Bern . . . Grandma didn't fail to notice that her husband's daily programme frequently ended with a recital from her niece, Lone Bang.

28

'Hi, Litla!'

1940

The ambassador's residence had now been transferred to the district of Kalvebod Brygge, and it offered a wonderful view of the harbour. Grandma Georgía described how she and Grandad had stood at the living-room window a month before, on the evening of Monday, 8 April, watching a fleet of German cargo ships file past. The old lady had a nose for major events and immediately sensed what was about to happen, but she and Grandad were perhaps the only people in the country who knew the Germans were preparing to occupy Denmark. The Icelandic ambassador had heard it mentioned at meetings in London before Christmas, a secret that he had tried to whisper to the Danish authorities on several occasions but that was always met with total denial: 'That will never happen!' At five thirty the next morning, on 9 April a thousand warplanes appeared in the skies of majestic Copenhagen.

Dad came in mid-June. He had broken his arm in the military academy and been given three weeks' sick leave. 'My God, did you break your Hitler salute?' Grandma asked in Danish, without waiting for an answer, marching towards the living room along the glistening corridor with such force that the ash fell from the small cigar she held at the height of her right hip, as if she were towing a toy on a string.

Mum kissed him on the cheek with her bright red lipstick. He carried her kiss until dinnertime, when Helle asked him if he'd injured himself.

It was strange to see the Nazi novice so intimidated by two women in civvies. His coyness seemed particularly at odds with his SS uniform. At home every general is reduced to a private. There was also something slightly pathetic about the way he greeted his fellow soldiers outside Tivoli with a Hitler salute in a cast. Dad always thundered in German with an Icelandic accent, and I frequently got the feeling that the Germans answered him with a 'Hi, *litla!*' – hi, little one.

As a polite little girl, I answered them with a 'hi,' much to my father's horror, since 'hi' was pure American.

'The Hitler salute is no laughing matter! You shouldn't make fun of war!'

I was allowed to continue sleeping with Mum because Dad slept alone in the guest room, in line with the theory that a German soldier should sleep only with his ideals and Fatherland.

'And the Führer...' Mum added with a laugh as she and Grandma sat in a corner of the kitchen crocheting, chatting and smoking, while Helle stirred the macaroni stew.

'As soon as men stop loving their women and start loving other men, then we get war,' said the cook over the pot.

Dad was quick to realise that there was no point in fighting the female army at home and turned his attention to me instead. In my memory those were the best times I had with him. We were welcomed everywhere outside the house, and he took me to the royal palace and cafés. His uniform guaranteed us timorous smiles from every waiter and driver. And my friend Åse frequently got to tag along. She was the daughter of the Norwegian plenipotentiary who lived on the floor below us, a lively girl of my age. She taught me how to play ping-pong and rummy and introduced me to Shirley Temple and ringlets. Dad took us to a salon to get professionals to put some into our hair, and we danced and sang 'Animal Crackers in My Soup' all the way home. Dad's presence ensured us the right to laugh in the street. Grandma obviously wasn't a bit happy about our ringlets, and the day after, when she saw we had shed them in our sleep (I've always had impossible hair), she gave the SS man a stern lecture on the stupidity of squandering money. But the old woman descended from a bean-counting race and always had problems with the spendthriftiness of Icelanders.

Åse was dark haired and jovial, but well brought up and placid in that Scandinavian way. She never crossed the yellow line the era had drawn across every moment, every social class. Her parents were collaborators, of course, and I therefore gained a lot of esteem in her eyes when my father appeared in a German uniform. I myself tried to make the most of the situation, balancing myself between him, Mum and Grandma. I'd come running into the kitchen: 'Dad won't allow me to have a sugar cube, he's just a Nazi!' Or dashing out to Dad: 'Mum won't let me wear my Sunday shoes in Tivoli. She doesn't understand National Socio . . . Socianism.'

Åse had a subscription to the Tivoli amusement park. I made Dad buy one for me, too, and got her to guide me around it like Alice in Wonderland. We fantasised about being two orphans in a turbulent world at war, who always managed to scrape out alive from the Allies' torture machines, such as American bumper cars, British ghost trains and French Ferris wheels. The little women with the big war code names, Åshild and Herbjörg, ran out of the war park screeching but suddenly shut up when they met four German soldiers on the pavement outside.

'Why were you afraid of them?' I said.

'I wasn't afraid of them.'

'Yes! You immediately shut up. I thought you were with the Germans.'

'You should never laugh at a guy with a gun, my dad says. How come you don't support the Germans like your dad?'

'Mum says the whole war is to be blamed on one man. And that the only thing he needs is love.'

'But we all love him.'

'But are you sure he loves you?'

'Of course.'

'It's a weird kind of love, then. He does nothing but scream.'

'Hitler loves Germany like his own arm, Dad says. He's willing to die for it.'

'Why does he want to die for his arm?'

'Huh?'

'If you sacrifice yourself for an arm, you'll just leave one arm behind when you die. What can you do with a severed arm?'

'Oh, Herra, I just mean that he's prepared to die for his country. Wouldn't you be prepared to die for Iceland?'

'No.'

'No? If your country were in danger, if some dragon were about to eat it or something?'

'What would the country gain from me dying? Countries don't want people to die for them. They just want to be left in peace.'

'But if someone takes them?'

'You can't take countries, Mum says.'

'Hey! The Germans took Denmark. In ten minutes! And Norway in a fortnight. The British took you and . . . and the Danes have had Iceland for hundreds of years!'

'Yeah? And what has it changed for us? What am I? Danish, English or Icelandic?'

Åse looked into my eyes and opened her mouth, which uttered no sound. The answer was clear.

29

Death of a Soldier

1940

We were silent on the way home. I looked around at the people, streets and houses. You could tell Denmark was a dead country at a mere glance. It was clear that even the lamp posts were in mourning. Cars drove down the streets in a funereal silence. Many windows were concealed behind dark curtains, and pitch-black swastikas fluttered over public buildings like ominous eagles. All of a sudden I felt the chill of the occupation and broke into a cold sweat at the same time that I reached the height of my ten years, acquired a new maturity, and understood that Mum was right: it is impossible to occupy a country. It's like wanting to control someone in his own home.

I said goodbye to Åse on the landing and ran up the stairs into our apartment, which now seemed as vast as a whole region to me: the last free patch in Denmark, an Icelandic island in the middle of the ocean of war, inhabited by a few isolated people.

Yes, we were even more isolated than the people back home in Breidafjördur because now there was no longer any telephone contact with Reykjavík. The last phone call had come from Grandad to Grandma: 'They want me to be governor. It's a new post, temporary, while the occupation lasts.' Then Grandma passed the receiver to

Dad, and the future governor of Iceland spoke with Hitler's future soldier. I remember him standing in the long corridor, with one foot on a Turkish rug and the expression of a stubborn twelve-year-old as he listened to his father.

'Son, they . . . they say that a father who watches his son go to war feels . . . feels two things.' His voice quivered slightly. 'Pride, on one hand . . . and apprehension, on the other.'

'Yeah?'

'It pains me, son . . . It pains me to feel only one of those emotions.'

'Yeah?'

I think Dad was spared a death on the battlefield by the fact that he was already dead before he left.

30

Mashed Turnip

1940

The uniform-obsessed man was, of course, always in his grey jacket, complete with shoulder straps and a collar marked 'SS.' Grandma had asked, if not ordered, him on several occasions to spare her these horrors under her roof, but Dad said that he couldn't be seen in civvies.

'But we have guests this evening and I would prefer it if . . .' she'd answer in Danish.

'I'm afraid I can't, Mother. The rules of the Third Reich are very strict in this regard. Apart from the fact that it's very difficult to take off the jacket with this cast on.'

In the evening the seven of us sat at the table: seven little dwarfs from a snow-white island that had absolutely no impact on the history of the world and yet each one of them was a world unto himself. On this occasion we were dining with Dad's siblings Puti and Kylla, and Jón Krabbe, a half-Danish Icelander who now headed the embassy after Grandad's departure and whom Grandma sometimes invited for dinner. I remember him precisely because of how unmemorable he was, as is often the case with diplomats. He was a handsome but wooden man in his seventies with a straight nose and white hair, a flash of exuberance in his eyes, but stiff lips and slightly oversized ears. They were the best weapon in his diplomatic arsenal: here was a man who listened. Jón always tilted his head slightly before he spoke, to emphasise the fact that the words he was about to speak did not necessarily reflect his own personal opinion or that of the Icelandic government but were open for discussion.

Grandma sat at the end and glared at the SS insignia on my father, as he slipped into the place furthest away from her. I sat opposite him and felt as if I were sitting at a negotiating table. Because it was a tricky situation. Grandma was a Danish aristocrat who was married to an Icelander and despised the Germans. Dad was a German soldier who was married to an Icelandic woman and despised the Danes. Jón Krabbe was a half-Icelandic official, married to a Danish woman, who every day had to bow to the Germans. Puti was a half-Danish, but optimistic Icelander who allowed himself to dream of an independent Iceland. Kylla was also Icelandic Danish but married to a Faeroese man who considered the idea of Icelandic independence utterly ludicrous. Mum was from Breidafjördur and saw everything from the perspective of the sea. I was still a work in progress.

So in came the good old rosy-cheeked Helle, who convinced herself that the deadly silence was due to the utter failure of her mashed turnip and rabbit pie, and started to blab nervously.

'Have I ever told you the story about Ebbe Roe?' she began, with a nervous laugh. 'No? Haven't I? There was once a turnip farmer back home called Ebbe Roe. One day he found a giant turnip in his garden. It was so big that everyone told him to take it to the agricultural fair in Hobro, where it won a prize. To celebrate, Ebbe took it to an inn, but there it was stolen from him.' She became more animated, chuckling as she continued, 'Ebbe searched for it all over town and finally found the turnip in a gambling club on the outskirts. Someone had bet it and lost, and after Ebbe Roe –' Helle paused to catch her breath, laughing harder, 'After Ebbe Roe had lost his house, cattle, wife, children, shoes and braces, he finally managed to win the turnip back and walked out into the dawn with it. Then he got hungry and decided to take a bite from the giant turnip. BUT. IT TASTED. BAD.' She howled, between shrieks of laughter. 'It tasted so bad that he gave it to a poor family he met on the road, ha-ha-ha. And then he walked towards the rising sun in his socks with his trousers around his heels . . . That's a story from Jutland for you.'

This was followed by an awkward silence as the ambassador's family stared at the cook with a strained smile. They had learned from their very first years in the Icelandic foreign service not to interrupt people, however loquacious they seemed, and not to pass judgement on them, even if they were servants. It was something we could be proud of, to be the only Icelanders who understood the protocol of international courtesy.

'Oh, what a delightful story,' Grandma finally exclaimed in Danish, half-closing her eyes. Then she smiled and nodded at the cook, who clocked her expression and light-footedly choo-chooed out of the dining room, parting with a sentence that hovered in the air like a trail of locomotive smoke.

'I just hope you haven't lost your appetite for my turnip! Ha-ha.'

'A typical Danish parable. No one's allowed to be better than anyone else here, and the worst thing that can happen to you is a stroke of luck,' said Dad as soon as the door closed.

'It's never good to have a stroke of luck,' answered his sister, Kylla.

'You've lived here too long,' said Dad.

'Do you think you've had a stroke of luck?' Puti asked, grinning with his chubby cheeks.

'What do you mean?' Dad said.

'Come on, you must be able to see it. You think you're going to get a slice of that giant turnip that's growing bigger and bigger and will soon be the size of Europe.'

'Are you comparing the Thousand-Year Reich to a turnip?' Dad asked, indignant.

'No, not a turnip, a giant turnip,' his brother said with a smirk.

Kylla sat between Jón Krabbe and Dad, and now, leaning forward, she said, 'Have you thought this through, Hansi? What will you do if Hitler loses the war?'

Dad had the expression of a rooster that had just entered an empty henhouse. He'd never heard anything like this before.

'Loses? What do you mean?'

His sister fixed her gaze on him without moving her head, and said, 'It's very likely. No one can win a war in five countries at the same time.'

'Then he'll just cash in his braces and shoes and get his turnip back,' said Puti, in an effort to lighten the atmosphere.

It didn't work. Everything froze at the table. Krabbe exchanged glances with each brother in turn, like a chaperone at a kids' dance, as he scooped the remains of his sauce onto his fork with a knife. Mum had emptied her plate and smoothed the napkin on her broad lap. Puti sat between Mum and me and, after a generous gulp of red wine, deflected the conversation back to Grandma.

'Isn't that story by what's his name . . . H. C. Andersen?'

'No, it's just a typical old Jutland tale,' said the ambassador's wife, stabbing her meat with a fork.

'Which is now German,' Puti added teasingly, and to complete the joke he clicked his heels under the table and raised his right arm: '*Sieg Heil!* What made it really funny, though, was that Puti lifted his arm as if it was in a cast, like Dad's.

I released a laugh, but Mum managed to swallow hers. Dad darted me a glance of disapproval and surprise. He'd turned bright red and sat at the end of the table like a beetroot in a grey jacket. Grandma stared at her Puti in astonishment. His joke seemed to have caught everyone off guard. Dad didn't know how to respond. At first he pushed his chair back from the table as if he intended to leave, but then he stopped and instead delivered a sermon in defence of Hitler and Nazism. He didn't get far, however, because Grandma halted him to remind him that we were not sitting under German rule and that freedom of speech reigned here, and then she asked him in the kindest of tones to stand outside on the windowsill if he wanted to sing the brown shirts' praises. Then she looked away to avert her son's stern gaze and said that while she didn't make a habit of imposing her politics on her children, she asked him to please ponder on his father's words when, on returning from a business trip to Berlin, he had said that Nazism struck him as a society turned upside down, where the beer cellar reigned over universities, parliament and church.

'But . . . but those are precisely the institutions that failed,' Dad said. 'The times called for new and unconventional solutions. Isn't Dad going to be governor at the service of the British? The civil servant who takes over from the king! Isn't that turning things upside down?'

Puti looked at his mother in surprise.

'Is that true, Mother? Is Dad going to be governor?'

Lady Georgía didn't answer.

'He'd never do that. Dad would never betray the king of Denmark,' said Kylla.

'Betray the king? How can Iceland serve him when it's been occupied by the English and the king by us?' Dad asked authoritatively. The blushing was gone now.

'By *us*? Tosh!' Grandma thundered in Danish. 'You're not German, Hans Henrik! You're my son!'

Grandma wasn't used to outbursts, and a new kind of silence descended on the table and lasted until she hesitantly stretched out for a sip of wine. Puti tried to revive the conversation: 'Krabbe, what exactly is Iceland's position with regard to Denmark now?'

Krabbe tilted his head before commencing his reply, and carefully averted all our gazes while he spoke.

'I think the Danes fully understand that the Icelanders need to, to some extent, take care of their own affairs in their current predicament in full cooperation with the occupying forces, in the same way that we Icelanders must understand the predicament of the Danes with regard to their distinguished invaders.'

In its journey around the table, Krabbe's gaze had locked on Dad's eyes as he pronounced those last words: 'with regard to their distinguished invaders.' Then he bowed his head again, as if waiting to be absolved of his impudence. The guests sat without batting an eyelid. No one seemed to comprehend these tactful words with their soporific effect. And to quash any protest that might be voiced by anyone who had understood his words, the official snatched the napkin off his lap and painstakingly raised it to his mouth, as if to prevent it from uttering any further indiscretions. That was the role of the diplomat: to shock people with courtesy.

The table was therefore silent again until Helle returned to carry away the dishes. Recovering her senses, Grandma turned to Mum.

'So what do you make of that Ebbe Roe tale, Massebill?'

'Yes, well, they sometimes caught giant halibuts in the nets back home in Svefneyjar, but it always caused problems, destroyed the nets, and made the lads too cocky. They always had to sail straight to Flatey to show it off. And it doesn't taste particularly good either.'

31

Danish Primary School

1940

We were stuck in Denmark until autumn and beyond. There were few trips by ship to Iceland and they were risky. German and British submarines were locked in a relentless ship hunt and there wasn't a single whale in the sea that was unaffected by the war. Grandma Georgía went back to Iceland in autumn, on the famous Petsamo trip, in which two hundred Icelanders living in Nordic countries were offered the option of sailing home on the *Esja* but first had to make their way to Petsamo, a fishing village on the northern tip of Finland. Grandma insisted on our not coming with her. 'You don't put all your golden eggs into one boat.' Puti immediately feigned offence and said, 'Am I not a golden egg then, Mum?' since he was to accompany her on the trip.

'No, you're a balding egg,' I answered.

Mum and I were due to travel on the next crossing. But it never happened. Dad had vanished to his war job in midsummer, and the two of us were left in the embassy residence. In light of events, the embassy had been shut down, but the sale of the upstairs apartment had been delayed for many months because of the occupation. Initially we held on to our heroic chef Helle and chauffeur Rainer. He descended from Franco-German nobility but had lost all the papers that proved it in the mess of World War I. The genes were still firmly implanted in him, however, because his heels always clicked when he was forced to wait in a corner or on a pavement. He spotted three bushy black eyebrows on his face: two on his forehead and one on his upper lip.

At the beginning of September, I was placed in the local school. The first day didn't go well because I came home with 'scrap wounds.' The kids had surrounded me in the yard and jeered at me: '*Klipfisk! Klipfisk!* – Salted fish! Salted fish! A day later the teaching started. The teacher was a fat gentleman with a high-pitched voice.

'And here we have a new pupil from Iceland, Miss Björnsson. Perhaps you'd like to tell us a little bit about Iceland? Is it true what they say, that no trees grow there?'

'No. But they're very short. They say if you get lost in an Icelandic forest, you only have to stand up.'

The class laughed loudly to show they were laughing at me and not my joke.

'But they also say that to see Danish mountains you have to bend down.'

For that impudence I was beaten up in the school playground and came home with a torn ear. I refused to go the next day, and a week-long school strike followed, until Mum found a cosy little school for me up by the Rosenborg Park that went under the charming name of Sølvgades Skole, Silver Street School, and every morning Rainer drove me there.

The bullying of Icelandic children in Danish schools seemed to have been approved by the parliament as part of the national syllabus, since I got the exact same treatment from this elementary school as I had from the previous one.

'Salted fish! Salted fish!'

The teacher was a tall blond man with thin hair and thick-lensed glasses who finished his introduction by mispronouncing my name to gales of laughter in the classroom, and the nickname 'Hebron' was whispered around the room. The Hebron Hotel was a notorious brothel at the time, so the children thought it was hilarious.

'Hello, Hebron!'

That was how all my classes started, but worst of all were the breaktimes, when I was pushed around like a pest-infested goat. I tried to go on strike again, but Mum stubbornly insisted that things would get better and pushed me into the car every morning. Things only got worse. Sometimes I literally had to flee school. Luckily I had three big gardens to choose from and a rich variety of trees to hide behind. Then on the next corner there was the National Gallery of Denmark, where I sometimes took refuge and managed to shake off the kids down its maze of corridors. Ever since that time, I've been able to move through museums at high speed, thanks to my well-trained eyes.

In autumn of 1940, the National Gallery was, of course, under German control. There was no Cubism, Fauvism or Expressionism on show, just Nazism. Athletic men brandishing spears and obedient women breastfeeding. It's amazing how staid all tyrants are when it comes to art. The Nazis sent an entire race to the gas chambers but couldn't tolerate the slightest mutilation on canvas.

32

Other People's Poop

1940

Children are cruel animals, with a bestial sense of smell and sharp intuition. They immediately sniffed out that the newcomer was not only an Icelander but something even worse. It's no coincidence that 'The Ugly Duckling' happens to be the Danes' national tale.

Mum had sent me to school warning me never to let the other kids know I spoke German. But she herself had made the mistake of sending me there with traditional Icelandic rye bread (Grandma Georgía liked it so much that she taught Helle how to bake it) stuffed with seal meat sent from home that we had carried around since Lübeck. Moreover, she'd cut the bread widthwise instead of lengthwise, the way the Danes have done by royal decree since the year 1112.

'What are you eating? Seal-shit bread? And cut widthways! Is everyone cross-eyed in Greenland like you?'

'*Nein!*'

With that my fate was sealed. German discipline terrorised adults during the occupation of Denmark; no one dared to criticise the Germans or German-speaking Danes. The so-called Danish liber-ation struggle didn't start until liberation day, when everyone wanted to have been a hero. But children were another story. The things that were only whispered in their homes were repeated out loud in the school playgrounds. Yes, the yards, lanes, alleys, corridors and paths. Actually, the Danish resistance only existed among children.

The Danish word for hell, *helvede*, is far too soft to describe the things I had to suffer in Sølvgade. Girls burned my hair with candles, and boys put smelly hot turds in my boots and then stood there sneering at a distance, watching me in the cloakroom. I struck the pose of a submissive nation – proud, proud, proud! – and acted as if nothing were wrong, slipped my feet into the Danish shit, and then walked past the rapturous piercing jeers of the Lasses and Björns. As usual, the car was waiting for me outside, but I slipped out of a side exit and took the street. I didn't want to soil Iceland's private car.

It gives you an odd feeling to walk on someone else's shit. And ever since, I've had problems walking the streets of Copenhagen; I always feel the hot excrement pressing up between my toes. With tears in my eyes and a lump in my throat the size of a grenade, I crossed the City Hall Square and headed down to Kalvebod Brygge. Mum wasn't at home, and Helle embraced me alone. She had massive breasts that were good to sink into, a short lady with perennially bare arms that reminded me of hot, fragrant loaves of bread (which are not baked in a mould but allowed to rise on their own on a plate). Her face was always sprinkled with yeast and possessed a fully baked expression, creamy teeth, tasty lips and pastry-brown cheeks peppered with freckles that looked like sesame seeds on buns. But on that day it was difficult to abandon myself in her Danish bosom.

'Are we a bit sad today?' she asked in Danish. 'Oh dear, what a mess! Now we'll just take a bath and it'll all be fixed!'

She promised not to tell Mum that I'd had a little accident in my boots today. No one could find out. Not even Åse, my Norwegian friend. She went to a German school and got invited to birthdays by upper-class kids. The quisling's daughter was the beautiful fruit of the occupation. She was secure, but I was *wrong* everywhere I went. To Åse I was too Danish. At school I was too German. And to everyone too Icelandic. I never fitted in. At any time in my life. In Argentina after the war, people thought I was German and looked at me askance. In Germany, when they realised I'd been to Argentina, people looked at me askance. And at home I was a Nazi, in America a Communist, and on a trip to the Soviet Union I was accused of 'capitalistic behaviour.' In Iceland I was too travelled, on my travels too Icelandic. And I was never elegant enough for the presidential residence in Bessastadir, while in Bolungarvík, where I lived with my sailor Bæring, they called me a prima donna. Women told me I drank like a man, men like a slut. In my flings I was deemed too keen; in my relationships too frigid. I couldn't fit in any damned where and was therefore always looking for the next party. I was a relentless fugitive on the run, and that's where the endless escape that's been my life started – in that elementary school in Sølvgade in September 1940.

33

Anneli

1940

By mid-November I'd simply stopped going to class. I'd met a kind woman who took pity on me when she found me crying on a bench in the Rosenborg Gardens. As soon as the embassy car vanished around the corner, I walked towards a dark red door at the bottom of the street and rang a bell marked 'A. Bellini.'

Her name was Anneli, a well-groomed lady with a red rose in her coal-black hair and pale, padded cheeks. She generally sat at a white-clothed table under a tall window, gazing through the blurry glass with a beautiful but melancholy countenance. One could see a white gable and part of a brick wall and, between them, a portion of the street. I felt she was constantly peeping between the two buildings, as if she were expecting someone.

She was married to an Italian countertenor who was now a pilot in Mussolini's air force. He had participated in the invasion of France, one of the most ludicrous operations in the total absurdity of the Second World War: Italians in the flower of their youth sacrificing their lives so that the word TABAC could be changed into TABACCHI on some tobacconist's signs in a few Alpine villages.

That was in June and now it was November and the little rose lady no longer knew where her tenor was singing – whether he was stuck in his wreckage on some cold Alpine peak, delighting the inhabitants of heaven with his high Cs, or happily gallivanting in his boots down the streets of Nice having traded in his Danish love for a French one, singing his arias through revolving hotel doors and hot vulvas.

We sat there for long mornings and played cards, listening to Caruso spinning on the gramophone, and I told her all about the Icelandic ambassadorial couple while she instructed me on the tragic nature of love: 'Happiness is the most dangerous thing. Because the higher it takes you, the greater the fall.' Otherwise we just sat there for long stretches in silence, an eleven-year-old Icelandic girl and this beautiful Italo-lovelorn Danish woman, who in my mind was forty, fifty or sixty but was probably only thirty. She was prone to shutting up mid-conversation and staring out the window for a long moment, like a dead-still porcelain doll who only occasionally fluttered her eyelashes – long, black, and so even they seemed to have come out of a factory. On her forehead were three birthmarks that formed a love triangle.

She grew paler by the day, and every time I said goodbye she would give me a gift: a notebook, a gramophone record, a pearl necklace, earrings, lipstick. 'Use dark red during the day and vermilion at night.' Instead of memorising the names of Russia's big rivers and Sweden's lakes, I was learning how to become a lady, taking classes in makeup and jewellery.

'Have you ever wanted to be called something else?' she asked.

'Yeah.'

'What?'

'Dana.'

'Dana?' she said, stretching out the vowels. 'That's a nice name. You can be Dana whenever you need to be, then. We women need to hang on to whatever we can.'

Anneli was mourning two lost loves – the good and proper Per, who had loved her too much, and the Italian for whom she had abandoned him. Emilio had sung to her and a throng of enraptured women on the deck in the Scandinavian twilight, and she married him on the same day the luckless Per stepped in front of a bullet in the Funen forest.

Now she sat in her high-ceilinged apartment at Sølvgade 6 discussing the logic of the heart with a snivelling little girl from the outer islands. 'Never allow yourself to be ruled by the heart or the mind. Get the approval of both.' That was a lesson that was worth more than thirteen years in a Danish school, and I would have done well to follow my Anneli's little piece of advice. But needless to say, I forgot it as soon as I passed the door's threshold and only remember it now, a whole lifetime and a hundred men later.

34

Sexual Science Class

1940

Maybe I was distracted by the fact that on the ground floor there was a dolled-up chick who sold herself to German soldiers? I sometimes encountered them on the stairs, excited on the way up, satiated, down. Anneli told me all about this nocturnal profession, which, being the child that I was, I couldn't fully grasp but was nevertheless excited by.

And one day I saw her appear at her door, a buxom, broad-shouldered woman, who under other circumstances might have happily served in a bakery – your typical average Scandinavian blond – but now stood all dolled up at the crack of dawn in a salmon-pink negligee that struggled to conceal the tools of her trade, her bare toes protruding from open-toed high heels. She nimbly stepped back to make way for knee-high German leather boots, offering a discounted red smile. But even though she had the big, bulging eyes of an owl, her gaze was as dead as that of a whip-tamed circus animal.

One day my classmates spotted me on the pavement, and I dashed towards the red door of number 6 so fast that I rang the wrong bell. I ran up the dark stairs as soon as the hall door closed behind me and on the first landing was faced with an open door.

'Oh, good morning, my little friend.'

It was a smoky voice, dark and slightly slurred. I see now, at the distance of a lifetime, that she must have been drunk.

'I . . . I'm just going up.'

'Oh? Do you live here?'

'Yeah . . . well, no. I'm just . . .'

My brain had been completely overtaken by my eyes, which were so busy absorbing every single pleat of her glistening negligee and the rough skin of her throat that it could no longer hear or control my vocal cords. The woman wore a small gold chain around her thick ankle, and her toenails were varnished in gaudy red. Her hair was glaringly blond, a magnificent lion's mane, a wig no doubt. Through her alcoholic haze she must have sensed how insecure I was, pale and breathless.

'Do you know someone in this building?'

'Er . . . no.'

The bell rang and downstairs the voices and shouts of children could be heard from the other side of the door.

'Would you like to come in?'

'Yes.'

It was dark inside the apartment; the long corridor was dimly lit by wall lamps giving off a faint yellow light that brought out the green of the dark wallpaper. Cautiously, I entered, passing the woman, as if I were scraping past the side of a mountain; the cliffs of her breasts loomed above and an odorous mist filled my senses with a mixture of exclusive German perfume, Danish sweat and soiled sheets, perhaps even the hint of aftershave. Her stomach protruded slightly and my eyes followed the belt of her gown like a sheep trail along these great slopes. Then she closed the door and walked ahead of me down the corridor to the sound of the floorboards. As mystical as an elf woman but heavy as a mare.

'Can I get you something? Some cola?'

At the end of the corridor was a cubbyhole that had been converted into some kind of waiting room: two old, narrow, dark red rococo sofas, glowing lamps with tasselled shades and ashtrays on stands. Pictures that predated the invention of photography hung on the walls: Zeeland country vistas and Jutland cows, drawn with European meticulousness. I'd always been slightly fascinated by the realism of these etchings, boring as they are, because my country had never been honoured with images of this kind. Iceland had been a land totally devoid of pictures until our first photographers were born. No Icelandic Sagas or paintings had ever yielded us pictures of fjords or lava fields. But here on the mainland they had gone over every tree, every single leaf, with a pencil and etching tool with Rembrandt-like precision.

'Can I get you something, dear? Cola?' she repeated. I came to and took my eyes off the pastoral bliss on the walls, Danish cornfields and lakes annexed by German lightbulbs.

'Yes, please.'

She disappeared behind a door she closed behind her, but soon reappeared with a small glass bottle of black liquid. I'd seen people drinking something similar in the Tivoli Gardens. She invited me to sit on one of the sofas – I straightened my school skirt, dark blue on dim red – while she sat on the other one, slipped a cigarette into the corner of her mouth, and struck a match.

'Well then, dear. What have you got to say for yourself? Aren't you at school?'

'No.'

'Why not?'

'I have a disease.'

'Oh dear. You look like a perfectly young, healthy girl to me. And what disease is it?'

'I'm Icelandic.'

'Icelandic? And is that really serious?'

'Yeah. I can't be in a Danish school. The kids might be infected.'

She broke into a cough that turned out to be the beginning of a laugh and she sipped at a crystal glass of brownish cough mixture. I sipped my cola, which was full of strange gaiety: the liquid danced on my tongue and tickled my palate. I'd never drunk soda before and reacted to it by sneezing; black drops spluttered out of me, sprinkling my coarse woollen skirt.

'And what are the main symptoms of this disease?'

She grinned, and it was obvious from the way she spoke that she'd once walked down a university corridor, even sat in a lecture hall.

'Symptoms of the disease?'

'Yes, how does it manifest itself?'

'Well, it makes you kind of . . . alone.'

'Alone?'

'Yeah.'

'Is the Icelander always alone?'

'Yeah, there are so few of us.'

'Isn't it better to be rare than common?'

'No. Then everyone wants to own you.'

'But isn't it more fun to be gold than iron?'

'Only boring people want to own gold. Gold isn't even beautiful. It's just what everyone thinks.'

'Isn't gold beautiful?' she asked, surprised.

'No. The most expensive things are always the ugliest. And free things are the most beautiful.'

'Says who?'

'Grandma.'

She was silent and stared at me for a while, then took a sip from her glass. I ventured to take another sip of the cola, which tasted delicious despite the strange fizz in my mouth.

'But . . . aren't you in the war?'

'We've got some men in it.'

'What men are they?'

'The English. They're not like the Germans. They've got gin. Do they lie on you?'

'Huh?'

'The soldiers, do they lie on top of you?'

'Yes, sometimes.'

'Doesn't it hurt? Don't their guns press into you?'

'No, no, they take them off first but . . . well, they've got other guns, actually,' she said, pursing her lips to suppress the grin that was bound to follow.

'Is that the weenie?'

She was speechless for two seconds and stared at me, fighting back the laughter and biting her lips. But cigarette smoke escaped through her nostrils, and the woman now looked like a polite dragon who doesn't want to spoil a good party with her fire and smoke and retreats into a corner.

'Yes . . . ha-ha. It's . . . he-he . . . it's the weenie. You're funny.'

'Is that like a gun?' I asked sceptically.

'Yes, don't you think so?' she answered, tightening her lips again to smother a smirk, as she pulled the cigarette out of the corner of her mouth and killed it in the ashtray on the high stand, which wobbled slightly from the strength of her stabs.

'Our cook says a weenie is like an upside-down flower.'

Now she burst out laughing.

'An upside-down flower?'

'Yes, a tulip she says.'

She found this equally amusing and repeated the word 'tulip,' which made her laugh even more.

I rushed to the defence of Helle's simile and added with a serious air, 'But isn't it difficult to get it inside . . . ? I mean, it's so narrow and . . . the tulip, I mean, is so flabby.'

'Yes, of course, it's a bit . . . a bit flabby.' She had to make a brief pause in her speech to wipe the tears from the corner of her eyes. 'But no, no . . .' She could barely continue from the laughter, which had now become totally silent. 'That's why you have to start with some magic and transform the tulip into . . . into a cucumber.'

Now I'm baffled: 'A cucumber? And how do you do that?'

This class was turning out to be even better than the education I was getting on the third floor. I had completed my elementary school in two months and was now attending the high school of life, where I was learning how to become both a lady and a whore.

'That, shall we say ... is something we do with our charm.'

'Charm?'

'Yes, when a man sees a beautiful woman he changes into ... a vegetable, a vegetable!' The burst of laughter that followed now was more like an epileptic fit. 'They change into vegetables!' That was the beer-swilling, smoky laugh that everyone has heard in a Danish pub.

I was embarrassed, like anyone in the presence of someone who has lost control of herself, and forced a smile. I felt the teacher had lost the thread of the subject, and I decided to steer her attention back to the topic that was most likely to come up in the exam.

'But what is it that comes out of the weenie? Doesn't something come out of it?'

The prostitute came gliding down from the heights of her laughter like a long-winged owl and perched on these words: 'It's called ... sperm.'

She let out a hoot and bent over, covering her eyes, those big eyes.

'And is there a lot of it?'

She looked up and stared at me in surprise.

'It's ... it's kind of like jam. As much jam as you'd put on a slice of toast.'

'Have you tasted it?'

'Yes.'

'And what does it taste like?'

'I don't know. It's a bit like ... have you ever tasted oysters?'

'Yes.' The previous summer I'd been on a trip to Flanders with Mum and Dad and had oysters in Ostend. They tasted like walrus snot, Mum said.

'Is it like oyster jam, then?'

'Yes,' answered the blond with a light laugh.

'Yuck,' I said, pulling a face. 'But you can still make babies with it?'

'Yes,' answered the big-eyed Dane, with an exclamation point stuck in her throat.

My God, what a weird system they had in this humongous project called life, and such strange rules, too. In order to create life, women had to paint their lips red and wear tight blouses so that the tulips would turn into cucumbers. Then they had to churn it until oyster jam came out of it and it was spread over the 'eggs,' where it had to wait a few days for a face to start forming out of all that mess.

'And do you have many children?' I continued to question the Danish prostitute, like a land-thirsty seal who had finally reached the shore.

She hesitated, and her voice had left the laughter far behind when she finally answered.

'Yes. Two.'

'Only two?' I asked like an ass. 'But Annel . . . but men come to you every day!'

'Huh?' she answered absentmindedly.

'But men come to you every day. How come you have only two children?'

She stared at me with her saucer eyes and fell into a bewildering silence. She could have chosen a variety of answers but opted for the simplest.

'No, I . . . I have just two. Just two children.' And there was a touch of grief in her voice.

'And are they at the Silver Street School?' I continued like the most idiotic kid in the world.

'No.' She sniffed. Sometimes tears take the first exit they can find and slip down the nostrils. 'They . . . they're with their grandma.'

'And is it good?'

'Good? What?'

'To do that thing with the weenie . . .'

'Good?' She pondered on this a moment, took a sip of her medicine, put the glass down, and then half opened her twisted mouth as her index finger stroked the lower rim of her left eye. Looking at me, cheeks quivering, she said, 'No.'

Then she added on an in-breath: 'No, it's not good.'

To fend off the tears, she took another sip.

'Why are you doing it, then?' I asked mercilessly.

She didn't answer, just sat there staring into empty space like a weary train driver who has been tracking across the globe all his life and is suddenly halted by God, who demands to hear the purpose of his life.

'Is it for the money?' I continued like the worst kind of Nazi.

'No,' she finally answered in a perfectly calm voice. 'It's not for the money, it's for my husband.'

'Are you married?'

'Yes,' she said, and now she finally started to cry. 'This is all . . . all for my husband. They were going to . . . send him away to Germany, to a prison . . . prison camp. But with this' – her crying intensified as she spoke, releasing feelings that had been locked away in a cell for months – 'he . . . he'll get decent food.'

The tears trickled eye shadow down her cheeks, forming blue streaks, which, on meeting her face powder, developed white edges, and the horseshoe shape of her mouth gave her lipstick a tragic clownish appearance. All of a sudden her entire cosmetic edifice had crumbled; the beautiful woman was reduced to a heap of flesh and tangled hair.

'All for my husband!' I think she muttered through her wails.

This was therefore no ordinary flesh vendor, but a war victim. And maybe this was the real Resistance, a woman who fought the occupation the only way she could, by saving a man's life with her charm.

She stopped crying just as abruptly as she had started and began to laugh. In a sudden temper she glared at me, told me to get going and not to utter a word of this to anyone, and asked me what I was loitering around her place for anyway. An Icelandic brat who should have been at school! It was no excuse that I was from a cold country and that there was a war going on, there was no war here, there were no battles being fought, practically no danger at all!

'Is there no Icelandic school for you?! You must be able to go to some Icelandic school?'

'No. I'm the only Icelandic kid that's left in Europe.'

We had walked all the way to the door now, and her rage seemed to intensify the scent of the perfume that engulfed me from her unruly hair and chest, which was veiled no longer in silk but in a wartime beige bra, since her negligee had come undone around her waist and dangled loosely on her sides, like drooping theatre curtains framing a great tragedy.

'Bloody rubbish! Enough nonsense out of you, now. Get out! You shouldn't be poking your nose into other people's business. Out, I said!'

'My schoolbag,' I quacked.

'Yeah? Where is it?!' she yelled like a hysterical teacher.

Without answering, I ran back down the corridor all the way to the sofa and grabbed the leather bag the boys called Germany because it was similar in shape.

Before I could return to the door, the bell rang. The teacher swiftly swallowed her fury, fastened the belt on her negligee, adjusted herself in the mirror in the hall, and transformed herself from a person into a tart in the blink of an eyelid. I slid past her, my schoolbag rustling against the wallpaper. The school bell rang again. The woman came after me, gave me a frosty smile before opening the door, and chirped, '*Guten Tag.*'

Outside stood a chubby young *Offizier* in a cold green uniform. His moustache twitched slightly as he eyed me quizzically: Was this (a) the prostitute's daughter, (b) the youngest practitioner of the oldest profession in the world or (c) her previous client? I left him with his speculations and dashed up the stairs, determined never to ring the wrong bell again.

35

Bitch's Belly and a God Named Dust

2009

Lóa is gone. Did she leave some treat behind? Yes, there's something. What's that? *Skyr*? Porridge? I forget everything, poor me. I must have been eating that earlier. But now I can't remember if I'm still hungry. Whether I was hungry, I mean, and am now full. I seem to have lost all contact with my stomach. It's running its own show.

I don't know what day this is, but it must be close to noon. There's no way that it's a good enough reason to draw breath. I'll say it loud and clear: the closer I get to the furnace, the more insignificant my days become. What's that rude knocking on my window? Wind? Allow me to respond in kind! To that liver-grey sky and the wind-bent trees with shrivelled leaves that look like overused hankies. Which shows you what a head cold the Icelandic summer is. I spit on this crap they try to pass off as everyday life to us who have lived under a more radiant light than the vile sputum of this rain could ever give. And it falls from a sky that looks like a damp and foul-smelling bitch's belly. Yes, that's our fate as Icelanders, to crouch under the belly of a stray bitch. Under erect teats that have nothing to offer but sterile, freezing icicles.

I, the sentenced bed-bird, say: The days become more diluted as life goes by. At first, existence seems so immense to us and we so incredibly insignificant; we gulp it all down. We spend our lives swilling it until we discover that there's nothing left to suck from it, because we realise that we ourselves are so much more significant than days, time, and all those things they call reality, a phenomenon that men have venerated for centuries but that pales into insignificance in the face of unreality. It was my good fortune in life to have freed myself from the former and subscribed to the latter. It was such a complete liberation for me to no longer have to get out of bed, pour milk into a bowl, totter over to open envelopes, watch TV, and make phone calls. That was when I first started to enjoy life, when I no longer had to live it and therefore got to cherish it in secret. Therefore let no one pity me for vegetating in this cramped garage in a dreary neighbourhood, because I've finally found life itself. And God. I can make him out with my glasses, on the floor by the sink: a transparent, tiny, lightweight dust ball, who moves only when the door is opened. I call him Dust. And honour him with this verse:

Praise be the Lord named Dust
For he exorcises all my lust
And sanctifies my mould and rust

Happiness is to own nothing. And believe in Dust.

36

Everyone Loves War

2009

I peep over the end of the bed and see myself down there in life, as tiny as a freckle on a distant face and so weary of the bullying from those Danish kids, but also glowing with excitement for everything that was in the air.

Human beings have always had a need for disasters. If nature doesn't provide them for us, we create them ourselves. And of course the war was fun. Of course I wouldn't have missed it for anything. One lived so intensely that sometimes the moment simply vibrated like the black gear stick of an old tractor. There will obviously always be departments of the human soul that welcome events of this kind: heads of divisions will leap into the air, flex their braces over their chests, put their feet on their desks, and toast with their employees: 'Well, dear colleagues, now we'll see some action! The war is here!'

Here's pretty much what a Hungarian told me right after the war, somewhere deep in an Argentinian train carriage. 'I sometimes don't understand how I was able to endure it, crawling through ice-cold mud for maybe days on end or trembling in graves of snow for weeks, weeks of hell without anything happening! That was worst of all. Or walking three hundred miles with holes in my shoes and sixty pounds on my back and ... Yes, well, I wore the same underwear for four years! But somehow you just couldn't complain, in some odd way you were happy. Now men wake up to birdsong and the smell of coffee and spend the whole day worrying about whether their bosses will like their reports or their wives are two-timing them. And miss having their hair grazed by bullets.'

War makes us all happy, because no one is given a choice. In peacetime, people become unhappy because they have to choose and reject. All wars therefore stem from man's insatiable longing for happiness. There are few things that men fear more than peace on earth.

Man prefers to be a passenger on the great wheel of destiny, rather than determine its course. Least of all does he want to assume responsibility for that destiny, which is why he worships those who do.

And when it comes to destinies, wars provide the most radical of them all. That's why we feel so good in war, we find our inner peace in war. And World War II was the ideal war because it was, as Goebbels put it, *der totale Krieg* – the total war that was everywhere: it spread across the entire continent and plagued every soul, leaving no one unscathed.

37

Womanhood

1940

Yes, that's what the war was like. On every single staircase in Copenhagen there lived women . . . No, let's put it like this: On every floor in every European city – Oslo, Lyon, Lublin – there were locked doors, and behind each one of them, major destinies. You could have knocked on any of them, and the doors would have opened like a thousand-page novel – tragic, dramatic, sad, exciting, incredible, and far, far too long. Every door to every house in every city was like a book cover with big burning letters: *He Left Me for Hitler, Mussolini's Bride, I Did It for My Husband* . . .

Anneli came to the door in a pale dressing gown and went straight back to bed. Her hair was unbrushed and tumbled over her shoulders. It was considerably longer than I had imagined. I followed her and leaned on the edge of the bed.

'You're late today,' she murmured feebly.

'Yes.'

She was incredibly beautiful as she lay there so languidly with her head half-sunk into a big, thick pillow. Her eyelids drooped at the end of every sentence.

'Where were you?'

'I . . .'

That was as far as I could get. It was the first time I'd been unfaithful. And with a whore, what's more. A drunken whore.

'You can't stay long today. I'm so tired.'

'Yeah, no, no. I'll just go. It's late.'

'Will you remember one thing for me, Dana?'

'Yeah, what?'

'Always remember, for the rest of your life, not . . . not to let them get you.'

'Right . . . Get me?'

'Yes. They will try to.'

'The Germans?'

She gave a faint smile.

'Men.'

'Men?'

'Yes. Beware of them.' She shut her eyes ever so slowly, her eyelashes fluttering like butterfly wings.

'All men? Not just Germans?'

'All men are Germans.'

She seemed to be aware of the ambiguity of her words, because I felt I could discern a smirk in her eyes. But still, I was only eleven years old.

'Not Dad, he's Icelandic. And your husband! Isn't he Italian?'

'Dana, and also promise me . . .'

'What?'

'Don't become a woman.'

I was totally lost now.

'Don't be a woman?'

'Yes. Women have such a rough time. Just be a person. Not a woman.'

'Huh?'

'Yes. Promise me. Not a woman.'

She repeated this almost inaudibly, like an exhausted runner who'd finally crossed the finish line and was gasping an important message to someone who still had the whole course of her life to run. And she closed her eyes after every sentence she uttered. But how beautiful she was on that pillow. I almost felt like kissing her, those red lips, strange as it may seem. I longed to give her a big, juicy kiss, to rub her thick lips against mine, lick her tongue. How come? 'Don't become a woman.' Had I become a man? With these words, the heartbroken Anneli had probably transformed me from a girl into a man, igniting some hitherto unknown fire in me. All of a sudden I stood there like a wet-dreaming dwarf in front of his Snow White, frozen with her coal-black hair, snow-white skin and blood-red lips.

'Look at me. I'm just lying here because . . . to be a woman is like being . . . it's just a disease.'

'Huh? What?'

I'd grown deaf with desire. She seemed to sense it, because she now appeared to be addressing her delirium more than me.

'To be a woman is a disease. A deadly disease. The only cure is to become a man but . . . because they call us the weaker sex and for the whole of our lives plot to get us . . . into bed, to have us lying in bed . . .' She cast a fleeting glance at the glistening white bedside table. On it was what looked like a letter over an open envelope. It had been folded and one third of it stood up so that the light from the bedside lamp illuminated the paper from the other side. Through it I could see clumsy handwriting in blue ink. Then she looked at me again and said, 'All men are Germans. Remember that, Dana. And promise me you'll never wear a yellow star.'

She uttered those words with a calm that belied the suffering that lay beneath them. She half-closed her eyes for a brief moment again, then looked at me and repeated, 'Never wear a yellow star.'

I hadn't realised that this woman, who looked like the model for a wine and rose commercial, had the blood of a fighter. I thought that love was her only god. That she was a woman first, then a person. But this lesson etched itself in my memory much more than her classes on the organs of love, perhaps precisely because I didn't quite understand her warnings about yellow stars and men being Germans. We sometimes remember better the things we don't understand. But I took in the lesson and decided never to love to the point of ending up in bed for love (unless for my own pleasure) or for the simple sake of being a woman. I never managed to live up to the latter part but succeeded at the former. I never loved anyone 100 per cent. Because that wouldn't have been sensible. No one should cook their heart in a single piece. You're better off slicing it in four, frying one or two pieces in the pan, and storing the rest in the freezer.

Anneli was worn out at the end of her lecture and now spoke with closed eyes. I stood up. Raising her eyelids with great effort, she took my hand with her soft, pale hands (it's only now that I realise that the woman's cheeks and hands were, of course, swollen from the drugs and heartbreak). I bent over her, kissed her on the cheek, and felt its autumnal freshness on my springtime lips. A kiss without a single trace of lust. I had locked all my sexual desires inside me before kissing her. And this brought a definitive end to my innocence. My first adult repression had begun.

Inside my soul the stem of a flower had sprouted a minuscule bud, black and hairy: a passionflower had taken root, an eleven-year-old exhibiting the first signs of womanhood. And I had immediately entered into denial. But wasn't that precisely what Anneli had told me to do? I was totally befuddled by all the signals I'd received on that big day.

She smiled at me and then, with her eyes, indicated a small ornate box that stood on a chair by the open door. It was the size of Grandad's cigar box, square and varnished in black, adorned with black pearls and a small mirror on the lid; I could see my greed reflected in it. It was a jewellery box. I loosened its tiny latch and lifted the lid. The box was empty, but at home I had various small artefacts that she had given me in the previous weeks that I could put into it. The inside was padded in a rosy velvet that gave off a scent that beckoned me, luring me down into the box's inner pinkness. I inhaled the pungent fragrance; it felt like a blend of different perfumes that had been sprayed on tantalising flesh in moments of pleasure and fused with the products of the body, neck sweat and armpit dew.

And I felt those feminine flavours drawing me in. Come here, come here, little girl. You, too, shall be a woman, woman. Don't think you can slip, slip away. Come here with your puerile organs and dimpled smile and let me fill them with doubts and dilemmas. You, too, will have to struggle under the weight of breasts through life, plaster yourself with creams and scents and colours, grapple with fat and endure bleeding and difficult births, and then lose your value as you're exiled to the land of wrinkles and thrown into the dustbin of life. Woman! Woman! Blissful pain awaits you behind the blood-red curtain. You thought you were a child who would turn into a person, and now realise you'll only ever be a woman.

38

Young Witch

1940

At the end of a long day in the School of Life at 6 Silver Street, Copenhagen, I stepped out into the November afternoon with the precious box. The shadow of the opposite row of six-storey buildings reached the fifth floor on my side, and further down the street the yellow leaves of the Rosenborg Gardens shone in horizontal rays. Copenhagen was as beautiful as before. The occupying forces had not yet conquered the trees and the light. The air was saturated with a pleasant coolness, which in my infantile mind I attributed to those thick stone walls of the city containing a frozen core (the Danish tundra), where winter was kept and sweated in isolation in the summer but exhaled cold air as soon as the sun stopped shining on them.

I waited awhile on the steps and cautiously glanced around the pavement. There were no schoolmates in sight, so I ran to the corner in a single sprint, then slowed down and strolled towards town, on the side of the park to catch the sun, with my schoolbag slung over my shoulder and the box in my hand.

There were few people about, and I allowed myself to walk in the new stride that the day demanded; I had acquired a feminine electricity in my gait; I walked straight and skillfully, thought I was a little bit more Dana. I felt the coarse wool school skirt flirting with my chilled legs, which were bare down to my high white socks and black lace-up shoes. They had been flat earlier that day but now felt like high heels, I thought. The black, hairy bud grew with every step. Yes, I had definitely turned into a woman, which was precisely what Anneli had told me not to do. This confident, graceful stride was accompanied by a sense of guilt, and what could be more adult than feeling guilty about having become sexy? Irresistibly, tongue-foamingly sexy.

A man in a bright coat and dark hat came walking towards me. I held my stride with the feminine box in my hand. He moved swiftly along the pavement with a slightly tilted head, his hat concealing his face like a shield, obviously a German. As he drew closer, I could make out his chin, then his nose. There was no question that the man was the spitting image of Tyrone Power, the heartthrob from Tinseltown. And he would now be the first man to witness my newborn femininity! The thought of it fanned the flames of my new magical powers; with them I could easily make the man in the hat fall at my feet. Within seconds he would be foaming over the delectable dish my body had become; nine steps later the German Power would fall on his knees like a shot soldier and tearfully beg the girl who had just burst out of her childhood to have dinner with him at the Hotel d'Angleterre and then go to the cinema with him at the Dagmar Teatret. The night would then be crowned by red-hot love games in the cabin of a ship anchored in the New Harbour. The girl couldn't picture the amorous encounter in any great detail, just a simple still life of a fireplace, a hat and a girl's bare knees.

I broke into a devilish grin when I realised my certain victory; I could barely understand how women could feel inferior to men when they held this power over them. We were drawing increasingly close to each other, and I fixed my gaze on the rim of his hat; soon two sparks would escape from under it and stoke my inflammable frenzy, setting four eyes on fire. To be safe, though, I wanted to open the sexy box to release the female genie to support me. But the lock was stuck. I couldn't open the damned box. When I looked up, the German Power had walked by. I stood there watching him, my first perfect prince, disappear down Princess Street.

I sighed in frustration but bent over the box and, after some effort, finally managed to pry it open. I must have looked like a powder addict when I stuck my nose into it and greedily snorted all its feminine vapours into my brain. And if women really are the weaker sex, that must be why I suddenly went weak in the knees. I felt a twig burgeoning between my legs and a numbness enveloping my nipples. The bud burst into a flower that spread across my stomach and below. Hairy, black. Black and hairy. Everything started to blur, but instead of collapsing I staggered along the garden railings with the open box, salivating and limping with lust.

Soon the fence led to a small brick hut, some kind of neoclassical temple that was later converted into a restaurant, I think, but that in those days served as a public convenience with Danish signs and German cleanliness. There was no staff in sight. I slipped into the ladies' room, locked myself in, put down my schoolbag and box, and greeted myself in the cloudy mirror. Unbuttoning my collar, I was gripped by an even more potent desire at the sight of my own flesh: I grew excited until my heart pounded when I uncovered one breast and suddenly found myself rubbing my life bud against the glacial rim of the sink and then the corner, which turned out to be even better. Then I spotted a mop in the corner, which I instinctively grabbed and shoved between my legs and started to ride like a demented witch, crying out in Danish, 'All men are German. All men are German.'

The sorcery between my thighs intensified with every thrust, pouring satisfaction into my body and soul like porridge into a bowl. Finally, I firmly grabbed the handle and rammed it against my crotch with all my might, with my skirt and knickers in between, and then allowed myself to slide down the hard stick and experienced what women would possibly call the hint of an orgasm. It was far from being a full orgasm, of course, but plenty to keep me going for now, plenty. Because I stiffly sat on the dirty floor a good while and stared at the glistening white tiles, bombarding myself with questions that were about as numerous as the stars that twinkled in the air around me, most of them yellow.

Through the gap under the door I caught sight of thick, weary female feet in worn-out wooden clogs, shifting stiffly on the pavement outside, dragging her soles to the accompaniment of a broom.

I sprang to my feet and flushed the toilet unconvincingly, like a poor sound effect in a bad play. I picked up the box and schoolbag and was on my way. Outside stood the old witch in a blue smock clutching a broom, her best friend for half a century. And now I understood why men had labelled all the women who preferred brooms to their weenies 'witches.' I was a witch. And that idea has followed me all my life and has never been as strong as now, even though I gave up those kinds of pleasures long ago, since I'm a semi-invalid now, a wicked pillow cripple with a wig. I was never able to look on myself as a beautiful, lovely woman. Some men found me attractive maybe, fun, beddable. But I was never a beautiful, lovely woman. I wasn't. No, no. I was a witch.

39

Birthday Boy

1940

The jewellery box turned out to be the last gift from Anneli because the next day she didn't come to the door, nor did she answer later that day after I'd roamed through the museum and gardens, with flashes of anxiety. Maybe she was dead or maybe just bored with me? Maybe she would spend the next four years in bed writing an immortal love story that would never be published, because no one would suspect that such a beautiful woman could write.

The war more or less revolved around breaking people apart, making them lose each other. In war everyone was alone. Even the soldier who trained to be a helmet in a squadron of a hundred. Even his wife who worked on an assembly line back home with hundreds of others. Even the prisoner who slept in a jam-packed cell.

But no one was so desperately alone as the Führer. I doubt if any figure in history was ever as lonely as Adolf Hitler. He therefore insisted on everyone in his territories greeting him by name: 'Heil Hitler!' And never has so much been done to soothe the psychological hang-ups of one man. First, a whole nation was turned into one giant daily birthday party in his honour, with everyone in their finest outfits and water-combed hair, both friends and foes sporting armbands for the sake of clarity, singing in his honour, showering him with gifts (generally their lives) and clicking to attention before him, forming giant birthday cakes and thrusting their arms in the air to symbolise candles, a thousand candles for the Millennial Reich, for the lonely little boy to blow out and boo at from his rostrum, his high chair: Adolf Hitler, the eternal birthday boy. But that wasn't enough, because after the cake the boy wanted to play with his tin soldiers, and get to use all his new toys . . .

Little Hjalti's solitude was so great, in fact, that it was a black hole, an over-famished vacuum that sucked in everything on its path, that constantly demanded new victims to prevent himself from being sucked into the hole. *'Blut muß fließen!'* 'Never enough human sacrifices!' But once all the blood had been consumed, the black hole swelled up over his head and he drowned in his own isolation. Yes. The last war was more or less about making all the inhabitants of this planet about as lonely as the one who started it.

In war one is always alone and, frankly, I think this solitude has shaped my life; I always thought it a bit pathetic, this need to spend one's life living with the same people.

40

Surf White

1940

Mum and I were left behind in two hundred square metres, like two stray sheep stuck in a chapter of the history of Iceland that had already been written but was still waiting to be printed.

Time after time, I went back to knock on Anneli's dead door, and my school days soon came to an end. The assistant head had finally phoned Mum to tell her how things stood: her daughter hadn't been seen in school for five whole weeks. Mum took it very badly. After swallowing the shock, she switched from defence mode into attack and unleashed her fury on the Danish schoolmaster in that glacial Breidafjördur manner: Why the hell did they wait five whole weeks to tell her this? The child could have been led astray!

And started stripping in public toilets, I silently added, secretly kneeling by my bed arranging my jewels in the box.

Her shrill islander's voice resounded down the floorboards and echoed against the rosette on the ceiling. 'But this is really *un-of-heard*!' she exclaimed in bad Danish. Her mistaken vocabulary, furious tone, and poor pronunciation amplified the echo and the fact that there were two decent people here who were stuck in the wrong place.

But we tried to make the most of it, and the weeks leading up to Christmas were among the best I had in all those wartime years. I confessed how I'd skipped school and then told Mum about my time there, without dwelling too much on my bad treatment to spare her any guilt. Nevertheless, she cried and hugged me, pressing me deep into her thick black hair. I could have sworn I picked up a scent of seaweed. And then it was decided that she herself would teach me until Christmas; she had all the time in the world and enough money to last us into the New Year.

She taught me Danish, arithmetic and spelling. But also sewing and cooking: porridge, white sauce, potato purée and brown sauce. I learned how to make all those things with Mum, and they've lasted me a lifetime. There's far too much fuss about books in schools. Naturally, our best moments were the ones that were dedicated to nothing and therefore included everything. Exactly the kind of everything I still remember today.

Mum boiled eggs under a twelve-foot ceiling while I lay on the sofa reading letters from Dad – 'They wake us at four here, *früh am Morgen*, as they call it. The early bird gets the worm!' – or I browsed through the *Familie Journal* magazine and read about German film stars. But all of a sudden Mum would come gliding in on high heels and do a spin in the middle of the floor. 'What do you think of this fine, fine lady?' Then a big laugh. She enjoyed trying on the thirty pairs of shoes Grandma had left behind in the cupboard and getting me to rate her performance in the high heels. They made a nice clatter on the shiny waxed floors. My mother Massa: the massive woman. On the way back she sometimes paused by the grand piano to run a finger over its keys in her longing to conjure up some magical sounds from that three-legged creature. No doubt it's the same principle that applies to men fondling women. 'If you've no hope, then grope,' as Grandma Vera might have said.

I put down the letters and magazines and impatiently waited for the next fashion parade: this was a good opportunity to observe my mother and admire her, that marvellous, marvellous woman. Her thighs had thickened and her stomach grown, while her breasts had shrunk and fused to form a horizontal ledge over her rib cage. Her hair kept its thickness and created a strong frame around her vigorous face, which in its red-lipped whiteness reminded me slightly of Anneli's face, although they were, of course, very different. Anneli was a gentle rose and Mum a sharp-eyed seal.

Mum was beautiful in a rather Icelandic way, in the same way that the gravel slopes of the Thórsmörk Ridge are called beautiful. She had these beautiful eyebrows and then, of course, that islander's whiteness, that white, white skin, which I always envied her and which Dad had probably fallen for. The poet Steinn had called her Surf White. My skin, on the other hand, was just canvas stretched over bones, which I then managed to colour through smoking and drink. Grandma Verbjörg was just as bad as I was, so Mum had clearly inherited her beautiful skin from her father, Salómon. The phenomenon wasn't uncommon in Breidafjördur, since for centuries the islanders had been fed on seal fat, as soft as fire and as white as milk.

'Mum, have you left Dad?' I asked when the fashion parade was over.

'Didn't he leave me?'

'But I mean, when he comes back, don't you want him to come back to us then?'

'If he co . . .' She halted the thought that travelled through every European woman's mind in 1940, out of consideration for me, and instead said: 'I don't know, what do you want?'

'Me? I just want Hjalti to choke on his own screams and for all this to be over and for Dad to come here so we can go home to Iceland. No, home to the islands. Tomorrow.'

It was a strangely infantile statement to come from a newly crowned woman. She smiled through tight lips, leaned forward, and then burst into a laugh.

'Ah, you little thing.'

Then she rushed over to me, threw herself on the sofa, ruffled my hair as if to say what a pipe dream it was, and then finally hugged me. It felt good, so good.

'Tomorrow!' she mimicked me, laughing, before switching to a serious tone. 'I certainly wish this madness could end tomorrow.'

'And would you take Dad back then?'

She directed her blue eyes into mine; under her dense black eyebrows they looked like a heavily overcast fjord. But then she looked away and stared out into the living room a moment, out beyond the grand piano and through an open door into the crystal-crowned dining room, yes, all the way into the kitchen, where two white eggs boiled with reckless abandon in the pot. She was thinking not about them but about other objects that were just as fragile and boiling; I sensed it. She was quiet a long moment, as parents sometimes are with their children when they need to express something about life that cannot be communicated in words. Then she stood up and walked out of the living room, past the grand piano, through the open door into the crystal-crowned dining room, and all the way into the kitchen, where two white eggs boiled with reckless abandon in the pot. She did this in white high-heeled, laced boots: the sound of her footsteps resounded like a soldier's all over the house, all the way into the kitchen. It was clear what the heels were saying.

41

Farewell, Copenhagen

1941

After Christmas, everything changed. Jón Krabbe, the courteous crab, appeared with the New Year's sun in his white hair to announce that the embassy apartment where Mum and I were living had been sold. Within a week, some new eminent German was expected to be moving in with his wife. 'He'll be working in the Ministry of Education, where he'll be responsible for the teaching of Danish children. They intend to implement reforms,' Krabbe explained, without, as usual, suggesting any judgement in his words. I left a note in the refrigerator for the new tenants: 'Children who speak German get beaten up in Danish schools.'

Wasn't that just collaboration?

Mum and I moved in with Dad's sister, Kylla, who lived in Zeeland with her Faeroese husband. There were also some of his fellow countrymen there, amiable and squinty-eyed people whom we welcomed in the dearth of Icelanders during those war years. Since the Faeroese make up an even smaller nation than ours, we get along famously. We don't have to strive to be their equals the way we do with other Nordic countries.

I enjoyed our time at Aunty Kylla's and had fun moving the mountains of Zeeland by throwing stones at them – cattle are the only formations that rise above the flatness of their fields there. Once, we went down to the shore and saw the 'Danish sea,' one of the most pitiful sights I've ever set eyes on. Mum soon grew anxious, however. She felt uneasy in other people's homes. Solutions were explored. It wasn't easy for her to find a job, perhaps because of the language, and having heard all the stories about the Danish school system, she wasn't too keen to enrol me somewhere where I might be bullied again.

Finally Dad came to our rescue. After several phone calls, he had managed, through some acquaintances, to find some housework for Mum with a doctor's family in Lübeck. The only snag was that there was no room for another child, since there were already six living there. After even more phone calls, the following short-term solution was found: a colleague of Dad's from the Nordic Studies Department in Lübeck, Dr Helmut Baum, who now worked at the War Accountants' Office in Berlin, kept his wife and children at a safe distance from the horrors of war on the island of Amrum in the North Sea. I was welcome to stay with them until the spring.

42

Night Mail

2009

Oh yeah. I lie here through long nights, illuminated by the blue light of the computer screen like some dishevelled, grey-haired goddess with a russet tail end (bed sores) and a red glow on my lips (the cigarette), and peer into the void, whatever that might mean. I launch the occasional adverb into the world to tease young men on the other side of the planet and poke my relatives under false profiles but am otherwise mostly busy dying. *Smoking kills*, the packet assures me, but it's taking ages.

To die ... Oh death, please do come soon so that we can start our honeymoon.

Death dwells at night but is still resting with his big backpack, stick and bundle, on the stub of a tree trunk in the deep, dark forest, black browed, with a weary, jaundiced grin. He's still waiting there but casts his glance down the leafy path to here. Through the thick, quivering mist of seconds I see his brazen stare.

He's coming. He's coming soon.

The November night is dark and humid with stormy sounds. The Almighty Farmer Above occasionally whips my corrugated iron roof with shivering branches as if he wants to punish me.

And e-mails reach me with chirps, perching on my quilt like birds, after a long voyage from sunny cyberlands, here into my darkness, shiny-eyed and beaming. I read those that catch my fancy. The Aussie tells me he's proud of Bod, who's reached his long-sought-after goal of 300 pounds on the bench and will be celebrating by inviting fourteen eggs for breakfast. I immediately reply that I, Linda, will now have to talk it over with my lover, that sluggish Icelander can handle only 210 pounds. There won't be much sleep in Melbourne over the coming nights.

Out in the darkness the planet spins towards the sun, tossing in space like an old man in bed, with all its African trees and Icelandic mountains, midges in Lofoten, towers in Toronto, and the swarming throngs of Bombay and Delhi. Oh, I wouldn't mind being God. An old lady and God at the same time. Who both seduces and torments men. And controls the lives of all the Jóns of this world. Nothing is impossible to the one who is willing to die, as that ancient Icelandic saying goes. And I therefore send a late-night e-mail to my sons:

The end is drawing closer now. There is clearly no life after death, so it's probably a good idea to grab the opportunity while I still have blood trickling through my fingers. You will hopefully live on for some time, but I'm on my way to the oven. I'm told it'll be a thousand degrees, which makes it easier for me to send you warm thoughts. Once upon a time you were my life, but now I've nothing left except this very life, nothing but the pretentious old beating of my heart and a few stale thoughts that swirl at the bottom of my brain like dregs around a plughole. I can't say that I've missed you, because no one misses those one has betrayed, and there's no point in crying over spilled milk. You are still, however, my sons, try as you may to fight that fact. And that is and will undoubtedly be your everlasting handicap. I am as I am, and no one can flee his genes. The kitten takes after the cat, as they say.

Farewell, my sons.

I bid you a tearless farewell. And leave you nothing, apart from a white chamber pot and a pretty good swivelling chair. You've already gobbled up my life's savings and shitted them, if I've understood correctly. I've no intention of pestering you after my death, although I'd have every reason to do so. I take my leave from this life utterly consumed and exhausted and don't expect to feel any longing to return as a ghost. Be happy, my dear kings, far and near. May the Almighty Farmer on the Farm Above bless you and all your children.

Wishing you a good night.

– Your Mum.

A quarter of an hour later an answer arrives from Norway. They get up early over there on the West Coast. My Ólafur is brief and to the point: '*Hi, Mum. Didn't you get the Christmas card from us last year? Regards –* ÓHJ.'

'*No. That's one of the luxuries of living in a garage; you can do away with all that paper mail. Was it anything special?*'

He doesn't answer.

43

Mother of Kings

1959–1969

Haraldur, Ólafur and Magnús, my sons are called. By coincidence I opted for the names of three little Norwegian kings: Harald Fairhair, Ólaf Tryggvason and Magnús the Lawmender. And I'm Herbjörg, the kings' mother. In keeping with my rank, I tried to maintain as low a profile as possible in that baby-making and to disturb the royal paternal genes as little as I could on their journey into and out of my uterus. They therefore inherited none of their mother's facial features nor anything of her gentle, loving temperament.

Haraldur arrived in '59, with a huge, pelvis-shattering head. He was an obnoxious child (so much so that I fled from his cradle), an insipid adolescent, and a dry stick of an adult. The mercantile genes obviously didn't stretch very far. Haraldur had many interests and swallowed up anything that came his way. But all the knowledge he picked up vanished into the mop of hair that was his head, never to be seen again. He sucked in the whole world but never gave anything back, just like his father in his business. He always reminded me of that old blotting paper used in offices in the days of yore. And right in its core there was a blob as black as ink: the sentence he had passed on his mother for having put him up for adoption at his granny's so that she could debauch herself on *Die Sexyger Jahre in Deutschland*.

There was no point in taunting him with tales of his mother's party exploits on the Continent. He was never able to stomach the Beatles.

Haraldur is a born lawyer who could have spared himself those years of academic studies. I offered to testify that the boy didn't need to take any exams, since he had mounted a case against his mother for neglect in the Kangaroo Court of Iceland before he'd even reached the age of four and had filed several lawsuits against her since. Greed, however, has always prevented him from defending anyone but himself. Speculation therefore became his area of expertise. Haraldur's main activity is the acquisition of houses and apartments that other people live in. The meaning of life clearly wasn't a subject covered by the law faculty of the University of Iceland.

Ólafur Helgi arrived in 1965. The name was chosen unconsciously. Despite his holy name (Helgi), my Ólafur was more like the Viking king Ólaf Tryggvason than like his namesake Ólaf the Holy. With his stubborn brain and missionary heart, he has travelled the globe spreading the good word about himself. He developed an interest in gastronomy early on, and I blame myself for that, being such a lazy cook, while he always went hungry. After dipping his finger into this and that, his path led him into all kinds of kitchens around the world. For a long time he managed the kitchen of a spa centre and for a while ran a catering service in Newcastle, but he found the Limeys a bit too stingy.

Now he lives in Bergen, where he's been for many years, delivering smorgasbord buffets made by his own company, I think, but what does he tell his mother? Nothing, of course. Not a tiny sausage. Since I visited him some years back, he's sent me nothing but bone-dry Christmas greetings.

The youngest is my Magnús, Prince Potato, born in the spring of 1969, my third attempt at giving birth to a genius. And now you can laugh if you like, but he truly can be called Magnús Lawmender because he got higher qualifications than his father, the post-Jón genealogy expert, ever had. How generous of me to have married and given birth to all these lawyers, considering how lawless I am. Magnús followed his brother's example and earns his crust in the world of finance. He's the banker in the family, or bankster, as they call them now.

His job was to dangle the carrot in front of the asses and lure them into the self-deceit that they could instantly borrow a better life, as of today, that they didn't have to slave away all their lives to buy a dream house to die in. Back home in Breidafjördur you needed the sweat of sixteen generations to acquire a half-decent roof over your head, but these people wanted it all before the weekend. So my Magnús was close at hand to dish out lifetime credit, those infamous *currency basket loans*.

Instead of paying down the principal with every instalment, each instalment got added to the principal. So the next payment would be even higher still and the principal rose over and over again until the mortgage on a first-floor apartment shot up to the fourth. By the end of the crash, and the crumbled currency it left in its wake, people owed as much as the value of the entire block but were still forced to clear out and build themselves nests in the bicycle shed.

It's always been a bit strange, life in Iceland.

These loan sharks (e.g., Magnús's bosses) clearly capitalised on the credit slavery of these common people and then took their gains to the market, where they traded in spiralling bonds and shares, until they came home, like the old father in the folktale with four rotten apples in his sack. That was the genius of the Icelandic economic boom for you. They even managed to sink the Eimskip shipping company, which Grandad Sveinn had founded in 1914. Which only goes to prove that new saying: He who owns nothing can do anything, but he who owns everything can do nothing.

He was therefore badly hit by the crash, my Magnús. He too had taken out some sky-high loan that came tumbling down on him. The patio went, and the house, although the car survived with a dent. And to think he was just getting back on his feet after his divorce six years ago, an event that hit him so badly that he eventually put himself under house arrest. Misfortune comes in truckloads, but luck always rides alone, old people used to say. The enterprising Ragnheidur, Magnus's ex-wife and the mother of his children, didn't restrict herself to two-timing him in the disabled toilets around town, as her mother-in-law so shrewdly discovered, but she also stripped him of his possessions, and that after having played the part of *primus motor* in a plot to sell off my dear old house. She is and will always remain my favourite enemy.

I call her Rainmaker because she generally brings heavy downpours. Once, she even managed to reduce the four-times-over widow that I am to tears. But she herself always sports a steely smile, looking nice and lovely. Lies and treachery are the last things that would come to people's minds as she pecks them on the cheek, let alone wild passion. A frigid haddock, more like it. And this is something my Prince Potato confirmed to me as he sat weeping in this garage a year ago: she was ice cold in the bedroom department. Back west, women like that were called frozen fish. He therefore came out of that marriage completely frozen, poor fellow, and couldn't get his tool to work again until, years later, a short woman with a Buddha smile managed to thaw it with her tantric fingers.

As for Rainmaker, she took her freezing appliance all over town, enticing unsuspecting men who mistook her frost for love, abandoning their children and homes. My Dóra, who reads all the gossip mags, told me about two fathers of families whom she had lured into her freezer, only to wake up frostbitten in their own gardens at the crack of dawn: their wives had found them there naked and trembling, with freshly broken hearts and pubic hairs on their lips.

44

End of Childhood

1941

So, after about a year in Copenhagen, Mum and I ventured into the Nazi empire with smoked Faeroese meat in our picnic basket and Icelandic thoughts in our heads. It wasn't easy to discern where Denmark ended and Germany began. The villages all had the same Third Reich atmosphere. The train slowed down going through Flensburg, giving passengers a chance to observe the freshly washed flags, immaculate streets, and glistening shop windows full of photographs of the Führer and all his blond children. There was no denying it: every door handle of that redbrick city radiated the joy of victory and self-confidence, and even the cobblestones couldn't conceal the pride of their most recent territorial conquests: Hungary, Czechoslovakia and Romania were now in the bag. We stepped onto the platform and changed trains, sat in a smoke-spewing carriage that transported us noisily towards the North Sea. There was, and still is, the port town of Dagebüll, which turned out to be the terminal, the end of my childhood.

Naturally, I was excited to be 'leaving home' and discovering new horizons, but our parting came as a shock. The train halted in the centre of the 'town,' which was little more than two houses, a hotel and a platform. From there we walked down to the harbour, two coated women, tall and short, blond and dark. Owing to a shortage of funds, Mum hadn't been able to afford two tickets for the ferry and intended to say goodbye to me on the pier. I was to board the ferry alone and be greeted by strangers. To boost my morale, Mum told stories about Grandma Vera and sang to me:

Sailing boat, oh, sailing boat,
Sailing into the salty cry.
Let our bodies in coffins float
Together into the big goodbye.

Sailors sometimes sang this verse to defy their fears if they had to head out to sea in uncertain weather. But it was of no comfort to me, since my mind was too preoccupied with a brand-new feeling that mounted inside me with each step. A little pupa had insinuated itself into my gut and was mutating into a caterpillar, then a worm and finally a small hamster. And when I saw the sea stretching out beyond the pier, the hamster suddenly expanded into a full-grown beaver that pressed his snout up my throat and repeatedly started to click his tongue against my gum. I loosened my red scarf, but to no avail. I couldn't fathom what was happening to me. I'd never had a visitor in my chest like this before. He had taken over my body. The only thing I could cling to was the knowledge that I no longer had any control over it, a fact that only helped to exacerbate my sobbing and the lump in my throat, a phrase I only learned later.

It was a small ferry, but the tide had raised it, making the gangway almost horizontal. Several well-dressed passengers stepped on board. As we headed down the pier, Mum gave me her main advice: 'And remember to pray for your father.' Then she stopped, put down the hard wooden cases, hers and mine, and asked whether everything would be all right now. I couldn't utter a word, nor could I squeeze a single sound past the beaver whose snout filled my throat and who relentlessly clicked his tongue against my gums. Through some formidable effort I nevertheless managed to swallow, but then my eyes exploded and I started to wail. Inside I was screaming: Mum! Mummy! Don't send me out to sea! Don't leave me! Don't leave me alone!

I couldn't understand any of this. I who had been so much looking forward to this! But no, now I couldn't lose my mother. She drew me into her arms and managed to speak some comforting words before she, too, erupted. At first I thought she was laughing. But when she pulled out her white embroidered handkerchief, I realised she was just as devastated as I was, if not more so. I looked at her in astonishment, the greatest woman ever to be born on this earth, who now stood with her soul in shreds and her face in pieces and a thin handkerchief as her only refuge. All of a sudden I felt that she was smaller than I was and that I needed to console her, a feeling that was so sad, however, that I started to weep again. A gentleman in a hat walked by and glanced at us, two bawling women. Then the male world sounded its horn for the departure.

'Remember, Herra, dear, I love you. Your Mum loves you and will miss you every day and night. And we'll see each other again in the spring.'

A uniformed man carried the case on board, and I slowly moved along the gangway, which undulated to the rhythm of my tears. Then I hurried to the front of the ferry, as it backed out of the pier, and waved hopelessly at Mum. On that bright, icy January day she stood on the German pier with her hair tossed to the northern wind and waved goodbye to her child. Her chest heaved and contracted. And she continued to stand there waving, even after the boat had turned and I had moved to the back of the deck and we'd sailed a considerable distance. I watched my mother shrink to a girl, then a doll and finally a tin soldier. She kept on wiping her eyes with one hand. In the end she was the only person left on the pier and then she disappeared like a sinking sun on the horizon of the sea.

My darling Mum.

My subconscious, which had already read my biography, of course, knew perfectly well that our separation would last well beyond January, February, March and April 1941. And even her little and superficial sister, my consciousness, could sense that this was a crossroads in my life. My childhood was over.

It is written in the book of life that every chapter of our existence concludes with a nervous breakdown. We show up at the next one as if reborn, having cried away all our tears, weakened by the wailing that still echoes in our souls. And this was my state when I reached the island of Amrum – a lonely little Icelandic girl who had lost her father and mother in a round of poker with the ruthless rulers of the world.

45

Amrum

1941

Amrum is one of the Frisian Islands, those white sandbanks that glisten like multiple earrings dangling by the throat of Germany, if we look at Denmark as the head.

Frau Baum stood on the pier in an impeccably ironed raincoat and rolled-up hair, splay-footed in high-heeled boots that made her look like Mary Poppins in that film I didn't see until several hundred pages later. But as we drew closer, her face was grey and stern. The woman, just under forty, seemed to be afflicted by her big lips and overly small eyes, and enveloped in gloom. Her eyes immediately reminded me of two little peas on an empty plate, although her lips were more like two curved sausages. Her children stood shivering in her shadow, three obedient German mice, and further down the pier stood a girl of my age with a wrinkled brow. Her name was Heike, a German through and through, who just like me was kept here away from the war. Her mother had perished in the first British bombing of Berlin, and her father was currently unleashing his sorrow on French farmers.

A crew member carried my case ashore. It contained most of my clothes, brand-new rubber boots, two old, bound Icelandic Sagas and the precious sexy box from the heartsick Anneli. Frau Baum laid claim to it all with a single austere glance.

Like the other Frisian Islands, Amrum is a slightly convex sand dune, shell-white on the sea side, with tufts of grey grass on top. It's six times bigger than our biggest island in Breidafjördur, and during the war about a thousand people lived there: women, children and incapacitated men.

The Baum family lived in Norddorf, a village of 365 on the northern tip of the island. The house was in the classical Frisian style, white with a steep, dark straw roof. Its interior was dominated by squeaky-clean floors, and every piece of furniture served its purpose. The walls were bare and white except in the living room, where a black-and-white photograph of the master of the household in a Nazi uniform hung, and the kitchen, which was adorned with a coloured picture of the Führer with a lupine expression. It was an old European tradition, rooted in centuries of penury, for people to eat under the watchful eyes of the emperor in the hope that his gaze would nourish their half-empty stomachs.

With clear zeal in her voice, the lady proudly showed me around the house, but she soon revealed her penny-pinching nature when she launched into a long lecture on the quality of the down in my quilt, which she had specifically bought from a farmer on the island, and then insisted on unpacking my luggage herself. I watched helplessly as my case vanished into her room, and was unable to say which of its contents mattered to me the most, except maybe for my German, which I seemed to have buried way at the bottom.

I was mute for the first few days. A nervous breakdown doesn't blow over in just a few hours. I felt insecure and insignificant, and missed my mother the way a boat misses the sea. Besides, the Frau didn't inspire conversation, and Heike looked askance at me, told me she didn't speak any Danish, let alone Icelandic, and carefully kept her things to herself. The women of Copenhagen had seen their share of hardship, but in the eyes of this twelve-year-old girl for the first time I could read about all the misery the war had to offer. Her life was clearly a smouldering ruin. On my first night, I lay awake missing Mum and observed the girl, Heike, in her sleep. At regular intervals she jerked in her bed and buried her head under the quilt. That's how the soul works; it tries to wear down each shock by endlessly replaying it until it has exhausted all its pain.

The next day I followed her to school. But once we were in the classroom, she acted as if she didn't know me, and didn't seem to have any friends in the class either. I later discovered she didn't speak the islanders' language. Because even though classes were taught in German, all the kids spoke Frisian to each other. It was a bizarre language. Somebody commented that Frisian was like shipwrecked Dutch. To me the locals always sounded like a dead-drunk Dane on an English merchant ship trying to speak German to a Dutch whore. But to be more poetic I'd say that Frisian is the only true language of the sea. When the North Sea comes ashore and meanders up to the nearest pub, it orders a beer in Frisian.

But I'm told that the Frisians have now lost their language of the sea, and that their noble tongue is spoken by only three old biddies in an old folks' home in Husum, and that attempts are being made to keep them alive at all costs.

I had come well armoured, of course, after the Danish treatment, and was determined to integrate into the group. It turned out to be easier than expected. The school was completely free of Danish-style torture. Maybe because German was almost as alien to Frisian kids as it was to Icelanders. Moreover, our teacher, Fräulein Osinga, made sure none stepped out of line. She was a blond, pale-skinned woman in her forties, peculiarly beautiful in her own humble way, a kind of Marlene Dietrich with a hair bun but no lovers, like the rest of the women in Amrum. Most of them were real or grass widows. Here there were only a few elderly gentlemen who were too over the hill to face the war and had therefore developed feminine sensitivities. (Men believe in the principle of an eye for an eye and a tooth for a tooth, up to the point when these bodily parts start to drop off.)

The island was virtually a *Fraueninsel*, or Island of Women.

The school therefore gave me a warm welcome, and being a wind-beaten islander by birth, I blended into this world with a great ease. After a month in Amrum I had not only acquired a Frisian friend but also started to sing in that bizarre language that still resounds in my head, like a ragged flag on a rusty pole. No doubt I should donate my skull to the United Nations Museum of Extinct Languages.

Frau Baum wasn't too happy about having another mouth to feed in the house, although I know Dad sent her a decent amount of money to cover my keep. And they certainly weren't poor. Herr Professor Dr Baum was a high-ranking and well-paid official in the Millennial Reich. He was seldom in Friesland. One often forgets that the commotion of war generates a monstrous tangle of red tape; he rarely got a break from his rubber stamping and filing. Their home in Amrum had initially served as the family's summerhouse, but it now seemed wiser to keep the Frau there with the children until the Germans had won the war.

British Spitfires flew over the island almost on a daily basis, making a big racket on their way to bombing Hamburg or Berlin. The boys in the village had fun counting the planes and cheered heartily if they reckoned two or three were missing on the way back. Amrum wasn't a target, of course. It was an island outside the war zone, a natural air-raid shelter. I'd actually found a peaceful island in a continent at war, and I tried to make the most of it once I'd recovered from my collapse, although Heike and I would naturally have to wage a war against the Frau.

46

Heike and Maike

1941

We shared a bedroom, a white-plastered cave with a square porthole set deep in the wall and two mattresses on wooden legs as thick as tree trunks, and gradually Heike started to loosen her tongue. She told me about her beautiful family life before the war, on the fourth floor in Prenzlauer Berg in Berlin. Her father was a tram driver and her mother worked at night in the box office of a theatre. 'She was far too fond of cabaret and that kind of thing, but fate punished her for not following the Führer wholeheartedly. We must all stand together.' Yes, of course, I thought, picturing my father.

Heike briefed me on the exact meagre rations she received. Which certainly didn't increase with my arrival. The little children got to sip skimmed milk while we were expected to drink water. And every single morsel of meat was counted. The Berlin girl knew that 'under martial law' everyone was entitled to a minimum amount of food. But Frau Baum would have stolen the *pfennig* off a dead man's eyes. Day after day we went to bed hungry, hungry to school. But I, of course, was a wind-beaten islander, who had been reared in the food chest of Iceland and knew that the sea always carried some nourishment to shore. Heike gawked at me with big eyes when I fried the first piece of freshly fished seal for her. And finally I won her over when we secretly managed to open some shells in a boiling pot. In return I offered her a share of the native friend I had acquired on my own. Her name was Maike, blond with squinty eyes, red cheeks and a quivering laugh full of fresh sea breeze. She lived close by in a redbrick house, with her mother, grandparents and brothers. Her father was abroad, a perfect family man whose new job at the front was to drop firebombs on small English towns.

After school we would walk along the shore in search of food, Heike, Maike and I. To the north was Sylt Island, which stretched like a white streak on the steel-green sea. We wrestled against the terns (they arrived earlier there than they did at home), hunting for their delicious eggs, and ate sun-dried seaweed and even roasted some eel on a skewer. When we saw an inquisitive seal approaching, Heike dreamed of stealing Maike's father's rifle, while Maike had the good idea to collect driftwood. The shortage of firewood was a perpetual problem in Amrum, but to our surprise there was plenty of it floating on the white shore.

We collected it all on a tiny trolley, which we towed back to Maike's house across the sand with great effort. There we sawed it to pieces singing this jolly refrain:

Ran an den Feind! Ran an den Feind!
Bomben auf Engelland!

That was how I teamed up with the devil without having the faintest idea of it. On the cold periphery of the Thousand-Year Reich a little Icelandic girl was lending a hand to the cause by sawing wood to fuel the furnaces of Hitler's machine, singing a bloodthirsty Nazi song:

War needs a hand! War needs a hand!
Let's drop a bomb on England!

Then we went from house to house and traded the wood for freshly baked bread. But when our Frau caught wind of this, she demanded to see the spoils we carried home. The fact that her tenants were being fed in another house obviously didn't reflect too well on her housekeeping. Our first windfall went straight into her larder and only earned us half an extra slice of bread the next day.

Apart from the Tieck family, Frau Baum was the only German in the village and was disliked by the islanders. The Frisians are actually not unlike Icelanders: freethinkers and independent spirits believed to be the descendants of the Wends, fearless ocean Vikings who had sailed bravely across the globe and never counted their bread in slices. We decided to take our future spoils to Maike's house, where we made our own larder in a small cubbyhole. This was where we headed straight after school and held feasts right until dinnertime. Bread and cheese had rarely tasted this good. But as soon as the Frau noticed our diminished appetites. she took further measures.

'I'm not putting any food on the table for full stomachs.'

'We just had a tiny piece of rye bread at Maike's,' said Heike.

'You've no business eating in other people's houses when your place is at my table. Everyone has to think for himself. This is wartime we're living in. Besides, I think I know how you get your bread.'

'But we get so . . . sometimes we're still . . . left hungry here,' Heike dared to say.

'Everyone feels some hunger in times of war!' Frau Baum snapped as she loomed over us, Heike and me, her three children and two heads of cabbage in a kitchen that had stunk of sour boiled cabbage since my arrival. 'We all have to make sacrifices.' No doubt she'd noticed that I'd glanced up at the face of the Führer as he watched over our meal from the middle of the wall, because she added: 'For the Führer and the Fatherland.'

She then gave us a brief lecture on the German nutrition strategy. People in her house had to live frugally because our troops needed all the food they could get; it was sent to them at night in special provision carriages across the lands they had swallowed that day. Here everyone had to make sacrifices, and the Führer himself provided the best example because he had denied himself meat a long time ago and ate solely vegetables for all his meals. For the first time I felt a tinge of sympathy for this well-combed man who denied himself meat and women for the love of his adopted land. The Frau had told us previously that he had no wife because he was 'married to Germany.' That night I asked God to take good care of Mum, Grandad and Grandma Georgía and Grandma Vera and Dad, too, yes, and . . . Adolf Hitler.

I'd spent only a week in the land of war, and the Führer had already crawled into bed with me.

47

Red Lips, Black Shoes

1941

Frau Baum sniffed out our driftwood business and managed to confiscate our trolley. We therefore had to search for other shore treasures. Maike taught us how to read seagulls, and bit by bit we turned into two-legged beach rats and observed these companions of ours in the sky as they hunted for food and other goodies. And naturally they found plenty on those shores. Submarines were busy torpedoing ships, and the currents of the North Sea took care of spreading their cargoes all the way from Skagen to the south of Ostend. Once, we found a half-broken barrel of herring, and on another occasion, fifteen hundred lightbulbs that wouldn't screw into any lamp. It was hilarious to see the birds struggling with those glistening glass pears. Our most valuable catch, though, was two wooden boxes full of shoe polish in small jars, which we transferred to Maike's deposit and then sold on the black market, without the Frau ever finding out. She did, however, once mention at dinner how shiny the villagers' shoes had become. We managed to suppress our grins as I answered, 'Yes, that's because of the feast.'

'Feast?'

'Yes, the Biikebrånen. It's next week.'

The German woman hadn't spent a winter on the island yet and was therefore unaware of this particularly Frisian tradition, which probably dated back to heathen times: On the night of 21 February, people wander down to the shore, where each village builds its bonfire or *biike*. They sing and dance and also burn a straw man, which some consider the symbol of winter; torching him was meant to reawaken the spring from the earth. Maike's grandfather told us that in the past, women used to light the bonfire to say goodbye to their men as they headed out to hunt whales. Her grandmother jokingly added that this was Frisian women's way of letting the lads know that there were no men on the island.

'Are people really going to light fires on the beach? That's just like ordering missiles from the Brits,' Frau Baum said, leaning back on her chair with her legs wide apart, sweating in her apron, and shaking her head.

'Mum, what's *misfiles?*' her daughter, a little blond flower with weather-beaten rosy cheeks, asked.

'Missiles are bombs that bad men who live in England drop out of their planes to blow up houses and make people die,' Heike answered swiftly.

'Why do they want people to die?'

And then I said: 'Because they speak German and not English.'

'Mum, I don't want to die. I want to speak English!' said the little girl, starting to cry. Her mother's face burst into a blaze.

'Why did you say that to her?! What kind of bleeding nonsense is that! And I don't want you lot going around the village speaking fri . . . frigging Frisian! You're in GERMANY, you go to a GERMAN school, so you should speak GERMAN!'

'No, Mother, I want to speak English,' the little one whined.

Although we were only eleven years old, our feminine intuition understood the woman's hysterical outburst. The woman's heart was trapped on an alien island in a frightful meltdown. Her fury had nothing to do with us; it was about something else, something bigger. We couldn't take it personally. Earlier that day I had read a letter from Mum, which was also full of exclamation points. 'Oh, if only I had you here beside me! I miss you so much, Herra, love! Remember to pray for your father!'

Men fight, women take fright.

Frau Baum wasn't the only person who was anxious about the imminent bonfire. It was being discussed all over Norddorf. The other Germans in the village, the Tieck crowd, were fuming. Their daughter Anna raised the issue at school and warned them that anyone who went to the bonfire would be shot by English bullets. Heike furrowed her brow. Finally an order came from Berlin banning the lighting of any fire on the shores of the Third Reich. On the other hand, there were no swastika officials in this little village, and it says a lot about the pluck of those free-spirited Frisians that they fearlessly built their bonfire regardless, as they had done every February for thousands of years.

Heike dropped out of the Fris-Icelandic club and berated me under the cold quilt back home for getting carried away by this nonsense.

'It's true what Frau Baum says. Old traditions have to go. We have to stand together.'

'But we're not responsible for this. We're just . . . watching.'

'Herra, we're at war. Neutrality is cowardice. Those fires are a threat to the German Reich.'

'Yeah, let's go and try to put them out, then. Are you coming with me?'

She didn't answer. And was silent as she had been when Maike and I discussed Biikebrånen. We were full of both fear and excitement. And pride. Because we had obviously left our mark. Every shoe that walked the dull grey streets of this humdrum village shone like obsidian in the sun. And in that very same week things got even better when we discovered two silvery metallic containers on the shore, the size of suitcases. Heike and Maike strictly forbade me to go anywhere near them and pointed out that our dear hunting dogs, the seagulls, were keeping well away from them.

'That's only because there's no smell from the boxes. There's no food in them,' I said.

'Yes, exactly! Bombs don't have a smell!'

But my Icelandic nature refused to submit. My reckless, stupid curiosity compelled me to peep into the boxes. The girls held themselves at a screaming distance as I crept up to the metallic cases and finally undid their simple latches. Oh yes, there were bombs in them all right: thousands of tubes of war-red lipstick. I yelled triumphantly and called the girls over. And after trying several colours out and laughing ourselves silly, we filled our pockets with these treasures and dragged the silver boxes out of view, burying them behind a dune.

On Biikebrånen Night every woman arrived at the ball with shiny black shoes and fiery-red lips.

48

The Man from the Sky

1941

Frau Baum forbade her girls to go to the bonfire and locked us into the bedroom to be certain. The German Heike agreed with the mistress of the house, and we argued bitterly from our beds as the evening twilight gradually filled the room. I was dead set on going. A Reich that couldn't put up with one bonfire could never last a thousand years. Maike and I had worked hard on lending a hand and carried many logs to the pile, which had grown into a tall and impressive mound. I wasn't about to miss it.

'Do you want to get yourself killed?'

'Killed?'

'Yes, it'll end with an air raid when the Brits see the bonfire.'

'I don't care.'

'Don't care? Do you really want to get yourself killed?'

'Yeah, sure.'

'Why?!'

'Because . . . because I'm curious! Icelandic!'

Maike knocked on the pane. After a brief scuffle, I managed to free myself of Heike and crawl out the window. Maike and I ran down towards the beach and reached it just before the fire was lit.

It was a cold and still night. Frost hung in the air, but there was no snow on the ground. The sky glowed with all its candles in a silence that was as thick as the sand and the darkness, until an old fireman ignited the fire with three sprays of petrol. About a hundred people had ventured out of their houses and stood there by the crackling flames and sighing sea. Naturally, there was some apprehension in the crowd, but the tensions of the past months had drawn them closer together. Finally someone started to sing. Men and women joined in, slipping their hands onto the next person's shoulders and swaying together to the rhythm of the waves, fire and song. It felt like a cosy scout bonfire or even a Christmas dance, but there was a strange sexual energy in the air. The women, who had dolled themselves up with red lipstick and shiny shoes, looked like Spanish flamenco dancers. The twin blond sisters from next door, who always walked around stooping under the weight of their new budding breasts, radiated with joy in the glow of the fire. Furtive glances shot back and forth like sparks out of the fire before dying in the dark of the night; there were no inflammable young men here to transform those sparks into flames. They were all far away, in Ljubljana or Libya, stuffing themselves with horsemeat sausages in the open carriage of a goods train. The only males left here were old-timers who swayed between virgin and motherly breasts, letting the last rays of their sexual sun lick the peaks where they once stood.

My God, I can still hear those ancient Frisian verses in my head:

Klink dan en daverje fier yn it roun,
Dyn âlde eare, o Fryske groun!

May the heavenly thunder sound in thine old honour, oh Frisian ground! But it was as if they had invoked the devil; in the middle of their anthem a peal of thunder was heard in the sky. People instantly stopped singing and looked into the air. There was nothing to be seen, but the noise grew louder. The Germans had been right. The fire attracted English bombs. We immediately ran away from the fire and fled the beach, some people throwing themselves into the sand. But Maike and I didn't get far, because the sound of an overhead plane turned into a crash and we looked around: an indistinct form, adorned with white and red rings, appeared out of the dark sky for a very brief moment before vanishing into the sea with a big splash at a short distance from the shore. We spotted half a wing protruding from the sea and white smoke rising from it with a faint hiss.

I noticed that the German girl, Anna Tieck, or Anna Tick, as I used to call her in my letters to Mum, was a few yards away from us. So she'd come, after all. And was now looking at Maike and me with a contemptuous air.

A brave old man, who obviously didn't care about his life any more, finally clambered to his feet and tottered down to the shore. Maike and I edged our way back towards the fire and passed it, following the old man. Others did the same. Soon more movement stirred the surface of the sea, and after a few tense moments, we spotted a man swimming towards us.

'Who goes there?!' the old man shouted in German.

No answer. A young man in a glistening jacket emerged from the sea, stumbling towards us, exhausted. He didn't seem to be armed, halted on the water's edge, and observed us for a moment before he bent over, steadied himself on his knees, and caught his breath. Seawater streamed from his head.

'Who are you?' the old man repeated in German. By now more people had returned to the beach. The blazing fire crackled behind them. The man straightened and asked, 'Is this Wannsee?'

'Huh?'

'Am I in Wannsee?'

He spoke German with an English accent.

'Are you English?' a young female voice asked behind us.

'Yes,' he answered in English, and then, holding out his hands in total submission, he said, 'Arrest me.'

The Frisians looked at each other, the man, and then each other again, without uttering a word. He was a young soldier with dark wavy hair and a handsome face. His lips and shoulders quivered from the cold. Staggering up onto the shore, he turned and pointed at the sea, at the wreckage, and was about to say something when he had a coughing fit that smothered his words. Finally he retched and left a coat of bright spew on the shore. An old lady approached him with a blanket and threw it over him before another younger one ran to assist her. Together they helped the pilot up the beach towards the fire. He was wearing a leather jacket with Royal Air Force badges on the front and sleeve, and a pretty white scar stretched from his lower lip down to his chin. The Englishman took a few tottering steps and then stopped to tell two men in his poor German that his companion was still stuck in the wreckage. As the women ushered the young man to the fire, the two men waded towards the debris. But they were old and wouldn't venture any further than up to their knees; the water was ice cold. No further movements could be discerned in the wreckage, which finally succumbed to a small wave as its vertical wing sank into the sea with a splash.

Moments later the old men turned around to join the group by the fire. The women had stripped the Englishman of his jacket and shirt and wrapped a blanket around him. Someone then added to that by enveloping his shoulders in a red shawl. He sat in the sand with crossed legs and stared vacantly into the fire, a faint chatter in his teeth, surrounded by the daughters and mothers of Friesland. Maike and I stared at him, spellbound. I'd never seen such a handsome man, except maybe on a silver screen in Copenhagen. They just didn't make beautifully chiselled faces like that on this side of the North Sea. And I had thought that the British were bomb-crazed, murderous dogs with Dickensian noses and Victorian double chins.

Our teacher, Fräulein Osinga, who spoke pretty good English, crouched beside the new arrival to act as interpreter and informed the others that the boy's name was William and he thought he had crashed close to Berlin, in the Wannsee Lake. She got no more out of him. He was clearly distraught by his error, a mistake that seemed to have cost his companion's life. It wasn't easy to make him realise where he was.

'Freezeland?' he said in a quivering voice.

He was clearly wet behind the ears in more senses than one, handsome as he may have been: a charming twenty-year-old boy who had obviously been standing in a London pub the night before, playing darts.

The women ogled the striking fellow with dreamy eyes and fiery-red lips. Few things inflame a woman's bosom more than the sight of a pitifully beautiful boy. The teenage girls coquettishly adjusted their brows and lips. Yes, all of a sudden, a treasure had fallen from the sky. *Eine Sexbombe aus England.*

'He's terribly handsome, don't you think?'

'Yes,' Maike whispered. 'He can't be English.'

Another rumble was heard, this time from the sea. A boat was rapidly advancing from the south with a powerful searchlight that scanned the shore like a frantic sniffer dog until it spotted us by the fire. Those who were sitting by the English soldier immediately sprang to their feet, and finally he did, too. The rumble of the engine began to fade but the spotlight was fixed on the bonfire. A stern male voice boomed through a megaphone: '*Feuer ausmachen!*

We all stood there rigidly, watching the despotic long coat wade to the shore. But in the corner of my eye I saw how Fräulein Osinga surreptitiously buried the pilot's leather jacket under the sand with one foot where it lay, close to the fire. The officer in the long coat was tall and moved stiffly, as if he lacked flexibility in his knees. He wore knee-high leather boots and an officer's visor hat, sported a bulky, menacing jaw, and held the megaphone in his left hand. In the other glistened a long-barrelled revolver. Two privates appeared behind him with rifles. The commander was no longer using his megaphone but waved his gun about as he roared at us to put out the blasted fire. What kind of craziness was this?

'FEUER AUSMACHEN!'

He wore his visor low; his eyes were veiled by its shadow. The Englishman started shaking again. Two boys suddenly made a run for it, up the beach, but were noticed by the commander. It was Maike's brothers. As quick as a flash, their mother turned her head to watch them flee, suppressing a scream, but swinging it back again she saw that the officer was levelling his gun. With the lightning instincts of a lioness she charged towards the barrel and managed to deflect the bullet that shot into the darkness. The gunman shook her off and was beside himself with rage. He fired two shots at the dunes and then pointed the gun at the woman who lay at his feet and whimpered in German: 'Yes, shoot . . . shoot me instead!' I observed the petrified look on my friend's face.

But the man in the long coat didn't have enough time to shoot the mother, because now the two privates walked up to him, pointing at the sea. The searchlight had been turned away from the land and illuminated the wreckage of the British plane. They all stomped away from the fire back down to the shore again. In the same moment, Maike burst into tears as she threw herself on her mother, who was still crouched in the sand with her hands buried deep in it, as if she were disappointed not to get it as her grave.

The boat moved towards the wreckage, but the officer hurried back to the fire. His men followed with buckets and ordered the males to put out the fire with seawater. The officer nudged the visor off his eyes and, stiffly but calmly, started to walk from one person to the next, grinning at the weeping mother and daughter who cowered together at his feet. But once he finally realised that these were nothing but war rejects – women, adolescents, children and old men – he seemed relieved, and his sense of duty yielded to a smile.

'So you are Frisians? All of you Frisians? And you think you're not at war? You think you can just continue to celebrate your

TRADITIONAL TWADDLE as if there were no danger? Light a fire, no less?!'

Behind him the fire hissed as the men's first buckets of water were unleashed on it. Maike was still snivelling in the arms of her mother, who wiped her own tears with the back of her hand.

'And what happened with the plane over there? Did you see it crash?' the officer continued.

'Yes,' our teacher answered.

'Didn't it fire at you?'

'No.'

'And what happened? Was it shot down?'

'No, I don't think so. It just crashed.'

'Is that so, yes? It just crashed and you continued with your little Frisian party? As if nothing . . .'

He suddenly shut up as his gaze froze on the Englishman, and he walked towards him.

'Who are you?'

The group held its breath in silence.

'Wi . . . William,' the pilot muttered.

'Willem?'

'*Ja*,' the drenched boy answered without any trace of an accent. A straight and simple *ja*. And there was no way of determining what language the word belonged to. It could have been German, Danish, Frisian or even Dutch.

'And why is it you are wet?'

The boy tried to utter something, but no words reached his lips, which now started to tremble as never before. The old man who had first walked towards him answered in his place.

'He . . . he swam out to . . . to make sure the pilot was dead.'

I had noticed that Anna the tick was standing close to me on the left. And without having to look at her, my left ear could sense her tensing up.

'And what? Was he dead?' the officer asked.

'Yes . . . well, no . . . not quite . . . he had to fight . . . fight him, didn't you?' The old man shot a glance at the Englishman, who suddenly looked at him but then cast his eyes on the sand again and nodded with a low head. The bucket men reappeared with another round of seawater, and the light from the fire faded some more with a fizzle.

'Yes? So we have a hero here?' The coated officer sneered sardonically before raising his voice again: 'But heroes don't hang their heads!' And he lifted the English jaw with his German gun, peering inquisitively into the boy's eyes. 'And what is a hero like this doing at a woman's ball? Why aren't you at the front? Are you a deserter?!' he snapped, tugging the shawl and blanket off the shoulders of the soldier, who was left standing in his white vest. Judging by the look on the English lad's face, he couldn't remember whether the vest of the Royal Air Force carried an RAF badge.

The officer threw down his megaphone now and tore the garment off the Englishman with great brutality. It was a beautiful torso that appeared to us ladies and eunuchs against the golden embers of the dying fire. The boy hung his head with a deep shyness, if not fear, but the officer grabbed his right shoulder and turned him halfway, and then, in a sudden fit of sadistic homoerotic glee, he ordered the lad to take his trousers off as well.

William was now shaking in nothing but his underwear.

The officer took a long pause to contemplate the boy. One could hear the lust boiling inside him. Then he took one step towards the young man, slipped the nozzle of his revolver behind the elastic of his underpants and eased them down. He ordered him to stand upright. '*Stillgestanden!*'

A naked man stood before us, a true Apollo in all his burning magnificence. Through the faint crackling, one could hear a deep, almost inaudible female gasp. Here in the presence of fire and death, sea and stars, the moment had stripped us of the garments of time and we now stood there like ancient, primitive souls on their first beach, by their first fire, experiencing their first desire. I've never forgotten it. I shall never forget it. Not even now as I lie here seventy years later, decrepit with my wispy hair on my deathbed. I still see it as it hangs there before my eyes, like the very purpose of life itself. Never before had I seen anything so terrifyingly beautiful as that, so boorishly ugly, so overwhelmingly true. 'An upside-down tulip.' Despite the frosty night and the hundreds of female eyes, the Englishman's organ held its substantial size and stirred almost imperceptibly to the tremors of its owner under a shelter of dark hair: a cock gilded by fire. Like everyone else, the man in the visor hat seemed entranced. He delighted in this wonder another short while and then found his voice again with a laugh as he shouted to his men.

'This is precisely what the German army needs!'

They laughed raucously and he repeated his punch line to squeeze out even more guffaws. The show ended the way it had started, as soon as three old Frisian men threw a final round of buckets of water over the fire. Everything plunged into darkness. The fog light on the boat was now the only source of illumination on the shore. A shout was heard from the sea, but the officer paid it little heed and instead asked the naked man for his full name. The Englishman mumbled faintly into his chest, concealing his jewels behind his hands.

'Well then?!' the German roared.

'His name is . . . Willem . . . Willem Wannsee, sir,' said Fräulein Osinga.

'Aha, Willem Wannsee . . .' the officer muttered, pulling a notepad and pencil out of his leather coat to jot down the name. 'You will receive notification!' he said to the soldier, and he walked over to him to stroke the English member with the barrel of his gun. Another shout came from the boat, and the coated man shoved his notepad back into his pocket. He was on the point of withdrawing when Anna Tieck unexpectedly stepped forward and opened her mouth. But before she had the time to give away the English pilot, I jumped behind her and covered her mouth with my hand. She struggled and we fell into the sand. I landed underneath her but managed to lock her arms and legs and hold back her German tongue. Fräulein Osinga shouted over us: 'Girls! What's got into you?!' And people turned towards us but kept themselves at a safe distance. The officer snorted at this infantile sparring match with slight bewilderment, without suspecting that this was a matter of life and death. But as he started to walk away, Anna managed to free herself from me and was about to stand when I grabbed the elastic on the back of her skirt with two fingers and dragged her down again. 'He's Engl—!' she yelled at her fellow countryman before I smothered her voice with the palm of my hand. She glared at me with crazed eyes, finally slipped away, and was about to run down to the officer on the shore when the people, who had formed a semi-circle around us, deliberately barred her path.

'BUT HE'S ENGLISH!' she yelled out.

People's faces tensed and no one dared silence her. She repeated herself but was unable to break through the throng that had silently formed around her. Many looked at the coated officer wading towards the boat in the water. He didn't look back.

Maike and her mother ran away from the group towards the bank of dunes that separated the shore from the village. Far in the darkness they could be heard calling out the names of the boys.

'We found the pilot! He's dead!' the men called out to the officer from the sea. Moments later he was on board and the boat vanished with its searchlight pointed to the north. Total darkness descended on the beach. Only the candlelit sky gave people the glimmer they needed to recover from the evening's events. Under the faint sunlight from other solar systems the numbed people started to make their way home. Three women helped the young man into his trousers, shawl and blanket under the watchful eyes of another three. The twins with the burgeoning breasts coyly giggled, their hair mingling together. The German Anna looked daggers at me. Or so I thought in the darkness. She stood with her back to the sand dunes and Germany itself behind them. Her coal-black pupils were the glistening twin lenses of a pair of binoculars; I felt I could see deep into them, fourteen days' travel away, all the way into the Chancellery in Berlin, where two raging torches burned – torches that from here were the size of needle tips but that loudly and clearly declared: You have betrayed the Thousand-Year Reich and you shall be punished.

49

The Leather Jacket

1941

I was still a bit shaken after the fight and didn't have the energy to follow the group, so I lingered by the ruins of the bonfire. White vapours were still rising from the sooty wood. Close to the fire, I stood on something that was more than sand. I bent over and dug out the aviator's jacket. It was made of leather with a thick lining and was heavy because it was saturated in seawater. Nevertheless, I took it with me as I moved away from the beach and followed the locals as they threaded along the lyme grass–crowned dunes towards the village.

I couldn't find Maike or her mother, but on one of the village's illuminated corners the twins came dashing from Maike's street and told me the boys were in one piece. I heaved a sigh of relief, but the sisters' eyes were focused on the jacket in my arms and they were desperate to know whether there was something inside it. The internal pocket contained a salty, wet ID card with a photo of the English prince. 'Oh, he's so handsome,' they gasped like adolescents through the ages. In a side pocket we found a bar of chocolate wrapped in damp paper. I gave them a piece and had one myself. It tasted bitter, like strong baking chocolate. 'But where did Anna go?' I asked, extinguishing the chirpy expressions on the twins' faces.

In the same moment we heard a rumble in the sky and looked into the air. Four English bombers flew over the village, from east to west, and then vanished beyond the sea. We felt a tinge of shame as we stood there with the jacket in our hands and the sweet flavour of the enemy in our mouths. I shoved the ID card back into the inside pocket but the chocolate into mine, and asked the sisters to hold on to the jacket. I didn't fancy taking it home to Frau Baum. They took it and told me the English soldier was now at Fräulein Osinga's place, where he would be spending the night. They started gasping again, talking about how beautiful he was, but then bit their lips, casting a westward glance towards the sky as the rumble of the planes faded slowly.

50

Branded

1941

I slipped into the garden, moved along the wall of the building, and was about to climb up to our bedroom window when I heard a strange sound coming from the one beside it. It was the bathroom. A faint light glowed behind the pale green curtains, and the Frau could be heard panting loudly inside. Was she ill? The more her sighs persisted, the more I realised they belonged to the realm of pleasure. I rejoiced for her, clambered to my bedroom window, crawled through it, and slipped into my bed.

Heike lay with her head on her pillow and her quilt pulled up to her chin. She was pretending to be asleep, but I could see perfectly well in the starlit darkness that here lay a child who had just shut her eyes to a world full of gloom. I watched her a good while, waiting for her to give up and open her eyes.

'Traitor.'

'Do you want some chocolate?' I asked, handing her the half-eaten bar.

'Chocolate?'

'Yes, we got chocolate at the bonfire.'

'No, I've brushed my teeth.'

'Hey, when a man is naked, he's . . .'

'What?' she asked.

'When a man's naked, then he's just a man.'

'Huh?'

'Then he's neither a German nor an Englishman. He's . . . you know . . . if he doesn't say anything. If he just shuts up.'

'What are you talking about?'

'Then there's no way of knowing whether you're supposed to kill him or not. Look . . .' I said, rolling up the sleeves of my jumper and blouse and placing my arm on her quilt. 'A bare arm, flesh and bone. You can't tell whether it's Icelandic, Danish or Frisian . . . or German . . .'

She scrutinised the arm in silence.

'You can't tell what country it's from.'

Suddenly her hand shot out from under her quilt and grabbed my bare arm. Then she stretched out for a pair of scissors in a basket on the bedside table, sat up, grabbed me with all her might, and pinned me to the mattress with a strength that took me so much by surprise that it left me defenceless. In just a few moments she'd managed to carve a whole swastika on my skin with the scissors, just above my elbow. And then let me go. Blood started to ooze out of one of the arms of the cross. I winced in pain and rushed towards the bathroom. Or intended to. But of course the door was locked. On the other side of it, the Frau was still releasing her wanton sighs. I hesitated and listened to her mounting the ladder of pleasure. When she'd reached its peak, I heard the scraping sound of a chair or table, or maybe even a drying rack, followed by a heavy sigh. Then silence.

I hurried back into my room, cursing Heike to hell. She had curled herself into the corner, so that I could barely see the crown of her head, but then answered in a voice that was half smothered by her quilt. 'You deserved it.'

I tied a sock around my wound, undressed, and got into bed. Heike seemed to doze off quite swiftly, but I couldn't sleep a wink. The turbulent events of the night shot through me, causing my heart to beat wildly.

Finally I decided to fetch a glass of water. My throat was extremely dry. The red tiles of the kitchen floor were illuminated by the light outside, which projected the shadow of the window frame. The moon was shining now. I let the tap run the Icelandic way, having learned from my winters in Reykjavík to allow the water to run until it got cold. But then the bathroom door burst open and Frau Baum stormed into the kitchen.

'Oh, it's you? What are you doing?'

'Getting some water.'

'Yes, drink the water, then! Don't let the tap just run,' she said, grabbing an empty glass, filling it, shutting off the tap, and then handing the glass to me. 'Where were you? Where did you go? Down to the beach? I forbade you! I was terrified about you. When did you get home? Did you get in just now? And what's wrong with you, child? Why are you looking at me like that? Did something happen? Have you been drinking beer?'

That was nine questions I could choose from. But I limited my answer to pointing at the pearl necklace she was wearing. This threw her at first, but then she recovered.

'Yes, I was just trying it on,' she stuttered awkwardly.

I had never seen this stiff, wooden woman in such a flattering light. With the fiery-red lipstick, she had managed to draw out a certain beauty in her face with the same effect that is obtained from painting a dilapidated house in bright colours: for a moment the eyes are beguiled into believing it's beautiful. She was bare-shouldered in a silk nightdress and wore the pearl necklace I knew so well. Now I knew what she'd been up to that night.

'That's a truly magic box,' I said.

'Huh?'

'My jewellery box. There's something very special about it. I can't quite explain it, but didn't you . . . feel something?'

'When?'

'When you opened it?'

The Frau stared at me with her small grey eyes, wondering if these were matters that could be discussed with an eleven-year-old child. 'Yes, actually, it . . . it was . . .' She spotted the sock I had tied around my arm. 'What's that?'

'Nothing. I scratched it outside against . . .'

'What?'

'Germany.'

Then I excused myself, telling her I wanted to go back to bed, and politely thanked her for the water. The newly unmasked Frau was unusually affable, just said *bitte* and told me to sleep well. And after that conversation of ours in a moonlit kitchen, she never raised her voice against me again. But I couldn't sleep a wink and nibbled on some more of the pilot's chocolate and stared at the face of the German orphan on the pillow. She was so beautiful when she slept. Damn her. Was I going to bear a swastika scar for the rest of my life? (Let's see. I roll up the sleeve of my hospital gown. Oh, yes, I can still see the clumsily carved swastika on my shrivelled upper arm.)

I decided to call her *Hækja* from then on, the Icelandic word for crutch, Hækja Hitler, the arm molester. And she had no monopoly over being motherless and fatherless. I was just as much an orphan as she was, even if my Mum wasn't dead like hers. Or maybe she was dead? No! And Dad wasn't dead either. That couldn't be. Where were they tonight? What were they thinking? Were they sleepless like me? Now I could never wear short sleeves again except maybe with Dad. He'd be happy to see his daughter branded with his ideals. Oh, why did he have to become a soldier? Why couldn't he just follow Mum's example, the wisest person who'd ever walked on earth?

My darling Mum. You're now sleeping on a hard bed in a doctor's house in Lübeck dreaming of Breidafjördur. Oh, what love didn't do to you. It had pulled you up by the roots and planted you here and there. Maybe you weren't the wisest person who'd walked this earth after all? Yes, you were. Brains have nothing to do with love. And love nothing to do with brains. When it comes to love, we're all equally stupid.

51

A Night in Norddorf

1941

I couldn't sleep and finally got up again. I could hear some laughter coming from outside and stepped out in my pyjamas. A magic atmosphere hung in the air; the garden glowed under the moonlight. The white orb perched on the church steeple like a slice of lemon on a cocktail stick, illuminating the narrow chimneys and steep straw rooftops. And in the garden next door the blond twins were playing badminton. The theatrical silence of the night was regularly broken by the girls' shots. The object they were striking back and forth at each other was no ordinary shuttlecock but some featherless, slimy object that glistened in the moonlight. As I drew closer, I realised it was an eyeball. They were whacking an eye between them. I asked them three times where they'd got it from, and they finally answered that it was Frau Baum's eye. And then they laughed themselves silly. But carried on playing with a human eye under the full moon.

My heartbeat quickened faster than their shots. There was something in me, something that was driving me, some unknown force. I walked past the twins, out onto the street, and into the village. HALEMWAI, DÜNEMWAI, OODWAI, said the signs, nodding at me. There was something unreal about this nocturnal light that was almost like sunshine. It was a small village, so on every street I could hear the echo of the badminton game, giggles, and squishy strikes of the rackets.

I reached Fräulein Osinga's house and saw a light in the window. On the street stood a small-chinned woman with combed-back black hair and burning, male-famished eyes. She became embarrassed and swiftly disappeared. I stood on my toes and peered through the window and saw my teacher sitting on the edge of the bed feeding the soldier, who lay bare-chested against a high pillow. Pretty puffs of steam rose from the spoon. Fräulein Osinga was dressed in a burgundy silk nightdress, with her back turned to me. Her blond hair was pinned behind into a huge kind of layered bun, which stood on the back of her neck and followed the movements of the head but otherwise didn't budge, as if made of wax. It was moving slightly now, though, as she turned to the English patient with a steaming spoon, and into that insignificant gesture I read something far greater. I saw it so clearly: the teacher was going to lose her life for the sake of Willem Wannsee.

For a good long moment I stood watching the English face, mesmerised, totally content not to have reached the age of love, totally content to be a free child who didn't have to lie down with princes but could make do with the handle of a mop. Then I continued on towards the moon, across the village, until I was standing by the last house at the end of the street, looking down at the eastern shore of the island. A few moments later I was on top of a tumbledown shack that stood behind a fence. From there I climbed the roof of the shack, and then a ladder that was attached to the straw roof, all the way up until I stood on the ridge of this alien house, holding onto the chimney.

It was a very tall building that offered me a good view of the village behind me. The straw roofs sucked in the moonlight but didn't reflect it. Only the cobblestones on the streets returned as much light as they got. The heavens were pouring with stars. In the distance, on the other side of the steeple, I could see the Frau's eyeball shooting over the dark rooftops at regular intervals. Frau Baum always found some way to keep an eye on people. I did wonder, though, whether the relentless whacking from the badminton rackets might have a bad effect on her eyesight.

Down on the street below, some girls in coats were chatting. They were heading towards the teacher's house. The English pilot probably didn't realise he had crash-landed in Pantiesville.

Then I turned to look out at the eastern coast, which glowed as white as marble in the lunar incandescence, and then beyond at the strait between the islands and the mainland. A patrol boat slowly crossed the surface, dutifully followed by the reflected sparkle of its lights on the waves. Its engine murmured from within its bowels, and I felt its sound echoing inside me. I was at one with everything, and everything at one with me. And beyond the strait an entire continent unfolded. I stretched out my newly branded arm and touched France, stuck out my nose and smelled Poland, then rolled up the sleeve of my other arm and felt a breeze from the North Pole. My spirit burst out and could no longer be contained in that tiny, light-footed body it now considered its toy. Two sluggish seagulls flew by the gable of the house with gentle flapping sounds. My first reaction was to follow them: I knew I could fly, but I also knew I could sit here for another three hundred years, like the chimney.

I took the second option and continued to gaze out over the countries with those sharp eyes the night had given me. Then I saw Dad tottering into the dark dawn with a towel wrapped around his waist, along with eighty other wretches; they were granted three seconds under the shower each. And just a bit further up the continent, Mum had just woken up with bags under eyes, on her way along the cobblestones of Lübeck. They were two unlucky Icelanders who, through an error of destiny, had become the slaves of strangers, the completely wrong strangers, instead of taking care of their child, who sat here intoxicated on the rooftop of a lovesick village.

52

Herr A

1941

The following day it transpired that the British pilot's chocolate had contained a powerful dose of amphetamines. The father of the twins, the tubby pharmacist, came raging over to us, confiscated the booty, and then delivered a stern lecture on the dangers of these substances, particularly for Frisian girls.

I was still high. And went to school in that state. And knew everything, could do everything, did everything. But in the evening the effects finally started to wear off, my heartbeat slowed down, and I changed from an all-seeing roof hen into a weeping child. Frau Baum sat over me, and Hækja fetched a glass of water. The pharmacist returned and gave me a calming milky mixture. Shortly afterwards, I managed to fall asleep.

For days the thought of my climb filled me with terror – I had stood on top of a chimney! – and I always lowered my gaze when I passed a lit window and prayed for the Frau's eye every night. Then I covered my ears to block out the stories that were spreading around the village, which Hækja, the arm molester, repeatedly tried to tell me: The English Adonis had betrayed Fräulein Osinga for her sister. Someone had stumbled in on him with the cobbler's daughter in a basement close to the graveyard. And then two girls were seen leading him down to the shore.

He was the only real man in Womenville, a status he got to enjoy for ten days, until two uniformed Nazis appeared on the streets of Norddorf. They came to our house and demanded to speak to Herr A. These were two menial young officers, peasants who had been posted to an insignificant village on the remote periphery of the Reich chancellor's empire but were eager to prove themselves worthy of more central missions and therefore extremely dangerous. As is often the case with upstarts of this kind, the uniform meant everything to them, everything from their shiny, polished boots to their beautiful, glowing buttons. They looked like two small-town kids who had come to pick up their dates for the masked ball, as they paced the kitchen of their compatriot, Frau Baum, waiting for the extremely dangerous leader of the resistance, Herr A, to step out of his hiding place. Hækja stood in the corner, proud of her impeccably dressed soldiers. Had she denounced me? Their caps tilted back from their eyes as they saw me treading down the corridor: Herr A was an eleven-year-old girl. Nevertheless, they ushered me into the living room and ordered the Frau to leave with her children, before locking me in with them. The living-room clock started to count the seconds I had left to live the moment I sat on the hard, creaking wicker stool.

'Do you recognise this jacket?'

'Yes.'

'Where did you get it?'

'I found it by the bonfire. Down . . . down on the beach.'

'What accent is this? Where are you from?'

'From Iceland.'

'Ah, Iceland? And are you living here with Frau Baum?'

'Yes. My father's in the army. He's Icelandic, too. He's in the Landsberg Military Academy. I think he's in the SS.'

'Really? Good for him.'

'And Mum is working as a maid for Dr Krewald in Lübeck. He's a friend of Himmel's.'

'Himmel?'

'Yes. Heinrich Himmel.'

The man questioning me turned to his colleague, who despite his higher rank sat in lower seating, since he had comfortably settled into the deep sofa under the photograph of Herr Baum in his brown shirt, and stroked his thick moustache. The interrogator laughed and his superior smiled.

'Ha-ha-ha, you mean Heinrich HIMMLER?'

'Yes. He's high up,' I said.

'Yes, yes. He's high up! Ha-ha. So she's a maid at Dr Krewald's? But what were you doing with that jacket? The jacket of an English pilot? What did you do with it?'

'I . . . I let the sisters have it, the twins next door.'

'Precisely. And why?'

'Because . . . because they . . . thought he was so handsome. The pilot, I mean. And there was a photo of him in the jacket.'

'Precisely, yes? And did you find him HANDSOME, too?'

I listened to the clock a moment.

'Yes.'

'Yes? Why? Why did you find this Englishman . . . this pathetic Englishman so HANDSOME?'

The clock ticked four seconds.

'Answer! Why were you fond of him?'

This was the tone I was destined to hear many more times in my life, from a recently ditched husband or newly betrayed lover. Men are instruments with very few strings to their bows.

'Come on, girl! Answer!'

'He was very . . . beautiful.'

'Really? More beautiful than a German? More beautiful than a GERMAN SOLDIER?'

Young ladies are quick to learn the art of lying.

'No.'

'Good. Do you know a girl called Anna Tieck?'

God Almighty, of course, it had to be her. The clock now started the countdown to my execution.

'Yes.'

'She claims you stopped her from denouncing the Englishman, is this correct?'

I might as well sign my own death warrant.

'Yes.'

'You know what this means? How old are you?'

'Eleven.'

'And already a traitor to the Fatherland!'

Now I broke down and started to cry.

'It is forbidden to cry during the interrogations of the Third Reich! It is punishable by death. I order you to stop immediately!'

Frau Baum was heard trying to turn the handle on the other side of the door. Then her pleading voice: 'My husband works at the War Ministry in Berlin! Professor Dr Helmut Baum! I beg you!'

My good old Frau.

'Silence!'

The clock ticks twice. I hiccup twice.

'Why did you prevent Fräulein Tieck from revealing the truth about the English pilot?'

'I just . . . I just didn't want anyone . . . to die.'

'To die?! Don't you know that war is ALL ABOUT DYING? LETTING PEOPLE DIE!'

I felt the ice-cold nozzle of a revolver pressing against my forehead. It was accompanied by a terrifying and rather peculiar steel odour that I've never been able to erase from my memory, even though names and faces have started to fade. It wafts out of the recesses of my mind from time to time, like an invincible gas, a death omen from Hitler that smells of German metal. I needed to come up with a good answer.

'No,' I whined. 'I'm just . . . Icelandic.'

'Icelandic, yes? That's . . . where do you stand in the war?' he asked, momentarily thrown, it seemed.

'We . . . we are . . .' I was about to attempt a factual answer but suddenly remembered a better one and rolled up my right sleeve, all the way up to my elbow, peeled the plaster off my scar, and with feigned pride showed them the scissor-carved swastika.

'I see, yes? Good. But why is it covered with a plaster? There is no need for a plaster over the swastika!'

'Because there was a bit of . . . blood.'

'Blood? But blood must flow!'

Blut muss fließen. He was now quoting the god of thunder himself. But instead of putting a bullet through my head, the soldier shoved me back, causing me to fall off the stool.

'Stand up!'

I struggled to my feet and stood there trembling.

'Chin up!'

I tried to straighten up.

'Where is the Englishman now?'

'I . . . I don't know.'

He pressed the nozzle of his gun against my forehead again. 'WHERE IS HE?!'

'Don't know . . .'

I heard something pop. Not a gunshot. Just a pop. The same sound you get when you pull the plug out of the universe and it shrivels like a balloon. That kind of a pop.

'Say the name! Where is he staying?'

'Fräulein . . . Fräulein Osinga.'

'Fräulein Osinga. Good. We thank you for your collaboration. Heil Hitler!'

He clicked his heels and swiftly extended his right arm in the air. I clicked my heels, swiftly straightened, and swung my right arm into the air as well, with my blood-carved swastika and floppy plaster.

'Heil Hitler!'

I was still standing frozen in that position when they had left and the Frau entered.

'Poor child.'

My face was as pale as a sheet, locked in that cramped posture: a child trembling in terror. And neither she nor I managed to get my arm down again. She led me into the bedroom with it still stuck in the air, and I lay in bed with my paralysed Hitler salute, remaining like that for the rest of the day. 'Trauma block' was the pharmacist's diagnosis. Children streamed in from time to time to silently gawk at this bizarre condition, which didn't wane until two days later. I was able to eat my breakfast with one hand but was spared the ordeal of attending school with my arm extended into the air for a whole day, when classes were cancelled for dramatic reasons: Later on the day of my interrogation, news spread that the English boy had been found in a boathouse by the shore with the cobbler's daughter. They shot her and took him away. The twins were also arrested but then released again, their backs even more hunched from concealing their breasts than before. And in the evening, Fräulein Osinga was found in her garden, as stiff as marble, in a pool of her own blood.

I had become a war criminal.

53

Daughters-in-Law

2009

And now I dabble in cyber-crime – but only to keep in some kind of contact with my daughters-in-law.

The last dose of family I had was when Haraldur's daughter, Gudrún Marsibil, visited me here before Christmas last year. She left me a box of chocolates – which I still have, even though its contents have been eaten – before she disappeared to Australia, where she is studying some kind of tourism thingy and trains as a swimmer. They're bouncing around in bright, sunny pools now, those ancient Breidafjördur fishing genes.

The real hassles with my family started in the mid-1990s when, to my misfortune, they managed to convince me that a patient with advanced emphysema and chronic cancer would be better off vegetating in the company of other zombies. By then I was completely bedridden and out of it, owing to the wrong medication. I left taps running and kept milk cartons under my bed. Things often got pretty smelly as a result. In the end, Haraldur threatened to sue me for slipping up on the amount of pills I was swallowing, and his wife had a smoke detector installed in my room, which screeched at me from the ceiling, like a wrathful god, every time I blew smoke out of my nostrils. 'We can't allow her to smoke in bed, she could set the house on fire,' I heard her say down the corridor. I paid a kid next door to disconnect the detector, but she was as stubborn as hell. My addiction reached new heights when I lay there puffing under the piercing screeches from the ceiling, enjoying some of the best smokes of my life.

In the end, though, I gave in, being so deeply moved by their sudden interest in their mother and mother-in-law. But I looked on it as a temporary stay and always aimed to get back to my parents' house, on Skothúsvegur, where I'd lived after Mum's death in autumn of '88. Naturally, I immediately missed my smokes in bed and the view of Reykjavík Lake through the blinds, where I was free of long corridors and social intercourse. They drove me up to a place that masquerades as a nursing home but is really nothing more than a wing of a famous retirement home for old sailors. The institution was called Skjól, the Shelter, but all I ever experienced there were battles and storms. I called it the penitentiary, a place where they dump people who insist on surviving and refuse to die. Everyone is served a life sentence there.

Haraldur and his wife said goodbye to me with far too much glee. Naturally this had all been concocted for their convenience, not mine. They could finally stop worrying about the old biddy; she was now in the gelid clutches of the system.

That's what society is made for.

So I'd been dumped in an old folks' home, not even seventy years old. For a while, even I believed I was condemned to accept their services and care until I'd kicked the bucket. But after three years I snapped out of this institutional coma; it dawned on me that maybe I wouldn't die today or tomorrow, that maybe I'd live for another year or two. That was eight years ago.

I decided to escape. And I did so by disguising myself as rubbish on wheels. I threw a black bin bag over myself, slipped into the goods lift on a wheelchair called Thunderbird, pressed the right button, and, before I knew it, was sitting in a van. I stayed with the driver that night, in a basement apartment. He offered me a drink. I asked him if he needed a woman. He reacted by disappearing into a cupboard and returned with a wig, which I have worn ever since. Then he crouched over me with his pungent smell of sweat and lay me on the sofa. I slept like a baby under some ghastly paintings and a collection of poems. And dreamed of Dad as a young man.

A day later I'd been tracked down. The supervisor from the institution (a broad-shouldered heroine with thick lips and three or four sets of breasts) showed up and I did some crying for her, managed to squeeze some tears out of those dried-up lemons my eyes have become. But she wasn't moved. 'Now you're going to come with me in the car, Herbjörg, isn't that right?' It was only when I threatened a poop-to-rule strike that she picked up the phone, and she was already out on the steps when she finally got hold of Dóra, who had an empty garage. For a whole week, I slept in the newly vacated room of a young girl, under pink bookshelves, while Gudjón worked on getting the garage ready. Rarely has a man radiated such joy as when he was asked to set up a kitchen unit and toilet in his own garage.

The supervisor from the institution asked whether I didn't want to let my 'next of kin' know. I asked her to notify my three sons that their mother was now living in cyberspace, planet no. 15.463. Gudjón then went off with his pockets full of my money and bought a computer and state-of-the-art router for me. HP, it's called, and it's still working.

Gudjón and Dóra turned out to be better than my own children. The garage is a fine old folks' home in its own right. Generally speaking, Icelanders use their garages not to keep their cars in but to store the junk they don't need in their race against time, stuff like wind-bent tent poles, obsolete lawn mowers and old people. I know of at least three other contemporary paupers like me in this city, or garage relics, as I like to call them.

It was certainly no thanks to my boys that I found my shelter. And as I've already mentioned, two of my sons have never seen me in here, in the eight years I've lived here, and the third one has only looked in twice. But this no-show is, no doubt, also due to the old bags, that is, me and those women called my daughters-in-law. My boys actually all ended up marrying the same woman, same mould, as they used to say, and as different from their mother as they could possibly be. They belong to that purely Icelandic species of busybodies with smooth blond hair, deep-set eyes and a big tangle of nerves, fast-talking women with heavy heels who do their makeup in the car and answer their phones during hospital visits, never stopping, always rushing off to here and there, saying 'Hi!' like chainsaws, and only smoking when their cigarettes are lit, but at all other times declaring that they have quit smoking. Just like the diets they obsessively follow between meals.

I sometimes wonder where these women came from in our society, because I can't remember meeting them in Breidafjördur before the war, nor in Reykjavík in the post-war boom. They call themselves girls, which is in fact what they are, since they've never reached womanhood, never walked in a long dress, never owned a fur or a pearl necklace, gone to an opera, read Doris Lessing, sat on a train, or danced their way below deck, locked in the arms of a tango man, and they have therefore never known chivalry, and I don't blame them, since our country is a whole three hours away from good manners. On top of everything, they can't even pronounce a word of French; my daughters-in-laws' greatest aspiration is to sip a glass of 'camembert sauvignon.'

I myself came back to Iceland three times after spells abroad and on each occasion was referred to in the gossip columns as a 'lady of the world,' just because I wore lipstick and bought men drinks. And on each occasion I managed to drink that label away because I've always felt best as one of the boys. I was in my element when the women had gone home and I was left sitting with the gin-sodden doctors and smoke-puffing wholesalers. That was when all the good stories and stuff came out. It's terribly boring to be a lady but such great fun to be a mister.

54

Rainmaker

2002

In my first months in the garage I was served by a young man whose life was on pause; he didn't know whether he wanted to be a priest in Iceland or an IT expert in America. While he was waiting for the answer to come to him and the acne to clear from his face, he had fun wiping old people's arses. Bóas was his name, a boy with gentle hands who wore ginormous glasses and trainers and was a true guru in all things technical. Bit by bit, I told him my sad story about how my clan had looted all my belongings. In a two-week course, he taught me how to become a computer cracker or hacker or whatever it's called.

'Now you're a hacker, man, as cool as any high-school nerd,' he told me, pushing my glasses back up the bridge of my nose and then his own.

He taught me how to break into my demonic daughters-in-laws' mailboxes. Now I could read about all their scheming ('We should just hurry up and sell, immediately') and I could even reply to e-mails under their names. Life in Garageville was finally turning out to be fun.

Through all that research, it transpired that Magnús's wife, Ragnheidur, aka Rainmaker, wasn't altogether devoted to her marriage and was engaged in a steady exchange of e-mails with a colleague from work whom I nicknamed Engelbert Humperdick. He was one of those insipid men who generally started his e-mails with a quote pasted from someone else and the words: 'Have you seen this?' This was followed by a brief and unimaginative commentary on Rainmaker's appearance. 'You were so cute when you came into work this morning. Red really suits you.' Then I immediately answered: 'Yeah, I'm red hot to fuck you tonight.' Of course they weren't my words. Although one could hardly call me a prude, that kind of language just isn't my style. It was Bóas who typed that in – the future priest – for the sake of his protégée, totally convinced it would 'work like dynamite, man.'

This kind of dirty talk was also very unlike Rainmaker, and in this way we managed to inject some entertaining tension into their erotic shenanigans, which, judging by their correspondence, mainly took place within the walls of their workplace, in broom cupboards and toilets for the disabled.

'Look, I mean it's one thing to park in a disabled parking space, but to desecrate their toilets, that's just . . .' said Bóas, shaking his head as he formulated messages that occasionally went over my head but always achieved the desired effect. He had worked with people with disabilities and was angry on their behalf for the sacrilege these 'healthy' individuals had committed in their bathrooms. As was often the case with deceitful people, my daughter-in-law had a very elegant writing style, using beautiful metaphors and tasteful humour that was often lost on the fairly square Mr Humperdick.

'Sorry about this morning, it's cock and bull anyway,' she said in an e-mail one morning.

'Huh?'

'Never mind, I'll treat you to cock and bull for lunch!'

'Lunch is great, but sorry, I don't eat meat any more.'

It was fun following these exchanges.

'Wanna go for a picnic?' she wrote.

'Isn't it a little bit cold today?' he answered.

This is what Bóas and I answered: 'Nothing beats white dew on green grass. Let's go for a picnic.'

'Wow, that's like poetry, man,' said my apprentice priest, elated by our collaboration, as we waited a whole twenty minutes to see Mr Humperdick's answer.

'I don't get it, what do you mean by white dew?'

'Spunk,' Bóas swiftly typed.

'I'll come down.'

They worked together in a brand-new, shiny building that had sprung up on the shore during the boom, and we'd taken our spying to such extremes that Bóas once took a trip down there to catch a snapshot of the couple slipping out of the toilet after a quickie. We then sent them the photo in an e-mail from a fictitious address. It turned out to be a bad move, however, because it burst their bubble, and the days that followed were pretty dull, although it might have given my Magnús a better night's sleep. But I later regained my destructive zeal again. The ingenious Bóas created a new e-mail address for me: bishopoficeland@church.is. From it, Rainmaker received the following e-mail:

Dear Sinner,

It has come to the Church's attention that you have committed adultery in the disabled toilets of public buildings. As is known, acts of this nature violate the laws of God.

In accordance with the regulations of the Church of Iceland, you shall do penance by attending mass over the next forty Sundays in forty different churches.

At the end of this period of contrition, you shall send us a letter in your own handwriting confessing to your sins. You shall list them all in detail and without omissions. The eyes of the Lord are all-seeing.

Once these conditions have been fulfilled, you shall be absolved of your sins and receive the bishop's blessing, but not before. Should you, on the other hand, disobey, the Lord's servants will chain your soul to the anchor of his celestial wrath and cast it into Satan's molten lava.

Reykjavík, 14 July 2002, in the name of the Lord.

Bishop of Iceland, the Right Reverend Karl Sigurbjörnsson

55

Prince Potato

2002

A few weeks later, there was a knock on the garage door. Obviously there was nothing I could do about it. I was unused to visits and hadn't had a bell installed, so naturally I couldn't traipse to the door with the gimpy legs and catheterised bladder I had in those years. So no invitation this time.

But several days after that, there was another knock, and I was so lucky, oh so lucky, that my Nancy, the girl who took care of me after Bóas and before Lóa, happened to still be in the house. She was able to open up for the visitor, who turned out to be my son Magnús, born in May '69. He had acquired a rather feline air. I calculated he had to be thirty-three years old.

His father had grown fat at an early age, so fat, in fact, that I was forced to drink myself silly to get on top of him, after which it took me three years to clamber down. So now my little Magnús had outlived his hair, poor thing, and insulated his body with some extra layers for the winter that awaits all men over the age of thirty. With his sad look and helpless hands, my little prince was a clear disappointment to the woman who had thrust him into this world.

Nancy rushed towards the bed to grab the swivelling chair on wheels that had been waiting for visitors for two long years. I noticed that the boy was still badly pigeon toed; I who throughout his upbringing had tried to knock it into him to stand like a man, not a poem.

'Hi, Mum,' he said with a sigh, pushing his glasses up his little feline nose and stroking his cheeks, causing his bristles to make a scratching sound.

His late father, Jón, had rampant facial hair and had to shave twice a day. He was Mister Twice in other ways, too, because he was bald and energetic below the belt, despite the flab. Sex was the glue in our relationship. But once Magnús arrived on the scene, twice turned into once, then rarely, and finally never at all. That fat fire cooled bit by bit until I called him the cab. 'Did you really have to be born?' I once let slip when I was drowning in maternal misery and the Potato Prince was driving me nuts with his whining. He deserves a decent welcome from me now, I thought to myself, since he's come to me with his problems.

'So you're here?' he continued, looking around as he shuffled the chair closer to the bed with his bottom, pulling off his swishing anorak and allowing it to crumple in the chair behind him, which caused my skin to crawl.

I tried to pull myself together and turned off my laptop, put it away under my duvet, and stroked the hot spot under it with my cold paws. Nancy, who had promptly slipped into her winter coat, gave us a timid smile and said goodbye in her New Zealand accent.

'Who's she?' the Prince asked as soon as the girl had shut the door behind her, a door that was frozen on the outside but lukewarm on the inside.

'Her name is Nancy McCorgan. From Home Care Services.'

'Yeah?' he said, and then he shut up, just pulling a face and nodding several times, absentmindedly. 'That's . . . that's good.'

Here my plump boy probably did a rewind on our entire mother-son relationship in twenty seconds, how painful it was to see me in a garage of all places, alone and abandoned, although

I nevertheless deserved it, having turned his childhood into one protracted hangover morning and given him fifteen fathers.

I used the time to marvel at the fact that I had such a young man for a son. How could a chronic care crow with rattling lungs like mine have a thirty-year-old son? Oh, well, of course I was only just over seventy, but according to the doctors I was ninety. Smoked meat always looks older. I must have been over forty when I had Magnús. Almost past the childbearing age and at the risk of conceiving an idiot. I'm afraid he may have come dangerously close to the borderline. Oh, go on then, my princely cat.

'And what, have you been . . . ? Been here since . . . ?'

'Since last autumn. I seem to remember looking at that plane crash . . . the Twin Towers, I mean, on the TV here.'

'Oh yeah? And what . . . are you . . . ?'

I paused a moment, fluttered my eyelids, and finally said, 'You're having problems finishing your sentences, Magnús, dear.'

'Yes, I . . . sorry.' He heaved a heavy sigh and then burst out with that social studies sincerity: 'I'm not feeling too good, Mum.'

'Mum?'

'Yes, you are . . . my Mum.'

'Am I now?'

'Forgive me.'

'I'll forgive you nothing, Magnús Jónsson. Where's the money?'

'What money?'

'Where's the forty million kronur your wife got for the house on Skothúsvegur?'

'It wasn't forty million, Mum. Twenty at the most. The apartment went for sixty-three million.'

'Really? That's not what the estate agent said.'

'He must have confused you.'

'Are you telling me I'm losing my marbles?'

'No. I just know it was about twenty million that we . . . were supposed to . . . keep for you.'

'Keep for me?!'

'Yeah, like we discussed. Mum, the money is yours.'

'The money is mine? What am I doing in this garage like some Oldsmobile, then?'

'You can have it whenever you want.'

I clenched my teeth, denture against denture, and growled each word.

'Magnús, why do you think I moved in here?'

'Calm down, Mum. We've got that money for you. You can have it anytime.'

'Where is it?'

'I . . . I don't know exactly. Ragnheidur's been taking care of it.'

'Ragnheidur?'

'Yeah.'

'And you trust her?'

'Er . . . yeah, she . . .'

'She's a wonderful wife, distinguished and respected?'

'Yeah . . .'

'Are you divorced?'

'Huh?'

'Have you left her?'

'Left her?'

'Yes, you're not going to hang around in that adulterous marriage much longer, are you?'

'Adulterous?'

'Oh, forgive me, Magnús, I'm just a tactless old woman. And halfway into the oven. But just take this from an old-timer: Ragnheidur has been rowing on more than one boat, as they used to say in Breidafjördur.'

He squinted his eyes like a sailor bracing himself for a wave.

'What's . . . that supposed to mean?'

'How's she doing, apart from that?'

'Just fine. She's just become a bit . . . she goes to church a lot.'

'Church?'

'Yes, all of a sudden she's going to mass every Sunday.'

'Really? Holy shit.'

'Yes, it's a bit weird. And she never goes to the same church. Last Sunday she went to Hafnarfjördur and the one before that up to Mosfellsbær.' He shook his head, took off his glasses, wiped away the mist, and was silent a long moment. Meanwhile, backstage in my brain, I was having a laughing fit, jumping up and down on enormous spring shoes, the most peculiar scene.

'Yeah . . .' he said, heaving a leaden sigh. His eyes lay deep in his pudgy-cheeked face, like two glistening raisins that had been pressed into a thick lump of dough. 'She's left me.'

'What are you saying? Left you?'

'Yeah, or . . . well, I was still the one who moved out.'

'She left you but you moved out? She threw you out?'

'No, no. I . . . I didn't feel good there and . . . just left.'

'Oh yeah, I've heard of that. Of women leaving their husbands and then just walking into the kitchen. And have you been left to roam the streets? . . . Staying in some wino hotel in town? Where are the children?'

'With her. But I get to meet them, OK.'

'Do you, now? How magnanimous of her. And has the other guy moved in?'

'What guy?'

'That bearded twat. And where's the money?'

'The money?'

'Yes, didn't you just say she was taking care of it?'

'Yeah? Sure. But Mum, everything's fine with that. It's kept in some book that she—'

'Magnús. Let me stop you right there. One massive stop. She's already taken my house and now YOURS as well. You've still got your car, though?'

'Erm . . .'

'You kept your car?'

'No, but I've rented a car and—'

'What kind of a ruthless bitch is this woman anyway? And bouncing off the walls in disabled toilets with that mister . . . that mysterious . . . mysterious style of hers.'

Oh, now he was looking at me as if I was some kind of rambling nutcase talking nonsense. This was followed by a deadly silence that was crammed with all of life's failures and said: Here are two frustrated individuals. The only thing they've managed in life is to have each other. But we didn't face each other as equals. I had managed to bring him into the world, but he hadn't yet managed to bring me out of it.

'Does she come here every day, that . . . Nancy?' he said at last.

'Don't you worry about me.'

'Mum, you have your money. It's in the accounts, you know.'

I gave him a good, long stare. And then slowly and calmly said, 'Magnús. No one's come here for . . . for fourteen months. Neither you nor Haraldur, Ólafur, nor your children. Not since you got your hands on my life's savings. I haven't even had an e-mail from you, let alone a phone call, yeah . . . except for Gudrún, who called me on my birthday. Do you think that's . . . ?'

I couldn't go on, a lump had swollen up in my throat, bloody bitterness and self-pity. The hot water was buried deep inside me, but once it was tapped it came bursting out.

'Are you on e-mail, Mum?' he asked, clearly amazed.

'Of course I'm on e-mail,' I snapped. 'I've got a net connection here, I'm permanently connected, on the computer! What kind of bullshit is this? You don't know your own mother, yeah . . . no more than your own wife. Have you smacked her yet?'

'Smacked her?' he huffed, scandalised, as if he were the spokesman for a new species of men, cultivated in a partnership between the state and the media, that never laid a finger on women.

'No, no, we parted on good terms.'

'Good? And she with another man between her legs?'

'No, no, Mum, there's no one else.'

'Magnús, the last thing I want to be is the mother of a wimp. I want you to go home now to the house you own and tell your lascivious wife . . . to . . . to join you for a picnic, where . . . yes, where the white dew falls on the green grass . . .'

I froze. He was staring at me with such surprise that the raisins protruded slightly from the dough.

'Am I to go and . . . recite that poem to her?'

'Oh, it's best if I just write the name down. Tell her you have proof and cause for revenge, that you're absolutely furious and demand your apartment, your car, your children, and the forty million that belongs to your mother.'

'You mean twenty?'

I scribbled Engelbert Humperdick's real name on the back of a used envelope, which he found on the kitchen counter and handed to me as if I were a vengeful mother from the Viking age. He read it with quivering lips. His face said, Am I really supposed to kill him, Mum? His tone of voice was unbearable.

'And how . . . how do you know this, Mum?'

'He who is bedridden has the all-seeing eye.'

He asked no further questions but folded the envelope in two, as if it were his manhood, and shoved it into a pocket. Then I watched him slip back into his anorak and lean over with his strong scent of the outside world.

'Bye, Mum.'

It was a clumsy kiss he gave me and I had to wipe my cheek afterwards. But as I watched him moping towards the door, I suddenly didn't understand anything about this life and how I, a wreck of a woman with a raisin for a liver and a glove for a breast, had managed to give birth to this 220-pound male body. It was as incomprehensible to me as a desiccated cactus being informed that it had a grown kangaroo for a son. He exited with sadness in his dark blue eyes, and then, needless to say, I didn't hear from him again.

What a dreadfully wicked thing for his mother to do, and above all, how inconsiderate. My son's peace of mind was gone, and my bitchy soul was to blame. Even on the cold summit of my old age, I hadn't managed to tame that ferocious beast. That's always been the way with me. The person that I am, Herbjörg María Björnsson, has never had full control over her voice and actions because there's a far greater power at the helm, which I choose to call 'Herra's life force' and which radiates inside, deciding on everything, taking control, and hurling bombs, causing flashes all around me, the only flowers in my garden.

56

Break-in

2002

Several days later another unexpected guest appeared out of the Advent darkness. It was early in the day, and Nancy opened the garage door. A long coat on high heels stepped in onto the concrete floor and clicked, performed half a swirl, and swung a scarf, looking around. Her blond, waxed hair was shoulder-long, and her lips glistened with what I think they call gloss, that slimy stuff that dry women lubricate their words with.

In a moment of confusion I was afraid she might be an inspector from the city council, or the Health or Social Services Department, who had come to peer up my colon or close down this illegal old folks' container, but instead I got a loud chirpy 'Well, hi there!' And when she reached the bed, I realised that this was Rainmaker, a woman who had cultivated children from the manure of my own blood.

'Hi,' I answered.

'Nice to see you. And sorry for being so lazy about visiting you.'

'Yes. Laziness is a vice.'

'Huh?'

'Laziness is a vice.'

'Huh? Yeah? Ha-ha-ha. Always so busy, with the kids and, you know, all that stuff. But how's life, Herra, dear?'

'Life is just as I want it.'

'Oh yeah? Ha-ha. The kids send all their love. They're always asking about Grandma Herra.'

'Oh, they must have forgotten me by now, those creatures.'

Damn it if my heart wasn't beating faster. I hadn't realised that old thing was still capable of changing gear.

'No, no, not at all. We always talk about you as one of the family. You can be sure of that!' For a moment she paused stiffly, and a hint of misery darkened the jolly facade of her face, before she cheerfully recovered and said, 'I brought you some magazines!' And then she pulled out some glossy rags about life behind the finest walls of the city, with all the shattered hearts that were to be found there. She placed the reading material on my covers, beside the computer that I closed like an eyelid. Rainmaker gave it a probing glance but then suddenly turned her head when Nancy said goodbye, inspecting her thoroughly as she brushed a lock of hair off her eyes. Her disdain was palpable: there's nothing that irks a wanton woman more than the sight of a pure, timid maiden who is already faithful to the man she has yet to meet.

'Yes, magazines, you say.'

'Yeah, I thought it might be fun for you to . . . just gossip mags, really.'

'But not about you?'

'Huh?'

'Not gossip about you and Magnús?'

This clearly threw her. A heat wave flushed across her face and she fluttered her eyelids. 'Ha-ha! No. We're not that famous.'

'I always say that everyone is famous in Iceland except for the president. Nobody knows him.'

'Ha-ha. It's always so much fun when you come out with these sayings.'

And now I sensed that she'd actually missed my warped mind a tiny bit. Missed her good old mother-in-law's banter, mouldy as it had become. I remember how well I'd welcomed her at first, when Magnús had first shown up with her for lunch on Skothúsvegur, a shapely graduate in business administration. She'd had great fun with this strange lady who cooked sausage with sauerkraut, smoked cream-yellow Roth-Händle cigarettes, and talked about our days at the presidential residence the way some people talked about children they had and missed. And I was rather happy with her. My Prince Potato had finally nailed a wife. There was joy in the house back then.

There wasn't the slightest trace of remorse or grievance in this Icelandic 'girl.' She had locked away that freshly skinned dog that was her divorce in the dungeons of her palace, and the echo of his piercing howls didn't travel as far as this frugal garage.

'So you've split up?' I said without accusation.

'Huh? Yes, that's right. Yeah. Unfortunately. But that's just life. And I want you to know we parted on good terms and remain the best of friends.'

'No one parts on good terms.'

'Yes! Magnús and I did! Ha-ha.'

'That'll be the first time in the history of the world, then.'

'Yeah, ha-ha, perhaps.'

'What's happening with the money, Ragnheidur?'

'The money?'

'Magnús tells me you have it. My money.'

'You mean the money from Skothúsvegur? Yes, right, that's precisely what I wanted to talk to you about. I find it very hurtful that you think we intended to take this money that is in our keeping. We just decided to spread the risk and to divide it between us so that—'

'I haven't heard from you in more than a year.'

'No, and I'm very sorry about that, Herra, dear, very sorry. But I think that's something between you and Magnús. And Haraldur and Ólafur . . . I was always saying that we should pop in to see you, but—'

'Where's the money?'

'The money? Now? It's . . . it's in a . . . we just decided to spread it
. . . not put all the eggs into the same basket, you see. So it's here and
there, in so-called investment funds. But we can take it out, if you
like. Of course, it's . . . your money, in that sense.'

'In any sense.'

'Yeah, no, no, but naturally maybe the boys will . . . yeah, I mean,
obviously you weren't going to start spending, you know, sixty
million, ha-ha, I mean being bed-bound and all that, so maybe it
wasn't such a bad idea to . . .'

All I needed now was a good kitchen knife, because the rage made
me sit up against my pillow so that this old hag could finish off the
bloody tart.

'Ragnheidur, dear. Up until now the unwritten law in most
countries around the globe has been that you don't start spending
the inheritance from a parent until they're dead. That means stopped
breathing and six feet under. Locked in a coffin with the lid tightly
screwed on.'

The words had caused me to tremble and strained my lungs.

'Yeah, no. That's . . . of course, that's right.'

'What did the money go into? The patio?'

'The patio? No. What makes you say that?'

'I . . . keep an eye on things, even though I'm—'

'Yeah? You *keep an eye*?'

'Yes . . . yes, yes.'

I'd painted myself into a corner. I tried to get back on track again.

'And you think . . . you really think I believe you haven't used any
of that money?'

'I mean, we might have used, you know, some of the interest . . .'

'Interest?'

'Yes, we just felt that, you know, since we were working on
growing this money for you that . . . but the principal hasn't changed.'

'Well, well, that's really something.'

'Don't get me wrong, Herra, and of course it's a lot of work to take care of big amounts like that because, as they say, money is like flowers or something, you have to look after them, and we felt it was only natural to get something in return for all that work, and maybe that's why we've been just . . .'

She shut up. She couldn't continue. She couldn't tell me she'd rooted through my deathbed, stretched under the yellow catheter, rummaging for everything under the mattress.

From where did this generation enter into Icelandic history? My foremothers had rowed across Breidafjördur, fishing for food to stuff up their noses. Nothing was achieved without hard work. Then Mum came along with all her scruples. Making no demands. Offering her heart to one man and then keeping it wrapped in a ribbon for seven years when he forgot to pick it up. Together they had nothing and still lost it all. Then they got back on track again and scraped enough together for the closing chapters; they were over fifty by the time they could finally buy a proper house.

Ragnheidur fiddled with her blond hair a moment, pumped her lips with air, glanced artificially at her watch, and then planted her gaze on the computer and said, 'Could I use your computer for a sec? I'm actually on my way to a meeting later and I'm expecting . . . an e-mail.'

'You're expecting an e-mail?'

'Yes.'

'In my computer?'

'Yes, I can check my mailbox if I go online. It'll only take a minute.'

I didn't like it one bit, but I couldn't think of anything smart enough to protect my files. She was already standing and walking towards the end of my bed. Then she snatched the computer and yanked out the plug with her wine-red nails and took it over to the kitchen counter. What a sly little bitch she was.

'Do you have a bad connection in here?'

'Huh? No. No, no.'

'It drops out . . . the connection.' Then unnaturally natural: 'I've got a connection in my car. I'll take it out to the car for a minute.'

She closed the screen again, placed the computer under her arm, and smiled at me. 'I'll only be a sec! You can take a look at the magazines in the meantime!' It took me so much by surprise that I could hardly get my brain to function, let alone my voice. She had simply vanished with my computer! A connection in her car? I'd never heard of such a thing. I'd always seen myself as a cunning she-devil, but now I'd met my equal. And so niftily executed!

She was away a hell of a long time.

57

Rat

2002

Finally she returned, Rainmaker, with all her glacial charm, and put my computer back down on the quilt.

'Thanks for lending it to me. Really saved me. That's obviously a very . . . very good computer you have.'

I couldn't read anything into her words, whether she'd found anything reprehensible in my files.

'It's not bad, the old gadget.'

'Yes . . .' Here there was a slight hesitation in her chirpy tone, a hint of insecurity in her eyes.

'And are you that . . . computer savvy?'

'Yes, I learned typing at the Commercial College, back in the days when the letter z was still part of the Icelandic alphabet, and then I worked as a secretary for various people, on and off. Back when men barely knew how to pick up a phone.'

'Right, and you . . . you keep up with the times . . . and technology?'

'I've always been savvy. Particularly when it comes to *tools of communication.*'

I'd said that last line to wind her up, and it hit the spot. She glanced at her watch and said, 'Right, then, listen, better get to this meeting.'

'Lovers' meeting?'

Her eyes widened.

'Lovers?!'

I wasn't about to let her get away smiling.

'Yes. Haven't you read what I've read?'

'Read what you read?'

'I mean, seen what I've seen? I gave Magnús his name.'

'Magnús? Whose name?'

'He should have done it by now.'

'Huh? Done what?'

'And hidden the body somewhere. He was going to do it for his mamma's sake, poor thing.'

Now there was a silence. And then the crust started to crack. Slowly but surely. There was no visible change in her smile. It was as screamingly amiable as before. With well-stretched lips and smiling wrinkles. But gradually the material started to crack. A web of fissures spread across her face, finally reaching the eyes, and then that delicately thin facade of loveliness started to crumble.

'Who ... who gave you permission to poke your nose in my private business?'

'Adultery is no private business.'

'Oh yes. It's ... it's private and none of your business. Magnús and I ... we ... our life as a couple is NONE of your business!'

'I'm only looking out for him, the lad.'

'Looking out for him?'

'Yes, it's what mothers do. Look out for their children.'

'How old is he? How fucking old is Magnús? Thirty-three! He's thirty-fucking-three and you're watching over him as if ... as if he ...'

'The soul is always the same. Always a one-year-old. He was crippled when he heard it, poor fellow.'

'Heard it? ... Did ... YOU tell him about this?!'

'I'm his mother.'

'Erm ... yes, but ... but that doesn't mean that you have ... the right to—'

'Don't talk to me about rights, Rainmaker.'

'RAINMAKER?!'

Oops, silly lapsus. Just let that slip out. The blond took it to heart, because her eyes started to fill with drizzle.

'What do you think you know about what it's like to be a woman TODAY?! Always having to rush from one place to another with those hundreds of chores and yet, at the same time, never getting what you need, and then when someone finally offers it to you, you can't take it and enjoy it because it comes with such a SHITLOAD OF GUILT!'

'My Magnús is fine in bed.'

She was speechless. Gaping.

'Wha . . .'

'He might be a bit lazy, but there's no impotence in my family. And never has been. His father was a super lover. Mr Twice. And I've never been a shrinking violet either. I think you should look into your own bosom, the little you have left.'

She was stunned again. Then she came out with, 'Are . . . are you . . . a RAT?'

'Yeah, sure, I can get ratty sometimes, but never a frigid haddock.'

'You . . . you . . . !'

Now I'd finally outraged her. It was such great fun to finally utter this word I'd never spoken out loud. I let her spin out of control in her fury like an off-roader on wet mud, without holding out a helping hand, until she finally managed to grope forward.

'You're just a fucking rat that lies here in this . . . yeah, a fucking garage rat that thinks she has the right to spy on the members of her own family, just because they . . . because they . . .'

' . . . don't bother to come and see her?'

'Just because she thinks she has a right to, because she's so twisted, because no one comes to see her, because she's so DISGUST-INGLY REPULSIVE and has never so much as expressed any affection for – '

'Where's the money?'

'The money? It's gone! You'll never see that fucking money again! BECAUSE YOU DON'T DESERVE IT! FAREWELL, MRS HERBJÖRG!'

Once she'd gone, I picked up a few tiny scales of skin that lay on the edge of the duvet. Remnants of the crumbled wall of niceties.

58

Frozen Stone

1942

How did I become an orphan in the war? It happened in March 1942. My short-term stay at Frau Baum's had dragged on and by now turned into a whole year. We all thought the war would end in a few months, while Hitler swallowed countries like a seagull gobbling herring. But the situation was about to change. Mum now had her own apartment. And since Dad was on a week's leave from the army, he was advised to come collect me in Amrum, after which Mum would meet us in Hamburg. From there I'd travel on with her to Lübeck. I had mixed feelings. Of course, I looked forward to seeing Mum and Dad again, but I'd immediately started to miss Maike and Heike and our peaceful lives on the white beaches.

Dad was a changed man. His expression had hardened like that of a dry fish, and there were traces of frostbite on his nose. He also spoke German more confidently than before. He frightened me when he launched into his long rants. He had graduated from the military academy the previous spring, but without any distinction. No doubt his age was to blame. The SS insignia had vanished from his collar and he'd now become a lorry driver. He had spent the whole winter driving back and forth across the plains of Ukraine, transporting weapons, people and food on the tented back under muddy downpours or in such polar temperatures that not even an Icelander like him had ever encountered them before.

He'd had no experience of battle, other than some crossfire in the woods, and never reached the frontline himself (which at that moment was behind both Belarus and Ukraine and was now extending into Russia at a crawling pace), so he hadn't killed anyone. Yet he wasn't the same man who had counted the steps up to our attic in Lübeck with me and spontaneously danced with Mum and me in the living room, without any music. The military academy had stiffened the corners of his mouth, and the Russian winter had, in addition to nibbling off the tip of his nose, frozen his gaze. Even though he managed to pull out some of his typical old Hanseatic jokes, his eyes were like two pebbles on the tundra. It was a subtle but perceptible change. The difference between a stone and a frozen stone.

59

Hamburg Central

1942

Seldom has such a splendid building hosted a more dreadful event than the one witnessed in the Central Station of Hamburg in March 1942. Oh, dear me. Do I really have to drag this up again?

My father and I slowly made our way through the ruins of the city at the crack of dawn, observing the semi-destroyed buildings and downtrodden faces. Some factories were burning in the distance. The station still seemed to be in one piece, however, and we followed the stream of people entering it. We found platform 14 and stood there in silence, I full of anticipation, he full of dread.

But the train Mum was on didn't arrive at 12:02 as the timetable had promised. Fifteen minutes later an announcement resounded against the steel ceiling: Owing to a malfunction on the line, the train would be delayed by two hours. But an hour later, new information appeared on the board, extending the delay by four hours. Dad squinted his eyes, peering into the hinterland of iron and rails, and pulled out a cigarette, discreetly, because this German soldier was smoking English cigarettes that I had procured for him in Amrum: the previous week the girls and I had found the carcass of a plane on the shore, which contained four cartons of Chesterfields, almost dry. He lit it with an SS match, however.

He was stuck in a conundrum. He was supposed to report back to the barracks in Berlin at midnight, when his leave expired. His train was scheduled to leave at 3:32 p.m. You couldn't mess with German discipline: if Dad returned later, his Hitler salute would have been axed. But he couldn't abandon his daughter in a dilapidated train station in a city in ruins, which was being pounded by a thousand bombs every night. Mind you, she was twelve years old now, soon to be thirteen. He drew on his cigarette out of restlessness and despair, locked in his thoughts, while I tried to enjoy the smell of the smoke. Few things were as good as the scent of tobacco in fresh air.

Dad cast away the cigarette, killing it with his military boots, and sighed heavily as he looked down at the tracks that extended all the way to Lübeck.

'Damn it.'

'That's all right, Dad, I can just wait here.'

He looked at me. A glimmer of hope flashed across his marine-blue eyes. Maybe he didn't need to choose between his daughter and Hitler? Maybe she was right? Maybe it would be all right? But the glimmer vanished just as fast.

'I'm just not sure that train . . . they may have bombed the line . . . those damned Brits.'

'Have they blown up the tracks? Do you think . . . ?'

'I don't know.' He shook his head in the hope that his thoughts, which had spun into a chaotic muddle, would be shaken back into place again, in a slightly more rational order. 'Don't know.'

Dad glanced at his watch. It was two minutes to three. It was now or never. All of a sudden he slung his bag over his shoulder, told me to grab mine, and then swiftly led me away from platform 14 into the main hall, past a newspaper kiosk and a small elderly lady who was selling roses.

God Almighty, I still remember that flower woman, smiling with her rosy cheeks like God's only daughter, offering colours to the grey and war-weary multitudes. Where did she find flowers in Hamburg, where every garden was buried under rubble? In her flinty black eyes I read her secret: She got them from her church, her roofless church. In her galoshes she clambered over the mounds of dust that had once been a brick facade but now covered the church steps like a coat of Icelandic lava, and she tiptoed along the floor, climbing over roof fragments, into the choir stalls, where she knelt before the altar and stretched her arm beyond it, into a hole from which she pulled out the flowers that the good Lord sent her from His celestial garden through a pneumatic tube, like the messages that were exchanged between offices before the war. Apparently this was the good man's only contribution to the Second World War.

Dad dragged me down a dark tunnel, which stank of pee and led to two toilets. We waited for the traffic at the door to abate (a chubby-calved woman wobbled out of the ladies' room, and a coated man with a stub in his mouth wandered into the men's), and then Dad bent over his bag, swiftly pulled a heavy steel spherical object out of it, and handed it to me.

'Take this. It's a hand bomb, a grenade. You hold it in your right hand, like this. Then pull out the safety pin with the other, like this . . . you pull it off here . . . and then throw it away from you. You have to remember to throw it away. Remember that. Throw it away. Then it explodes. See, you do it like this. And then you throw yourself on the ground as soon as you've thrown it. Got that?'

I nodded. Although he'd explained it far too fast. He seemed to agree, for he went over the instructions again.

'I'm giving it to you for your protection, Herra. Remember that. And you should use it only in an emergency. Understand? Only when your life is in danger. If you're surrounded by Brits. But you have to be one hundred per cent sure you're in danger, because you have only one bomb. *Eine einzige Bombe.* Do you understand?'

I nodded again and stared at the steel egg in my palm. A whole war had been handed to me. It was so heavy, as heavy as . . . a heart. Where was I supposed to keep it?

'Where are you going, Dad?'

'I . . . I'm going where . . . I need to go. I just obey. Most likely the eastern front. We all have to support the struggle, Herra, remember that. The world can't be de-Germanised again. And this brings great hope for us, too, for Iceland. Hitler looks on Iceland as the original source of the Teutonic race, he looks on us as the custodians of the flame.'

As he completed those last words, he squeezed his palms around the bomb in my hand and shook it for greater emphasis. 'Custodians of the flame.' When he loosened his grip, I stared at the grenade and felt like a mythological statue guarding the spark of life.

'But Dad, who'll win the war?'

'We will, of course. Hitler.'

'But when?'

'In the summer. It'll all be over in the summer. Once we've taken Russia. Then the others will surrender. Then we'll all meet in autumn and move to Moscow. They've promised me a post at the university there. They'll be setting up a department for Germanic studies and the Nordic section all to myself. The world is ours, Herra. Copenhagen, Berlin, Moscow . . . What do you think of that?'

Not a lot. This was the third time he was telling me this, in the exact same words. He seemed to sense my scepticism and added a line I hadn't heard before.

'Imagine, Herra. Russia . . . You'll be an elegant lady, go ice skating and study piano, travel in a horse-drawn carriage, stroll through the city in a mink fur, just like Anna Karenina!'

All of a sudden the door of the ladies' room swung open and a grand Nazi Frau stepped out with a swaying behind. She didn't notice us, but Dad straightened up.

'Listen . . . don't hold it like that . . . people mustn't see it. Here . . . let's put it in your bag.'

'But doesn't it explode if . . . can't it explode?'

'No, only if you remove the pin. No, keep it in your pocket

instead. No, well, in the bag might be better. There, yes. It'll be all right. Hitler is with us.'

And here the child asked, 'Does he know I have this . . . ?'

And the child answered the child: 'The Führer watches over everything. He's everywhere. He knows everything.'

Then he became an adult again and gazed at length into my eyes.

'Take care, Herra, love. Daddy has to go. And remember to wait here on platform 14, you know where it is. And if the train doesn't come, wait by the *Billettverkauf.* Your mother and I agreed that if something came up we would meet there. The *Billettverkauf.* It's where they sell the tickets. Tickets for the trains, *die Fahrkarten.* You know that, right? Good. It's there in front of the main hall, the *Wandelhalle.*'

And then he grabbed my head with both hands, as he knelt on one knee before me, and said to me in an altogether different and more Icelandic tone: 'Oh, sweet God. My child . . .'

The loudspeaker announced the imminent departure of train 235 to Berlin from platform 9. It also announced some tears. His sky-blue eyes welled with sea and he pulled me into an embrace before I could see anything flow out of them.

'God bless you and protect you, my child. I . . . I love you, you know that.'

He had started to cry now, and his voice quivered.

'You must never forget that your father loves you.'

I felt his body sobbing against mine like an old car engine against a cold-water tank. He now realised he was about to leave his only daughter in a train station in a big city, at the mercy of everything, in the middle of a war, just so that he could get a chance to make her fatherless. I didn't cry. I had a mission now. I'd become the torch-bearer of the Germanic race. A custodian of the flame. I couldn't permit myself to shed a tear on that sacred fire.

'God be with you,' he repeated finally, before he abruptly broke out of the embrace, trying to pull himself together by swallowing twice and vigorously rubbing his face. He was in a risky position. Although it wasn't explicitly stated in the military rules of the Third Reich, he knew of two SS men who had been executed for the mere crime of shedding a tear.

'Right, I must go now. Goodbye.'

He swung the bag over his shoulder, stood up, and took several steps away from me, casting a swift glance at his watch. Before he could turn his back on me, I said, 'Dad!'

'Yes?'

'You're not allowed to die! Remember that.'

He froze for an instant and opened his mouth as if he were about to answer, but then closed it just as fast, not just because he didn't know what to say, but also to prevent his eyes from watering again. He stretched his clamped lips into a forced smile and exhaled noisily through his nose, as if he thought that my words would best be answered by the breath of life.

Then he was off to the eastern front to hand more arms to the rising sun. I could see the soles of his shoes as he ran down the passageway. They were white, but one of them had been blackened by the burn of a cigarette.

60

Whining *Verboten!*

1942

Mum didn't arrive that day. Nor that night. The train pulled in shortly after midnight, dragged itself into the station like a mole with a twisted snout, and vomited a flood of faces. I swallowed hard as I stood there on platform 14, famished and newly armed. Every face bore the scars of hardship; people rushed towards the exit with their reinforced cases, as if it had just been announced that the station would blow up in five minutes. What a mass of people. What a load of eyes. What a multitude of beating hearts. It was as if a whole small nation had disembarked on a narrow platform and been given appointments in gas chambers for later that day. What did all these people want from this burning city? Why didn't they just go and hide in a forest and live on homegrown beetroot until the front line had invisibly crossed their garden, leaving behind a black Audi and a white AEG washing machine?

Oh, dearest Mum. I couldn't even remember what you looked like. Hadn't seen you in over a year. Since the port of Dagebüll, like a pier puppet that slowly shrank to a dot, the full stop to my childhood. Using my eyes as if they were hands moulding clay, I tried as best I could to recompose my mother's gentle expression from the myriad of faces – the hair from this one, nose from that one – but every imagined face immediately transformed itself into another, and moustaches and caps constantly distracted me from my search. How could God be so cruel? He had just squeezed two thousand women out of his iron sleeve, but he still couldn't let one of them be my mother?

By the end I was starting to hate all those weary women who pressed themselves out of the dark night into the light of the station, which was nevertheless kept as dim as possible, with a camouflaged roof to outwit His Majesty's bombers. I toyed with the urge to throw my bomb at this mash of eyes that endlessly poured into the station, that endlessly mocked the absence of my mother.

Finally, I was left standing alone on the platform, alone in that vast hall, and wondered whether I was entitled to cry a bit. But then I spotted a sign in Gothic letters, which in my agitated state I read as WEINEN VERBOTEN! – Whining forbidden! – so I turned back into the *Wandelhalle* and went looking for the *Billettverkauf*, which by then was closed, of course, since it was past midnight. I slid down on the dirty stone floor and leaned against the locked door, staring at the wall opposite me in despair: A billboard showed five smiling children waving out of a train window. The caption under it read: KOMMT MIT IN DIE KINDERLANDVERSCHICKUNG! – Let's send our children into the country!

Why wasn't I still in Amrum?

There were still some scattered people in the station. A well-hatted family was engaged in a loud discussion under the big clock. Around them, cases sat silently awaiting a decision on their accommodation for the night, while tenor male voices echoed from the gathering like sparks from a bonfire. Beyond the people, one could see out into a half-burned urban landscape decorated with flames. An elderly man hobbled across the hall on makeshift crutches. One of his trouser legs swept the floor. Passing him, a young, attractive, well-dressed couple swiftly came walking, most probably some Swedish members of the Social Democracy Party, who knew exactly where they were going.

In those years in Germany, one never saw a couple or pair of lovers under the age of sixty. All the men were scattered far afield, busy killing or dying. I watched the couple storm past.

The thought of exclaiming a brief Nordic *hallo* to them crossed my mind – after all, these were, yes, almost my people – but I didn't want to disturb that beautifully important air they exuded. And I've always felt like that about the Swedes (even after three of them proposed to me on a ship on the same night). They considered themselves to be superior to other nations, and they were, of course. Having invaded half of Europe in previous centuries, they had moved on from those warring tendencies and now contented themselves with the production of 'neutral weapons' for others to use and financed Nobel Peace Prizes to alleviate some of the guilt that entailed.

The young man glanced at me as they dashed past, and what did he see but a forsaken Icelander in the corner, a dirty, emaciated wreck in a blue skirt, helpless in front of the locked gates of the world. I observed them as they moved towards the eastern exit of the hall. The night would be their ally; in the consulate's bed they would be shielded from all bombs, and between silk sheets they would conjure up good ministerial material. Yes, I could have sworn they were some prime minister's future parents.

A moment later I found an armed guard, if not a soldier, looming above me. A wooden-headed boy with a square face, thick lips and pale eyebrows under an oversized helmet. He ordered me to the nearest air-raid shelter. Hadn't I heard the alarm? That showed you what a state I was in, the fact that I hadn't heard the sirens.

'I'm waiting here for my mother. She . . . she's a prison warden in the Fuhlsbüttel camp . . . but gets the weekend off. We're going to . . . watch the air raids.'

With a hand grenade in my luggage, I had grown more confident. I didn't even stand up to answer this Nazimodo, who swallowed the information by nodding his big-eyed wooden head and even smiled at this good and obedient Nazi child. Nevertheless, he was about to say, 'But . . .' when he was interrupted by an explosion. We both turned our heads out of the hall. At the other end the family meeting scattered, and people grabbed their cases. Fires reignited outside in the dark ruins, and in the close distance we could hear the whistle of falling bombs as they plunged vertically through the night sky, the way our common snipes do back home, and then produced those deafening bangs as they built their nodular nests on the rooftops and harbour warehouses. Damned Brits.

'But . . . unfortunately, there are no more trains tonight. Not until the Kiel train comes in the morning at six fifteen. You have to leave. No one is allowed to stay here tonight. You must go to an air-raid shelter.'

'Why aren't you in the war?'

How cheeky I'd become.

'Huh?' the startled Nazimodo asked.

'Why aren't you in the war? My father's in the war. All real men are in the war.'

'In the war? I am in the war. I'm taking care of the station.'

'That's good. Then I'll stay here.'

That was the right answer, because he seemed content and wandered away. But I continued sitting there and must have looked like the Kid in Chaplin's film.

And that made sense, because a short time later he was the man who appeared to me.

61

Half Hitler

1942

The big white clock over the main entrance was about to strike three and the station was now almost completely deserted. I sat in the middle of the hall and pined for Mum and Iceland. At some distance to the left of me, two stout and sluggish Dutch countrywomen were sleeping, enveloped in black, reminding me of two seals wrapped in shawls. I'd allowed myself to dream of a warm place between them, but they spoke from the bottom of their windpipes and didn't understand the most basic questions in German, although they gave me a slice of sausage. Outside, through the darkness of the city, I could hear the crackle of gunfire and, in the distance, isolated shots from anti-aircraft guns, even though not a wing could be heard in the sky.

I had managed to slip into a semi-dormant state, which ended when a strange being appeared in the hall, to my distant right, on the corner by the newspaper kiosk, looking around. It was a dark creature with two short hind paws but long, strong front legs. The first thing that came to mind was an ape or a two-legged dog. It spotted me, the only sign of life in the hall, and edged towards me, thrusting itself on its two front legs.

As it drew closer I realised it was a man, half a man. In half a coat with half a cap on his head, hairy cheeks but a bare chin. Under his big nose he sported a short, curly moustache. He had lost his legs but transferred all their power to his arms, which enabled him to cross the hall surprisingly fast. Then he sat beside me. No doubt he'd deluded himself into thinking he'd finally found a girl of his own kind, because I could read the disappointment in his eyes when he saw I had legs. Out of some unconscious Breidafjördur consideration, I had tucked them under me, but now he saw that his dream princess was fully limbed and, moreover, a child. But even though this was only half a man, his voice was whole.

'Good evening, good evening. "Goodnight" would be more accurate, but that's more of a farewell than a hello. Therefore I'll say good evening, even though it's morning. What's your name, young lady?'

'Herra.'

'Hair ad?'

'Herra. With two rolling *r*'s.'

'*Ach so?* Herrrrra. With the Führer's *r!*' And suddenly he was impersonating Adolf Hitler: '*In unserrrem Deutschen Rrrreich!* Yes, what I wouldn't give for two rolling *r*'s. Then I could rrroll all the way to Amsterdam and from there across the North Sea on my yellow arse.'

'Yellow arse?'

'Yes, I'm Jewish. Jews have yellow arses. And a yellow star. Aaron Hitler, delighted to make your acquaintance.'

'A . . . Hitler?'

'Yes, Aaron Hitler.' He held out his hand. It looked more like a foot. It was covered in a thick black fingerless glove; his palm was protected by a piece of wood that was hidden inside the mitten, out of which stretched long fingers that together seemed to have the power of a Beethoven string quartet. He noticed my hesitation.

'Yes, forgive me if my hand is a foot and therefore soiled by the salt of the earth.'

I took his hand. It greeted me gently, although I felt it could easily have broken every bone in my hand in an instant. His trunk seemed lean, however, and his face delicate, with smooth, pale skin, even though the hair under his hat, his sideburns, and his moustache were all deepest black. He must have been about thirty. Two soft stubs protruded under his short coat; he'd been amputated at the groin.

'Did you say Hitler?' I asked.

'Yes, Aaron. Aaron Hitler. His Majesty's brother. His little brother.'

This was some kind of joke, some kind of nocturnal entertainment that was being performed in Germany's train stations, sponsored by the Ministry of Culture, no doubt, to provide some distraction, boost the morale. But children are serious people.

'The Führer's brother? But you said . . . Jewish?'

'Yes, and therefore . . . shush!'

He mimed a giant knife with his right hand, accompanying his shush sound with a throat-cutting gesture and pretending to chop off his legs. I felt this was my cue to laugh at this cabaret number, that he probably expected me to, but I couldn't and blurted out, 'Yes?' in my confusion.

'But where are you from, you pretty creature? I hear the sea in your accent.'

'Yes, I'm from . . . I . . . the islands.'

'An island girl? Travelling alone?'

'Yes, Dad just left. I'm waiting for Mum. She was supposed to be coming from Lübeck tonight but she wasn't on the train.'

'Oh, Lübeck. The British gave it a nasty pounding yesterday and the day before. Whole neighbourhoods reduced to dust. What a pretty city it was, at least seen from the gutter. They wouldn't allow me up the tower, the bastards.'

'Huh? What do you mean?'

He saw my anxiety mounting to despair.

'But . . . no need to worry. Your mother is in no danger.'

'Huh?'

'Yes, safe and sound. I know that for a fact.'

'How do you . . . know that?'

'I know it for a fact.'

He said this with such a warm smile that I immediately calmed down in an almost supernatural way.

'And are you Jewish?'

'Yes, the last Jew of the Third Reich. Once they get me, that'll be it. *Ein Volk! Ein Rrrreich! Ein Führrrer!*'

'But how ... how did you get away?'

'Why ... Dolfy, my brother, of course,' he said with a shrug, which indicated that 'his brother' wasn't quite as ruthless as the war led us to believe. He didn't seem to have anything to add to this, because he gazed across the hall at the Dutch country seals and beyond out the other entrance, as if he intended to move on. The Führer's brother couldn't be wasting his time consoling a moping kid from Iceland. But I suddenly felt an urge to hold on to this street beggar. He exuded a strange sense of well-being.

'So he has spared you?'

'Yes. Although I didn't altogether get away, my legs did, they ran away. To Sweden first, then on to America. Which is where they're living now, little things. I sometimes get a letter from them. The right one is in Ohio and the left one in California. They were used to living wide apart, I have such a huge crotch, see? I'm sometimes asked if it's a hassle lugging this around, but I say no, oh no, because under me I've got two pouches full of gold. Two entire nations to be exterminated later on. I just need to get myself into a harem. I'm working on it. But unfortunately there aren't many females who are into big-dicked dwarfs. Women get pretty touchy about no legs, I've come to realise. They prefer men who can "stand on their own two feet." SS men, for example, or men like my brother Dolfy. But, on the other hand, I say, happy is the man who has no legs, for what are legs but instruments of stupidity? Just think of what the legacy of legs has brought us!' He held out his big, strong hands. 'All of this is the work of men with legs. A foot will trample, a hand will sow, I say. But I'm willing to take over when my brother Dolfy loses the war. Then they'll call me and make me the chancellor of Germany.' And then he started to mimic his big brother again, rolling his *r*'s. 'Because we shall rrrrrise from the rrrrruins! We shall stand on our feet!'

That was one thing I found funny and could finally laugh at. He gave me an encore.

'Because who else but I can lead the German nation out of the depths of its despair? A man who has experienced the miry pits first hand!'

And he beat his woody palms against the stone pavement, making it echo. I laughed even more. He jerked his head at the end of every sentence, just like the Führer did, and for a moment looked so much like him that I was beginning to believe he really was his brother.

Finally he straightened, threw his head back and his arm up in a mock Hitler salute, but in such a way that only his elbow went in the air, as if his arm had been amputated, and yelled out loud and clear: 'Half Hitler!'

62

The Hymen Cap

1942

A night of bombing in Hamburg felt like four or five nights elsewhere. The planes arrived in groups, loaded with fire, and relieved themselves over the beautiful old residential neighbourhoods before vanishing west again like satiated hyenas. This gave us a pause for a nap until the next round arrived and sirens and anti-aircraft guns sounded once more, followed by a downpour of whistling bombs, and those horrific bangs started all over again.

'I wander about on my stumps at night. I need only half a sleep,' said my friend Aaron with a wink.

'Where do you sleep?'

'Oh, I try to spread myself around. Once I slept in a drawer, another time in a swan's nest. If I sleep on something light I sleep heavily, and if I sleep on something heavy I sleep lightly. If I sleep inside I sleep in, if I sleep outside I sleep like a dog, with one eye open. It's good to sleep in the gutter because then you dream of tea parties with God. Oh, those cakes! But the safest place of all is in a bomb crater because Tommy's a miser and never drops a bomb in the same place twice. Besides, nothing scares me, least of all death. Whatever will be will be, no point in doing things by halves!'

It was as if it had all been scripted long ago. Like an old play. He had rehearsed answers to every question and never ran out of words. And every line contained some ear-soothing energy; they came sparking out of him like electrical cables out of a power plant, and his voice was like red wine to the ear, gently flowing, savoury, and intoxicating, from that death mask of a face.

And then he sang for me:

Out in the forest, like a stone,
The King of Love is sleeping.
And if he doesn't wake alone
His kingdom is hers for keeping.

God, I was bewitched by that tailless centaur with his Chaplin moustache! But then my other friend reappeared again, Hans Smartypants, the one with the white eyebrows and helmet. He started by shooing off the Dutch countrywomen, who clambered to their feet and were on their way. Then finally he came to us.

Hitler's half-brother launched into a brand-new routine.

'Good morning, good morning, good boy. And what pretty boots you have! If they made boots like that for the arms, I would have dashed to the front line ages ago, to smack the arses of those Russians east of the Don and then find my feet in the infantry, because in war I'm good at everything, except legging it, of course!'

'Who are you?' Hans asked, slightly thrown off-kilter, before turning to me: 'Is he with you?'

'Peace be with you because the war sure won't. But you've managed to protect this fortress and that is good. Yes, an honourable achievement, which I will be reporting to my people in due course. My name's Aaron and I'm a Hitler, the little brother of our great father, his majesty's half-brother, to be more precise. Yes, half a Hitler, as it happens, but the other half bore no relation to my brother and me and therefore had to go,' said Aaron, making a whistling sound over his stumps and an appropriate gesture.

The white-eyebrowed soldier stared at this freak a long time. Who was . . . no, WHAT was this lump who spoke up to him like a slave but down at him like some high-ranking aristocrat? Was THIS (!) his BROTHER? Yes, maybe they were not that unlike, although this one's hair was curly and his nose seemed to be squeezed out of the depths of Jewdom. The boy pondered on the sacred name a while.

'Heil Hitler!' the young Hans exclaimed, his voice echoing against the hall's 121-foot-high ceiling, thrusting his arm into the air as he straightened and clicked his heels.

I've witnessed many comical scenes in my life, but the puerile reaction of that soldier had to be considered one of the funniest. But I didn't laugh, except on the highlands of my soul, in the shelter of a little shed that stands there. On the other hand, I could see that my friend Aaron was heroically struggling not to smile as he responded to the salute. It was a comedian's smirk in the middle of a performance. And finally I understood that man, that half-man, half-reckless flippancy.

The soldier continued: 'Footman Hans Jürgen Rupert, sir, from Air Defence Division 161 B, under the command of Sergeant Major Gunter von Affenberg. North Hamburg Defence Unit, transport and construction.'

Aaron was still struggling with himself but did his best.

'End of communications, message received, hand at ease. You are a splendid specimen of the Aryan race. The future is ours. Have you procreated?'

'I beg your pardon, sir?'

'Produced offspring?'

'I have no children. I'm still young.'

'How old are you?'

'Nineteen years old, sir.'

'Good. Can you sire frogs?'

'Huh?'

'Got any seed in your mill?'

'Erm . . . yes, I think so.'

'Aryan seed is the gold of this earth. Mark my words. Once the tap has been connected, it's got to be turned on. Superiority is one thing, but expansion is another. Every boy must supply his yield; every maiden must nourish her stock. Just think about it, my good Hans. You produce hundreds of soldiers a day, allowing them to colonise the palm of your hand, precious conquests no doubt, but ones that do little to expand our land-thirsty Reich. You must find a hundred women today and two hundred tomorrow. Our shelters are full of them! Go fill them to the full! That's what we need. Why do you think we're getting nowhere in the mud graves out east and making no headway against those Rrrandy Rrrrussians? Because we're running out of people! We need soldiers!'

I looked up at Hans Jürgen, who was staring down at the man on the ground with a Hitlerian glint in his eyes, a glint that yelled: I recognise him! This is his brother!

'This is something I often bring up with brother Dolfy. "You should have children, my dear brother!" I say to him over a mug of beer. "You should be fucking women, three a day, so that you can have thirty thousand children in ten years!" Think of what that would do. Our men would be standing outside Peking, not Moscow. I myself have performed my nocturnal duties and produced seventeen children in seven months in the villages of Bavaria but had to flee when the farmers saw Jewish noses popping out of their daughters' crotches. I ran so fast that my legs ran ahead of me and now live far from their torso and back, totally childless in America.'

'Jew . . . Jewish nose?' asked the soldier, just as I had done before.

'Yes, sorry, did I forget to introduce myself? Aaron Hitler, the last Jew in my brother's empire. I was so high up on the alphabetical list that they accidentally skipped over me.'

The clown lifted his hat, revealing the yarmulke that lay on the crown of his head beneath it, a black rag buried under his dirty hair. The soldier swallowed this sight with difficulty; his Adam's apple momentarily jammed above the tightly buttoned collar of his jacket, hanging there from a few stiff bristles. I was therefore relieved when Aaron slipped his hat back on again.

'Don't misunderstand me. I'm only half-Jewish. Both my legs were Catholics. Clean-living priests, the pair of them, who lived to make children hop on their knees. But they had problems being branded with a yellow star. But no worries, dear Hans, our beloved brother is Aryan from head to toe and not to be blamed if his brother is Jewish. That was our father, Alois, who so badly forgot himself when he took Dolfy to school one day, made the poor fellow wait in the corridor while he was having it off with that tart of a mother of mine, triggering an outrage that set the whole of Europe ablaze. Yes, I'm... I'm all to blame! My conception, my birth! Me! My father's original sin! My brother's revenge! The suffering of mankind! Oh my, oh my!'

He waved a hand in the general direction of the city, and in the same moment another bomb fell out by the Gänsemarkt.

'But according to our Jewish faith, every conception brings shame to our tribe, and that is why we circumcised men wear a hymen on our heads.' He lifted his hat again to reveal the *kippah*. 'Crowned by original sin, we roam the earth hunched under the burden of sex and are daily reminded of our fathers' sins. I myself wear the ancient relic of my foremother's hymen, that of Rebecca the daughter of Salomon of the Jordan Valley in southern Judaea, who lived in the first century before Christ. My ancestors and grandfathers, six hundred men, have worn this on their heads for two thousand years across two thousand mountains, all the way down to the beer cellars of Bavaria. Care for a sniff?'

He removed the hymen hat from the crown of his head and raised it to the soldier, who by now had turned crimson. I struggled as before to smother my laughter, while at the same time remaining awestruck by this torrent of words. Hans Jürgen hesitated, then finally bowed to the name of Hitler and stuck out his nose to get a whiff of the two-thousand-year-old hymen.

'According to our faith, the oldest male in the family must dip the hymen in his sperm before passing it on to the youngest offspring at his circumcision so that here' – he turned the skullcap over, making it look like a primitive bowl in the palm of his hand – 'here in this cap we have preserved the life juice of generations, from Abraham to Alois! Yes, yes, him as well, Dolfy's and my father, he contributed to this cap, too.' I had started to laugh out loud. I just couldn't keep it in any longer, it was impossible. 'So here you have it, in one yarmulke, the original Hitlerian sperm from which the Führer sprouted ...'

A gunshot resounded and the yarmulke glided to the floor as the half-man keeled back and his stumps swung in the air. The comedian had completed his performance. The laughter froze in my throat. I looked up. I hadn't noticed the soldier lifting his rifle. The shot was deafening. A threadlike trail of smoke oozed out of the barrel. A threadlike trail of smoke also seemed to ooze out of the ill-fated soldier's head as he stood over his newly fallen victim, perhaps wondering if he really had killed the Führer's half-brother. That gave me time to clamber to my feet. By the time the soldier had finally come to himself and prepared to shoot me, I was standing on the floor and was threatening him with a hand grenade.

Dad might have been a Nazi, but he was no fool.

63

Funny Corpse

1942

The shot had struck the heart, and blood spurted out of it onto the dirty floor like black wine. When the soldier had left, I edged towards the body. We were alone in the hall. Air-raid sirens sounded in the distance. I peeked at the half-man, who was now fully dead. His eyes were completely open, perfectly 'lifelike' but so utterly empty inside, like eggs that had just cracked, staring at what had just flown out of them. I gave a start and backed off into the hall. Seen from a distance, the body looked like a small black sack that had fallen from the sky and from which the black contents were now leaking.

I looked alternately at him, at the ticket office, and out at the city, squeezing the grenade in my skirt pocket, and no longer knew what to do. All of a sudden I burst into tears. And the beaver's snout was back in my throat knocking against my gums.

I edged back to the unmoving half-man. I bent over him and closed his eyes the way I'd seen a farmer do once, back on the islands, when he had found a body on the shore. His right hand twitched, as if the body wanted to thank me for the service. I took it, and then took his left one, too, and dragged him like a long-armed ape into the corridor of the toilets and tried to mop away as much blood as possible on the way. There I left him, in the same spot where my father had left me the day before. I couldn't bear the idea of Mum meeting me over a corpse. Then I went back into the hall and tried to sleep the night away, pulling the steel jewel out of my case and wrapping myself in the red scarf that Mum had knitted for me earlier that year. In that way I carried both of them with me. Mum's blood flowed around my neck, and my father's heart pounded in my pocket. Finally I managed to catch some sleep between rounds of explosions and dreamed of dwarfs dancing on a green meadow, where a baroque-bearded poet laureate recited poems in a white tunic.

At quarter past six the station started to fill with people, mainly women and children, who for some unknown reason felt it was safer to come to Hamburg than to stay in Kiel. Some of the women gasped at the exit when they caught sight of their city. A number of them turned back into the station with one or two children in tow and vanished down a platform again. This was a nation in turmoil. People were prepared to settle anywhere so long as there was hope of shelter from the bombs. I enviously eyed the girls who had a mother's hand to hold. And continued to struggle with the lump in my throat.

A grey-haired, uniformed woman with glasses finally opened the ticket office from inside. I decided to wait there in front of it, but so as not to obstruct the ticket-hungry customers, I moved to the front of the canteen, which the Germans call the *Imbiss*. And there I waited for a whole day. With a hand grenade in my bag and my head full of Mum.

She never arrived. After twenty-four hours' guard duty in front of the *Imbiss*, which included a long conversation with a bag lady **who** stank of fish, and an obscene offer from a fat officer's son, I came to the conclusion that my mother was stuck under the gable of a fallen house, but that she had luckily had her knitting with her and was now sitting all dusty and humming in the shadows of the ruins, knitting herself a jumper, because the nights are cold by the Mecklenburg Bay.

It crossed my mind to buy a ticket back to Friesland. After all, I could still have a shelter at Frau Baum's, I who had left her my good old sexy box. In his confusion, however, my father had forgotten to give me any money before he left. But maybe I could sell the grenade for something? Finally I swallowed the lump in my throat and gave up on the chance of Mum's coming to meet me here. I took my case and headed down the corridor to the toilets one last time. Two rats were now sniffing the body. I let them be – we all have our part to play – and I bid my friend farewell from a distance, asking him to watch over me. Then I moved back into the main hall, passing the lovely flower lady, who was still in good contact with the heavens above, and stepped out into the war.

64

Humanity

2009

It's strange to think this old-age machine can still produce tears. I just don't get it. And wipe my ancient cheeks. Rancid, darn sentimentality. And the fact that this ancient bag of a body is forced to keep up its shit-making all the way to the nailing of the coffin is clearly nothing more than a celestial mockery, some kind of divine punishment to keep us needy to the end.

Spurred, spurred, spurred, till the very last turd. But man is kinder than his monstrous Creator, because man had the decency to invent rules that allow people to stop working at seventy, whereas our cruel God grants no exceptions, never gives us a break, keeps us traipsing to the toilet until our very last breath.

In any case I attach no importance to God. It's nothing more than arrogance for us humans to consider ourselves any more significant than all the animals, flowers and plants. Cows never created a bovine Jesus for themselves. Not even a dandelion believes in God, and that's the most stupid plant of them all. They possess an intelligence that is superior to humankind's, what I call earthly wisdom. Yes, those blessed animals and plants know how to live. They know what life is. And that's why we're so terribly scared of them, the beasts. Because our souls know they know more than we do.

I just say: if anyone is God, it's got to be me, someone who has survived eighty years without losing her wits and has woken up in four different continents, on top of hundreds of men, who's had and lost children and created an entire solar system of problems, but managed to solve most of them with perseverance and above all stoicism, plus the drop of generosity I managed to squeeze out of my grandma's desiccated corpse.

Old people talk about soon going to the Lord, how they look forward to finally meeting their maker, without realising that this is as close to him as they'll ever get: to have experienced human existence and overcome all the trials that life places in our path and to now face up to the most human thing of all, death. To bow to the god that dwells in the core of every man. Because when we die we don't vanish into the air but into ourselves, into that human kind of divinity called *humanity*.

65

A Polish Stallion

1944

The horse trots on. And quite a lovely feeling to have four legs underneath me. Step by step, he carries me by the edge of a pine forest through the rustling grass. Some bird, undaunted by the war, breaks into flight, singing of summer in Europe, poor fool. The woods are alive and the sun climbs up the dense pine trunks like a sluggish but quite luminous forest cat. The flood of rays occasionally bursts through the wall of pines, stinging my eyes. A beautiful day, a good day. Full of brand-new pain. A fire flickers between my legs. But a maroon Polish horse carries that fire with care. He has lived through four years of battle and knows that his load is a fourteen-year-old girl who was raped last night.

It's been more than two years since I became an orphan and entered the war from the Hamburg Central Station. I've been roaming around the Reich of war, through ruins and raids, seeking refuge in shelters and sleeping in courtyards, attics, here and there, in Münster, in Minden, in Kassel – oh, how many cities they have – and spending the best six months with a family in Munich, until one night they managed to flee to the post-war era. And all this time I managed to fight off the hands of war and keep myself a child, all the way up to this eastern forest, all the way up to last night.

But the morning has brought me a horse, a Polish horse. He's taking me to a better place. He knows of a better place. He knows of some tiny, peaceful village where no men, soldiers, or hatred live. Oh, but the bareback rocking hurts. Oh, come now, elderly me, come down with a saddle from the ocean heavens above!

Lying on a pillow a whole lifetime later, I find myself peering over the edge of the bed: a fathomless abyss opens up below me. At the dim bottom I can make out a faint glimmer. It must be the sun rising over the shattered continent on a sore horseback morning. And yes, there I am, in the dark embrace of the forest. Slowly advancing like a six-legged ant.

This forest seems more Polish to me than German. There's something Slavonic about the foliage. Not a tank can be heard here, and all the bombs are fast asleep. They sometimes shine beautifully in the night, under the drone of aircraft in the sky, on the horizon out west. 'Unlucky city,' a gaunt woman in the underground shelter had muttered, 'unlucky city.' I can't remember what city it was; they were obviously all unlucky. The frontline is far away, to the east of the Don and to the west in France, but sometimes the line cuts through our heads and down between our eyes. And then there's nothing to do but shut them when we hear the bombs drop. But now that the sun is plucking its radiant melody on these evergreen violins, not even the whisper of a gun can be heard. Nothing outside the ears. But inside them, armies are marching. I was raped last night.

The horse hangs its head to sniff the trail, which he's either taken before or is improvising as he goes along. We don't know each other, just met earlier, at the rosy blue dawn. I call him Czerwony. And he hasn't objected. Therefore he must be Polish, like the boy who screamed himself into me last night. That was the Polish invasion of Germany. I didn't want to disappoint him by telling him I was Icelandic. Besides, I was no longer Icelandic after three years of roaming through this war. Unless that is precisely what being Icelandic means: to be tossed from one calamity to the next.

It was a dense, green summer, no different from the previous or following ones, with the number 1944 embroidered on every leaf. Oblivious to man, nature just followed its course. And strange to see flowers and bombs erupt in the same field.

66

Among the Sorbs

1944

Earlier that spring, I had climbed out of three weeks' basement confinement in some nameless farm in eastern Germany. It wasn't considered wise to keep me above ground, since the district was being combed for Jews and I was both unregistered and without a pass. Some very kind people had taken me in, joyless peasants with veinous noses and narrow-minded eyes. They had a hunchback son who did the work of three men.

They didn't speak German with each other but Sorbian, which, like Frisian, is one of the forgotten languages of Europe. I managed to catch only some fragments of this ancient Slavonic language, but the woman of the family gave me a glimpse into the history of the Sorbs, the people they belonged to, which no one knew then any more than they do now. According to her, they were descended from a tribe of nomads who had gone camping in the sixth century, roaming across half the continent until one night they finally set up camp on the banks of the Spree and didn't make it any further the next day, and were still there. And yet they'd had to put up with ten centuries of harassment on their camping site from beer-swilling Germans.

They called their land Lusatia, a beautiful name that the Germans deformed to Lausitz. This territory, which rapidly vanished into the

German woods and is nowhere to be found on a map, has a symbolic shape, in that it looks like a severed tongue. The Internet now tells me there are only sixty thousand Sorbs left above ground and yet they are still struggling for the independence of their land and language, to the deaf ears of the powers that be in Brussels. But I can console the poor devils by telling them that we Icelanders were no more than forty thousand when things were at their worst and our country was plagued by the Laki eruption in the eighteenth century, yet in the end we became a nation among nations, with our singing Björks and crashing banks, Olympic silver and Nobel Prize medals around our necks.

I had stayed with these people a month before moving into the basement, and I tried to earn my keep. Had ended up there after a few hours wandering through the woods, following a fight with some women on a horse carriage. The black-skirted lady taught me gardening, made me plough the garden beds and sow cabbage, turnips and potatoes. She spurred me on with the same harshness her own unhappiness inflicted on her. She had learned her German from two poetry books and chanted the sentences in the most peculiar way, decorating them with rhymes.

'Stand not under the sun. It's bad manners, child. Your bowing bend before sun. Bowing bend. Till workday end.'

She said this on the go, because she was always on the go, on her way out the door, across the garden, with potatoes in her apron, water in a bucket, constantly waddling and never pausing. (At least the women in Iceland used to sit at the table every now and then.) In the city they would have considered her mentally ill, but here in the country she yodelled in tune with hens and plants. Nature is tolerant that way, which is why the countryside will never be completely abandoned.

To continentals, light is precious. We Icelanders have never known how to handle the sun. We see so little of it in the winter that it's barely worth its while to rise. But in the summer we have so much of it that we can work twenty-four hours a day. This is why we Icelanders are always at work, yet at the same time forever taking a break, having no respect for that burning star. On the contrary, we curse the sun if it doesn't show, but curse it even more if it's shining, while we pull down the blinds. We hold the world record in curtain pulling.

For that reason I welcomed the subterranean darkness for several weeks, even though we were at the height of spring. But my seclusion in the dim basement was a hot topic above the floorboards. I was starting to understand Sorbian a bit and heard the man say he wanted to get rid of the stray girl, it was asking for trouble, taking in a stranger like that, and who actually believed the girl was really *Icemandic*? It was obvious she was a Jew. Because they're a race of poisonous liars, as the Führer calls them.

'She's a good worker,' said the old lady.

'But she puts us in great danger, woman, and . . . yes, you better stop speaking that rhyming German when they come.'

'My German is beautiful.'

'They'll think you're making fun of them. It could be fatal.'

'Iceland,' the hunchback then bellowed. 'I want to go to Iceland.'

Like many a pea-brain, German or otherwise, he had embraced the Icelandic faith. I had told him ludicrous tales about polar bear islands and huts full of women in a country with no trees.

'No trees? So you don't have to chop wood for the fire?'

'No. No chopping.'

He half shut his eyes and dribbled from the corner of his mouth.

'I want to go to Iceland. No chopping.' But then he suddenly grew pensive.

'But how do you make fire, then?'

'You . . . just burn . . . grass.'

'Grass?'

'Yes, we have grass cookers and grass ovens.'

'Grass ovens? I want to go to Iceland.'

In my later trips around the globe, I would regularly come across specimens of his kind, Iceland fanatics, who all carried some kind of chip or hump on their shoulders. The two good gentlemen, God and Christ, who normally provide psychological care to people like this, seemed to have forsaken these damaged souls, who then for some reason directed their hopes towards Iceland and venerated this distant country, lost in the glacial seas of the north, as if it were the promised land.

'Here it comes, your mouthful,' said the countrywoman in her strange vernacular as she passed down the rye bread to me in the dark, with the occasional dab of butter or the odd bowl of soup, Lusatian bean soup, which was probably awful but to me was like a warm salmon from heaven. I tried to kill time by carving a horse. The shavings shone in the darkness, like water lilies at night. The horse was as deformed as my stay, since it had been sculpted in haphazard blindness. At night the walls exuded an icy dampness. I shivered in the corner.

On two occasions they erupted into the building in a fury, bursting onto the floor above. My silence was so deep I could hear my heartbeat. They shouted so loudly that cupboards broke. When I later lived in a basement flat in Reykjavík, I always left a light on, 24/7.

'You, Slavonic lice on Germany's head! Where is the Jewish child?!'
'Never was she here. Of that have no fear.'
'*Was?!*'
A rhyme could be dangerous. But down in the darkness I clutched the good old hand weapon that Dad had given me as a parting gift two years earlier. 'You must never forget that your dad loves you.' Ever since then I'd carried that eagle's egg across ruins and squares, in and out of garments, and at a time like this it was good to feel the strength of German steel.

They were back again and paced the floor with even more shouts than before. I could hear the rhyming housewife trembling in the corner. But how was one supposed to use a hand grenade in a cellar? Could it be thrown upwards, perhaps?

I hadn't found any answers to those questions when the trapdoor was thrown open and one or two of them clambered down the ladder. In the meantime, however, I had slipped into the wall cupboard: I lay there flat on a shelf, counting the Svefneyjar islands, with every single islet and skerry, donating a heartbeat to each one. The cupboard had an odd design. Its middle shelf was half built into the wall, so that only part of it was visible when the cupboard was opened. I managed to hop into it so that my head and arms were hidden by the wall, and only my legs would be visible to whoever opened the cupboard. I managed to hide them, just in time, with a piece of shredded curtain and some empty sugar boxes, and then poured starch into my blood just as a soldier threw the door open. I excluded one eye, though, and kept it on blinking duty, floating above my head, clutching the grenade to my heart.

The eruption was accompanied by a thin ray of light that fell from the open trapdoor, and the floating eye now caught a glimpse of the blood-polished barrel of a gun as it swept the dusty sugar boxes off the shelf. But the invisible soldier let the shredded curtains be, and now I was finally happy with the spindly legs I had so often cursed in my puberty, which stood there like thin curtain rods under the threadbare material. Then I heard them rooting through things in the next room and thanked God I was in the habit of hiding the wood shavings in a crack in the wall every night. I stood in the cupboard until the starch had lost its power or receded from my blood. That was long after they had gone back upstairs, closed the trapdoor, shouted more at windowpanes and pottery, shot bullets out of their mouths, and finally stormed off.

A deathly silence descended on the house.

I clambered up on my delicate porcelain legs and then had to climb over the bulky bodies to get out. The couple's blood had mixed on the kitchen floor. The son, however, lay in the garden with his bleeding hump. And his soul flown to Iceland. But on the other side of the house, the vegetable garden was singing green. Potato and carrot leaves, cabbage and who knew what else. They were all there, joyfully and vigorously leaping out of the soil. It pained me. The godless God had forgotten himself over his heads of cabbage while his blessed children were being murdered in broad daylight.

I ran away, retching.

67

Marek

1944

In the days that followed, I was a Little Red Riding Hood without a basket, roaming through the woods, and regretted not taking some carrots and turnips from Mr God's garden, although I was still enraged by that universal idiot. Already on my first forestial day I gained a clear insight into the nutrition universe of caterpillars, only to discover later that they themselves were, of course, the best nutrition. And I occasionally still feel the patter of tiny feet on my tongue when I'm slipping a morsel of hairy food into my mouth. For two nights I stayed in a lovely ant hotel, in the black, mouldy hollow of a tree, and on the third day I met the good old Big Bad Wolf: a bucktoothed wild boar suddenly appeared on the floor of the woods like an ugly ambassador who insists on dancing with a colleague's daughter. But by then Riding Hood had acquired wild forest eyes and managed to chase the beast away with a simple glare.

The odd thing about wars is that although they always employ all the latest weaponry, they always take you back to antiquity; here the war had catapulted me back into the Middle Ages, into an authentic Brothers Grimm tale.

I can see now where I was, on my ramblings through the woods on the last days of my virginity, by peering beyond my bed at the landscape that fills my flashback and comparing it with what I can see on Google Maps. It seems to have been in some Nieder-something forest east of Cottbus. Strange name for a town.

I ended up sailing across a vast river with a peculiar family of refugees and then accepted a place in their carriage, entering yet more woods. But eventually they ran out of food and I was dumped by a small stream, becoming Little Red Riding Hood again. This was followed by a wonderful forest life, crammed with despair and disorientation, howling hunger and hooting owls. Then finally I found myself wolfishly ravenous in front of a small lumberjack's hut. I'd obviously stumbled into what had once been Poland because they spoke Polish there. In a dark window a pale and big-eyed creature with a prominent chin appeared with the expression of an imprisoned cat. He turned out to be a Polish war tourist, a boy of about twenty, who after ten hours of reflection decided to offer me a scrap of bread that was as hard as glass. Outside the birds were singing, but we ate in silence: I had entered my first live-in relationship.

Marek was incredibly shy and his eyes were full of horrors. He gestured slitting his parents' throats, and the loss of two sisters flashed across his big eyes. I myself tried to communicate how I'd lost Mum at the train station in Hamburg, but I didn't mention Dad, out of respect for Marek's parents and their demise. Where was my father now? A soldier, prisoner, corpse? On the other hand, I had great difficulties explaining to the Polish boy that I was an Icelandic girl who had grown up in a vast fjord up north by the Greenland Strait. But how was I supposed to mime that?

There in the spring of 1944, I was so incredibly lost and war weary, after two years of travel with my friend the hand grenade, that I was barely Icelandic any more, just *Celandic*. I had started to think in German and had forgotten all those whale-backed sunsets in Breidafjördur. And of course I had become a teenager, a fourteen-year-old lass with my hair in a bun and a body in full bud, the male-enticing flesh had risen, and my breasts still hung together. I probably wasn't a bad-looking girl, but I had no way of confirming this because I hadn't seen a mirror in months.

I can't remember how I was dressed, but anyway, war has a way of extracting the pizzazz out of any piece of clothing and bestowing it with a kind of emergency glamour that turns every man into a prince in rags. I must have been wearing a skirt of some kind. A skirt and a torn jumper. Yes, it's coming back to me now. And the old shoes of a delicate-looking man who hadn't stood up after an air raid, in an underground shelter in Leipzig. I had learned from the boys to hang on a bit in the shelters while everyone rushed outside. More often than not there was some old lady left lying there, who had been trampled on or had sailed away aboard her soul, suffocated in the stampede. And then the body could be searched for *pfennig* in the pockets, cheese in a bag ... and, once, an old man's shoes. I remember his face, oh my God, I can still remember it. He had a small globular head, the old fellow, like an old Icelandic countrywoman, with round spectacles that I left on his nose, valuable as they were. He looked like a musician who had lost his violin. But I took his shoes, and the heat of life still ran through his feet when I removed them. And now I feel a jab in my aching old heart: was he still alive, poor thing?

Bit by bit, a tacit arrangement developed in that primitive home. Marek would roam the forest in search of food, with his lumberjack's axe over his shoulder, while I fetched water from a putrid stream nearby and fiddled with the contents of the cabin, sheets and cups. He was a cunning forest cat, particularly at making traps. One night we ate a wild hare under the anodyne light of the moon. In the faint distance we could hear brick walls crumbling, while the train to the eastern front rattled by in a nearby wood, and in the clatter one could make out its heavy clutching of the rails; those carriages were full of fodder for stomachs and canons. But the two of us sat outside the cabin door, chewing on roasted ears and crispy legs.

Marek took care of the fire, all the cutting, lighting and frying, but allowed me to cook the swallow eggs and wild plants. The only thing missing in that home was a child. But I didn't fancy the forest gangling in that way, with his chess-player airs. The strange thing, though, was that as each day in those woods passed, the lad grew increasingly attractive.

Then one beautiful summer evening he finally managed to light my fire. It was in the middle of my Polish lesson. He had taught me the Polish words for fire, wood and pot and wanted to teach me some courtesies, asking me to repeat: Can I get you something? '*Czy można* . . .' I started, and then he burst into laughter. I had said *moszna* instead of *można*, an organ he thought was funny to see inside my mouth. He laughed in staccato, like a coughing tractor, and I burst into a shrill Icelandic giggle before we fell into a timid silence as our faces turned the same tint of red. He leaped to his feet like a stepped-on rake, crammed his pockets with fingers, and vanished into the darkness while I collected the glasses and plates. In a distant tree an owl hooted its ode to mice and midges.

68

Yagina

1944

The days were long. Marek, the forest animal, went out to see his furry friends and sometimes didn't return until just before dark, more often than not with scratched, empty hands. I was left alone, recounting island stories to the butterflies and writing long, imaginary letters to my mother that always ended with the same words: 'I hope we meet again after the war, you, Dad and I, and move to the Svefneyjar islands together and live with Grandma and all the other people who dwell there.' Still it never occurred to me to leave. How was I to know what might await me in the next neck of the woods? I'd seen enough destruction and disasters to know that no news was probably the best news. Sometimes I just sat on the cabin step and marvelled at the arrangement of the forest.

One day a dark figure appeared from the east end of the woodlands and waddled straight towards our cabin. I was alone at home, sitting on the threshold, carving, and I watched the black hump transform itself into a vagabond woman in a wide coat with flappy red cheeks. She approached with heavy steps and, without any greeting, plonked herself on a pile of wood and gasped, saying something in Polish that seemed to mean: 'Oh dear, what a day.' As casually as if she'd just got home. Fatigue makes sisters of us all.

She was an elderly woman and I couldn't stop staring at her legs: her calves were swollen and of the same width all the way down to her ankles, like a telegraph pole, but her feet were tiny and her shoes almost invisible. It was as if she had worn her feet away from walking and now travelled across pastures and plains on her two remaining stumps. Her face was virtually wrinkle-free, violet red with thick, black eyebrows and sun-yellow teeth. Her hair was raven black but singed with silver around the ears, which protruded like rocks in a waterfall. She had broad features with high cheek bones but a hollow face between them. She had beautiful teeth, even though they were as crooked as hell. It was as if the Creator had intended to mould a beautiful face with his clay, but run into trouble when he was trying to get the teeth inside her mouth, and finally overdid it, by pressing his thumb too hard against them, without realising that he had caused the middle of the face to cave in. As a result, the woman had a completely flat profile with her nose concealed by jutting cheek bones.

In fact, the woman had a slightly oriental look, although she wasn't from the Tundra countries. She said her name was Yagina Ekhaterina Volonskaya and was from the Grodno region in Belarus. Like a true country woman she expected me to be fully familiar with the area and her beloved farm, Volkonskaya, which was renowned all over the country for the quality of its hens and hay, although it had recently suffered from the fluctuations of the frontline. In one year the frontline had moved four times through her farm, which had meant eight different army shifts.

She seemed to have told this story many times because, although her German was limited, she managed to tell it swiftly and efficiently, with the help of some sign language through her black fingerless mittens.

First the Russians had come charging in, she said, speaking of them as a foreign nation. They'd burned down her granary. Then the Germans came attacking. They shot the cows and boiled the meat in their helmets. Then the Germans again. *Kaputt!* And they had pounced on her, the bastards. 'That was pretty rough, but they were satisfied I think.' Then the Russians came again, all jolly and victorious. And took away her good-for-nothing husband, Evgenij, but he wasn't with them when they came back, then they took the hens and sucked the eggs out of them as they fled, but not before they had blown up the farmhouse by way of goodbye. Then the Germans were back again but then there was nothing left but some cabbage in the garden. Then they returned once more, but this time Yagina had hidden herself in a nearby ditch and missed out on the krauts' retreat – no rape this time. Shortly after that, the Russians came darting through on their motorbikes. But one of them stopped to piss in the ditch and Yagina asked him when the front would be coming back to Volkonskaya again? Never, he'd replied, shaking his pecker and zipping up his fly. Then the old one got bored with nothing left to do but watch the cabbage grow so she decided to leave.

'I'm on my way to America,' she said, blowing through both nostrils. 'Zhivago, to be more precise. Is the sea far from here?'

'Erm . . . yes. I think so.'

'Yes, I expected as much,' she said. 'Is that Germany?' She then asked as she looked around and peered into some tree bark.

'I don't know. The instructions in the cabin are in German but there is . . . someone has carved *Polska* into the wall.'

'I see. Everything is German today. Our land was German for two weeks. I was hoping it might yield more that way but couldn't see any difference. The last time they left, my neighbour Fedor came and wanted to drink a toast while we still could, toast to the independence of Belorussia. He's such a dreamer, you know, one of those . . . with his long beard and wonky legs. But the independence didn't last very long. We barely managed to finish our glasses and there they were again, the Russians. Do you know how it's going in the West?'

'The West? No.'

'They launched an offensive at the beginning of June. You not heard? No? They're retreating, the Germans. Now I just need to squeeze myself through the Western Front and get me aboard a ship.'

'Yes? But . . . but how's it going in the east?'

'There was a hell of a racket, booms and bangs. But they're slowly gathering ground now, the Russians.'

'Are the Russians winning?' I asked, surprised and anxious. I never expected Dad to be on the losing side.

'Yes, they're getting there, but slowly. I managed to overtake them, even though I'm no race horse.'

'Is the war almost over then?'

'No, it's only just started. Soon Hitler will have to put his helmet on. Have you seen him?'

'Hitler? No . . . well, yes, I've seen his arm.'

'His arm?'

'Yes, I was in Munich when he drove through town.'

'Hey, have you heard anything about my Vasily? Vasily Volonsky?'

'No.'

She followed this with a long story about one of the most famous deserters of the war, a history I didn't understand at the time, but would read about years later. Vasily Volonsky was a pilot in the Russian Air Force. At the beginning of Operation Barbarossa, launched by the Germans, he was dispatched along with nine others to fight them in the air. But because of an engine hiccup he lagged behind his comrades and watched the battle from afar: he witnessed nine aircraft being shot down in ninety seconds. Instead of being the tenth man to go down, he veered towards the north and headed for the coast, over the Baltic Sea to Sweden, which he knew to be a neutral country. There he landed on a tiny airfield in the woods and ordered them to refill his tank at gunpoint and then flew off again, over Norway and out across the Atlantic ocean, then north of Iceland and finally landed on the western coast of Greenland where he refuelled and accepted a seal steak from a frosty Danish couple.

Then he took off again and flew over the Greenland glacier and half of Canada until he landed on the frozen Hudson Bay, abandoned the Russian plane on the ice and walked to the town of Churchill, jumped on a train and reached Chicago in two days, whereupon he just vanished into the crowd with water-combed hair.

That was why Yagina wanted to go there. The famous deserter was her son. She pulled out a letter from him, stamped 4.3.43 by the General Post Office of Chicago and showed it to me. Had she been travelling for a year then?

'No, it's not long since I left. I didn't leave until the war had eaten my house and I was in the ditch. It was so damn boring living there alone and henless.'

I made the fire and put on some water, wanted to give her some forest tea, but she pulled out her own supplies, bread and ham, luxuries I hadn't seen for months. I now realised there were fifteen extra pockets sewn into her coat, full of all kinds of goods. In one she even kept a small lantern and in the other, her post.

'Do you need to send a letter to America?' she asked.

'Huh? No, but . . .' All of a sudden I had an idea. 'Maybe your ship will stop off in Iceland?'

She lent me a pen and paper. 'Dearest Grandma and Grandad. I'm alive. I live in a forest with a boy called Marek. We are fine. But I want to go home . . .' I got no further because I had started to weep. The travelling woman stood up with great effort and gasps and approached me. There was a strangely good smell from her, even though she looked dirty, a mystical fragrance of apples. She pressed herself down on the doorstep, drew me into her arms and I disappeared into her Belorussian embrace, vast, warm and soft. Her coat was unbuttoned and I could feel her hot breasts and some very friendly sweaty odour rose from her lap. My tears dribbled down the black material of her coat but I noticed that they fell off it like raindrops from a horse's fur. *Oh my, how sweet it was to rest in a woman.*

Marek came home before dark and greeted the guest with the same suspicion he had shown me on that first day. They had problems understanding each other and finally stopped trying. We sat alone in silence, staring into the fire like three shattered nations.

I offered her my sleeping space but she told me she was no longer able to sleep lying down; since moving into the ditch she'd grown accustomed to sleeping up against something, did I have a wall, a cupboard? Otherwise she could just as easily sleep outside, she was well used to it.

'For three nights I slept on a coal barge and snored all the way down the Neman River, from Masty to Hrodna. We came under fire, the captain and I, and he didn't come out of it too well, poor thing, and I couldn't steer a barge. Besides, the body in the wheelhouse had started to stink so I just settled down in the prow and watched the landscape and cows float by. But rarely have I slept better as in a bear's lair close to Bialystok. There I dreamt that I was Catherine the Great and throwing parties in big palaces in the Kremlin and elsewhere, surrounded by handsome young soldiers I allowed to rock me every night. It was so cosy I spent an extra night there, even though I had no time for it. I'm on my way to America. Zhivago to be precise.'

She left the following day. I should have followed her, of course. But I didn't feel up to it. Something held me back in the cabin. While Marek was sleeping on his Polish ears I watched Yagina limping between the tree trunks into the daybreaking woods, without ever turning, with fifteen full pockets and a sack, heading for Berlin. How did she keep her course? 'Oh, I just let the sun push me on in the mornings and drag me to itself at night.'

I was missing her already.

69

European Fields

1975

In the summer of 1975 I was in Florida and popped into the only bookshop in Orlando and, by a sheer twist of fate, I was sent to the toilets at the rear of the air-conditioned shop. On the way back I passed the history section and my eyes fell upon a book bearing the title: *How I Beat the Russian Army to Berlin – The Incredible Journey of Yagina Ekhaterina Volonsky* (by Gail Huddenshaw, A. Knopf, 1967). On the photo pages I saw a picture of an ecstatic Yagina under her son's arm on a reception roof in Chicago, in a white evening dress with her hair done up. Wes Volonsky had become a famous businessman in the city.

Naturally I bought a copy and devoured it in two days, much to my boys' dismay. Afterwards I wrote to the publisher and received a reply to say that the positive woman with the caved-in face had died at the beginning of 1969 at the age of seventy-five. The book ends in a flower shop on a busy corner in Windy City, which Yagina owned and ran, she had given it the beautiful name of 'European Fields.'

70

Skin Song

1944

The travelling woman left solitude behind her. Marek continued to teach me Polish in the evenings, with varying degrees of success, but showed no signs of flirtation. I was infuriated by him. What a scandal. Here were two young specimens in the glorious prime of their youth, isolated from all of society's restrictions, and we couldn't even come up with a kiss. After two bright June weeks in that forested paradise, I was beside myself with desire. It wasn't love, of course, but just the demand that he pay me a minimum of respect. I wasn't a piece of wood, was I?

His muteness certainly didn't help the situation. In order to be able to be quiet together, people have to speak the same language. I frequently felt the urge to lock my arms around him out of sheer boredom, so that our tongues could speak a language of their own.

In the end I decided to follow the Pole into the woods. Keeping a good distance. He wandered unusually far that day, and to be honest, I was afraid of losing the trail back to the cabin. But then he reached a small lake on a high clearing, put his axe down, and started to undress. The birds expressed my appreciation of this sight, echoing across the woods. I drew closer. His back was turned to me, and he had removed all his clothes except for his underpants, which were soon thrown on the leafy bank of the lake. My reaction to this unexpected vision was strange. All of a sudden I was possessed by the certainty that I would die before the height of summer and was absolutely determined to get a taste of Adam's apple before it was all over. Full of death-given courage, I stepped forward and called out, 'Marek!'

He turned and covered his member, petrified. I walked over to him, in all my smallness, with my soft cheeks and rock-hard determination. 'Marek.'

I tiptoed across the stones like a forest creature the other animals had never seen before. All the way over to him. Breathless.

'Marek.'

He was a bundle of nerves with startled eyes, as he stood there naked with a hand over his crotch like Munch's painting of puberty. I touched his shoulder. The weather was warm, so he wasn't at all cold, but his lower lip nevertheless started to quiver. I gently stroked his chest and smiled up at him; he was a head taller than I was. He was trying to smile back, I could tell, but nothing reached his flesh, skin, lips. I stretched up towards his face, half shut my eyes, and kissed, but only reached his chin. I kissed a chin. He was still so bewildered, so stunned, so totally confused, that he couldn't move. Not until with a smile I stroked his lower arm and loosened the grip over his groin.

There he was again, my friend Penis. Not as big as the British pilot's jewel, but just as beautiful and surrounded by black bushes. I allowed my hand to slide down his stomach, as taut as a drum skin. His consternation now reached all the way down to his bladder, but I allowed myself to continue. His bush was as stiff and dry as steel wool, causing a moment's hesitation, but my fingers trod lightly along the path. I looked up at him again, but he stared beyond me, at the leaves around him, as if he missed their protection. I ignored it and with my hand started to make his skin sing (an expression I owe to Bæring). I had never received any training in these hand movements, never seen any films or read any booklets about them, and no authors had ever instructed me on how to handle the tool of life. But my studies in the art of pleasuring at the School of Life in Copenhagen now came in handy. I followed what my tender instincts had taught me, and the uprising soon started. Then I took a step back and started to unbutton my childhood. He stood there dumbfounded and watched, but still seemed like the most famous lover in the world, patiently waiting for mistress number 4013 to make herself ready.

A caw was heard from a corner in the woods: a crow laughing on a high branch.

Finally I was free of my clothes and naked for the first time since 1941, when I'd climbed into a bathtub by the North Sea. But there was no mirror here. I could only see my nudity reflected in the eyes of this man, and it was obvious how magical I appeared. Beauty like this hadn't been seen in the Nieder-something woods for over two thousand years. I was a flower that had blossomed in chains and was now all the more beautiful for being able to break free, because its beauty was virginal. I read all these things in his Polish eyes. They had never seen anything like this.

I took a step towards him, on a lichen-covered stone, and pressed my skin against his; we embraced and kissed. My first kiss in the adult world. Sure, I'd been slobbered teeth-to-teeth by a murky boy in an underground shelter, and tongued by a postman on a train one Easter night, but this was a *kiss*. We kissed voraciously, like two famished animals that had never been fondled in their lives.

My breasts in his hands, my hands on his flesh: we were one naked animal, one four-legged beast of love. By a lake in a Polish forest. And all of a sudden the gnarl between my legs had turned into a moist sponge. That had started to sing. Like a small transistor radio it emitted a distant humid sound, a bewitching voice accompanied by a gypsy orchestra. I led the Pole's hand to the right place and the singing suddenly stopped, as if the speaker had been plugged out and the singing now came out of my mouth instead. I started to pant to the music, which was now starting to lose its rhythm. Although his fingers were Polish, they were no Chopin hands, and started to hammer out a raw modern piece that couldn't stick to a melody but turned out to be extremely interesting nonetheless.

Life said hi.

I led him into the cool lake. We changed into little children playing in the still water with splashes and spurts. But in the middle of these water sports, his eyes caught sight of the drawing Heike had carved into my arm. All of a sudden, his laughter sank to the bottom and his smile disappeared. I tried to explain, but he rushed onto the bank and got dressed. Then he walked home, making sure he was always ten yards ahead of me. As I hurried after him, breathless and sweating, I remembered him describing how the Nazis had killed his parents and two sisters. And here I was, running back to him, back to the hut, with a swastika on my upper arm . . . Why didn't I escape?

71

'Germany Girl'

1944

That evening we ate in silence. Some grilled fish he had caught in the lake the previous day. I tried twice to smile at him and touch his hand, but he withdrew it and ordered me to put out the fire before it got dark. We couldn't allow ourselves to sit outside at night, fires attracted guns and bullets. For the first time we went to bed straight after dark without lighting a candle and just lay there staring into that black blotch of ink that follows every sentence in the book of time. I felt this period was bigger than the others. Outside, the forest was buzzing, and I killed time by trying to decipher the sounds but couldn't attribute them to anything other than the growth of early summer.

Every leaf, blade of grass and ant was busy at work, and each gave off humming murmurs that were inaudible to the human ear on their own but when combined with millions of others created a buzz that was similar to the loud silence of a philharmonic orchestra when the conductor has just entered the hall but no music has begun. Maybe we could expect some music in this hall? Or maybe nature was just saying shush because it wanted to listen to the war news? But there was none tonight. No drones. No trains. The bombs had probably taken the night off in the cities under the western sky, Dresden,

Cottbus, Berlin . . . I pictured dark, smouldering amusement parks swarming with one-legged people.

Occasionally I glanced over at Marek; he seemed to have his eyes open. And his head seemed to be buzzing to the beat of the forest, crammed with thoughts. Gradually it grew slightly brighter in the cabin. At first I thought my eyes had developed night vision, but then I saw that the table under the window had drawn a shadow on the floor; the moon had come out. I tottered outside for a pee. The heat of the elapsed day still lingered in the midnight stillness, and it was clear that the evening shift in the woods was far from over. The mice and ants, maggots and midges were far from being asleep and shifted about in a nocturnal frenzy. If you listened carefully, you could hear the singing labourers in the next anthill.

The moon had risen in the north and seemed to be stuck in the branches like a phosphorescent parachute. Against the starry brightness of the sky, the foliage was black and only stirred when it was stirred. A long-tailed bird suddenly recovered its memory when it saw me, remembering that it had a family in the thirty-fourth tree from the moon, and darted over the roof of the cabin, leaving a shaking branch behind. I watched it grow still again as I added a lukewarm discharge to the forest buzz.

I could see that my roommate was still awake when I tiptoed back in, but he didn't look at me. I laid my head on the moist-smelling pillow and thought of home. How could this have happened? And why me? All fourteen-year-old Icelandic girls had their maiden years delivered between the blue mountains, in the arms of their fathers and mothers, with the warmth of a bedroom and a slice of raisin cake. But here I'd had to survive from one meal to the next, a lonely kid in Europe, spring after spring. Would the war ever end?

But this was undoubtedly tougher on them – Mum, Grandma and Grandad. Two years had now passed since I'd vanished in time; they had probably given me up for lost by now. I'd written them several letters that I'd taken into post offices, whenever I came across one, and even allowed a postman to grope me in return. But obviously there were no ships from the port of Bremen to the ports of Iceland, and the writing on the envelope, 'Sveinn Björnsson, *Botschafter*, Reykjavík, Iceland,' faded in three different cities.

But what did I know? Maybe Mum was dead? Maybe Dad? Both of them, even? But Grandma and Grandad were certainly still alive. Old people didn't die at war. That was more for young people. Like Marek and me. Maybe the Polish boy would snap out of his gloom and we'd have a baby in the New Year, here in this snowy cabin, and would then be married in Wrocław when the bombing was over. I would teach needlework at night classes for female factory workers and return to Iceland every second summer.

Half an hour later, a car was heard. And now the Pole finally moved his head; we looked each other in the eye from our beds, under the table that stood between them. The car sounds were accompanied by an eruption of laughter; they obviously weren't far away. Then the car stopped and we heard some shouts.

'*Lasst mich raus. Ich muss pissen! Pissen auf polnischer Grund!*' And then more laughter. '*Polen, ich pisse auf dich!*' Leave me, I have to piss! Piss on Polish soil! Poland, I piss on you!

Marek was about to peep through the window when there was a frightful bang and fragments of glass blasted over the table and floor. The Pole retreated into his bed and buried himself under the covers, while the curious Icelander stretched towards the shattered window with one eye. It was a drinking binge: four SS men on a drunken rampage in an open convertible had halted at about a hundred yards from the cabin, brandishing peaked caps, bottles and guns. Another shot was fired and I ducked for cover. But this time the bullet didn't hit our cabin; it was probably on its way to the moon, because now they were all yelling something at it in the sky. The plan was obviously to invade the celestial body in the autumn.

I leaped out of the bed, slipped under it, stretched out for my bomb, and then climbed back in again. Marek was observing me, but I didn't allow him to see my beautiful weapon, hid it under the covers, and clutched it with ten fingers, though not too tightly. We lay stiffly in our beds until they had emptied their guns and fleshy pistols, then we froze in terror. The vehicle could be heard crawling through the undergrowth and, as far as I could tell, was headed for the cabin. Yet again, I went over the instructions on how to use the hand grenade in my mind: 'You pull off the pin, like this . . . pull here . . . and then throw it away,' I heard my father say to me for the hundredth time.

As soon as the car reached the cabin, I would jump up, open the door, and throw the steel egg. The pin could only be pulled just before. I had to be 'one hundred per cent sure.' It took me a good while to break out of my paralysis, regain my hearing, and realise that the noise in my ears was just the buzz from the forest. I hoisted myself up on my elbows and looked outside.

'They're gone,' I said in pidgin German.

The Pole didn't answer but lay there motionless, with his head under the covers. He was still visibly tense, a bundle of nerves.

'Germany girl,' I finally heard him mutter in the corner under his blanket.

'Huh?' I said.

'Germany girl,' he repeated, and I realised he was speaking German. 'Germany girl.'

He flung off his covers and stood up stiffly with bursting veins in the middle of the cabin in his wartime underwear and yelled at me: 'Germany girl!' Then he ripped the covers off me in one move but was startled by what he saw: a scantily dressed girl with her father's heart in one hand and her virginity in the other. I managed to hide the former, but he took the latter. By force.

72

17 June

1944

I didn't get away until two hours later. Away from that hellish man I had so hellishly longed for. Naked I fled into the nocturnal light of the forest, with my luggage in my hands, clothes and belongings and a red stream down my thigh. In the film of my life, I see myself fleeing that lumberjack's cabin and cursing the twigs that bite my feet. Determined never to tarnish myself again in anything that might be confused with love!

Away, away, away!

I did, however, pause at a grenade's throw from the cabin and was on the point of hurling my father's heart at it, which the Polish bastard had managed to momentarily seize from me, along with my virginity, which was no ordinary virginity, of course, but a sacred international relic that I had managed to preserve across an entire country for half the war. What an idiot I'd been! To have stroked that mortal enemy's groin and awoken his poisonous pleasures. But I managed to make the brute bleed with a sudden bite when I grabbed my weapon back from him. Was on the point of using it, felt this was the moment – a 'Germany girl' with her German grenade! – but the forest whispered into my ear: 'There will be other rapes after this one.' And I shoved the steel egg into my torn bag, walked away and into my clothes, with burning blood between my legs, a red scarf around my throat.

Bit by bit, birds started to sing to my glory. Nature clearly wanted to honour me for the sacrifice I had made in its name. Yes, God was godless. I cursed him and cursed myself, cursed Marek and cursed the birds, as I stepped out of the leafy blackness into the semi-dark grasslands. Dawn broke with a feeble light and a sunless sigh, as if the earth were exhaling its light towards the celestial darkness.

But when I'd reached the next stretch of woods, the birds greeted me with a new song, new lyrics. From their throats one could now hear, 'Trumpets are sounding loudly.' For they knew something I did not, that today was 17 June 1944, the day Iceland became a sovereign state.

73

Red

1944

At the same moment that my groggy grandfather was fumbling with the morning blinds of Bessastadir and realising that he was about to become the president of Iceland for everyone's sake but his own, I was walking through my Polish night forest, towards the rising sun. I now found myself in some kind of fern kingdom, waist high in plants of unknown origin. High above, the tree crowns silently kept watch. The fire still crackled faintly between my legs, but my head was numb, as if it had been struck. And the strangest thing of all was that I could no longer conjure up Marek's face, and my memories of the incident were confused. My body had formed a protective bubble around its lost virginity and solely tended to Herra's soul and self, dismissing anything that had to do with the where, who, and how.

Maybe it was triggered by these primordial conditions (the forest and the dawn), but all of a sudden the legacy of foregone generations, which I unconsciously carried inside me, flared up like an emergency flower that opens in the blink of an eye, offering shelter to all the other plants. No doubt Mum, Grandma, Great-Grandma and all their foremothers had been raped as well. In farms, in barns, in ditches, on hills, on heaths, in bedrooms, in kitchens, in larders, at balls, in woods, on ships, in castles, cabins, gardens and the Garden of Eden. And bit by bit the female species had developed soul protection, which now shot up and enveloped me like a flower out of the earth and prevented me from seeing what had happened. Now that I was wearing my skirt and jumper, I bore none of the trademarks of a rape victim; I hadn't even cried, just silently cursed myself for having been stuck for so long in a time-bomb relationship instead of following that good Yagina woman across the Atlantic. By now I would have been the owner of a whole chain of flower stores in the state of Illinois with super American sons: a Senator, Michelin chef and stockbroker. And I wouldn't be living in a garage but a bungalow.

All of a sudden I was distracted from these heavy thoughts. By a red horse in the green woods. It appeared as if out of a magic lamp, standing to the right of me, and swiftly shook its mane, causing a ripple in the ferny green overgrowth, when it noticed me, and then bolted slightly to the side in a few impetuous dance steps. I was equally startled and froze on the spot. This was a huge continental horse, probably a draught horse, with thick lips, bulky knees and furry legs, a horse that we associate more with man than with nature. When he turned his head and looked into my eyes, I could see in his two ink balls that he was just as lost as I was. We stood perfectly still for a long moment, facing each other, and I felt a need for him. At this juncture in my life the only thing in the world that could help me was a horse, a Polish horse. And in his equine heart he, too, felt that a violated damsel from Iceland was precisely what he needed to carry on his back. We were destined to spend the day together, the sunniest day in the history of Iceland.

After a few awkward moments, Red stretched out his head, a two hundred-pound piece of craftsmanship the size of a boat engine. I touched his forehead with the back of my fingers. What lay behind it? He rubbed his imposing chin against my stomach, as if he wanted to sniff the man's deeds. Then he moved lower, pressed his forehead against my groin, massaging it up and down over my skirt. Was this a rape rescue horse? Red from the Red Cross?

It finally dawned on me that he wanted me to mount him and was offering me his mane as a ladder. I picked up my bag, slung it over my shoulder and, hesitantly, I grabbed his stiff, rough hair and climbed over his ears, which were as big as folded napkins. The pain in my groin returned, but I clenched my teeth and managed to bestride him with the help of Red, who tactfully lifted his mane and then set off. On his right flank he bore a large but superficial wound, and he limped slightly on that side. It seemed to improve as we travelled but returned if we paused for too long. The pain lay in his skin; movement softened the lesion, and it stiffened when we stopped.

The workhorse seemed to know where he was going, because he constantly headed east, towards the sun, transporting me under green-leaved chandeliers across floods of spruces, between a collection of rocks and coniferous paths, over streams and rivers. He moved at a steady pace, with heavy and weary but sturdy steps that bore witness to his endurance. When the sun freed itself from the highest treetops, a path appeared, crossing our way. Red halted briefly and swivelled his ears in each direction, but then lowered his head again and trotted over it, heading into the woodland shadows before us, snorting and foaming.

Was he maybe a Nazi horse who was collecting Jews in this region? Was I on my way to a camp? The late Lusatian couple had told me about these *Konzentrationslager*, which were some kind of camps or warehouses that Hitler had built for his friend Death so that he would never run low on stock. And the Führer had personally selected the best elements of his nation because there is nothing despots fear more than ideas and talent. The greatest honour for any German was to be escorted into a gas chamber: the concentration camps were the honorary German academy. How could I trust this horse? After three years on the run I had developed a solid intuition, which had been shattered by my harrowing night with Marek.

In fact my life had been reduced to pure fiction at this stage of my existence. It was just some worn-out paper on which time scribbled its various unexpected incidents, forming a thick volume of unlikely tales in which the only connecting thread was me, like some kind of ledger, a thousand entries for the thousand items I had been forced to put my name to. I had long ceased to live my life, but instead resigned myself to reading it like a book. And what next? I wondered. Only the God of woes knew what kind of fucked-up, crazy creature would emerge from this chaotic writing. If he had taken a photograph of me at the end of the war, it wouldn't have been a black-and-white picture of a sixteen-year-old curly-haired girl, but a Cubist Picasso portrait of a Breton fishmonger with a face deformed into a hundred dice.

And one of those dice had just been thrown between my legs. A phallus yesterday, a steed today. And a red one according to the state of my skin. Czerwony means Red in Polish. We trotted towards the day and never crossed a clearing, let alone a human settlement.

74

18 June

1944

It's 18 June 1944. Paul McCartney is two years old today. Little thing. If I were to dismount and press my ear against that Polish tree trunk, I would be able to hear the bells his mother, Mary, is shaking over his cradle in a brick house in Liverpool. Their echo reverberates across Europe, under the ground, under the war, with beetles announcing the beat that will be resounding here in twenty years' time when all the leaves start to sing in English 'Love Me Do' in front of Polish and German forest rangers who won't understand a word.

But today it is 18 June 1944, and Paul McCartney is only two. I, on the other hand, am fourteen, doing my third year in Inferno High with another two whole war terms to go. Czerwony the horse had been carrying me across Poland for a whole day. And finally took me out of the wild forest back into human territory, with cultivated land, roads, and houses in the distance. The horse recovered his joyful trot again and moved at a canter along the dusty road. The pain in my groin returned.

The country road was so glaringly white in the summer heat that I had to squint my eyes and didn't see the cloud of smoke coming against us until the tank hidden inside it had stopped. Czerwony slowed his pace and eventually stood dead still against the war machine. The road was so narrow that the tank occupied its full width, and its edges were two manes of grass, fenced off by barbed wire, making it virtually impossible to pass.

The tank was clearly German, marked with a black cross. It started to show signs of agitation, to shift on its tracks. I tried to direct the horse onto the grassy bank, but stubborn as a tripod, Red refused to budge. The tank edged forward another bit and halted. Its nozzle was approaching the horse's head now. There was no window on the front of the tank, which gave the impression that it was following a will of its own – two beasts confronting each other, a metallic dragon and a draught horse. Once more, the former pushed forward, but instead of stepping aside, the latter drooped his head. The tank's cannon was moving across the workhorse's mane. I leaned over to one side just to be safe, but there was no point, the nozzle halted right in front of my face. I looked into the black hole of war. And smelt its bad breath. I almost felt like pinching my nose but didn't dare offend this beast of war. Was this perhaps the moment to use the egg? Chuck it down that infernal trunk, like horseradish down a nostril? Czerwony wasn't intimidated in the slightest and didn't even stir when the tank treads rolled into motion again. Once more I bowed to avoid getting the tank gun in my head, but then I decided to wrap my hands around it, instead of getting annihilated with horse and hooves. The tank halted again and I clung to its sun-heated metallic shaft while Czerwony reluctantly stepped onto the side of the road. I managed to feel my way down the gun and clamber onto the tank. The hatch was open and I could see into the beast's intestines. There were two soldiers inside, a sweaty blond kid without a helmet and a cursing chubby one with a rifle and a red face. Lying between them was a beautiful white living goat.

'Heil Hitler!' I exclaimed, a child accustomed to war.

They parroted the same greeting, but I was already startled by the goat and asked, 'Is she in the army?'

'What? No!'

'Oh, a prisoner of war, then?'

'Get out of here with that bloody horse!'

'Yes, but he's Polish. Doesn't understand German.'

'In war, everyone understands German! Try to pull him to the side! We are in a hurry.'

I pulled my head out of the beast's intestines and yelled at Czerwony in Polish, the few words I knew. He raised his mane, the tank brusquely twitched again, and the draught horse finally sidestepped towards the barbed wire, digging around it with his hooves until it had loosened two pickets; the fence yielded just as the caterpillar beast bulldozed by. I leaped off the tank's rear into the cloud of dust and closed my eyes. When I opened them again, I saw my valiant friend wrestling with a tangle of barbed wire on the edge of the field, but he swiftly freed himself and scuttled with a loud snort out onto the arid field of dirt. I called him back, but he trotted away, his hooves kicking up dust as he cut diagonally across the field towards an old farm two hundred yards from the road. I carried on walking down the road, the pain between my legs flaring up again, and then turned up a path leading to the farm. Was this my four-legged friend's home?

75

Crackling Gravel

1944

The horse was standing in the yard as I approached, limping slightly in the final stretch. Beside him was a skinny, stooping man with an autumnal moustache, chatting to him in Polish. You didn't have to be a great poet to realise that this was the reunion of two friends.

The farm buildings were dark, traditional post-and-plank log structures with red French windows. But they had an exoticism about them; their craftsmanship was somehow slightly more fanciful than the more utilitarian German farms. Polish farmers clearly had more time on their hands between chores than their German colleagues and could dabble in carving patterns in the eaves and ridges.

Czerwony turned his huge head and watched me hobble into the yard. He then stood there like an awkward country bumpkin who doesn't quite know how to introduce his girlfriend to his father. Or did he resent the fact that I'd hopped on the back of the tank?

'Good Hitler,' I accidentally said in my bad Polish, instead of saying good morning. The old man greeted me without a handshake. The still heat of the sun buzzed in every blade of grass, and the gravel crackled like fire. How I loved that weather, me the Ice Maiden – I've always been such a tropical animal. I turned to the workhorse and scratched him under the jaw, feeling the perspiration in his greasy beard. He placed his forehead against my chest and pushed me away. If it had been meant as chastisement, the horse was quick to retract because he then stepped forward and placed his forehead in the same place again, between my breasts. I pointed out the wound on the horse's right flank to the farmer, and we scrutinised the bleeding scratch the barbed wire had left on his thighs. With a profound glance, the old man thanked me for returning his best horse. Decades later, a horseman told me that some horses are incapable of finding their way home without a rider.

I noticed one of Hitler's soldiers in the yard, gazing out at the countryside. Despite the heat, he was wearing a long leather jacket and a peaked cap, and he held his gloved hands behind his back. The farmer disappeared with his horse, and I stood alone in the yard with the Nazi officer. Judging by his manner and dress, he had to be high ranking. He turned and advanced wearily towards me. He moved gracefully but without arrogance, with his head raised high but his muscles fully relaxed. His gait suggested some hidden brilliance. Was he armed? Of course he was armed. I surreptitiously groped for my grenade. It was at the bottom of the sack I carried over my shoulder, I could feel its hard shell through the canvas material. He approached with slow steps on the hot gravel. Was he going to kill me?

My fear vanished in the face of an overwhelming fact: as the officer drew closer, I realised that this was the most handsome man I'd ever set my eyes upon. Forehead, eyebrows, cheekbones, lips. I was awestruck. The leather boots, jacket, gloves. Wasn't he warm? With a smile that half closed his eyes, he offered me his hand without removing his gloves. I had learned in Inferno High to avoid this kind of man assiduously and knew very well that there is nothing worse than a wicked man's kindness. I took his hand with quivering lips.

'Pleased to meet you, young lady. Where do you hail from?'

'From . . . from Germany.'

'From Germany to Germany. Everything is Germany now,' he said, waving his hand over the Polish field. 'Except for our house back home. That's empty.' He cast a vague and strangely dreamy glance towards the west. 'And where are you headed?'

I didn't like all this courtesy. Why didn't he just growl at me?

'The horse . . . brought me. I don't know . . . I . . . initially I'm from Iceland and—'

'What? Iceland?'

I'd said the magic word. He'd stumbled on a rare specimen. He babbled something about Iceland, the blue north, walruses, and romanticism and I don't know what, because my ears were deafened by my eyes. He was about thirty. Under other circumstances his face would have been considered perfectly handsome, but now it was fatally handsome. It possessed an exquisite pallor that evoked words like *corpse* and *death mask*. For some strange reason these words came crawling out of the dark cave of my mind into the moonlight that emanated from the officer's forehead. Those words precisely and no others. Like two hairy, earth-burrowing nocturnal animals.

76

Candlelit Dinner

1944

His name was Hartmut Herzfeld, he was born somewhere in Schleswig, and he had studied to become a writer at the University of Hamburg, literature and art. This all came out on our first date. He invited me to dinner in the Polish farmer's living room. We sat there, the two of us, over some wild boar in the candlelight, sipping red wine from the Carpathian Mountains. He was a perfect gentleman, courteous, refined, and totally free of philandering. However, I expected he intended to ravish my freshly raped body before he killed me with his gun or gaze later that night. I groped for my good old egg and promised myself I would escape at the end of the deed, before sunrise, for the second time in three days.

It wouldn't be easy, however. He had two helmeted heads under his command. Karl and a second Karl were eating back in the kitchen, along with their rifles and the moustachioed farmer, Jacek, who had served us chicken legs and mashed turnip. As a middle-aged twentieth-century peasant, he had naturally never boiled an egg in his life until a bullet deprived him of his wife and turned him into an expert chef.

For reasons I didn't inquire about, this little platoon had been staying at the farm for close to four weeks. My main suspicion was that they had something to do with Hitler's army-communication network, because from one of their rooms, I could often hear loud conversations in coded language through some kind of talking machine that spurted out crackles and buzzes. But I had obviously shot to the top of the hierarchy of this small community and was now sitting with the top brass in the living room, over crystal and silver, all thanks to my incredible nationality, my wonderful German, and my semi-virginal, yeasted breasts, which had risen in the bowl of war and were just ready for baking. They were like those flowers that smiled just as dazzlingly on the battlefield as they did in gardens at springtime. Nature is blind to the history of man.

'How many people live in Iceland?'

His voice came like a polished silver fork out of a majestic family sideboard.

'About a hundred thousand, I think. The last time I was in Iceland was before the war.'

'A hundred thousand? It's lucky you weren't all wandering around Stalingrad,' he said, grinning.

I didn't get it, of course, had never heard of that city; besides, my thoughts were elsewhere. But he didn't lose himself in flattery and continued the conversation in what could be called professional terms. Occasionally, however, I felt I could discern carnal thoughts in his eyes when he smiled at me between morsels or gazed pensively out of the windows full of darkness, allowing the candlelight to flicker over his perfect profile.

I looked out, too, to keep him company. Far off in the eastern sky a light hovered in the air, white and small, like a fading sun. I looked at the man again. He stared at length at the light sinking down the sky and seemed increasingly distant, as if his eyes were busy turning the light into a poem. But once it had vanished behind the treetops on the other side of the field, he snapped out of his reverie, straightened in his chair, and raised his eyebrows and glass.

'Yes, war.' There was a strange tone in his voice. 'There are many wars in every war.'

He chucked the words out of his mouth like pebbles into the dark. I was meant to hear them ripple on the surface of a lake far below and sense the depth they contained: this man was standing on the edge of an abyss.

But I was too preoccupied with the circumstances, appearances on the surface that a fourteen-year-old girl couldn't see beyond: it was here that I sipped red wine for the first time (I'd drunk schnapps with three men at a train station once), was on a date for the first time, was probably in love for the first time. Because, despite the circumstances, this was an extraordinarily romantic dinner. There we sat as two grown-ups (oh God, oh God, I still get butterflies from the thought, this freshly liberated thought of the young me who walks into the living room in the body of a child but turns into a woman the moment I sit down, just because of the way he pulls back the chair and invites me to sit with humble elegance), with three courses and sixteen years between us, a German and an Icelander, in a country house in the middle of Poland, on such a hot and still night that not even the candle noticed that the window was wide open as it gently illuminated this strange encounter. The flame played against the crimson wine in the glasses, and I sensed a bright red glow inside it that couldn't be pinpointed because it seemed to dwell *inside* the wine and shine from there, such a strangely intense red in the almost black liquid, like a soul in a military uniform.

Then he lifted his glass, not from the bowl but from the stem, like a true man of the world. My eyes locked on his pale, elegant, and sensitive fingers. I was suddenly so obsessed with his hands that I almost fainted. This would often happen to me in later years when I developed a crush, infatuation, or fixation. Fingers, hands and elbows had the effect of a drug on me. I was just so happy and surprised to see that my love had hands and not wings as I had imagined.

The most romantic thing, though, was the glow from the tiny, shiny swastika on his chest. I felt ashamed, but there was no denying it: Hitler's cross had the same effect on me as a beautiful rose. Nothing is as seductive as a taboo.

Beneath, there was the simmering awareness of the weapons we were both carrying (for safety I had shoved the hand grenade into the pocket of my skirt), and they were engaged in an erotic dialogue of their own: barrel and egg. I have to confess that there are few greater turn-ons than the knowledge that your host intends to murder you with a revolver once the carnal dessert has been consumed.

'But you probably know that you Icelanders are an extraordinary nation.'

'No. The only extraordinary thing about us is that we exist at all. That we survived this long. If we were to vanish in the morning, no one would miss us.'

'Oh yes. There are people who would miss you. People who believe Icelanders are the original Aryans who preserved the true spark of our race. That it was through you that Old Norse mythology came into being, yes . . . if not through you, you at least preserved it . . . and that it is the only true cultural heritage we Germans have, unlike ancient Greek culture, for example, which is totally unrelated to ours. Iceland would therefore be our Hellas, our Athens. The promised land.'

I'd heard my father say this hundreds of times. My eyes were glued to his swastika pin as I pondered on an answer.

'Hmm . . . mythology . . .'

He halted his wineglass a moment as he was lifting it to his lips, chuckled lightly, and then took a sip. 'You don't like mythology?'

I had developed an aversion to mythology at an early age. It's one of the most ludicrous pranks mankind has played on itself, to have created these superhuman models, giants and monsters to fight against and suffer from the comparison: an endless source of unhappiness. Why can't we just content ourselves with being human?

'No, gods are so boring.'

'Oh? How's that?' he asked. Was that a grin in his eyes?

'Perfection is no fun. I once met a man who was so ungodly and earthbound that he was already half-buried, as he said. His legs were missing. And yet he was one of the funniest men I'd ever met. He didn't survive the night, but in my mind he remains immortal. Three years later I think of him more often than of God, or what's called God.'

'What happened to him?'

'He killed him.'

'Who?'

'God killed him, out of jealousy. Because he was funnier than He is.'

'Are you funny?'

'Not as much as you.'

'Me? Am I funny?'

'Yes, in that uniform.'

In those years, people's words sometimes gambled with self-destruction. You could dig your own grave with the things you said. The war had gone on for so long, and the soul was so weary of the constant threats to its life, that you sometimes unconsciously flirted with ways out of it. Or was it the romantic element in me, maybe? Maybe it was an attempt to talk him out of those clothes that fitted his soul so badly? He took it rather coolly.

'Don't you like . . . don't you like the uniform?'

'Yes, but not on you.'

77

A Field Sparrow

1944

He was a disappointment to me. He turned out to be neither the Nazi he was supposed to be nor the poet I had imagined. He was only beautiful. As beautiful as a shiny doorknob that fits nicely into one's palm and bows its head when asked to open a door and then closes it again and shuts up for the whole night. He escorted me to the bedroom where Jacek had prepared a bed for me, and then wished me good night. As polite and neutral as a doorknob. And I had thought he had his eye on me. But no. He didn't even want to rape me, let alone kill me.

I was appalled and couldn't sleep.

Maybe he didn't want me because I was dirty and soiled by another man? These things didn't pass unnoticed by a sensitive poet. Maybe I was damaged goods for the rest of my life? No, with him, with that holy man, I'd become pure again. Love would save me! But what was I thinking anyway? I who was still so sore and numbed by that horrific event. Yes, of course, it was best this way, to sleep alone tonight and recover. But still, no. I longed for him like a thirst longs for water, and lay in bed with a stomach as taut as a stretched spring: the slightest touch from his finger would have catapulted me out the window.

Aargh and grr!

The next day he picked up the conversation where he'd left off at breakfast and lunch: 'Tell me more about Iceland. Are there many cars there?' Then he had to leave the farm for dinner. Second Karl drove him in the sidecar of his motorbike. I ate with Karl, who devoured his meat like a wolf (jerking his head back with every bite) and told me he was an apprentice with a blacksmith in Saarbrücken, a young lad with coarse features. He was bright red in the nasal area. It was as if his big nose had been pressed into his face only last week and the skin was still recovering. He had no interest in Iceland and was capable of talking about only one subject: flyovers, which he felt were a major innovation, if not Germany's greatest contribution to civilisation. 'These aren't bridges over rivers or lakes, but roads, other roads. Flyovers. Think about it. Flyovers.' Yeah, yeah. Get away from my ears, as far as you can, so that the bomb that kills you doesn't burst my eardrums.

Class divisions in the army were, of course, merciless. Unschooled helmets got dispatched to the front by the more highly schooled caps. Brains are the currency of life. And Hartmut had a whole treasure chest of those, whereas life had dealt the Karls only a handful of loose change. But the peculiar thing about intelligence is that it is rarely accompanied by good luck. It's the moderately intelligent men who are the most successful in life; they have enough wits to elbow their way through a crowd, but not so much as to make them shy away from the podium. The most pernicious specimens in any society are always the so-called uneducated intellectuals: the mediocre minds and phoney-schooled workplace preachers with artistic ambitions gone sour, or the megalomaniac dwarfs who inflate their egos with bullshit. That is why we never see truly cultivated people as prime ministers, just air hostesses and solicitors.

Although I spoke only equine Polish, I chose to talk to Jacek instead of that oaf of a blacksmith. The farmer was a calm and brave man whose serene temperament reminded me of Jón in Módárkot, a man who appears later in my story. He was a prisoner in his own home here and was forced to slave away for soldiers who were a lifetime younger than he was, had occupied his land, sent his sons running, and killed his wife in the shed. But from his manner one could see that his soul hadn't been conquered. He undertook all his chores at a sluggish pace because inside himself he had managed to conceal his vast green pastures, which the Germans had never set their eyes on and over which their war birds would never fly. It was an immense property; it therefore wasn't easy for him to move about the house and kitchen with all that inside him.

They came back at midnight, Hartmut and Second Karl. I waited with a calculated, nonchalant air on a chair in the kitchen, stooped over a Polish crossword, with my cleavage on view and bare knees in the air, by the open door, like an amateurish whore. But none of it came to anything. There was a dark cloud hanging over Hartmut when he appeared in the hallway, and he headed straight for the bathroom. My knees were starting to hurt when he finally reappeared. He cast a furtive glance down the corridor and into the kitchen at the bare-thighed tart who was sitting there, but I got nothing from that glimpse. It was fleeting and vacant. He then walked into his room and locked himself in. And I could dismantle my whorish pose.

I played around with translating his name and discovered that Hartmut means gallant, and Herzfeld, heart field. It couldn't have been better. As the days passed, I totally lost myself in that field and aimlessly roamed through it like a disoriented field sparrow, rummaging and pecking for that bloody heart hidden between the blades of grass. I was insanely in love. In the morning I came across him in the hall as he was standing in front of a small mirror on the wall, combing his hair back. I froze on the spot with a gaping jaw and couldn't snap out of it until he had completed his task and glanced at me, flashing a smile and winking before he rushed past. I staggered into my room and had to lie down, knocked out by his cologne. Day and night I could think of nothing else but that pure forehead, that straight nose, and those soft, thick lips, high cheekbones and strong chin. And yes, those eyebrows ... so perfectly drawn! Oh my God, his eyes ... His hair was blond but always darkened by water combing or the shadow of his cap.

Yes. There was some shadow over him, if not inside him, that I couldn't quite fathom. Wasn't it fun being an officer in the most victorious army history had seen? No, there was something troubling the Valiant Heart of the Field. The look in his eyes seemed to be somehow drowned in ink, and although he had a bright smile, it reached me like a watery glimmer from the depths of a dark cave. Bit by bit I realised that this beautiful boy had lost all joy for living. The little he had shown me on the first day seemed to have completely evaporated. One night he left the farm and came back with a heavy brow. Next day: no more questions about Iceland. Just rye bread with butter. He grew paler and more taciturn by the day. But it must have been the poet in him. Isn't that what poets were normally like? With paper-white faces and heads full of ink?

My crush on him, though, magnified in direct proportion to the darkening of his soul. I cared nothing about his mood, so long as I had his face in front of me. Love is sparked by two things: surface and substance. For a first-timer, the former was more than enough. I went out to the stable to talk it over with my best friend Czerwony; he was disapproving of it all.

78

SS Kiss

1944

Finally I burst into his room one night. He sat at a desk in the corner by his bed, in a sleeveless white T-shirt by an open window. Somewhere in the distant darkness a train rattled across a meadow. Small flies fluttered in the light above his pen like interested readers. He looked up but showed no surprise, as if it were the most natural thing in the world for a lovesick child to erupt into his room.

'Are . . . are you writing?'

'Yes. Scribbling really.'

'What are you writing? A letter?'

'No.'

'Can I see?'

'See?' he answered with a snorting laugh.

That was enough for me to step in and close the door behind me.

'What are you doing here?' I asked.

'Here?'

'Yes, on this Polish farm. Why aren't you in the war?'

'What are you doing here?'

'Me? I . . . it was a horse that brought me here. I have nothing to do with this place. I'm just satisfied . . . so long as I have a bed.'

He eyed me for a minute, then finally said, 'Herra María?'

He had called me that on the first night and chuckled every time he repeated it in Icelandic or German: '*Herr* Marie.'

'Yes.'

'Grab a seat. I just have to . . . finish here.'

He turned on his chair and stooped over the paper. Despite his broad shoulders and strong upper arms, his back seemed delicate and his trunk narrowed at the waist. Instead of sitting on a chair on my side of the rudimentary bed in the corner, I approached him from behind, halted at the end of the bed, and tried to peer at the pages on the desk. He was either writing a fan letter to Hitler or composing a poem. Sensing my presence, he turned his head without lifting it and chuckled through his nostrils again.

'Isn't your underwear marked?'

'Huh?' he said, without looking up.

'You're not wearing an SS vest?'

'SS? Yes, sure. All our clothes are army clothes, underwear, socks, shoes. Everything.'

'So why isn't there a swastika on the vest?'

All of a sudden there was anger in his voice.

'A swastika on my vest? There is a swastika on my vest. There's a swastika on the paper. There's a swastika on the pen. But they didn't manage to get one into the ink! They couldn't do it! It's so heavy that it sank all the way to the bottom!'

He was almost shouting those last words. The door opened, and the big-nosed Karl stuck his head through the gap.

'Is everything all right, sir?'

'Yes,' answered the commander, 'fine, just close the door.'

The handsome officer of my dreams bent over the desk but had stopped writing and buried his face in his hands. I toyed with the idea of escaping through the open window. What had I done? Knocked him off balance? Why was he talking about the swastika like that? Wasn't he a true Nazi? How could an SS officer allow himself to shout such things, such blasphemy? Was he writing a suicide note? He was still sitting there with his beautiful face in his hands. I hadn't a clue of what to say or how to react and therefore started to peel off my clothes, a solution that has served women well since time immemorial. I pulled the white blouse over my head, loosened my skirt, and took off my dirty socks. He straightened up and placed his hands on the table but didn't turn on his chair, just sat dead still, listening to the silent sound of a stocking being pulled down a leg. Then he picked up his pen and started to write again. I freed my breasts from my vest. Flies busied themselves under the working light that illuminated every hair on his left shoulder and neck. I felt the hairs were dancing to the rhythm of my every move, as if they were being charged by some precious electricity. Still I halted my stripping at the panties and stood on the rug at the end of the bed a moment, in nothing but my briefs, like a small nation at the negotiation table.

My left breast stood in the shadow cast by his right shoulder, but my right breast smiled at the light, making my pyramid-shaped nipple glisten. Oh, how small and innocent it was.

I carried on standing there and listened to the muted sound of his pen scratching the paper, until I grew shy and crawled into the bed under that thin quilt that must have been marked SS somewhere. He turned to me, put his pen away, and snorted again.

'How old are you, Fräulein?'

'Fifteen.'

'Fifteen?'

'Yes, I'll be fifteen at the end of the summer.'

'Then you're fourteen now.'

'Yes. But fourteen in war is like eighteen in peacetime.'

'Says who?'

'I've heard it. I'm not a virgin.'

Oh, the humiliations of love. The child from Breidafjördur had turned into a Nazi whore.

'I've even been raped.'

He stood up and lay down beside me, on the quilt, smelling of vanilla and talcum powder, and gently stroked my hair as if I were dead and he was in mourning for me, a Polish country girl who had killed herself in a dirty canal like Hamlet's Ophelia. In light of this, I was allowed to be delirious.

'You're so handsome. The most handsome man in the history of mankind. You are . . . can I call you Hartmut? I've had to say "sir" to so many people for more than four years now and I'm so tired of it. In Iceland you only "sir" people in hats, and not the ones who wear caps. But here they even say "sir" to their executioners. I heard one screaming: "No, for God's sake, sir, don't shoot!" just before he was killed, by a high wall.

'Do you mind? Can I call you . . . Hartmut?'

'In Germany you can be on first-name terms with a man only after you've kissed him.'

'Really?'

'No, not really.' He smiled. A broken smile. What was tormenting him? I couldn't allow myself to ask him all those questions or find answers for them, because now he was looking into my eyes. He put down his smile and vanished into seriousness and love. We kissed. A kiss marked SS.

79

Morning with a Dead Man

1944

The Polish nocturnal butterflies sang their song, and trains came and went. In the space of a night I'd turned fifteen, sixteen, and seventeen. I fell asleep all caressed and sore from bliss and woke up when a clap of thunder released its downpour. Hartmut stretched out to close the window. We lay there like a loving father and daughter and listened to the sky pounding the earth, a hundred million drops lashing against it. We had no future, but the moment kept us tight together, and what was life but a morning hour in the arms of a man? I started to think about all my misfortunes, the days of hunger on the streets of German cities, long nights in underground shelters, and the rape in a Polish cabin, and it all seemed so trivial now that I lay with this handsome man on the peak of ecstasy.

'I was lying. I was a virgin. That was my first time.'

'You . . . what a rascal you are. And are you maybe thirteen years old?'

'Yes. I'm going to be confirmed next spring,' I said in a mousy voice, waiting for him to finish laughing. 'What were you writing?'

'Nothing.'

'Yes, what? You've got to tell me. I gave you my virginity; you owe me.'

'A poem.'

'I thought so. A poem? About what?'

'Oh, just . . . some old-fashioned, romantic nineteenth-century nonsense.'

'Don't be like that. Can I read it?'

'No.'

'Are you allowed to write poems if you're in the SS?'

'No. Only kill.'

'What's it like . . . to kill?'

'He who kills dies. He who is killed lives.'

I didn't quite get the answer, but stored it to understand it later.

'But aren't you . . . don't you believe in the . . . swastika, then?'

'Do you think Christ believed in the cross?' He blushed as he said this, felt ashamed of the comparison. 'Forgive me, I'm no Christ.' (At this point the newly kissed girl felt like correcting this good man.) 'And yet I'm still . . . yes . . . I can say that I'm being crucified.'

Outside, the rain lashed against the windowsill, fields and countryside. Dawn broke feebly, watery grey upon the horizon, like a shoal of herring in the ocean darkness.

'Have you ever . . . killed anyone?' I whispered into his bristles.

'Only myself.'

'What do you mean?'

'I'm a condemned man.'

'Huh? What for?'

'Cowardice.'

We were silent a long time. I sat up in the bed to contemplate the moment. He was staring at the ceiling, the whiteness, and I at him, the white in his two eyes. The rain subsided as the light grew. The yellowing windowsill, as hard and thick as stone, gave off a peculiar glow in the grey dawn. And somewhere Czerwony was standing in his four-legged sleep, good old workhorse.

'Why . . . we can just flee! Here out of the window!'

'Flee? Where is it possible to flee to? There are eyes everywhere in Hitler's Reich. A friend of mine was killed on the run, like an animal, shot in the back. Besides, I'd rather look my . . . my mistakes in the eye.'

'Your mistakes? It's not because of your mistakes that the army wants to kill you. We can escape to Iceland!'

All of a sudden I saw a man standing in the cabbage patch outside the window. I covered my chest. He had a rifle on his back and glanced over his shoulder. Our eyes met for the briefest of seconds before he looked towards the woods, but his glance managed to express a whole sentence: I despise you, you little whore, you and your nocturnal pleasures, but I won't torture you to death, I'll look away, because a condemned man is entitled to enjoy the fruits of life before the final curtain falls, the fruit that will then rot as soon as he's gone, ha-ha-ha. (The eyes are generally far more eloquent than the mouth and tongue.)

'Who is it? Karl?' Hartmut asked.

'Second Karl,' I said, lying down again and cuddling up to him.

'Yes. They take it in shifts.'

80

Rose Blood

1944

I was restless. I wouldn't give up. I would save this man and take him to the warm shelter of Iceland, go home on the MS *Gullfoss*, covered in SS kisses, with the most handsome man in history on my arm. It wasn't just the Jews who had to be saved from Hitler's Holocaust.

I discussed the issue with Czerwony. He was as negative as always but pointed out that Jacek the farmer was the most skilled horse castrator in the district, as he himself had experienced firsthand, and he still had all the equipment required to squeeze the testicles out of a beast. I enlisted the services of the horse doctor, told Jacek all about my daring plan in the sixteen words of Polish I knew. Hartmut came in to me in the evening with a small folder crammed with letters and documents.

'These are letters from my mother and other things.'

'No, you keep those. Tomorrow we'll escape.'

'Tomorrow?' he asked. 'I'd still like you to have these, if—'

'Don't say if. History wasn't built on ifs, Mum says.'

The following morning I slipped into Karl's room, where he was still asleep with his big nose in a bed of dry sweat. He woke up to the smell of chloroform that immediately put him back to sleep again. For certainty I rubbed the cloth into his face. What a daredevil I was. Down in the yard, Hartmut approached Second Karl with the same substance from behind. The soldier immediately crumbled. We made a run for it, heading north, straight towards the field, me in front, dragging him out towards love and freedom, until a gunshot pulled him away from me. He lay there, face-down in the wet mud as blood spurted out of a small orifice in his back. I looked back and saw Jacek standing at the corner of the stable with a haggard face, as he lowered his rifle.

I threw my arms into the air. How naive I'd been. How stupid. Yes, a fourteen-year-old Icelandic idiot. Shoot me, shoot me, I thought, and I prayed to the Almighty Farmer Above to make his Polish colleague send me a bullet across the meadow, which wasn't actually a meadow but just a field. But my prayer fell on deaf ears. They were too busy dispatching other souls to heaven. Inside the walls of the farm, two other shots were heard. And there was no doubt that each of the shots contained the scream of a soul.

I dropped my arms and managed to shift the attention away from my small life to the death of a bigger man. Or perhaps he wasn't dead? With great effort, I managed to turn him on his back. His face was more beautiful than ever before, even though it was smudged with mud. A glistening black ant scuttled across his forehead. I'd seen a man blow life into a suffocated woman in an underground shelter once. And that is what I tried to do now. Like Juliet to Romeo. And when I could not manage to blow life into him, he blew his soul into me. I gave up and swallowed. His face now looked like marble, white and cold, sculpted by Michelangelo. Oh, why did such beauty have to disappear? Oh, my first and only. Groping through his breast pocket, I found the little folder. Like buns that were still warm on an extinguished fire, these papers lay on a heart that had ceased to beat. I opened the bundle and skimmed through a folded sheet of paper marked with skulls, swastikas and 'SS':

Once I had a rose so red
It shone as bright as light.

And like a guiding star it led
Me through the darkest night.

I wore that flower on my chest
And started the road ahead.
There came a crossing, I had to rest.
My beautiful rose was dead.

From rose's petals, rose's blood
trickled down my breast.
I watched it, buried in the mud,
Till darkness brought me rest.

Till darkness brought me rest. Hartmut Herzfeld (1913–1944).

The war tourist continued on her way. The SS bride cried across the fields and into the woods. And sent a sad farewell to Czerwony. While the Nazi whore mourned her scheme, the island girl thought of home, and of Mum and Dad, wherever they were, with their lonely hearts. On one of the pages in the folder, I could read my father's name: *Hans Henrik Björnsson, 100/1010 G4. 17. Bat. Leicht. Inf. Gross Deutschland, Div. Süd, G. Kursk.* Written in Hartmut's handwriting.

I had told him about Dad. He had promised to make inquiries about where this Icelander had ended up in the war. They had a telegraph transmitter in one of the rooms. But Hartmut had said there was no definite information. What did that word mean then? *Kursk.* Was that a code word for 'presumed dead'?

I swallowed the lump in my throat and crouched under a tree and called on the wild boars, wolves and bears to come and feast on sorrow-marinated girlie shanks. That bed of pine needles gave off a good smell. And now I pull that sweet and sad tree fragrance from the depths of my buried being, like a thread of gold out of a heap of dung.

The war is probably best described as follows: you experience what is called the 'worst moment of your life' about five times a day.

That night I called on a middle-aged country couple. The man with a Polish-sausage paunch sniffed the Nazi scent on me and sent me to the sty. Then he showed up in the night with a thirst for revenge and lust for virgin flesh. I immediately sensed where he was going but managed to prevent it by turning his assault into my handiwork, something a woman in Erfurt had taught me. I will spare the reader the details, and the story of my winter. It was a long, cold nightmare, but not as bad as the summer that followed, not bad enough to be recounted.

81

Pen Pals

2009

Aldon the Aussie is writing to tell me he's furious. He'd been under the impression that he and Linda were headed for the altar, but now shares the bad news that Bod has dropped out of the Melbourne tournament. He has taken the mention of a *lover* really badly and is now organising a trip to London. 'We need to talk.' The two buddies, Bod and Aldon, beg Linda to meet them at the May Fair Hotel earlier than planned. 'You can't do this to us. Bod is up to eighteen eggs in the morning and twelve in the evening.' I guess he'll end up with ovaries in his scrotum.

Then I get other e-mails personally addressed to me. I'm in touch with all kinds of people around the globe. Whiles the time away.

Susan Sommersworth is a sunshine lady from the West Coast of the US, one of those women who is in a relationship with her own hair and attends to it with the same dedication other people reserve for their pets or a sick partner. She's a pretty tedious pen pal, but I can't help answering her after, on a trip to Buenos Aires, she made a detour for me to the Chacarita Cemetery, tracked down a tiny grave, and laid down a flower. She's ever so chirpy and nauseatingly positive and wants to know everything about Iceland, sends me whole armies of sunny yellow smileys, and will no doubt be buried with a smirk stuck to her face. I don't know where the Yanks get all this cheerfulness from, but I guess Smilism beats defunct Stalinism. My Bob developed squinty eyes from all that Yankee smiling, laughed at everything I said, and always pointed his finger at me as if to emphasise that it was me and no one else but me that was being clever and funny. Oh, he was great, Bob was.

Now that we have the net, I can look him up. Robert McIntyre. I can't find him on Facebook but good old Yahoo! gives me sixteen thousand results. They mostly turn out to be about his namesake, a Scottish motorcycling champ born in 1928, but there are a few things here and there. My Bobby set up a film company sometime around 1970, then published a book, *On the B-Side of Life: My Years in Beijïng, Brussels, Berlin and Buenos Aires*. Might there be some mention of me in those pages? Here I can see that someone has found it in the middle of the Amazon jungle and read it. Gives the book one star. I can just picture my wrinkled Bob getting all excited about that; he embraced everything with enthusiasm, even when I called him a taxi. It would be nice to be able to send him a line, if he remembers his Ice Lady. He ought to; we were practically glued together every day for nine months.

Yes, I remember it so well. We were sitting together in an Irish pub close to the Plaza de Mayo, me and my masturbation coach Heidi, when he blew in all squinty-eyed with zit scars on his cheeks: 'Where are you from, girls?'

'We're from Dykeland,' I answered, thinking that would be enough to get rid of him. But he was quick on the uptake.

'Yeah? I've been there! Beautiful country but a bitch of a language.'

He said he wanted to import jazz to Argentina, tango was dead, asked us if we wanted to come to a concert the next day. I was going through the most difficult weeks in my life, but Heidi managed to drag me along. Three weeks later I'd go to New York with Bob. He was pretty well off. Although his father was a professor of literature, his mother descended from money, the daughter of some inventor of

Italian origin. I was charmed by his energy and enthusiasm and so badly needed it, having mourned my child for so many months, but I always awaited that *moment of seriousness* an Icelandic girl believed lay at the core of every love. But it never came, and we kept on circling around it on a plane.

I had probably experienced true love only once, love at a thousand degrees. It lasted for only one night. And many people got less than that. Years later, another kind of love came along, which lasted a bit longer. It was the love of a lifetime that didn't survive death, however.

The time has come to tell that story.

82

Iceland

1974

The summer of '74. What a time to be alive. It was a jubilee summer, and the sun shone every day, every night. God, how beautiful Iceland was back then. And it was so good to be back home.

I'd had enough of partner switching and my endless globe-trotting. After I'd called a taxi for Post-Jón, I got it into my head to move to Paris with the three boys, aged eleven, six and one. I hired a deathly pale babysitter and got myself a job at the Icelandic embassy. Boulevard Haussmann, *bonjour*. My family wasn't happy about the move, but still my dear paternal uncle Henrik got me the job because in those days he was the Icelandic ambassador in Paris with a jurisdiction that stretched from the Tuileries Garden to Tunis.

I still had France on my list. No one can consider herself a woman of the world without putting herself through the ordeal of Paris first. The older boys, Haraldur and Ólafur, went to a fine school and blabbed in French there with Pierre and Maurice, but Magnús was put into a crèche. They were pretty primitive in those days, crèches, and for a whole winter the child was fed on nothing but bread. Prince Potato still carries that baguette fat around with him to this day. We lived in the fifteenth arrondissement, nice and clean, all the streets lined with food. I knocked over ten melons on my sprint to the metro that ran over the district on stilts.

Life was good in Paris.

The city is so beautiful that every tramp feels he lives in Versailles, and the language so lyrical that every solicitor thinks he's a poet. But this creates arrogance. No other city I know has produced such an obscene number of snobs as Paris. It took me a long time to get used to that. But I wasn't totally immune to it myself and was classically starstruck when I strolled past Helmut Newton at the Deux Magots or met his majesty Sartre in a seedy bar.

The job suited me fine, being the polyglot-toasting creature that I was, and it did me no harm to be a member of the Björnsson family in the Icelandic foreign service, the very own niece of *l'ambassadeur lui-même*. A poet friend nicknamed me the Ambassadame, and of course I should have been that instead of a mere secretary, but I was a woman, used to taking care of children, so it was easy for me to add another. Because Uncle Henrik was soon transferred to Moscow, only to be replaced by a stale old politician, one of those men who only ever lifted a finger to salute himself and who in Paris was like a seagull in a puffin colony, alone and speechless, his only mission seemed to be to keep the chauffeur occupied. Almost every morning when I traipsed into the gentleman's office with the paperwork, he was on the phone to Iceland with his cronies back home, who had to blow off steam about their Lefty government. Men have always looked on their chatter as work, whereas we women postpone all that chin-wagging until the evening.

Back home my decision to move abroad with my children was deemed so significant that I ended up on the cover of an Icelandic gossip mag: ALONE WITH KIDS IN PARIS. A lot of Icelandic women went to France in those days, but few of them had children before they got locked into castles by counts and marquis. Many a jewel had been stolen from the crown of Iceland.

I lived in relative poverty, of course, but what money I had I splashed out on the au pair, perfume and Jean Marc. He was the worst squanderer I'd met in those days, one of those wizards who always managed to fill his glass after showing his empty pockets a few moments before. My children were so well acquainted with my catalogue of Jóns by then that they themselves nicknamed the Frenchman the '*Ah oui* Jón' because Jean Marc was from Avignon. He was a decade older than me. At first he was *charmant*, but three months into the relationship I realised he was actually nothing more than a pauper with a university degree, more of a moocher than a smoocher, as he sat there sponging off us for eighteen months.

I had to content myself with being called Erra because when the language god gave the French an alphabet, the letter *h* got locked up in the library and the French have suffered from its loss ever since. To them, hair is *air* and a heel is an *eel*.

I finally got into the Palais Garnier, and every month I strode up the stairs and corridors of the Louvre to see *The Raft of the Medusa*, *The Wedding Feast at Cana*, and my favourite, the Sun King himself, by Rigaud. I inhaled that metro odour and dined my way from one neighbourhood to the next, into the darkest *impasses* and *passages*, where I sometimes had encounters beyond the pale of biographical licence and then felt I had landed in a not so overly boring art-house film. In my memory, Paris lingers like an immovable feast in my soul. The years I spent there were a holiday from life, three wonderful winters in the company of pixies, because they're so different, those French *monsieurs*, minuscule, with their pretty profiles, smooth talking and elfin in all their seriousness. Humour isn't easily found in them, no more than any other word beginning with *h*, but their sense of poetry is second to none, and this they have chiselled into stone and cobble: it's not bad to enter a city that offers two ways towards the *rue du Paradis* – the *rue de la Fidélité*, on one hand, and the *passage du Désir* on the other.

But by the spring of '74, I'd had enough. I was forty-five years old and I hadn't settled down anywhere. I'd seen enough countries in my life. And enough men. Enough etiquette and diplomacy. I decided to go home before my soul got numbed by champagne and French menus. I'd had a belly full of three-course colon pampering and was starting to desperately long for crappy Icelandic food: a bad hotdog and lukewarm Coke out in the glacial rain underneath the light yellow gable of a sports centre in some ugly village out east. After spending half my life abroad, I yearned for my country in all its crassness. All its women's-club coffee, cake mania, cola binges and cold sauce orgies. All its wind and rain and bitter, grumpy men. All its myopic culture and Worst German architecture with its endless parking fields and petrol temples.

It was actually so strange that in the beauty of Paris, which never meets you without her makeup, it was the rudeness of Reykjavík I missed the most, the ugliness and its rough weather. I couldn't stand all those flowery balconies any more, baroque palaces and quaint, arty squares, not to mention the frigging fountains. This lava longing must have had something to do with the ugliness of our land, because Iceland obviously isn't all beautiful. Many parts of the highlands and around Snæfellsjökull are very ugly, for example, not to mention the Reykjanes Peninsula and Mount Hellisheidi, that uncooked gruel of gales and lava. No wonder tourists seek out these barren, desolate places, far from the standard EU beauty of stone cathedrals, vineyards and the apple-seller lady in a green bodice. I wanted to go home to the miserable drizzle of the lava fields.

Most of all, though, I missed my dear people, that collection of idiots at the far end of the ocean. I missed the raw communication and informal, febrile nature of Icelanders; the adolescent lives that are lived on this immature island that doesn't know how to behave any more than its inhabitants do. I was sick and tired of continental good manners, all those *bitteschön* and *seal-voo-plays*, and those tight-assed French gentlemen who opened car doors for you while their minds slid up your uterus. I'd even started to think fondly of Icelanders' pushiness in lines and traffic. I was dying to go home to jostle around stores and spit in flower beds.

I dragged the boys home and dumped them on my friend Gútta, while I toured my country, warming and breaking hearts. I literally gulped down the country and the nation, which, as it happened, was celebrating an anniversary under the sunny skies of Thingvellir that July: it had been 1,100 years since the First Settlement. The Parisian lady traded in her tailored coat for an Icelandic jumper, the woman of the world was just as much at ease in the West Fjords as she was in Versailles. At a country ball I sat smoking a Viceroy with a bulldozer driver while they showered us with soda and schnapps, and the band played the Viking version of a Beatles song. I'd never felt better. I was simply happy.

And I'd already thrown up twice when a new wave of schnapps washed up a middle-aged sailor on my drunken shore – a brute with sideburns and broken teeth and fingers so thick they could barely fit in his hands, even though he'd sliced one off. The man was so drunk he couldn't even utter his own name and kept on repeating the same phrase: 'Have you ever seen a sea goat?' as he swayed on his chair like a sailor in stormy waters. 'Are you my sea goat?' But finally the waves subsided, the man steadied in his chair and, staring into his glass, he suddenly started to sing:

Oh, Mary, oh, Mary!
My chubby little fairy,
Put your little berry
Into my open mooouuuth!

His voice was like a rum-and-aftershave cocktail. The band lost its thread, and some people turned their heads; a middle-aged woman smiled. At the end of the performance, the man slowly slid to one side, like a felled tree. I managed to grab him before he hit the soda-sticky floor. He recovered his senses, laid his head on my shoulder, enveloped my skinny yellow fingers in his sailor's paw, and refused to let go.

83

Bæring

1974

His name was Bæring, son of Jón. A Bolungarvík specimen from head to toe. Helmsman on the *Vesti ÍS 306*, he had spent half his life standing on the bridge of a ship, with an undulating horizon in the window.

And I, who wasn't going to tie myself down again. We spent a wild weekend together in his huge house and hit it off with a bang. I even shed a few tears when he said goodbye to me on the pier (he'd signed up for a long fishing trip) and then phoned the boys to tell them to hop on a plane: Mum had settled back in the West Fjords.

A week later I had filled Bæring's place with my gang. It was a typical house of that period, like a garage with glasses. It was a pretty weird change for Haraldur, Ólafur and Magnús, to finish school in Paris in the spring and start again in the autumn on the edge of the Arctic Circle. Hello, gloves and hats . . . No cafés, no metro, no *menu fixe*. And no glances or daily flirts. Just weary mothers with plastic blue berets in the freezing plant.

I got the old camera going again, though, and took a whole series of pictures of men down in the fishing huts, but then forgot about the camera while I was waiting for them to send me some printing paper from the south. Years later I sat drinking with a conceptual artist who was blown away by this dusty camera, which stored fifteen fishermen from Bolungarvík, anno 1974. 'This camera is a work of art all by itself!' he exclaimed, and he wanted to put the thing in an exhibition as a conceptual art piece, with his name on it. Then I blew my top and assured him that there was skill in those pictures, two years of study in Hamburg with all the maternal sacrifices and Beatle kisses that entailed.

I guess my spirits were dampened by this new housewife existence. Long winter days were spent sitting on a stool in the living room, smoking Pall Malls and staring out at the ocean through the huge window. I could sit like that for days on end. The island girl had missed the ocean and enjoyed seeing how time kept on drawing on it with a pencil that was sometimes sharp, sometimes blunted. In Iceland the sea is never the same. Currents are constantly changing, and every day is wacko. Occasionally my sailor would call me from the marine radio to tell me to have the bottles ready for his landfall, one a day.

Hitler's egg slept in the drawer of the bedside table.

It's wonderful to raise children out in the country, the cliché goes, but it was my children who started to raise me. For fifteen years, in my rebellion against male dominance, feminine instincts and historical trends, I had struggled against the fact that I was a mother, but here I was almost buried in the role of a housewife: the wife of a sailor in a coastal village. I was at home when they went to school, I was at home when they came home, and I was at home in between. I was always at home, goddamn it, barely left the house for four years.

And all for a man I couldn't even see through the window. Who only appeared once every three weeks like a seaborne Santa Claus. The lust was so great I normally had to pack my boys off to Bæring's brother when the sailor was on shore leave. But the lust was as short-lived as it was great: by the third day I couldn't wait for the boat to take this cargo away from me again.

I loved him when he was shore bound, but adored him even more when he sailed away.

84

Housewife

1978

He was a festive fellow. Short and strong, with a white crown on his head, pitch-black sideburns and a deadly charming smile, which derived all its power from that quarter of a front tooth he was missing. He was constantly on the rise, his body always seemed to be full of baking powder. With his tight belly, puffed-up torso and bloated cheeks, this man seemed built to last for ever.

It was so beautiful to watch him smoke. His right hand was missing a middle finger ('it died in the Easter storm'), but no gap was visible because his other fingers were so thick and prominent, yet that was where he held his cigarette and lifted it to his mouth. I always got the feeling that he sipped on his cigarettes as if they were straws. He normally kept the smoke inside him a good long while, until people started to wonder where it had gone – had it come out below? But then it would finally reappear through the nose, calmly and majestically, like white smoke out of the Vatican chimney.

Bæring Jónsson was fifty when we met, but everyone considered him to be younger than I, who by then was well marked by my seven lives. I was also stupid enough to think that this man was my last chance. My Bæring was a jolly man, but there was a menacing crater lurking inside him that would emerge from the depths of his soul on the fourth day like a boat engineer raising his oil-black head through the hatch door.

The first winter, I always waited for him down on the pier, trembling, with lipstick on. He was generally nuts by the time he reached the shore.

'There you are! Where have you been?'

'Oh, just here . . . ha-ha . . . up at the house.'

'I've missed you. You were hiding from me!'

'Erm . . . no . . .' I'd answer hesitantly, still thrown by his absurd sense of humour.

'Well then, have you been to the off licence?'

'Yeah.'

'And did you buy some mixers, too?'

'Yeah, Canada Dry and orange.'

'And some whore-ange? Ha-ha-ha.'

He'd always have a drink before we started, even at ten in the morning, and once the ritual was over, the proper boozing started, lasting well into the night. I couldn't always keep up with him, but I've often enjoyed the company of drunken men. Then he conked out and slept for forty hours. Then the second day of his shore leave would begin, a repeat performance of the first. He was an energetic lover, though finesse wasn't exactly his forte. As a young man he had been married to a woman who now lived up in Ísafjördur, and they had a daughter called Lilja, who was now twenty and would pop in for a drink from time to time.

And I also had some relatives up there, from my mother's paternal side, who still lived in Ísafjördur. I spent one Sunday showing off my boys to three strong-handed women who repeated one after the other: 'It was sad to hear about the coffee man, your mother's husband, he went rather swiftly.' Mum had had a second husband, Fridrik Johnson, a coffee merchant she met after the war, and he passed away in 1964, in the middle of a phone call. Mum held him a big and fancy funeral, and my father was the first to enter the church and the last one to leave the reception. A few months later they were back together. He cried the whole first year.

'But they're all right, aren't they? Is your father doing OK?'

That's how people talked about Dad. Is your father doing OK? Yes, he's OK, apart from the fact that he's shooting small kids out the window and is currently designing a gas chamber in the basement, but otherwise just fine.

It was fun for me to move to the west, where Icelanders are at their most Icelandic. Tenacious and humble marathon boozers. Naturally, I would have preferred Breidafjördur, but most of the houses there were deserted now. It all happened in a flash. As soon as phones came to the islands, people abandoned them for the mainland. A thousand-year-old civilisation drew to an end.

Despite my string of Jóns and all his bullshit, my Bæring was the most bearable of them all. He was *el hombre*, although I'm not sure I actually ever loved him. How could a person like me have fallen for an ocean lout like him? A man who had never been anywhere but out at sea and never read a book that wasn't an Icelandic biography, a literary genre I abhorred. But if we managed to forget our differences, sparks started to fly, and the fun engine was hot-wired into motion. I had finally met a man who was crazier than I was. What's more, I'd had a more difficult life than he'd ever had and fed on his joie de vivre like an exhausted crab that has finally reached a shore. And the more I fed on it, the more he produced. My laughter turned him into a star in our own hilarious universe: he played the lead and ran straight up from the pier to the house with a brand-new repartee each time, a love song he had composed in his cabin:

Oh, Herra! Oh, Herra! My heroine, my queen, my czar!
Tell me! Oh, tell me! Tell me who you are!
Are you from the constituency?
Or maybe Berlin, Germany?
Are you the grandchild of a king?

I don't really give a thing.
Just step into the riiiiing!

He could rattle on like that and was at his best until the drink took over. Love grew more numb with every sip, every kiss became oppressive, every caress a one-man sport. On the last day, he woke up in a vile rage with an aching hangover. The boat engineer stuck his engine-oiled black head through the hatch door and started ordering me about the house.

'You fucking presidential slut!'

I was scared and locked myself in the toilet. He banged on the door until the panelling caved in and he had to board the boat with a broken hand.

Three days later he returned on a US Air Force helicopter with an elephantine hand. He extended his sick leave indefinitely, and, humiliated, he was another man: we had happy days with a good family life. Bæring was at home and got to know the boys, he arm-wrestled with them with his good arm and let Haraldur win. I enjoyed having a man who loved all my sons equally because they weren't his own, and ate everything I served him. A man who woke up before me and made coffee for two. Came laughing into the bedroom and rounded off every day with a mighty 'skin song.'

Life was finally beautiful.

85

Hrefnuvík

1980

I found myself out in the shed with Hitler's egg, placed it in an old wooden box, and hid it under a trough. It was the end of June, so the stables were empty, apart from our ram, the one and only Sigvaldi, who was still in there. I paused by him on my way out. He stared at me stiff and strong-horned, with a macho glint in his eyes. They were all the same. And that's where they all should have been kept. Locked up in a sty.

The generator was silent, it was a beautiful bright evening, but there were still some small waves, dregs of the afternoon wind, breaking on the shores of the vast Djúpid fjord. The nocturnal stillness was gradually approaching, and a calm had already descended on the glacial lagoon beyond. Kaldalón, Cold Lagoon, is one of the most sacred places in Iceland. My goodness, how I could just stand there watching it, and my goodness, how it soothed me. As long as I could see across the fjord, every day was a Sunday to me. It was like an altarpiece in the landscape: the glacial tongue curved into the lagoon below and reflected in it almost daily, giving it the semblance of a holy picture.

Our farm stood on the edge of the rocky bay, a dwarf house painted in white with a green roof and a few eider drakes floating on the water's edge. It seemed to be high tide. This could so easily have been my final destination. Herra in the safe harbour of Hrefnuvík after decades of wandering across the open seas.

'Where were you?'

'I just . . . popped out.'

'Where?'

'Just, you know . . . to the sheep shed. Gave Sigvaldi some more food and—'

'I already fed him this morning. You shouldn't interfere. I don't want it! Understand? Were you chasing after Jón? You got the hots for Jón?'

'Huh?'

'Have you got the hots for Speedy Jón? What number would he be?'

'How do you mean?'

'Would he . . . will you be hitting the MILL-JÓN mark? Are you going to call him MILL-JÓN?'

'Are you talking about Jón from Módárkot?'

'You're a randy bitch.'

'Aren't you following the elections?'

'Randy bitch. You're such a nympho you're starting to have it off with the rams in the shed!'

'Where's the radio?'

'I bet you'll reproduce. Me-he-he! Herra Björnsson and Sigvaldi Kaldalón!' He thought that was funny. 'And will your offspring be a Kaldalón? Ha-ha. Won't it be a Kaldalón? No, what am I saying? You're passed the childbearing age. Nothing but empty rotten eggs inside you. And the stench, yuck.'

He sat on the edge of the sofa, stooped over the coffee table, bottles, glasses and an ash-sullied plate, and muttered those last words into his chest. With a bit of luck he would soon doze off.

'Where did you put the radio?' I repeated.

'Aren't you listening to me, woman?'

'Yes, I want to listen to the results.'

'Aren't you listening to ME? Listen to me when I speak!'

He sprang up from the sofa and nearly fell back into it again. He put down his cigarette and ran around the table. I tried to flee into the kitchen, but he managed to grab my arm; before I knew it, he squeezed me into a neck lock from behind. The smell was disgusting. Alcohol, tobacco and sweat. I'd given up being able to drink with him. They were hellish days. He tightened his grip and spluttered over my shoulder.

'Did you hear that, Herra? You should LISTEN TO ME, WOMAN! I don't want to be talking to the walls. Get your clothes off.'

He loosened his grip and I managed to breathe again. He threw me on the floor.

'Clothes off, I said.'

He hauled me towards the bedroom. It was a tiny cubbyhole that had been built for a dwarfy couple who had enjoyed a blissful marriage here, judging by the carpentry and lovingly painted boards. I had got used to this. It was best to obey and bite the bullet. It normally only took about fifteen minutes, probably longer now, though, he was so drunk.

It was strange, but I survived these daily horrors by picturing my boys, focusing hard on my children. Haraldur had moved south to the university, and Ólafur and Magnús were in the district school just three fjords away. I pictured them in their classes, swimming, leaning against walls. What were they leaning against the walls for? They hadn't started to smoke, had they? Oh, isn't he finished yet? Damn, it's bad today.

Maybe he thought so, too, because he couldn't manage to finish it off and finally stopped, kicking me onto the floor.

'Jesus, look at you. Like a sheared sheep. No wonder I can't come with a bag of wrinkles like you. Get out.'

I tried to clamber to my feet. God, how small I'd become. I was about the size of the folded shell of a tern's egg.

'Get out, I said!'

I staggered out and grabbed a blanket from the living room. He pushed me from behind, shouting, 'Out of the house! Get out of the house!'

Then he ripped the blanket off me, dragged me into the hallway, and from there hurled me into the garden, slamming the door behind me. I was a fifty-year-old woman with a battered soul and wounded body, deathly pale and naked, with grazed knees, and locked outside in the only five degrees the Icelandic summer had to offer that night. I hoisted myself to my feet and tried to get back into the house, when I heard him sliding the latch closed on the inside. I begged him at the window. Cried a good long while. My dearest Bæringur. My most generous, sweetest only love. I'll be good and do everything for you, if you'll only let me ih-hih-in.

Was he asleep? I looked around. The ocean wind was dying down, but I was so darned cold. Finally I decided to take shelter in the shed. A naked woman seeks wool. I hopped over tussocks and stones. The national highway was just above the farm, but fortunately there were no cars about. I entered on the barn side. The place was almost empty, apart from a small pile of straw in the far corner. All of a sudden I remembered the lambskin rug the previous owners had left behind. What had he done with that? I edged my way along one of the troughs. Sigvaldi stood there stiffly and stared at me. Yes, there it was. He had chucked it over one of the rafters. I grabbed the rug and walked back to the barn. I nested in the straw and wrapped myself in the fleece, black and crusty, but still a lot warmer than the hay. It made me think fondly of sheep. Blessed creatures.

And I stayed like that for the whole evening. A small, terrified woman who had lived half a century and learned nothing. I was still just the frightened girl who had been raped in a Polish cabin on the day of Iceland's independence and ran away in a fury. No, no . . . I was angry back then, now I was only scared and broken and drained of all life's energy. Come now, my young Herra, and give me back the courage I've lost. The courage I lost somewhere between Baires and Bæring. Yes, how had it happened? That a woman who, just a few years before, had swaggered down the Boulevard Saint-Michel, bursting with self-confidence and newly acquired Parisian arrogance, had fallen this low, naked and weeping in the five-degree corner of a barn in a forsaken part of Iceland, and allowed an illiterate juicer to transform her into such a little mouse that she didn't even have the guts to look a ram in the eye. I could hear him, the male with the horns. Moving around the sty. Oh, what a fate.

And to think that the fjord had seemed like such a dream to me. We were going to start a new and better life here and were both so relieved to free ourselves from old restrictions, housewife and sailor. Now we could live together in serenity and peace and take up farming, the most primordial lifestyle for any loving couple. The autumn had been wonderful and 'dry,' but then Advent had knocked on the door, with its holiday thirst. Bæring drove into town and returned with six bottles in a box. When they were finished, another six appeared with the ferry *Fagranes* on the pier. Five months of bottles and beatings ensued, and those bloody daily attacks that had become a constant in our household and followed the evening news with the same relentless regularity as the Icelandic weather forecast. On Good Friday I'd had enough and walked over to the next farm, Módárkot, in the pouring sleet. Jón the hermit wasn't one for asking questions but served me a hot toddy. Together we sat listening to some radio psalms as the night hammered against the windows. He wiped his glasses with Windex. 'It makes everything so shiny and bright,' he explained as I shed a tear into my toddy.

The next day I got a ride into Ísafjördur and spent the Easter weekend with my sturdy cousins Lára and Dadína. They lived together, loved receiving guests, and bombarded me with questions about the boys. On Easter Monday my Bæring appeared, as sober as a judge and totally adorable, and accepted some lamb leftovers. That evening the Easter holiday was over.

And I who had grappled with a whole world war had to admit that of all the conflicts one had to face, private battles were the worst. It's more reassuring to know that the enemy is in the next trench than on the pillow beside you.

At the end of May, the boys came home from school, two happy neon blonds. Since then, everything had been better, up until now, when they'd gone off to a football tournament. As soon as the bus picked them up, the bottle opened again.

All of a sudden I remembered the Hitler egg I had hidden in the shed. Maybe it wasn't a bad idea to . . . But before I could get it, I heard a creak in the door. The man stepped into the barn, slightly less drunk, but armed with his old hunting rifle. He sometimes shot razorbills at sea and ptarmigans on land. But now he was hungry for woman meat. I sprang up from under the fleece on the straw and ran across the barn and into the shed. He was too slow to react and shoot, but appeared along the trough, sniffing out his prey. The ram gawked at me when it saw me rise naked from the darkness of the sty with a golden sphere in my hand.

'If you dare,' I said in a trembling voice, and yes . . . almost forty years after my father had given me this weapon as a gift, I slipped a finger into the safety pin and prepared to pull. The moment had finally come.

'What's that? The perfume? Ha-ha . . . not only are you a randy bitch, you're nuts, too.'

'No, this isn't perfume. That was a lie. This is a hand grenade. A German grenade from the war.'

'What a load of horseshit.'

'Wait and see . . . If you so much as try to point that gun at me, I'll pull the pin . . .'

I was in such a state that not only was my voice shaking, but my hand and fingers were as well. And all of a sudden the pin broke! The bomb was alive.

'You and your war . . .'

I held the explosive at a good distance and mentally counted one, two, three, four, as I backed away towards the open door of the building. The floor was soft, covered in layers of sheep shit. Bæring raised his rifle and just as I was throwing the grenade at him a shot resounded. The egg was at the other end of the shed, and I got out in one piece, but the grenade hadn't exploded.

I dashed straight for the house. Before I reached the corner, another shot was fired. A window broke somewhere. I rushed in, locked the door, grabbed a jumper off a hook, and crawled under the table. I could hear him roaring outside. He wanted the 'presidential slut' to come out, open the door. Then he shot at another window and stuck his nozzle through the broken glass.

'Herra! Where are you?'

Yet another shot. It seemed to hit the armchair in the living room. I managed to wriggle my way forward on the ground, unseen, into the bedroom, found my pyjama trousers on the floor, and slipped into them while he wrestled with the window. Was he breaking in? 'Fucking hell,' I heard him curse. Then another shot and something shattering. I opened the bedroom window, clumsily leaped outside, and ran, limping, up to the road, heard him calling and shooting. A bullet ricocheted on a stone. I knew the sound from western films. What had my life turned into? I got across the road and threw myself behind a rock to catch my breath.

Why hadn't the grenade gone off? All of a sudden I heard him. He was up on the road.

'Herra. Forgive me, come now,' he gasped.

I peered over the rock and saw him standing in the middle of the road with no rifle. I retreated to another pillar of rock and picked up a stone. My foot was hurting me.

'Where's the rifle?'

'It's . . . down there. I . . . Herra, let's be good.'

His voice was slurred but then drowned in the sound of a vehicle driving over the blind hill behind him. Just then, a hunchbacked clunker of a Saab appeared. Bæring turned and moved to the side of the road, but the car pulled up beside him. A cheerful young man's voice asked for directions to the hunter's hut. I used the opportunity to slip along the road back towards the farm. Bæring looked at me as he was answering some question the kid asked about the elections. I found his rifle on the grasslands above the house and took it down with me for safety. Behind me, the car turned around and disappeared over the blind hill again. The tide had pulled out, exposing a vast shore rimmed with stones darkened by the sea and a silvery-white stillness across the bay. It was a stunningly beautiful night in the Djúpid, crowned by the majestic glow of Kaldalón.

'Herra!'

I turned and paused, feeling more secure with a weapon in my hands, in a dark blue sailor's jumper and chequered pyjama trousers. He edged his way down from the road towards the house, slowly. He was soon within a good shooting distance from me.

'Herra,' he said in a calm and sober voice. 'Forgive me, let's be friends. Don't be like this.'

I levelled the rifle to threaten him, but my arm was shaking.

'The ammunition is finished,' he said with self-assurance, stretching out his hand as he was approaching. 'Here, I'll take it.'

I lowered the weapon and backed away from him, down to the shore to the sound of pebbles. He followed. I turned and gripped the rifle with both hands; then, swinging it in the air, I threw it as far as I could. It smashed against the surface of the sea and sank below. Then I felt a paw on my shoulder and a roar in my ear.

'What the fuck are you doing, woman!?'

He turned me in a fury and dealt me a mighty punch with his clenched fist, striking my nose. I fell and struggled not to lose my senses, was soon crawling on all fours, and spat out a broken tooth. Blood dribbled over the stones. He looked around, trying to find new bashing opportunities, but I managed to break free, staggering towards the rocky reef to the west. I collapsed twice but got up again and the last time grabbed a stone to have in my hand. Soon I reached the end of the reef and stood there like a death-sentenced convict who had been granted one final thought. In front of me there was death, behind me the Djúpid fjord. He was moving in on me, a heavy brute in boots, with clenched fists and a fuming bull's snout. But when he was just a boat's length away from me, he slipped on a wet rock and knocked the back of his head against another and then lay there motionless. I waited a good while. How long? Half a minute? Half an hour? Then I approached him, slowly and trembling. I realised blood was oozing out of his head. Was he dead? Was my darling dead?

I bent over him. But then he suddenly muttered something, opened one eye, and lifted his right hand. I was so startled that I threw the stone I had forgotten in my hand at him. It smashed against his face, close to the temple, with a faint crack.

I was so distraught that I threw myself on him and tried to resuscitate him, stroking his cheeks and uttering some kind of words of love to him, the few drops I had left. But it was all to no avail. The man was dead.

I patted his chest like a nervous wreck and caught sight of the bloodstained stone and threw it into the sea. I then stood on the tip of the reef like a human lighthouse and looked across the bay over to the Kaldalón and felt I was strong, was cold, was me, was triumphant, was a woman. I had killed a man. That feeling lasted about half an hour because then I was cold and clambered over him, staggered back to the farm, and phoned Ísafjördur. They said they'd be there within two hours with an ambulance. So I'd finally called a taxi for him too, *el hombre*. I sank into the sofa and finished the bottle, then opened another and smoked cigarettes until my broken tooth stopped bleeding, and then finally switched on the radio.

Votes were still being counted; it was almost five. I landed in the middle of an interview: the reporter asked the newly elected president whether she considered this a significant step in the struggle for equal rights. Vigdís Finnbogadóttir had rarely sounded so proud.

'Yes, I think it is.'

Then I finally broke down and started to weep.

86

Bloway

1980

I cried for four weeks, lay in bed for the whole of July, a total wreck. But it wasn't the sorrow of a widow or the guilt pangs of a murderess. I guess I was mourning my life. Jón from Módárkot looked in on me, blessed be his memory. He had no telephone but had telepathic powers that kept him permanently connected to the truth and time, those two elements that tom-tommed between the rocks of our land, available to all, free of charge.

Jón always showed up when I was at my worst. Knocked twice and then walked in on his silent rubber soles, a supernatural man who smelled of Windex, with broken capillaries on his cheeks and nose, but otherwise pale with a drooping upper lip and ovine teeth. He never asked anything, but sat over me while the kettle did its job. Then he left a hot cup on the bedside table, with a Melrose's Tea label dangling at the end of a damp string. They nicknamed him Speedy Jón because of how slow he was to answer a question. If you asked him something in autumn, the answer would come in the spring. 'If I remember right, I think she was some Jósef's daughter.' His voice was particularly meticulous, almost feminine.

I said nothing about the circumstances of Bæring's death, just talked about rum and delirium. And there was no Sherlock Holmes in Ísafjördur. Everything was so conveniently primitive in those days. No combing the bay for guns or bloody stones. No one showing up with autopsy reports and demanding answers. People knew Bæring, where he came from, and what end he would come to. But whether I killed him or not, I'll obviously never know. Whether he wasn't a dying man already.

When does a woman kill a man and a man a woman?

I did go to Bolungarvík to bury the bull, however. Even though the local priest was a renowned 'burier,' with an appetite for corpses, who believed it was his mission to dispatch as many of his parishioners to God's kingdom as he possibly could, he also had a reputation for sitting up with the widows until all the bottles on the farm were empty, so I looked for someone else. There we sat around the white coffin, ten women and two boys. His crew from the *Vesti* sent a telegram. His daughter Lilja wept woefully. Haraldur sent condolences. My father wrote about him in the national paper, although he'd met him only twice. He and Mum took the boys south for a few weeks while I got on with my wailing.

In the end I had to get up because the summer was about to turn to autumn. Ólafur and Magnús came back west, and with their help I managed to make enough hay for the winter and the fifteen sheep, which became my salvation when school started and I was left alone again. Few things are as soothing to the soul as tending to animals.

Winter arrived, and life was blissfully simple. I always awoke at the crack of dawn and therefore always a few minutes later than the day before. I took care of the sheep, fed myself, grabbed a book. I dabbled in making blood sausage and cooked meat soup that lasted me ten days. I didn't wash up for a whole month. By seven, six, five o'clock the light was gone and I kicked the generator on. In the evenings I'd lie in bed listening to the Reykjavík intellectuals on the radio talking about art or politics. But sometimes I just lay there and let my mind wander, back to Bob and his silly jokes, back to Amrum and my old house in Svefneyjar. Because of the murmur of the generator and the small size of the bedroom, I sometimes felt as if I were in the berth of a ship sailing into Iceland's deepest fjord, seeking shelter from the polar winds.

The phone was kind enough to remain silent for weeks on end, although my dear Mum called a few times to see if I was capable of saying hello and to give me some news from the city. Our cousin Lone Bang had celebrated her eightieth birthday, but Dad's siblings, those who were still alive, refused to turn up because she hadn't invited him. Shortly after Grandma Georgia died in September 1958, the singer had decided to move to Iceland and currently lived in a Reykjavík basement with some actors where she honoured the president's memory and taught singing to a young and precocious Björk, and was feted by the small city elite with their pursed lips and minuet steps. Well, what do you know?

By the end of October, I was out of cigarettes, and I had almost forgotten my old addiction when a carton finally arrived by bus a month later. It was then that I realised I had attained a new form of bliss: the simple life.

In the middle of the journey of my life, I had been granted a spiritual retreat. I was finally free of children and men and free of all the whips and lashes that accompany contemporary life. The only happy people in our cities are vagabonds and tramps.

Was I just a countrywoman at heart?

Then, one cold Tuesday in Advent, the generator broke down. I welcomed the silence, but the darkness surrounded the farm like an army, with consequences that took me totally by surprise: suddenly an old ghost raised his oily head. The boat engineer of my life wasn't altogether dead. Within just a few hours I had plunged into the darkest inferno. I felt he'd come back, and I expected the barrel of a gun to come through the windows at any moment. I was terrified of the dark and lit candles in every corner. But couldn't sleep. Although it was totally still and silent, my head was about to explode. It was as if all the rapes of the past years were assaulting me at once, like hundreds of pinkish pale bats beating me, both inside and outside, with their spiky wings, snapping at me with their small teeth. That odd couple, Pain and Humiliation, joined the mob, as did Rage against the betrayal of love, and together they whipped the giggling animals and the biting intensified. In the middle of this ordeal, I heard a crashing sound in the kitchen, a heavy *thud*. Was he inside? Was he back again? No, it was . . . it was a *thud*, it was THE *thud*: suddenly a little girl appeared, my little girl, my beloved, dearest lovely child, who had died on a narrow street in another life. She appeared to me, over the end of the bed, hovering, with her golden locks all shiny and glowing in the candlelight, she was so beautiful, dressed in the same clothes she was on the day she died, and recited this poem:

Blo way, blo way.
Now go, Bloway.

My God, that voice, it was her, it was her, oh, my darling child, my angel, and so beautiful, so blond and blue eyed, Blómey, my Blómey. And yet so ghostly, so clearly pale and spectral, yes, almost as if she'd aged, a girl who had been three years old for thirty years, and she repeated her name, yes, she was saying her name, Bloway. And then she was gone.

All gone, Bloway.

I lay there stretched out in ecstasy. Hot water streamed under my skin, and I was filled with calm and peace, fell fast asleep half an hour later, and dreamed of beds of roses and gentle swings. She had never appeared to me before, and it was so good. She had saved me from madness. Oh my God, and I who had never believed in anything that hovers.

The next day, Jón arrived. I was fiddling with the sheep shed gate and felt my eyes water when I saw him walking over the blind hill, slightly curved. I was almost on the point of running up to embrace that wonderful man but felt it would be too *unwestfjordian* and waited for him by the gate. My eyes were completely dry by the time he reached me.

'Good day.'

'Hi.'

We stood under the drizzling snow for some moments. Across the bay, the ferry was on its way into the longest fjord in Iceland.

'The generator's gone?' he asked finally, and he moved slowly towards the shed.

'Yes. Did you hear it break down yesterday?' I asked out of my anorak as I followed him.

He didn't answer until two hours later, when the generator was working again and we were sitting in the kitchen.

'No, I've lost almost all my hearing powers now.'

Bit by bit, I came back to my senses again. *El hombre* slowly faded in my mind, like a dirty heap of drift snow on the side of a mountain; in the end there was nothing left of it except its sandy coat in the green heather, and it still lies there today.

I stayed put for another three years. Haraldur had mostly vanished. By then he'd started a relationship with his serious wife, Thórdís Alva. They lived together in Reykjavík and phoned me at Christmas and Easter. Then there were the little kings, Ólafur and Magnús, who normally stayed with me over the summer, but for the rest of the time I was alone. I had nothing to give to them, poor little things, and looked after them like a wounded doctor after patients and just couldn't wait to send them away again.

It was a mixture of solitary bliss, exile, and atonement. And my existence in this garage is no doubt some kind of prison sentence, too. If the judiciary system doesn't nail you, then you've just got to take care of it yourself. Apart from that, I categorically deny being a murderer. I'm no bloody murderer. A person who has been killed a thousand times over is unable to kill.

Looking back on it, those years of peace and isolation in the Djúpid fjord were among the best I ever had. First of all, I had discovered the virtues of frugality and then the inner peace, or at least some hint of the peace, that I had seen glittering in the eyes of a hermit whom we'd met years earlier. He was the only inhabitant of Skötufjördur, a man so free of us all that he wasn't even listed in the national register. The sad conclusion I had reached in life was that happiness doesn't come from other people, but by staying away from them. That's why I feel so darn good in this garage.

87

The Leaf and the Wind

1984

What did I do after my years in Djúpid? I moved south and . . . hang on, here comes my Lóa, bless her.

'What did you do last night?'

'Last night? I just stayed at home, watching TV with Mum. We watched *ER* together.'

'Tosh. You should go to Afghanistan and take care of women there. It's so good to get into a war when you're young.'

'I don't think Mum would be too happy about that.'

'Tush. It's good for all mothers to see their children leave.'

'But I'm her only child.'

'Yes, you're lucky. You just mustn't forget life, Lóa, dear. It's a lot more fun to live it than to watch it.'

She gives me my medicine and then I allow her to feed me, pretend to be feeling weak. I can't be bothered shovelling that stuff inside me, I'm tired of grub. But pretty soon I'll be able to give up all these ingestions. Advent is fast approaching with the fabulous fourteenth. One thirty, the girl at the crematorium had said.

Yes, what did I do after my years in Djúpid? I went south and moved in with my Prince Potato in Reykjavík, where we found our shelter. There I turned into a gardening hen, pecking at flower beds with a scarf wrapped round my head and rejoicing at anything green that sprouted out of the soil. We start off our lives dreaming of golden-green forests and end up marvelling at a single tree. That pretty much sums up our existence: it's all about chopping down our dreams. Liberating one's self from everything one wanted and everything one got. Now I lie here with just one egg left.

I forgot to mention it. When I threw the grenade at Bæring, it landed on the floor of the sty, bounced there into a corner, where Jón of Módárkot found it for me and brought it to my bed of sorrows. He mistook it for a 'carburetor,' but I corrected him and told him it was a Russian hip flask that my Bæring had found in the stomach of a catfish and that was very dear to him. 'Oh, really?' The safety pin was no longer on it, so it was no doubt unusable, past its shelf date like a fresh cheese from 1942. To be honest, I was sorry I'd never had a proper chance to use it, to see it shine. But now it's all I've got left, that and life itself: *Le seul souvenir de ma vie turbulente.*

The thing that pleased me the most about moving back to Reykjavík was renewing my contact with Mum and Dad, who had been living on Skothúsvegur for so long now that their holy spirits inhabited every single object in the house. In the corner there was a statue of the first settler, and Mum regularly dusted his helmet and spear.

My mother was edging close to eighty now but stayed in good shape, had kept her back straight with all the dignity of a Breidafjördur lass, which couldn't be said of her daughter, who excelled at back-bending activities in the garden behind the house. My father was seventy-five years old, with a smooth forehead and combed-back hair, but he looked good for his age, although in his eyes everything was still in ruins. Some journalists had written a book about 'Icelandic Nazis,' and there was a photo of Dad in it in full uniform, Hitler's soldier, 'the president's son.' Every five years for the whole of my life, I received a phone call from some zealous hack who was eager to dig something up about my father's misfortunes.

'Where can I get hold of him? Is he in hiding? Don't you think the nation has a right to hear this story?' And now they had finally put this book together. Half-truths about half the war. The other half was too complex for the media. My father had obviously already done his penance many times over. Even his children and wife had bled for their father's sins. But the reporters wanted to hang them around their own necks and proudly show them off around town.

'Don't you want to tell the story yourself?' I asked my father one snowy, bright autumn Sunday.

'*Ach*. Who wants to hear a leaf tell the story of the wind?'

I clasped him in the middle of the living room, and we stood there, locked in an embrace, until the deception that nothing had ever happened took hold of us. Never on his part, never on mine. Never between us, ever. Mum came in from the kitchen carrying a pot of hot chocolate, with white hair and dressed in a skirt, and said, 'Well then.' She couldn't bear *sappiness* any more than Grandma could, than I could. But did she really not know what had happened?

So many things had been buried in silence. When my father returned from the war, he promised Grandad never to mention Germany again, never to go there again, never to answer any letters from there. And on no account was he allowed to talk about his experiences during the war. This clear order from the father of the nation was in keeping with the traditional Icelandic code of silence. Dad had obeyed. Had he also neglected to tell Mum about what took place at the end of the war, and contaminated his, and my, life for the rest of eternity?

I never asked. Silence begets silence.

88

Funerals

1988–1989

Mum died in August 1988, and I said goodbye to her with waves of salty tears. Thórdís Alva wrote so beautifully about her in the paper that I sent her 20,000 kronur in an envelope. In a few eloquent sentences she had conjured her up for me again as the earthly goddess who had enveloped me in the fragrance of her sweat in the embassy bed that first Christmas of the war. Just two months later, though, that powerful umbilical cord had been severed, and I was able to just about reattach it only in old age. In many ways my life had been a long race up to the hospital where she lay on her last day. I just managed to arrive on time and stooped over the side of her bed, gasping for breath, and got to be a daughter again until the evening came.

Oh, my lovely Mum.

All the Johnsons came to the ceremony, and the entire Björnsson clan. I had never realised what a fine and noble figure my mother had become until I looked behind me in the church and, for a brief moment, thought that I was at the wrong funeral, that they were burying some aristocratic dame from a fancy neighbourhood, until I spotted faces from Breidafjördur: weather-beaten islands in an ocean of face powder and furs.

After the reception, I took Dad home and helped him up the steps of Skothúsvegur. He managed to insert the key into the lock but then crumbled on the threshold. I had to get the neighbours' help to get him into bed and then sat by his side, took his scaled hand, and held it for ten whole months, read newspapers for him, slipped records onto the turntable, and recited all the Schiller I knew. Every now and then, the poems seemed to trigger a memory and he muttered something. He had given up smoking for Mum's sake after they got back together again, but I got him to start again, gave him a drag from one of mine. I could tell he enjoyed it, even though he was in another world.

Once, I had the Hitler egg with me and allowed him to handle it. He held it for a whole half hour and then asked when the next train to Berlin was.

He went on a bright June day, just before dinnertime. Swans drew a cloud in front of the sun over the city lake; I sat alone with him and tried to bid him farewell in peace. But the strangest thing was that, as soon as he had breathed his last, my mind was assailed by a whirlwind of forty-year-old questions. Hadn't this man, through his confusion, wrong decisions, and relentless bad luck, exerted too much influence on my existence? I would have been only too happy to live my life without a father, but now I was stuck with a triune one because, in the end, fate had shaped him into my father, son and holy burden all at once. And yet he was the man I had given the most to in my life. A whole heart was needed to reconcile myself with him, which is why there wasn't much left of this piece of meat. I'm the woman who spent her life trying to love the man who robbed her of the possibility of finding true love.

Mein Vater, mein Vater . . .

I organised a nice funeral, which was well attended, and I stood stone cold on the edge of his grave, chucking six hundred conflicting feelings onto the coffin as it descended into the earth. And it wasn't until I visited his grave two weeks later that the tears came. I saw things as they were: my past had been buried. It had vanished out of sight. I couldn't brood over it any more. It's only when your parents are dead that you can start to live. And I got to live three whole years, until the doctors informed me of my death sentence in the spring of 1991.

89

Rib Report

2009

Oh, now I'm suddenly worried that I could die before the agreed time. I coughed up blood this morning and I couldn't hide the rattle from Lóa when she arrived at 9:40 on the dot with her dimples so wonderfully full of life. I have an appointment with the body burners on 14 December and I'm determined not to miss it. I'll ask the girl to put me into a nice dress on the thirteenth, maybe I'll send her to the shops and ask her to buy me a mortuary dress.

Oh, I can barely move, it gives me a stitch in the breast cavity on my left. Unless it's a rib. I didn't break one in my coughing fit this morning, did I? I try to raise myself, as my bladder demands, but there's just so much pain. The god of old age bends my ribs like a sailor bends a teaspoon. I have two bad choices. Either I allow my sac to leak into the bed and wet my bedsores, or I stagger to the toilet and break another rib. That's decrepitude for you. It makes you choose between two bad options, because it offers you no solutions except for that final punctuation that puts an end to our existence.

I see here that good old Aussie Aldon has arrived in London and has no doubt booked a double room for himself and Bod. As for me, I wouldn't mind getting rid of my own bod at the geriatric ward so that I could carry on dabbling here in the garage, without any urine or bedsores. When the body reminds me of its presence, with all its torture and humiliations, I always think of my father, who was forced to march across Europe several times during the war, spending two winters in the trenches and his summer holidays in prison camps.

Where was he in June 1944? When his daughter grappled with the great trio on the Polish plains: first rape, first love, and her first period, and his abandoned wife contended with her German suitors, while his father and mother were put in command of a new country, sailing it into the sunshine of the Great North.

90

Eye of War

1944

My father was lying on his stomach in the mud with his dusty Mauser rifle on the banks of a river that wasn't called the Don or Dnieper but the Dniester, no less, which flows down to the Black Sea, drawing the frontier between Ukraine and Romania. Yes, they had retreated that far, poor things, to fight over the land now known as Romania. Ten thousand Germans, in torn trousers and frost-gnawed shoes, pitted against one hundred thousand singing Russians, who under the veil of the night had crept across the river. There is a certain principle in life that says that no matter how much confidence the invading side may have, it will never amount to half the vengeful power of the home army.

All of a sudden the Icelandic soldier saw something white roll down a heap of earth and halt beside him. Some kind of white glistening sphere. A toadstool? Mushroom? No, it was an eye. A detached eye that lay there in the mud beside him and . . . yes, there was no question about it: it could still see. It looked him in the eye and asked him like a baby's head that had just popped out of mother earth, What are you doing?

He wasn't given enough time to answer because there was another explosion with a yellow blaze that scattered everything in his sight into the air. The eye had vanished when he opened his own again, and he noticed that above him, from the banks of the trench, a tall soldier came flying over him with his face locked in a grimace. He landed so close to my father, knocking his head against the edge, that Dad could hear his neck break through all the battle sounds: the emergency calls, blasts, and flying engines.

He told me the story later in a small bar in Copenhagen. We had an unexpected father-daughter moment and could finally talk freely beyond the jurisdiction of Iceland's law of silence.

Later that day, he marched with his buddy Orel, a pastor's son from Aachen, and a hundred other downtrodden soldiers, up the bank of the river that flowed peacefully on their right, moving upstream; they were retreating into the hinterland. Orel knew many poems and he liked to rattle them off to kill time. Dad said, 'I had to ask him to stop reciting them when I found out that most of them were by Heinrich Heine. His poetry was banned within the boundaries of the Third Reich, "because of the Jewish ink in the poet's pen," to quote someone more important than me.'

The banks were wide. Unbombed stretches of grass and mounds interspersed with trees. To the left of them rose the Carpathian Mountains, distant light blue summits, which darkened the forests in their shadow and lifted the spirits of a German soldier after three winters on the soggy Russia Plains, but on the other side of the river lay the endless expanse of that same unvanquished land. They avoided looking in that direction, but instead focused their eyes on their worn-out boots, which marched on the path back to Germany like homeward-bound horses. A number of young soldiers splashed themselves in a shallow stream that crossed the path, and two of them flung themselves into it fully clothed. An officer glanced at them in silence.

In the blue distance of the valley, a plume of smoke oozed out of a crooked chimney. Someone was expecting a defeated platoon for dinner. Close by was a roofless military camp hospital that had been set up under tall trees by a wheelless jeep that served as a kitchen. Roars of agony filled the air and pierced the soul. The men cast a furtive glance in their direction but then immediately looked away again. A leg had fallen off the operating table in the moment they had glimpsed it.

Orel kept on with his Heine verses about Napoleon's soldiers (Dad gave up trying to stop him), while the Icelander was still thinking about the eye that had rolled over to him in the trench in the middle of the battle like a latter-day lotto ball.

91

Women and Booze

1944

They carried on marching all day and in the evening reached a crooked-roofed village. The locals could be seen fleeing when the first helmets appeared between the houses. What was left behind was an unbombed village with a hundred warped houses, all of which were open, some with boiling eggs on their stoves. Ready-made beds and ticking grandfather clocks. The fellows settled into a small building on the edge of the village, with a tiny living room and kitchen, which soon filled with famished retreating men.

They ate their way into the pantry and under the beds and down into barrels. And found bottles: by evening the village had been turned upside down. 'Heil Hitler!' They had to drink to the memory of their dead brothers. The Russian campaign had unexpectedly turned into a drunken spree in the Carpathian Mountains. And a wild skirt-chasing expedition. As night fell, young women began to appear between the trees. Heavy-breasted girls with hairy foreheads and a party twinkle in their eyes. Someone went out for a piss and found a friendly gaze in the woods. Soon barns and sheds were rocking.

My father witnessed this game from the sidelines but saw a young soldier appear on the threshold of the kitchen with an older woman.

She stood out from the other girls because her face was pale and her eyes shone with intelligence. Maybe she was an office girl in hiding. Her eyebrows were thick and heavy and her profile so birdlike that her entire expression struck my father's head like a whiplash: for a minute he thought Mum was back. The illusion was so powerful that he almost addressed her in Icelandic. But after staring at her face for half an hour, he finally staggered into the bright night garden, drunk on alcohol and memories, and suddenly pictured the day when he stepped off that boat in Breidafjördur and rushed straight to the farm where the woman of his life was waiting for him. Massa in her crown of pearls of sweat, with a rake in her hands. And he was filled with nostalgia. A longing for her and for his life before the war.

Why hadn't he taken his wife's advice? He who had longed for her for seven long years but got her back again, only to ignore her wisdom. After a whole three years in the cold and mud, his faith in Hitler crumbled with the simple apparition of this woman's face on the threshold of a Romanian hut.

'Yes, and then men talk badly of women and booze . . .' Dad snorted, smiling and shaking his head in the small Copenhagen bar long after the war. And there was a hint of sappy juice in his eyes.

92

War from a Distance

1944

Wars don't need much sleep. Before dew saw daylight, Ivan arrived to send the battalion running. The men clambered to their feet, their cheeks still smudged by women, and peered out into the darkness of the night in terror. Soon bullets would be flying.

'Hans! Hans!' Orel's voice cried out between the gunshots as Dad sat in the woods under a tree counting the Svefneyjar islands. He sat there facing the village. A shower of bullets blasted over it like a hailstorm, and the highest gables glowed in the morning twilight.

'Hans! Hans!'

Was he a coward? Deserter? Traitor? Or just an Icelander?

He had wandered away from the village around midnight, over the stream and under the roofs of foliage. Lured away by my mother's face, he had abandoned this rocking, copulating ship in the middle of the forest and had found himself a tree to rest against.

Dad heard Orel yell his name a few more times, without running to his rescue or accompanying him to the Land of the Dead. And then he was heard no more. My father's ears told him that his companion was gone. The war had silenced six thousand lines by Heinrich Heine.

Few things are as dangerous for a soldier as viewing war from a distance. A sense of futility will take hold of him and there's no turning back. My father stood paralysed against a tree trunk, observing the massacre, an Icelander in the woods. And that was where the war ended for him.

93

Piglet in the Woods

1944

Mum saved Dad by luring him out of the war and leading him into the forest. But what then did the little pig do, the one that came running in the afternoon along the forest floor, pale pink with singed ears, and constantly shaking his head to rid himself of the pain?

My father regained his senses from where he had prostrated himself on the ground before God and mankind – Come, take me, take all my senses, because I used them to back the wrong horse! – and was resting his head on his helmet, with the summer sun on his forehead. The village crackled in the distance. Isolated gunshots resounded through the ruins. The war shift was about to end.

The pig was followed by voices, almost laughing voices, which echoed through the hall of the forest, and then a shot. My father hoisted himself up on his elbows. Another shot. The pig collapsed in spasms. His tongue slid out, thick and glistening, like a cryptic message from death to life. Dad fumbled for his rifle.

But the Russians got there first. They were suddenly standing over the pig, armed soldiers, and one of them noticed the 'German' who was gawking at them as if he'd never seen other humans before. The Icelander's life rapidly rewound all the way back to his childhood by Reykjavík Lake, and it was there that my father found the most appropriate response. Like a six-year-old boy playing Cowboys and Indians in the summer of 1914, he threw his arms in the air: I surrender! Then he clambered to his feet and held them even higher: I surrender! They didn't shoot. Maybe they didn't realise at first that the soldier was German. Maybe the absence of his helmet had saved him. Either way, my father had become a Russian prisoner of war.

94

Mrs Johnson

1945

Dad and I returned on the *Esja* at the beginning of July, with a large group of Icelanders who hadn't seen the country since before the war. On a bright summer morning we finally saw Iceland again. We stood on deck when the Westman Islands rose out of the sea, and then the glaciers behind them. The initial feeling was strange. It was like seeing one's own face emerge from the depths, slowly and arduously, trying to catch its breath again. Then I thought of this line from a poem by Laxness: 'My mountains rise, as white as curds and milk.' Because after all my misery, my country looked like a banquet: I literally wanted to gulp it all down.

Grandma Georgía made sure we were driven straight from the harbour out to the presidential residence of Bessastadir, where my father was kept in a room like a state secret. I was to bring him his meals up in the loft because he wasn't allowed to appear at official functions. He sat up on the edge of his bed, acting as if nothing were amiss, but ensuring that he avoided his daughter's gaze and focused on the food. I sat down briefly beside him and tried to find the key word that would unlock some dialogue about the horrors that were tormenting him and us and that I couldn't discuss with anyone but him, and he with me, but that were too big for two small beings like us to deal with. But the god of speech was too reluctant to release that word. At the end of his pancake, Dad looked at me, determined not to cry, and patted me on the knee.

'Don't think about it.'

Mum and I didn't meet until three months after our homecoming. Grandma couldn't forgive her for the sin of having, as soon as she returned home at the end of the war, thrown herself into the bed of Mr Johnson, the staid coffee merchant who, moreover, already had three children with another woman. The fact that the latter was dead was of no importance; Grandma felt Mum had betrayed the family and she therefore 'put her on ice,' which was her way of dealing with anger.

As for me, my relationship with Mum was never the same after I'd watched her vanish from sight on that pier in Dagebüll in 1942. A child's soul won't listen to reason. It felt her mother had abandoned her. She had sent me away, only twelve years old, on a boat to some unfathomable destination and then didn't come to meet us in Hamburg as she had promised.

She later told me how the trains had shut down for a month, how she had cried that night and many more, how she trusted that my father would take care of me, and how she remained in the Lübeck household until the summer of 1944, when a friend of the family invited her to stay at his country estate – the Loon Count of Loonyburg, she called him. Was she in love with him? 'He was a tease,' went the answer. But she did spend the winter of '44–'45 at his place. Sometimes a man is a woman's refuge.

The island girl was a resourceful woman. As soon as the castle fell into the hands of the Allies, she was in a jeep shooting west, with a giant wheel of cheese on her lap. After an adventurous journey, she reached England and from there sailed on to Iceland; she was home by April 1945, long before all the other Icelanders who, like us, had been trapped by the war. And shortly after her homecoming, she'd found refuge in the arms of that gentle, elderly widower.

I waited for her in the living room of the presidential residence in Bessastadir, a sixteen-year-old woman by then, with neatly brushed hair, on a sunny autumn day. The chauffeur parked in the driveway and Mum stepped out, like the sovereign of some other country, a country I didn't know. Alfred, the residence manager, received her, and without moving, I watched her in her high heels as she stepped onto the stone floor of the foyer and on into the cloakroom. She didn't see me until she came out again, coatless, in a light dress, adjusting her elegantly set hair with open palms on her first visit to the president's residence. I felt an urge to take a step towards her, despite Grandma's stern look, but couldn't. I couldn't step over all that had happened, and I waited for her with leaden feet.

Mum came sailing towards me smiling, broader and more heavily keeled than before, and started off trying to kiss me in a manner that was appropriate for a public place, even though Grandma was the only other person in the room, but then gave up and embraced me, as her head started to shake and a tear trickled from one eye. We embraced again and I vanished into her hair but could no longer find the smell of seaweed, just the scent of post-war boom. She had become Mrs Johnson.

I was unable to utter a word. Mum filled the silence with remarks like 'How you've changed and grown, my child . . .' I could sense from her voice that I no longer lived inside her, but stood outside, outside the sanctuary of her soul. And I felt it would take me a lifetime to penetrate it again. Unlike Mum, I didn't produce a tear, although my insides were screaming in pain. There was a fence in the sound of my mother's voice, insurmountable and bristling: the god of events had broken us apart.

Further inside the house, my father's heart was ticking, until he finally appeared in the living room, constantly stroking his forehead with the open palm of his right hand. When he finally stopped stroking it, he took the hand of the woman he had betrayed for

Hitler, and she could observe how the war had thinned his hair and consumed his being.

He didn't say anything and neither did she. But Grandma broke into Danish: *'Jæja, så kan vi gå ind.'* Right, then, let's go in. She had organised this long-awaited family meeting and directed it like a general. She sat us down by the window in the dining room, me beside Dad and Mum opposite us, and placed her chair at the corner of the table so that she could spring up and scuttle into the kitchen, while she watched over Mum like a guard, with her elbows on the edge of the table. Elín, the maid, brought pancakes and hot chocolate to the table. She was a country girl with dark hair and pure cheeks, adorably free of any sense of servitude.

'Would you like me to bring in the cream now?'

'Yes, that would be nice.'

'Whipped, then?'

'Yes, of course.'

'But you realise that's the last cream.'

The hostess nodded and smiled at the maid, while we silently stared at the steam rising from our cups, which turned golden in the horizontal rays of the autumn sun. Back in Breidafjördur, those rays were called cod-liver light.

Grandma addressed a few ice-cold questions to Mum, and I noticed that Dad's hand was trembling when he tried to lift his cup by the handle. But then it was as if the quiver transferred to Mum's voice.

'More than anything, I would, of course, want Herra to come live with me.'

Grandma immediately quashed that. Then Hans Henrik would be left all on his own while she, Massebill, not only had a husband but three children. Mum was speechless, Fridrik Johnson's children were grown-ups; she had seen only two of them twice. But Grandma remained immovable. One couldn't have everything in life. The negotiations ended with an agreement that I would visit her once a month. Dad sat through this in silence but finally started to cry without anyone but me noticing. He dabbed his eyes with a napkin and I lay my hand on his under the table. Mum was quiet and observed our alliance with broken eyes. In her eyes one could read that Dad and I were bound together by something that couldn't be found in a dictionary, something between the illicit and unspeakable.

95

Depression with Whipped Cream

1945

It was a strange summer. Bright sunshine on the outside but dark on the inside: one big depression with whipped cream (I ate sixteen pancakes a day). The dreams recurred night after night, pregnant with pain and suffering. One night I was being drooled over in Russian, the next I was squirming in a pit of worms in an air-raid shelter and the worms turned into people. At one end, children were being born, and at the other, human lives were being extinguished. I tried to crawl my way towards the light but was constantly being drowned by arms and legs and children's naked thighs.

For entire bright summer evenings I sat in the attic, staring out of the window and wondering what Mum was doing in the town on the other side of the bay. Why wasn't she knocking on the windows and doors of the presidential residence, howling with remorse?

By any contemporary standards, I should, of course, have been put in some psychiatric ward, where some shrink could have coaxed the horrors of war out of me, and that ultimate shock, but those institutions didn't exist back then and barely exist now. Instead I got to play bridge with Grandma and her friends, semi-Danish bourgeois ladies who discussed Mum's relationship with Fridrik in a coded Danish that I nevertheless managed to decipher. Here I got the gossipy version of events: that Mum had met him in England, that they'd travelled home on the same ship, but that she had, above all, fallen for his apartment on Brædraborgarstígur.

In the long, bright nights I stared at the man sleeping in the bed opposite mine, just as I'd stared at Marek in the old cabin, and asked myself how the monstrosity of war had been able to act with such precision, to have glued us together in this calamity, a father and daughter, the only Icelanders in the cast of 200 million people performing in the spectacle of that war. It defied belief. The demonic serendipity. It was as if a walrus had managed to thread a needle.

The atheist God clearly hated me.

96

'The Songbird of Spring is Here!'

1945

And what then could be said of the evil curse which, like a spear of darkness, pierced every hour that passed in this greatest residence in the land?

My father and I went on long walks, trying to escape the hundreds of black rats that followed us from one room to another. Maybe they would lose themselves along the shore? We walked out to Rani and sometimes even as far as Gálgahraun. The wind blew sunrays against our faces and corrugated folds across the Lambhús Lake, bringing a glow to the late summer hay. We talked about everything but what we needed to talk about. He told me about his summer evenings in Vejle, Denmark, and taught me about shellfish. One day we decided to take a stroll on the shore to look for mussels, despite the warnings from Elín, the housekeeper.

'There'll be no slimy shells going into this pot!'

On the path of the Bessastadir Peninsula we met Grandad and our cousin Lone. She had arrived the day before and they were now returning from a stroll. 'The Songbird of Spring is coming on Friday!' the president had announced from his office during the week, like a chirpy scout. I glanced at Grandma who was knitting in a deep armchair in the living room. 'Who?' she swiftly quipped, knitting her brow.

It had been many years now since the singing bird had made an appearance in their home. Lone Bang had lived in London throughout the war, rubbing shoulders with mammoth celebrities like Sigmund Freud and Elias Canetti, who many years later won the Nobel Prize for literature. She had performed several times in the famous lunchtime concerts of the National Gallery where there was nothing on show but songs. But now she had come home; the war was over and there was no peace any more.

The president was wearing a coat and hat, Lone a black coat with hair that flickered like a candle in the wind.

'Good morning!' said Dad vigorously. 'Did you walk down to the shore?'

They blanked us and walked past in grave silence, like a presidential couple following a hearse. Yes, of course, they made an elegant couple.

Despite everything that had preceded this, this was probably the most painful moment I shared with my father. I had seen him and his father chatting at the table in Bessastadir, but once Lóa had arrived their communications were severed. And here the father had virtually repudiated his son in front of his daughter, under the influence of his lover. We carried on walking towards the tip of the peninsula where the grass swayed to and fro like a demented soul. I took my father's hand, like a mother leading a child, and tried to say something to raise his spirits, something about the Arctic terns and mussels, but he didn't answer. I glanced back and saw the unofficial presidential couple of Iceland embark on the path back to the house – he furtively squeezed her hand. The backdrop to this moment was the residence, with its red roof and white facade that suddenly looked like Grandma's face.

When we reached the end of the peninsula, I realised we'd chosen the right time. The tide was completely out and the shore was covered in slippery, slimy seaweed. But there were no mussels or other shellfish in view. We had to struggle not to fall, but Dad stepped over the seaweed, staring straight ahead, advancing another two hundred metres, as far as he could go, to the border between land and sea. Stood there for far too long for my taste, with his back turned to me, gazing at the fjord and beyond it where the brand-new Reykjavík airfield had been built. But finally he decided not to drown himself on that day and turned around.

What did that woman know about Dad's fate? What right did she have to scorn the son of the woman who was the wife of the man she secretly loved and what's more, her maternal aunt? Who was she to judge, from her pseudo-Jewish standpoint? Grandad's destiny was to stand between fires. The president, who had seen through the divorce between Iceland and Denmark, was eternally trapped between his mistress and wife, and his roles as a lover, husband and father with a chronic lack of courage.

And why the hell couldn't he have chosen an Icelandic mistress?

As I look back on that image through the telescope of time – that furtive touching of hands by secret lovers on that blustery sunny August day of 1945 – I can see how it encapsulates the curse of a whole family. Those who live in hell breathe fire, the old people on the islands used to say, and Grandma had certainly lived in hell for half her life. And the effects were felt by her children, children-in-law, grandchildren . . .

Would my father have deserted the family nest had the house been whole? Had he embraced Nazism in response to the self-crowned 'queen of the Jews'?

Sometimes the king's love is the curse of the court.

97

Spite and Love

2009

Lóa, who was the purest of virgins when she first appeared here in the garage, has finally been deflowered. I can hear it in her voice. It isn't as prudish as it was. She's giving nothing away, except for a smile and talks about a 'friend.'

'Oh, there's nothing friendly about love,' I say.

'Why do you say that?'

'Spite and love . . . are flames from the same fire.'

'Maybe things were different in the olden days?' she says as she slips on a solar-yellow rubber glove.

'Oh no. It still burns just as hard.'

'Should one avoid the fire, then?'

'No one can. Because that fire is life itself.'

She seems to have lost the thread and is, moreover, trying to find the other rubber glove when she childishly asks, 'You've been in lots of countries, haven't you?'

'Countries are fine, but for no more than two weeks.'

'Why not?'

'Oh, because then it starts to get complicated. You fumble in people's pants and start to get phone calls.'

'You . . . did you fall in love a lot?'

'Nah . . . the heart is like grilled meat. There's no way it can be grilled again.'

'You mean one can only fall in love once?'

'Yes, of course, you can try regrilling it, but it gets terribly tough . . . terribly bland.'

'And how long did it last for you?'

'The first love lasts a lifetime. I still think about him.'

'But I mean how long were you . . . together?'

'We were a couple for two' – I pause for breath – 'two days, I think.'

'You were together for two days and you still think about him?'

'Yes. Love is measured in degrees, not minutes.'

98

Escaping Post-war Iceland

1948

Dad was an outlaw. After his prison sentence in the presidential residence, he tried to walk the streets unnoticed, rented a room, but got little sleep from the stones that got chucked at his window. I continued to live in the comfort of Bessastadir while he decided to move to the countryside in the east, where he traipsed across the moors in boots, drenched, with fencing wire on his shoulders.

Since the law of silence still reigned supreme in Iceland at that time, it took my father two years to understand his father's wish for him to get out of the country. At a small party in the presidential residence on 9 September 1948, held in honour of a certain nineteen-year-old lady, Hans Henrik finally managed to read the magic word in the eyes of the hosts that was to solve the problem: Argentina.

Life in Bessastadir had become increasingly unbearable for me, too. The daughter of war, I didn't always feel at home in Icelandic society. There was a ban on discussing anything to do with Germany, according to a tacit presidential decree. I was supposed to erase half my life. If only I could have . . .

But I had nowhere else to go. My mother's home was out of bounds, and besides, Reykjavík had turned into such an endless tea party I almost loathed going into town. How that clutter of huts could have turned itself into an American film in the space of a few years was one of the enigmas of the century. Old mud-puddle streets had been paved, and everyone went into town smartly dressed. People seemed to be following an urge to strut around town, to see and be seen: women with capes and hats, veils in front of their eyes and cigarette holders in their handbags, heavily made up from Monday to Monday, and men ready for the shooting of a big film, with hats tipped over their eyes and a cigar between their lips. In stores, boys pulled fat wads of notes out of their pockets and waved them in front of old people before they paid for their comic books. And Cadillacs glided down the streets like exotic animals.

Everything had become American, all the daddies were rich and the mamas good looking.

During the war, the Yankees had taken over from the British as the protectors of Iceland, and they hadn't left yet, despite their promises to do so. Grandad wanted to hang on to them as long as possible, being the cautious realist that he was, because otherwise there was the danger of a Soviet Iceland. Besides, no other nation had recognised Iceland's independence in practice. Though he'd been sitting on the presidential throne for three years, no king or other country had invited him out on an official visit, apart from that good old gentleman Franklin D. Roosevelt, the summer before he died.

The Yanks took care of us for fifty years, with their soldiers, money, TV and candyfloss, and then only left after little Bush got himself into a historical muddle in Iraq. He needed all the men he could get, and the base in Keflavík was shut down in late summer 2006. Then finally, against our will and with a lot of moaning, we Icelanders became an independent nation: free and devoid of an army for the first time since 1262. That was obviously more than we could cope with, since two years later the country went bust. In the autumn of 2008, we collapsed into the arms of the Global Capitalism

Rescue Team, and God only knows who will take pity on us once they discharge us from that ward.

The first winter after the war, I had tried to sit with other Icelandic kids in high school (most of them were two years younger than I was), girls who judged boys on the strength of their stamp collections and boys who drank milk at parties. To me the girls were children, and the boys did it in their pants if I drew close to them. I had to make do with fifty-year-old men, such as the occasional drunken ambassador who would stumble into my room while looking for the toilets at a cocktail reception in Bessastadir.

Life had once more put me up against the wall. And given me two options: to prolong my boredom in Bessastadir or go with Dad to Argentina.

99

Fair Winds

1948

The ship touched land on a bright sunny day, and once the paperwork had been completed, we were finally ashore. Owing to the crowds, there was no way of hailing a cab or a carriage, so we walked into town with our belongings in two cases, a timid and insecure father and daughter from a faraway land. I had realised that this historic day in our lives was a Tuesday, which in Iceland is a portent of problems, and I had bad premonitions.

My worries, though, were overshadowed by new feelings: We were stepping into a new world; a new continent welcomed us. Even though the stone slabs and lanterns were European in style, there was no denying that the earth and air exuded an exotic scent. Even through the asphalt, one could smell that the soil gave off a scent that was different from the one we knew. I still remember the first American tree I saw; it cracked through the pavement like a thick-barked primordial dinosaur. For some inexplicable reason these trees were much wilder than their European colleagues, if not completely crazy. But nevertheless, some prim little gentlemen had travelled here by ship and train and tried to reorganise their little prim lives by raising their fancy stone palaces, full of law books and ceramics, after chopping down the jungle with a ruler and wiping out an entire civilisation with an eraser. On my first day, Latin America appeared to me as an anaconda in a bow tie.

The heat mounted with every step. It was summer, even though Advent was around the corner. And bit by bit the bustle of life also increased on the streets. It wasn't just summer in the winter here; pavements were turned into living rooms. Women sat peeling potatoes and men read newspapers, one drank coffee while another stuffed his pipe, children played barefoot football and beat a three-legged dog, while cars, buses and trams drove all around them, crammed with people who had been born or had originated in other countries but called themselves Argentinians now. Two horses were lining up at a bus stop, and up a side street someone was milking a cow. Buenos Aires was a city machine operating at full steam. No bombs had ever fallen from the sky here, and people streamed up from the harbour today as always: weary of Europe, bored with Europe, away from wars and strife, bearing dreams of peace and a piece of land in the South American country that resembled Europe the most. Buenos Aires had been home to a million people at the turn of the century, and that figure had now grown to three million. A city bursting with life: a poet once wrote that if you yawned on the streets of Baires, you risked swallowing a motorbike.

We found a room in a cheap guesthouse run by a moustachioed Italian mother and daughter as if it were on the Bay of Naples: Pensione Vesuvio. 'Buongiorno, signore.' Inside its walls, there was another country. They didn't even know who Perón was, and daily bowed to their leader Il Duce, who lived on in a photograph above the breakfast table.

Dad knew fourteen words of Spanish and scanned the papers every morning in search of work. The plan was to revive the old trade of importing clothespins from Germany. But on our first morning the city had greeted us with seventeen thousand clothespins: you could barely see the walls here from the laundry hanging on the lines, and for some reason it was all white sheets. In my simple mind I assumed

Tuesday had to be laundry day in Argentina. But two weeks later the lines were still loaded with bedclothes. I connected this to the lovemaking sounds I sometimes heard through the window at night or even at lunchtime. All of that love in all that heat and humidity obviously called for constant washing. I liked this country.

For safety, Dad had brought along the phone number of a man we had met in Paris on our way over, a Swiss Jew. He was a brash man with a twitching moustache who was starting to market an exciting new gadget: the meat thermometer. Argentina was the meatiest country in the world, he claimed, an untapped gold mine for a device of this kind. Monsieur Björnsson could become his man in South America, and he asked my father to contact him as soon as he had a business card.

In those years, Argentina was probably the most popular country in the world. Everyone wanted to go to the Land of Silver, even though Argentina was the only South American country that had no silver. And because of the huge inflow of immigrants, accommodation wasn't easy to come by in Fair Winds, as my father called the city in our early days there, after he'd heard that its original name was Santa María del Buen Aire (Holy Virgin Mary of the Fair Winds). Two months later we were still in the *pensione* run by the Neapolitan mother and daughter. Dad hadn't found a job but had learned an extra twenty words of Spanish. I wasn't doing too badly with the lingo either, since I'd found a gaucho, Alberto, a country lad with dark eyebrows who danced with me through the whole city and then dragged me up a long staircase at the end of the night. His landlady hung the sheets up to dry on the line. He was proud to belong to the 'shirtless ones,' *los descamisados*, as the supporters of the president were called. They came from the sweaty classes and had ushered Perón into power four years previously after massive demonstrations. My black-eyed country boy had Evita Perón on the brain. I wasn't amused when he called out her name in the middle of our act. On the other hand, I felt a change in his attitude towards me when I gave in to his wish for me to put my hair up like the First Lady's. After that, all doors were opened to me in Fair Winds.

Every week, Dad phoned the Swiss Jew in Paris, but the line was either engaged or there was no answer. The embassy had also lost trace of the strange man. Perhaps this was delayed Jewish revenge? The Icelandic 'Ans Enrique,' as my father's name was pronounced, didn't allow this to put him off, however, and contacted a German company that had recently started to manufacture meat thermometers. He had some samples sent to the guesthouse and sent me around the restaurants of the city with my Evita hair and red lipstick.

'Hola, ¿podría introducir la innovación tecnológica más útil para cocinar la carne? Un termómetro que muestra la temperatura en el músculo.' (Hello, may I introduce you to the most useful tool for cooking meat? A thermometer that measures the temperature in the muscle.)

Amazing I can still remember it . . .

But offering a meat thermometer to an Argentinian grill master was like offering a compass to a search dog.

When all our money ran out, my cowboy pulled a few strings and got us both jobs on a ranch out on the Pampas. I rewarded him for his efforts by calling him a cab.

That took us away from the city and the waiting. Dad was to be the caretaker and I was to serve an old man who virtually lived in a world of his own. Even though the wages were low, our accommodation and keep were free. This was a marvellous way for us to start in our new world.

100

At the Bennis'

1949

Looking at a map of the world, if you place the head of a drawing pin on Buenos Aires with its tip pointing towards the South Pole, that was where the ranch was, on the banks of the Salado River: La Quinta de Crío. Eighteen people lived here, all with the same surname: Benítez. It was clearly a Hispanicisation of the original surname Benni.

A few cows were milked to meet the needs of the household, but otherwise the flat land of the farm was split into two between its pale yellow wheat fields and luscious green pastures for the black cattle. The buildings were white during the day but pitch black at night. Never have I experienced the type of darkness they have on the Pampas. Around the house were a few ombu trees topped with huge crowns, and the path to the next farm was lined with spindlier plants. Their leaves seemed dark against the golden cornfields, like plumes of ash shooting out of a still sea. Otherwise the landscape was like the Great Steppe of Russia, *La Pampa*.

Beyond the trees, at a short distance from the farm, stood a shed that managed to include a bedroom, a living room and a toilet. Inside it sat a fat man in his seventies in a makeshift wheelchair, who because of his lack of a throat looked like a mountain of flesh. His small head rested on multiple chins like an ornament on a cake. It was the strangest face I'd ever seen: a big nose with an even bigger mouth. Without smiling, his mouth stretched from ear to ear. His eyes, on the other hand, were tiny and translucent yellow. His skin was thick and rough and lined with deep wrinkles, which were interspersed with tobacco-stained warts. He was the most hideous man I'd ever seen, a heap of flesh with jaundiced eyes. The first thing that came to mind was a lizard.

Dad was engaged in general farm labour, while my job was to milk the cows in the morning and at night and tend to the old man in the shed. He was deaf, dumb and blind. The door creaked every time I stepped inside with his bowl of porridge. The air was heavy and saturated with human odours. I couldn't help thinking, how could my life have been turned upside down like this? Just a few months previously I'd been sitting with Vigdís Finnbogadóttir and the other kids in a café by the lake in Reykjavík, and now I was sitting at the other end of the globe, feeding a crocodile with a teaspoon. Because despite his lizard-like features, he was known as the Crocodile, El Coco.

His two nephews, both men in their forties, sat inside the farmhouse with their extended families over loud meals, in white shirts with rolled-up sleeves that exposed their muscular, sunbaked arms. It was they who managed the farm and ordered my father about like a grovelling dog, and they called me Evita from the very first day, as soon as they'd measured me up with their goatish, wanton eyes. They'd never heard of Iceland and could never remember the name. Dad and I called them the Bennis. Their wives were real cooking machines, short, stocky creatures with nipples popping out in every direction. The house was crammed with children of all ages, everything from small floor lizards up to sixteen-year-old *señoritas*, who were as white as the walls they slid along and only became visible when they blushed. The matriarch of the Bennis had a yellowish-brown shrivelled prune of a face and never had a kind word to say about anyone except for the black dog who licked her hands and face after meals.

Watching over this entire herd was Gustavo, the head of the clan, hanging high on the kitchen wall, a big-nosed man in a black-and-white photograph that had been retouched in the manner that was fashionable back in the years before the war, with a crazed gaze that relentlessly yelled: *El día pasa! El día pasa!* (The day is passing! The day is passing!)

His widow, Dolmita, still lived: an elegant lady of Romanian origin, born on the banks of an Alpine lake in the mid-nineteenth century, who had once seen Wagner himself mount a horse. She tottered about the house with trembling hands, like a bird with shivering wings. A skeletal figure with skin stretched over her skull, she spoke Spanish with an unfathomable accent. Her nose, though, still kept its European dignity and attested to her aristocratic origins, which had, however, shipwrecked against that rock called Gustavo, because her descendants, who filled every courtyard and patio here, showed no trace of culture of any kind. Just a bunch of illiterate, carnivorous rodents. The old lady looked like a guest in her own house.

The couple had had three sons. The oldest had fled home at an early age with his father's mistress. According to the latest news, he now lived with ten dwarf Indian women in the Andes. The second son, the father of the Bennis, had been killed by a combine harvester in a work accident, and the third was the deaf, dumb and blind reptile in the shed.

I soon realised that the household despised the Crocodile. Even the mother with the regal nose would have nothing to do with him and assured me that he could neither see nor hear, knew nothing, and understood nothing, he was just a *dolor de la tierra*, a pain of the earth. His father must have felt some affection for him, though, since he had left him half the land. The Bennis strictly prohibited me from bringing the Crocodile anything that could be considered a treat. El Coco was given the exact same ration of porridge at almost every meal, and his weight was therefore a total mystery to me.

'Obviously some disease,' Dad said.

They were forced to keep him alive, however, because as a young man he'd had a son with a travelling whore from Paraguay. He was called Big Ben and had appeared in the fullness of time, a tall brute who demanded his father's money and made the farm his home by force. Faultless in appearance but cursed with a faulty temper, he managed to stir up every marriage on the farm and finally made off with the farm's savings. Rumour had it that Big Ben was now a renowned knife fighter in the bars of La Boca, one of Fair Winds' roughest neighbourhoods.

The big family in the kitchen therefore shared half the land with the Crocodile. If he kicked the bucket, his half would go to this son, the criminal. They couldn't allow that to happen. I therefore played an important role on that farm. My task was to keep El Coco alive until his son was murdered in a knife fight, as a fortune-teller in the village had prophesied. According to her, it would happen when the son reached the age of thirty-three. He had just turned thirty-two.

In the evenings the Bennis practised knife-throwing in the stable.

101

El Coco

1949

What kind of an existence was this? To be unable to hear, see, or express anything? Maybe they were right to call him the Crocodile, more beast than man? He always sat in the same place, under a tall chest of drawers on top of which a clock ticked loudly, beside a robust but lopsided bridge table. An intricate jigsaw puzzle lay on top of the green flannel. While his hands were working, he fixed his reptilian gaze on a small window on the southern wall beside the door that creaked every time I entered. This gave me an excellent preview of my future life in the garage. I played the part of Lóa, let him know I was there by touching his right shoulder. He greeted me with a sound that travelled from the depths of his throat and seemed to be full of prolonged suffering, like the groan of an unknown creature trapped in a dungeon so deep that no one could see it. But as time passed I learned to discern joy and even a smile in those guttural sounds.

He was generally dressed in a tan shirt and brown trousers that were fastened high above the waist. I was told he dressed himself and took care of his own bodily functions, since despite being in a wheelchair he had full use of his legs. The worn-out linoleum bore witness to all of this heavy man's leg movements from the bed to the toilet and from there to the jigsaw puzzle: a four-square-yard patch that was lighter than the rest of the linoleum – the kingdom of darkness and silence.

He never went out.

His father had made the wheelchair after the fortune-teller in the village had forecast that the deaf-mute would be paralysed at the age of thirty-three. It was the most loving piece of craftsmanship I'd ever seen; even the spokes of the wheels were made of wood. I later realised that El Coco never dressed himself but instead slept in his clothes in sheets that hadn't been washed since before the war. I soon started washing them, doing my best to ensure that no one saw me hanging up the Crocodile's sheets. It then took me a week to get him to change clothes and an equal amount of time for him to thank me. Even though his nostrils were clogged with hair, he could smell the odour of fresh laundry every time I passed him with clean bedclothes and underwear, and grunted with an ugly smile. I later allowed him to place his hand on my cheek in gratitude. His palms and fingertips were surprisingly soft, considering the roughness of the rest of his hands, and his fingers were surprisingly refined. He gently stroked me and smiled. I saw him in a new light. And put a pair of sunglasses that my father had bought in Baires on him. The human mountain sighed with pleasure, and his lizard eyes could now no longer intimidate me.

I started spending more time with him, even helping him with the jigsaw puzzle. It felt oddly cosy to sit with this massive beast, decoding the gasps he exhaled. And bit by bit a longing to bring cheer to this man grew in me. I managed to smuggle in some cups of maté to him, the Argentine tea, which the poor man had been denied for decades. Then I picked flowers from his mother's garden and placed them under his big nose. He responded with a palm dance. I also brought him honey, which he acknowledged by drawing a swarm of bees in the air. I took this as encouragement and found further things for him to smell: an open tomato, a rat's tail, fresh chilli . . . and each time, using his homegrown finger language (which gradually acquired as many nuances as the colours of a butterfly's wings), he could tell me which object belonged to what smell.

Finally, I came with a lump of lukewarm bull dung and placed it under his nose: then he sneezed and laughed for the first time. The laughter spurted out of him like a jewel that had been buried in the earth for decades. Coco wasn't the simpleton eating machine everyone imagined. He had the sense of smell of a hunting dog. That great nose that he had inherited from his father was his only funnel into the world; all his senses were poured into that. The deaf-mute could even smell my moods and was now starting to draw them every day: tired, happy, sullen, in love, hung over, homesick, or worried about Dad. I was starting to avoid his nose in an unconscious attempt to guard myself, as if it were a sophisticated X-ray machine.

And I could rely on his razor-sharp sensitivity for just about anything. A local boy had stolen a rose for me from Dolmita's garden and walked down to the river with me. The sun was setting and our long shadows shimmered on the surface of the water, almost reaching the opposite bank, though not in unison. In exchange I snatched his handkerchief from him, which I now placed under the nostrils of the clairvoyant's nose. He sniffed the material and passed his verdict with a simple gesture of the hand: the boy was too stupid for me. I, of course, saw that for myself on our next date and couldn't bear the sight of him after that. Diego was his name, and he had a head like an Easter egg: terribly sweet and brown but totally vacuous inside.

My respect for that unfortunate man in the shed grew from day to day. Conversely the low opinion I had of the Bennis sank even further. They behaved like a stupid mob in a simplistic fairy tale, underestimating the true treasure of the family by exiling him to a ramshackle hut where there was no heating on those cold winter nights that the South Pole blew in.

His original name was Johan Hector, born in Lucerne, Switzerland, in 1883. His mother descended from a famous line of goldsmiths,

Lupesca, if I remember right, and his father was an Italo-German brewer's son, Gustavo Benni. In 1900 the family had immigrated to South America in search of gold and green forests. After three years of roaming down the coasts of the Atlantic, they ended up in a silverless Silver Land and got into cattle breeding. Life was no better or worse than it had been back home by the Alpine lake, just different. The main difference was that now all their dreams had been erased from their lives, like the mountains. The future was no longer an uncertainty that glowed behind the next hill; it simply loitered in the courtyard like a black dog. It wasn't there, but here, not a dream but a fact. That's what life is like on the steppe. On the Pampas, every man stands alone, up to his neck in his own life without any escape from himself, not even with his eyes – he sees nothing but his own shadow.

Johan Hector Benni, who later became Juan Héctor Benítez, was born blind and slightly deaf but then lost all his hearing at the age of five when he slipped out of his brother's view and wandered to the mouth of a tunnel, where he got a train in his face. It was back in the pioneering days of rail transport in Switzerland. 'It passed so close to him that it left a streak of blood on his little forehead.' Since then he had lived in darkness and silence but learned to see with his nose, listen with his palms, and talk with his fingers.

I handed him a letter from my mother. He carefully felt the envelope and lifted it to his nose, sniffed the stamp, smiled, and gesticulated that Iceland was 'like a brass band.' Then he pulled the letter out of the envelope and read it with his nose like a myopic mole. He said that Mum missed me terribly but was fine otherwise. So it wasn't a lie, what she'd written on the sheet that I had hidden from my father.

102

The Milk Platform Uprising

1949

My father and I shared a room. He slept badly on most nights and I often had to stretch my arm across the floor until he fell asleep again. In the end we pushed our beds together at night and separated them again in the morning, so as not to give rise to any ugly suspicions.

Hans Henrik was a wreck of a man. The war had shaken every piece of manhood out of him, like coins out of a piggy bank. There was only one coin still ringing inside him. On one side was the image of the swastika he had tried to scratch away, and on the other a picture of a leaking heart.

'You think your mother left me only because of Hitler or . . . ?'

'Yes, I . . . you loved her more than you loved Hitler?'

'Yes, of course. *Love* her. Still love her.'

'But you were ready to die for him but not her?'

Tact has never been my forte.

'Yes . . . I'm . . . a man . . .'

Although those four words were all possible beginnings of a sentence, clumsy attempts to form a sentence, together they did form a sentence that contained a profound truth: 'Yes, I'm a man.' That really meant: 'Yes, I'm an ass.'

He fell silent. I, meanwhile, could hear the heartstrings snapping inside him until there was only one left.

'Do you think she's content with that . . . coffee guy?'

'I don't think so. He's never even been outside Reykjavík.'

Ah well. Maybe I wasn't totally insensitive.

After the first summer (winter), I realised that I had probably followed him here for his sake – out of pity. And I couldn't sacrifice my life for my father. No one does that. I couldn't turn his defeat into my own, I who had barely started the game of life. But where could I go?

'You can always go home, Herra, dear, if you want,' he said sometimes.

'If I want?' I muttered into my chest. We were walking along the gravel path in the sun, on our way home after a Sunday in the village, mass and market. The youngest Benni was ahead of us with the rest of the herd, while the old ladies had travelled by car with the elders. 'And what? Leave you here?'

'Yes, yes. You shouldn't be thinking about me,' said Dad, combing his hair back with one hand, his jacket on his arm. The afternoon sun was hot and the waist-high fields buzzed on both sides.

'Not think about you? I do nothing else but think about you.'

'Why do you say that?'

'I hold your hand at night, can't sleep from worry and . . . I've become my father's mother.'

'Herra, I . . . you mustn't forget yourself.'

'If only I could.'

'You mustn't. It happened to you, too.'

'Yes, that damned—' I snapped sharply, but one of the pallid Benítez daughters turned her head and cast me a glance through her hair. I shut up and we deliberately slowed down. I kicked pebbles at the sun, which now shone horizontally in our faces.

'Dad, why . . . why did you get into all that madness?'

'Why?'

'Yes. Why didn't you listen to Mum?'

'I . . . I should have.'

We had reached the platform where the milk was collected from under a handsome ombu tree on the pathway to the farm. Some flies carried the sunshine on their shoulders into the long shadows. The Bennis had almost reached the farm. I halted and looked at Dad.

'How . . . how could you be such an *idiot*?'

The angry tone even took me by surprise.

'Idiot?'

'Yes, if you hadn't . . . then none of this would have happened!'

'Herra, you can't look at it like that.'

'Yes! That's how it was! If you hadn't . . . it was just . . . you . . . you ruined my life!'

'Herra, dear, don't . . .'

'Yes, you've ruined my life. Just look at this,' I said, waving my arms at the farmland all around us, furious and flushing. 'What are we doing here in this . . . dead-boring shithole of the world?!'

'Herra, no one . . . no one's to blame.'

'Oh really?'

The sun was sinking over the ocean of corn; its long rays played on the wrinkles of my father's face. The cod-liver light was different here from what it was back home, not as clear and cold.

'No, it's just something that happened. War is war,' he answered wearily.

'Oh yeah? War is war and a father is a father and—'

'Herra,' he snapped, finally with some severity in his voice, 'I'm not to blame. It was just . . . just pure bad luck. Pure and simple bad luck!'

'BAD LUCK?!' I yelled so loudly I must have been heard inside the farm.

To see us there, such an unlucky father and daughter in a distant land, boxing the air, trying to punch the ghosts of our own making, which we would never be able to grab, seize by the throat, defeat. Fucking hell. Of course, he was right. It was pure and simple bad luck, which made it all so unbearable. There was no one, nothing we could hit except the air and the boring, doglike spectre we dragged behind us. It's one thing to suffer, but another to have no obvious culprit.

'I hate those words: "bad luck".'

'Yes.'

'And this bloody silence there always has to be. One is never allowed to talk . . . We're not allowed to talk. You don't want to talk, and no one else will . . .'

'I don't want to talk?'

'No. You're like all the others. One can never talk about anything . . .'

'Herra, dear, be careful not to—'

'No, go to fucking hell! You're not going to shut me up here in this . . . shitty South American dump, a whole seven thousand miles from Iceland? It's just sick!' I was starting to shout again. 'This is a sick family! You're sick! Everyone, this whole fucking family! All sick! Mentally sick!'

All of a sudden I heard what I had said and burst into tears. I fled him, bawling, up the path towards the farm. When I reached the courtyard, I couldn't face the idea of going inside and waiting for Dad in our room. I turned right and ran over to Juan Héctor's shed. I lay beside him that night. He played a concert for ten fingers and two ears for me on a crossbeam. It was the most beautiful music I'd ever heard, even though I couldn't hear anything. He had learned piano in the days of yore and still knew how to play. And it was fitting that the silent man should play a silent piece for the girl who was tormented by silence at the end of this day.

After that pathetic attempt to topple Iceland from a milk platform in Argentina, I made no other, but just collected all my secrets and locked them deep inside my soul. I was no better than the rest of my clan and my miserable nation. Just like them, I surrendered to the tyranny of Mr Silence, the despot who ruled Iceland in the twentieth century, and remained subservient to it all the way here into the garage.

And paid for that privilege with a sevenfold cancer.

103

Epiphany

1949

I considered going home but then pictured the kids in the café by the lake in Reykjavík. Even they were so limiting in their conversations that I could reveal only 33 per cent of myself. Maybe I wasn't a wreck in the way that Dad was, but the war had shifted me over to the other side of the wall of what you can call normal life. I had lived through things that others don't see until that wall comes down. In a 'group of good friends,' I therefore never sat at the same table as them but to the side, down in a smouldering bomb crater.

Here at La Quinta de Crío, on the other hand, I was trapped in a temporary setup I could see no end to. Dad was sinking into misery and had even stopped contacting employment agents in the capital. Should I have just left him to his fate? Headed out into the unknown over the Andes, got a sailor's diploma in Chile, sailed across the Pacific, and ended up as a governor on Easter Island? My life was just beginning; his seemed to be over. No, I couldn't leave him behind. But head to the capital, maybe? No, I couldn't bear the thought of dragging that zombie from one curtainless guesthouse to the next. So what were the options, then? While I was ruminating on all this, I got the strangest idea of my life. It could be argued that it was insane, but so was the situation that had generated it.

There were many German immigrants in those parts, and an Oktoberfest was being held in a nearby town. I managed to get the Bennis' permission to go and sat at a long outdoor table with some of the local kids. It was strange to be sipping German beer and eating pretzels under the eyes of green parrots. But you get used to everything, even waking up to the chirping of beetles on Christmas Day. At the next table some fatsos in leather shorts were chanting Munich beer songs. At the end of the first beer, I traipsed into the bar hut that housed the toilets. In the doorway I bumped into an odd couple: a young Germanic-looking girl and a real Argentinian cowboy, a gaucho. That sight triggered an unexpected idea, a solution to my and my father's future in Silver Land. Its execution required a great deal of dedication, but if it succeeded we could hope for better days before long.

A short while later I planned a visit to the doctor in the capital. 'It has something to do with my uterus,' I said to the people in the house, and I wasn't lying. Dad promised to take care of Héctor in the meantime.

104

Mollusk

1949

In a dark bar on a bright street in the Constitución district, I was told where the famous Big Ben Benítez knocked back his glasses. After a few false leads I stumbled on an unmarked underground joint where the knife and accordion led the dance. A warehouse had been converted into a tavern with a minimum of effort. A bunch of boozers filled one corner, and a barman sat on his stool, busy growing a moustache. Floorboards wobbled a long way down the room, and the smoky fog slithered as I strolled towards the bar. Inside this cave a gently drunk man played his *acordeón* and a wasted woman sang an unsolicited song while her partner danced solo on the floor; at regular intervals the woman alternated her singing with shrieks of laughter that were laced with the most loving hate.

I whorishly sauntered over and ordered myself a glass of coal-black wine, smoked a few Arizonas, and then discreetly asked about the famous boy. I was already quite tipsy and engaged in a passionate discussion with two Germans, who together had lost one arm in Normandy, when the fellow finally showed his face. Like a true man of power, he majestically strolled into the joint, flanked by sidekicks, two shady *mestizos* who were a head shorter than he was and chewed on Italian cigars. Big Ben was bareheaded and therefore immediately stood out, because in those years the whole world wore hats. He flashed an attractive scar on his right cheek, which he wore with pride, like an officer's medal of honour, and carried his chin high so that the nearest bulb would highlight his wound. His skin was thick and he had thick hands. His face was far from the ugliness of the Crocodile, although his nostrils showed the paternal genes at work.

I remained still at the end of the bar, casting a furtive glance out at the table and then at his beefy torso. It didn't go unnoticed by him: I sensed his confidence wavering. The knight even seemed flustered with the barman, whom he obviously knew well. Maybe he wasn't all that cool after all. The three men moved into a dark corner and slumped into seats with their drinks. Big Ben dumped his feet on the table while the other two kept their heels glued to the ground and occasionally turned their glasses but rarely raised them to their lips. They just shut up and smoked. Their calm concealed the same pent-up aggression you'd find in a pride of dozing lions.

So as not to appear too sluttish I allowed some minutes to pass before walking over to them. The leader sat up and greeted me with a grin. But he was clearly disappointed by my small stature. I always had more chances by staying seated. With a decent smile and a spellbinding stare, I could make most men believe I was a long-legged diamond goddess with a slim waistline and ample breasts. Many of them would then be very surprised when I popped off to the ladies' room and they saw this short tomboy of a woman with a flat maid's ass. But once I sat down again, I could reignite their interest.

I would have preferred to wind this up as swiftly as possible in the Icelandic way, but this cowboy was the kind of guy who preferred the hunting to the catch and first wanted to wear me down with a conversation about astrology. One of his henchmen happened to be an expert in Aztec astrology, and Big Ben allowed him to decipher my future while he borrowed his cigar. The minion pressed me for my date of birth and then made his calculations and drawings until he'd shaken half the cosmos for a precise picture of my trajectory on earth. He probably saw the garage as well.

'It's as if you can't get into your own life. Jupiter is so heavy here, see? It's always pushing you away. You're condemned to follow a tortuous path.'

We left the warehouse behind us, and the *dama de hielo* or Ice Lady was escorted to an even darker place. Big Ben was adamant to show me what he called knife tango. We finally found a sample of this suicidal dance in some narrow joint down by the harbour, but by then dawn was beginning to break. The night had come to an end and it was time for the morning work. I followed him up to a small loft apartment by the train station, where I vanished into the bathroom and came out again to face the greatest hesitation of my life. The sun had risen over the rooftops to the east, a golden orange eye that asked me the same question the eyeball had asked Dad in the trenches.

What are you doing?

I reviewed the situation. There I was, at the age of twenty, half-naked on a seventh floor in Argentina, on the eleventh day of my menstrual cycle (that was how well I'd planned this operation), a girl in the prime of her life who was finally ready for her big moment, when life lays down its strict law for a moment, transforms a tulip into a cucumber, and strokes it to extract some oyster from it that will then hatch an egg. Crazy stuff.

The sun didn't seem satisfied with the answer, because it repeated the question.

What are you doing?

Oh, for God's sake, I thought, as I slipped into his bedroom, closed the door behind me, and wrestled against my final doubts. But it was the same as before and after – some life force was pushing me onto a path that I knew perfectly well to be wrong.

The stud had started to snore. His scar shone in the wondrous morning light, white against his golden-brown face. The bed was like a white island in the middle of a smelly ocean of dirty clothes. I zigzagged towards the bed and lay beside him, stroking his chest and stomach. He had a beautiful and well-proportioned body. Finally he stirred, and I whispered something into his ear. His greasy hair smelled of cinnamon. I continued fondling him and loosened the belt of his trousers. His male member slept inside them, curled up and still, like an unknown species of mollusc resting in its shell. The knife man faintly smiled and we kissed. I felt I had finally reached South America. Then I helped him out of his trousers and shoes and slipped out of my pants.

It was probably Jupiter. None of my killing charm or sweetest caresses could make any difference; that tulip wouldn't turn into a cucumber. But I wasn't about to give up, and tried as best I could to get that mollusc on its feet. My future and Dad's was at stake. But it was futile. Long into the morning I tried to get some blood to flow into that golden-brown splotch of flesh, without success. I even prayed God to raise that limb from the dead. Nothing doing. Finally I dozed off on my watch, but I sprang up when the man woke, and gave it one final try. I pictured my happy father holding a tiny Benítez grandson, a babbling blond infant with a scar on its cheek, the legitimate heir to La Quinta de Crío. Once the Crocodile father and son were dead, we would build our own ranch down by the river, a long way from Bennis' farm. Grandma and Grandad would get a postcard with a photograph of a house that was bigger than the Bessastadir residence itself. But the result was the same. The knife hero just couldn't get it up.

'Is something wrong?' asked the Icelandic girl.

'No, no, it's just . . . why are you so keen to . . . ?'

I sensed unease in his voice.

'Am I that ugly?'

'No. Ha-ha . . . a curse was put on me.'

'Curse?'

'Yeah. A fucking fortune-teller. Told me I would never be able to . . .'

'Huh? Was this the same fortune-teller who predicted you'd die at the age of thirty-three?'

'How do you know that?'

'I know a few things.'

'Where did you hear that?'

'In La Quinta de Crío.'

'La Quinta de Crío? Have you been there?'

'I work there. Live there.'

'Huh? You don't say!'

'Yes, I'm taking care of your dad.'

'Dad? The old Crocodile?'

'Yes,' I said, and I had a sudden epiphany. There was another way of getting my hands on the Crío estate. I swiftly dressed, said goodbye, and ran down the stairs and all the way to the coach station.

105

Bad Seed

1950

On 4 July 1950, I gave birth to a daughter. And then wept for two days. A good-for-nothing like me had achieved this. I who had been raped by life had managed to bear fruit. I who was supposed to be useless had created something new. I cried out of joy, relief and sorrow and couldn't believe my own eyes when a healthy little girl was placed in my arms. Dad shed a tear of solidarity, took care of Héctor, and negotiated with the Bennis to grant me a week's maternity leave.

I gave birth at home. In Dad's and my room. The midwife was the fortune-teller from the village, the same one who had wrongly prophesied the Crocodile's paralysis but had nevertheless proved her powers when it came to the curse on his son's tool.

The child appeared almost blond straight out of the womb, with a white body that looked like a beam of light in the black hands of the midwife, who showed a considerable lack of human warmth. I said nothing about who the father was, but even when the baby had barely pushed its head out to show its tiny wrinkled face, the clairvoyant could see who he was. She roughly clasped the baby, like a calf out of a cow, and kept on muttering to herself: 'Bad seed, bad future.' She severed the umbilical cord with a wrinkled brow and handed the howling infant to me with a look of disdain.

But she was just a small gypsy cloud on my clear horizon. Because now I understood why children were called sunrays.

106

Night Coach to Baires

1950

Two weeks later we had to flee La Quinta de Crío. My father and I sat on a dusty coach for the capital, with a sleeping face wrapped in a cloth. The sun bathed the cornfields against the eastern sky, highlighting the dust particles that slowly danced in our eyes and seemed to have no idea of the sixty-mile-per-hour speed the Greyhound was travelling at. I was bewitched by those small particles that hovered in mid-air. Against the dark red material of the seats, they looked like minuscule suns, stars in a distant nebula, major events in an immense universe that was nevertheless compact enough to fit into the night coach to Buenos Aires.

'But how could you ... with ... with him?' was the only thing that was said on the journey.

A Slavonic woman wrapped in a shawl a few rows down turned to stare at us. We obviously looked like an unfortunate couple with our newborn child. A thin-haired man in his forties with prominent temples and his twenty-year-old wife, with slightly puffed-up cheeks and breasts that were swollen for the only time in her life. In a way that suspicion was correct. We had become some kind of damned couple. And now I had pushed out of me half a farm for the pair of us.

We spent a night in a seedy guesthouse by the train station. The blessed child slept under her mother's watchful wing as the new Grandad lay sleeplessly counting the *cucarachas* crawling across the floor and walls. He was in just as much shock that night as the family on the farm that morning when they had heard the news of the girl's paternity. I who had done my utmost to save and resurrect his life was now being condemned for all my efforts. The fortune-teller had pointed out the obvious: even though the child was a beautiful little blond, in some bizarre way she bore a strong resemblance to El Coco. Initially I denied it, but after some brief torture in his shed, the fat man had confessed to the conception in front of the Bennis, who went berserk on the farm. '*La puta mierda!*'

I managed to hide the baby in a ditch until the storm blew over. Otherwise they would have drowned her in a milk bucket. They gave me about ten slaps each and then threw me into the dung channel in the cowshed. I bit the bullshit and cursed in silence. My father had been sent off to the market with some slaughtered bulls and didn't come back until the afternoon. An hour later we had left La Quinta de Crío, but the heir was alive in my arms and that was all that mattered. In her name we would return and demand what was rightly hers.

But what would happen to Héctor now? Had I now signed his death warrant, as I'd done for my Hartmut Herzfeld, Aaron Hitler and Fräulein Osinga? What kind of a curse was I anyway? Spreading demons and death wherever I went. And hadn't the Sorbian family been massacred because of me as well? A housewife, a cripple and a farmer.

There was a trail of seven bodies behind me.

How the hell had I turned into this? There were no murderers in my family on either side. God had obviously cast me in the role of the jinx.

107

Up, Up, My Soul

1951

In the end my father and I parted ways. He'd had enough of me. No matter how hard we tried, we couldn't live together. He couldn't look at the child without seeing its father. What I had considered a brilliant idea was abhorrent to him.

'It's totally out of the question that I would exploit . . . *that* . . . to secure my future in this land. Herra, I don't understand you . . . How could something like this even have occurred to you?'

'Things like this have happened before,' was the obvious reply, but the only answer he could give was a deadly silent stare.

He would understand this once we had withdrawn our winnings from this little blond lottery ticket, whether it was in a year's time or in ten. In the meantime we'd go our separate ways.

Shortly afterwards I met a gangly boy who became my 'Ur-Jón,' and I moved in with him. Juan Calderón was a Spaniard from head to toe and good at everything except drinking, which was what he devoted most of his time to, however. He worked in a slaughterhouse and tried to provide for his little family, a fellow with elegant fingers and eyes full of loss.

We lived in a corrugated iron shack in La Boca, a Genovese slum close to the harbour. The shanty was also inhabited by cats and mice and stood in the port like an uninvited guest in a courtyard that belonged to a three-storey stone house. I was a housebound mother, since nurseries were still an unknown concept in the Southern Hemisphere in those days, and I killed the time by watching the people from the stone building stroll past my window, heading for the outhouse that stood in the corner of the garden. I could never get away from the feeling that our house was *inside* another one. In the mornings, when the fog chilled me to the marrow and my little one had spent the night waxing lyrical about her earaches and my Calderón was crawling home from one of his binges, bearing the scratches of men's fists and women's nails, I sometimes wandered over to the little mirror that hung on the rotten wall and asked myself whether my grandfather could really be one of the presidents of this world.

I was having trouble breastfeeding and was pointed to a wet nurse who lived in the neighbourhood. Twice a day I would take my little sunshine to her and join the end of the line. There were always another two or three mothers with their babies there. The milk cow, who kept a giant cask of red wine beside her, sat on a wicker chair in the middle of a garden under a shrivelled tree, wearing a perennial smile – a buxom Audumla, the primeval cow from Norse mythology. She sometimes had a baby on both breasts, but generally only one so that she could stretch out for sips of wine with her free arm. The milk squirting out of her must have had a high alcohol content because she was always quite intoxicated. The broad smile never faded from her lips, and she frequently broke into song. I had my worries about this but was assured that few things are better for a baby than a cocktail of mother's milk and wine. At least my little one slept soundly every night during that period. But I could barely stomach the sight of my child sucking the callous wart that had been chewed on by dozens of other babies that week, and I remembered what they said back home: 'One's mother tongue is passed on through the mother's milk.'

I therefore asked them to send me stories and poems from Iceland, which I constantly read into her little ears. No Icelandic child had ever received such an intense literary upbringing straight from the cradle. The first words that came out of her were, 'Up, up!' I had recited the opening of the Passion Psalms to her so often: 'Up, up, my soul and all my heart.'

Even though I was finally living in a metropolis and there was plenty of joy around Ur-Jón and his friends, I treasured my nights. I had found a purpose in life. Calderón could go on as many binges as he wanted, I didn't care. In my daughter, Blómey, I had found the most fun soulmate I'd ever known. The cohabitation between us two women was the best I'd ever experienced. Despite the poverty, cold and hunger and a whole autumn of solitude, I had found some hint of happiness.

108

Café de Flores

1952

Dad rented a room from a German woman who still nourished some hope of victory and secretly idolised Hitler. He shrugged his shoulders with embarrassment when the steel-breasted woman in her floral dress showed me a gramophone record of the Führer's speeches. He later told me that she had offered him a well-paid desk job for a Nazi association in Argentina, but he had turned it down. My father had obviously learned from his participation in the Second World War that it was best to stay away from that lovely crowd. Most of his time was spent working for a blacksmith, and he led a simple life but let me know if he'd met someone famous on the street. Once, when he was walking through the El Palomar district, he saw the presidential couple drive by in a car, and he talked about it for years. 'I looked Juan Perón in the eye.' Even the winter he'd spent in the Russian prison camp hadn't managed to cure him of his leader-induced paralysis syndrome.

Grandad suffered an unexpected heart attack and died in January 1952. Dad travelled home to the funeral, but I stayed behind. I didn't feel up to taking the little girl on such a long voyage. She was the apple of my eye and, by spring, was already chatting to me in Spanish and Icelandic. I could just stare at her for days on end and found it difficult to leave her in the care of Juan's sister, a fourteen-year-old beauty queen, to accompany him to a bar. For the first time, I was truly in love. Of course, I had loved the SS poet, but the love for a child is different from the love for a man. Children don't desert you, cheat on you, or allow themselves to be shot in the back in an open field. You can trust a child.

And the world had never seen a more beautiful child than Blómey Benítez. It was as if the inner beauty of her father had been able to make her in his own image. I did my utmost to dress her up as much as I could when we went out, even though I couldn't even afford a patched dress for myself. When the Italian women in La Boca saw me leading her down the path, they nodded their heads at her, but not at me. She belonged to another world. And in due time she would inherit three hundred hectares of land and three thousand living bulls.

On 1 May, the Perón couple held a huge event in the city centre. People poured onto the streets. Juan and I tried to squeeze our way into the main square with little Blómey in a pushchair in the hope of catching a glimpse of the heroes, but the size of the crowd made it impossible. Instead we sat at on outdoor bar on one of the side streets and drank in the atmosphere, which was unlike anything I had experienced. Even though we were in the heart of winter, the weather was mild, the sun sat in the sky, and joy radiated out of every face, not least those of women, who had their star in the First Lady. A number of things could be said about Eva Perón, but no one could deny that she had fought for a profound change that now enabled Argentinian women to vote for the first time. She moved through the city in an open car and waved to the crowds, stuffed with drugs and concealing a support brace under her coat. The woman was extremely ill and died only three months later, at thirty-three years of age.

Juan's friends had joined us and we had a nice little party there on the pavement. Our child tottered between tables, nibbling at a piece of bread, was given some soda water, and made friends with the owner's kid, a little boy. I had few worries about her. Like most of the streets of the centre, this one had filled with pedestrians and there were no cars about. But as soon as the speeches started in Plaza de Mayo, people moved away from the street to gather in the broad avenues leading to the square. The voice of the first speaker echoed across the rooftops, while down on the street we stayed chatting, laughing and smoking, the young people of Baires.

One of Juan's friends was a yellow-toothed poet with a wry sense of humour who was a great raconteur. I kept an eye on Blómey, who crawled under the next table to stretch out for a leaflet on the pavement. Then she stood up to triumphantly show it to the son of the owner, who had made paper aeroplanes out of other leaflets. I noticed that my girl had a dirty face and called her over to me; someone had given her chocolate. I was about to wipe her face when the boy called out to her and she ran after him. They ran straight across the street: the paper aeroplane lay on the other side. I shouted at Blómey to stay off the street, but Juan told me to relax, there were no cars around. The owner, a portly man with a smiling moustache, stood in the open doorway and had overheard us.

'That's okay, our son was brought up here. He's always careful.'

The name of the establishment stood over him in gilded letters against a green background: CAFÉ DE FLORES.

A cheer suddenly rose from the crowd when the president started to speak. Perón was a powerful orator with a manly voice. My Calderón idolised him, but now as many times before, I got the impression he was trying to contain his admiration. Here, among his cynical friends, it was unbecoming to be a *Perónista*. The poet launched into a bawdy story about Perón. Regardless of whether it was true, exaggerated, or fabricated, it was hilarious. Juan adjusted his beret and leaned back in his chair, red with wine but ill at ease. And all of a sudden he got on my nerves. Everything he said at home vanished here.

Blómey walked over to me and had learned the name of her new toy: *avión de papel*. I managed to wipe her mouth, missing one of the punchlines in the poet's story. Then she found another leaflet and asked me to make another aeroplane for her. Juan took on the task, relieved to be able to sidestep out of the story about the president, and he folded the paper with trembling hands. Then he fired the plane across the street in his tense and unthinking state and I bit my tongue. Blómey chased after it and tried to shoot it back at us, but the plane nosedived to the ground.

Perón finished his speech, and cries of exultation reverberated across the square and gardens. Then it was as if wind started to blow from every corner. It was impossible to describe it, but the neighbourhood, streets and city were electrified with expectation. Someone had turned on the radio in the bar, and a voice mentioned the First Lady's name, which echoed in every mouth all the way out to the pavement. 'She's about to begin.' I looked Juan in the eye and understood that, as usual, he didn't have a dime in his pocket. In irritation and pride I suddenly stood up and said I'd settle the bill and headed to the till at the very back of the café.

I had just reached the counter when I heard a *thud* behind me, when I heard the sound of an engine on the street and that harrowing *thud*. I turned and blacked out for an instant: it took a few moments for the sunny, bright image of the tables, pavement, and street to develop out of the darkness again. And then I saw that in the middle of it there was a car, an American convertible. A man with a bright hat had stepped out of it. I rushed out, saw Juan stoop over something in front of the car, and then saw something that I have replayed in my mind every day since: my daughter lying on the street and the stream from her skull glistening in the sun, her smile vanished. That was the most difficult thing, to see the look on her face, not even two years old, meeting her maker: it was serene, serious, full of reverence. She had vanished into another world.

I pushed Juan away and bent over the child, losing both mind and heart. The poet friend groped her little wrist and shook his head. Juan enveloped me from behind, and the last thing I saw was the bumper of that car. A shiny chrome American bumper. The sun glared against it, and the crowd's shadows stretched along it. On the right of the licence plate I spotted countless tiny drops that sparkled in the sun and looked like hundreds of small islands in a broad fjord. In my panic I tried to find those I knew best and the one where Grandma still lived, but I was dead before I could.

I wasn't reborn until two hours later. To a life different from the ones I'd known before. Life number seven.

109

Visiting Hour

2009

Oh, God rot them all. I'm tired of vegetating in this bed. I'll probably end up leaving this earth on foot, or isn't death always in good shape and free of disease? The elves in the cliffs back home were true athletes and, late at night, went to work spinning cartwheels in the nocturnal meadows of Iceland. Oh and, would you believe it, last night I dreamed of the Führer with his arm in the air, about as tall as a finger, on a rock, on a slip back home in Svefneyjar, yelling at the shore and the seaweed.

Then Lóa comes in to bring me back to reality, and she's dragged my legally registered son along, Prince Potato. Magnús, dear, are you here?

'Yes. How are you?'

Oh, he's here to say goodbye.

'Won't be long now.'

'Huh?'

'Won't be long now.'

'Yes.'

'It's all Hitler's fault.'

'What are you saying?' he asks again. My eyesight is seriously deteriorating. Now elves are lining up by the bed and demanding bottles. What's all the rummaging? Rumba and rum. I need some new music.

'Hitler is to blame for everything. You can blame him for how . . .'

Here came a couple of coughs.

'Oh, oh, hell and bastards, they're all demanding bottles now . . . demanding bottles . . .'

'Mum . . .'

And now many things happen at once, I lose a quarter of my mind, and my Dóra squeezes herself into the garage, greets people, slams a door and starts blabbing: Do I know an Aussie, some guy from Australia, who has been knocking on the door all weekend and now just this morning, big and hulky, a puffed-up troll with arms as thick as legs but a small head and blond hair, and demanding to see Linda, wants to talk to Linda, he's sure she lives here because her computer is here. Wanted to look through all the rooms, searching under the beds like a cop, got on the floor and was sweating profusely. She had to wipe the floor with a dry cloth after he left.

'The sweat was pouring off him. His back was wringing wet.'

'That's Bod.'

'Huh?'

'Tell him Linda has moved.'

'Linda? Who's Linda?'

'The Lady Inside.'

And then it starts to darken in my head again, and my ears fill with snow: I look at my Dóra, her beach tan and pink lips, but can't hear her, just watch her mouth moving, and Lóa, too, as in a silent film. Is my hearing gone? But my Magnús sits there in a state of virtual collapse, reciting a psalm of repentance like a Business Viking on the steps of hell. He conned fifteen hundred people in his name, raised their debts higher than their houses, and then requisitioned their cars.

'You've got to talk to those people,' I say when my hearing finally returns. Still my voice remains under the water but my ears above.

'What?'

'Do you reckon you'll be put away?' I ask, cheeky old thing.

'Away?'

'In jail.'

'No, I . . . I was just an employee.'

'Just a cog in the swindling wheel?'

'Yes.'

'You're a chip off the old block. It's all Hitler's fault.'

'The financial crash?'

'Yes, and that, too.'

Then there's a silence, which is odd because Dóra, that big blabbermouth, is there. 'It was good to see you, Mum,' Magnús finally says.

'Send my regards to Haraldur and Ólafur. Tell them that their mother did her best, but my eighth life wouldn't allow for . . . for more.' And then I had a new coughing fit that almost killed me. But I grabbed hold of myself.

'Just tell them to blame it all on Hitler. He's the Christ of our age and he's still . . .'

I had another coughing fit, but owing to some higher force I survived that one, too. Life was going to grant me another hour. I decided to use it well and started to tell them a story, the story of Dad in the USSR.

110

Hans Bios

1944–1945

Thanks to a fat pig in a Romanian forest, Hans Henrik had become a prisoner of war of the Russian army. The shame was so great that the days that followed never entered his memory; week-long roads, bridges and forest tracks flickered through his mind like a film fed through a projector, while his eyes were glued to the floor of a vehicle, staring at his dirty shoes and seeing Mum's expression in them.

He ended up in some nameless prison camp in a nameless place. Fifteen men slept in the same bed, snuggled up to each other against their own will, like different species of animals, and were woken at four every morning to chop wood until the first days of frost, and after that, sawing. His co-prisoners were all Germans and died at the rate of two a day, collapsing exhausted in the snow and freezing to stone in minutes. But there was a constant flow of 'new' arrivals. My father thought they were all the same men, he saw no difference between those who died on one day and those who came the next. Was he perhaps one of them? He couldn't exclude the possibility that he had died several times and then found life again, as if the camp were a playing field in which life and death challenged each other for the sheer fun of it.

The slaves looked forward to working in the hope of knocking some semblance of heat into their bodies. The food was unbaked dough the size of a fingernail, soaked in freezing water. My father lost a quarter of his stomach and two of his toe tips. But it was still better than being shot in a shitty Romanian village with six thousand lines by Heine in one's head.

I know all this from the letters he wrote me, in his many attempts to make peace with himself and the world and, by writing, to establish a closeness with his only daughter, writings that would have made good material for a biography but that were too implausible to find anyone willing to publish them in the Icelandic republic of silence, where people wanted to read only total or partial lies.

'I didn't utter a word for the whole time,' he wrote to me. *'German was frozen inside me. It was as if Hitler were wreaking his revenge on me by taking away my powers of speech. Some of them even doubted I was one of them. But many prisoners lived in hope and sometimes pricked up their ears at the western wind in the hope of hearing shots from the German army. Instead they got Russian lead in their bodies. It is particularly beautiful to see blood colour the snow. The red colour devours the white until it loses its heat. Then it turns black.'*

His muteness proved useful in the end. At the beginning of the year they combed through the camp in search of reinforcements because the final offensive was approaching. In the Russian books the Icelander had been registered as 'Hans Bios,' and someone was now convinced that this forty-year-old Old Norse specialist wasn't German at all but Estonian. An inner voice encouraged Dad to accept that honour. Three days later he was a free man and sat fully clothed with a Russian rifle over his shoulder in a vehicle of the Red Army along with a bunch of weary recruits. It was not far from the course that he had lumbered on at the German steering wheel three winters earlier, half a war younger, and about twice as optimistic. Yet the fact that he was now wearing another jacket, the enemy's, was not quite as humiliating as he had imagined. Anything was better than felling forests for Stalin, and when it came to the crunch, the uniform in itself was of no importance, we're all brothers in war, we're all enemies in war: surviving it was the only thing that mattered. Dad was now fighting solely for himself. He had to reclaim the small territory he had sacrificed to conquer a world that was now lost.

'*And when you go from Russia to Poland, at least you're heading for Iceland.*'

111

Daughter-of-Pearl

1945

Meanwhile I myself was sitting on the banks of the Oder. Children cried in the darkness and mothers were banging pots. The horses were on the ground, and ahead of us the river flowed from the south to the north, left to right. Slightly further down, a bridge was snorkelling in the water. A torch swayed in the air, reflected in the calm waters of the river, between two half-broken pillars and a semi-submerged bulk of steel. Gunfire resounded in the distance. No one seemed bothered by it. Fatigue had brought us tons of tranquillity. Only those who were hit by the bullets briefly paused in their walks to ponder their fortune or misfortune and then died. The others walked on, unperturbed.

A fortnight must have passed since I'd joined up with these people, German landowners and leaseholders who had ploughed Prussian soil over the centuries and were now trying to save themselves before it became Russian. This had prompted a great parade across the bomb-cratered landscape in the beautiful brown mud and occasional snowfall. The worst part was not knowing where my skin ended and the shoe began. But now our destination was finally within reach. If we could get across the Oder we'd be safe. Hitler would never allow Ivan to cross the river.

It was a beautiful and peaceful war night. We had left a lot of misery behind us, but here hope shimmered in the light of torches. Someone said that February was ending and that March awaited us on the other side of the river. The ground was free of snow and reasonably dry. People settled under the carriages and against the trees and scratched their gun bites. A boy had fallen asleep against the groin of a horse, and bone-weary mothers curled up around their newborn sorrows, the children they had lost yesterday or the day before. Our greybeard had fallen asleep under a horse carriage that had then started to roll; the wheel had stopped against the neck of the old man, who carried on sleeping in his beard. I contemplated his head, recalling all the stories it contained, which he had told us in a corner of smouldering ruins or a warm ditch. A female ancestor of his had been given a pearl necklace by her duke on a trip to Venice before the turn of 1800. This was no ordinary necklace, these were no ordinary pearls, but pearls made of mother-of-pearl that had been kissed by Casanova himself, thus increasing their value. Since then the necklace had been passed down in the family, from throat to throat, land to land, one war to the next, although the pearls had, bit by bit, slipped off the necklace.

'My great-grandmother and -grandfather lost their land in the first Prussian war and bought it back with eighteen of the Italian pearls. Grandma used four of them to survive the Franco-Prussian War. In the First World War my father saved the family by buying a carriage and two horses for twenty pearls from the necklace. In this war we've survived with the remaining few. I paid thirteen for the car journey from Lodz to Warsaw, even though those daughters of Casanova were worth considerably more than that. I paid two to have sixteen people sheltered in the basement of an embassy, four to buy a whole pig, one for a warmer coat for my Anna . . . and so on, see . . .'

He pulled a frayed necklace out of his pockets, which now held only two weary pearls.

'I have two left. Two pearls from the Casanova necklace.'

He looked us firmly in the eye, me and a thirteen-year-old freckled girl, and then slipped the pearls off the necklace, rolled them into his palm. Tiny rainbows appeared on the surface of the grey-white spheres that looked like small hard candies, and those rainbows seemed to have been woven into them like magical patterns made by elves. In the distance, bombs fell from the sky.

'Now I'm giving them to you, one pearl each.'

We protested vigorously, but he was unyielding. Said he'd lost half his family in Russian air raids and didn't give a damn about the other half, felt the historical jewels were better off placed 'in the hands of the future.'

And now I sat here on the banks of the Oder River, gazing out at the water with my hands in my pockets. One held a grenade, the other a pearl.

112

Break from Life

1945

Dad had never seen the war advance at such a speed. The offensive into Poland moved so swiftly that they seemed to be running for days. They were often pushing the front back by as much as sixty miles a day. Battles were almost welcomed for the break they provided from the running. Privates lay in makeshift snowy trenches while the artillery launched its attacks. Dad had a close call in the village of Białystok when he got a piece of a tank's caterpillar track in his helmet. Black smoke puffed across the white field.

The race was on again, in full uniform, with a rifle and bag on his back – but eventually the forty-year-old started to lag behind. He separated from his platoon and for two weeks moved through a wintry green forest along with four limping, wounded colleagues, shooting nothing but fallow deer and hares.

Finally they stepped out of the thick of the pines into a clearing where squadrons had set up camp. Moustachioed officers stood outside greyish-brown tents smoking pipes – the men seemed strangely calm. The carcass of a horse lay on a heap of wet snow. Some men stood shivering around it, chewing on slices of flesh they had cut out of it. Moving in closer, they noticed an increasingly odd odour wafting through the air, the type of odour no human nose had ever smelled before, some kind of burning scent that hovered over the encampment like an invisible fog. Slightly north of them, white smoke smouldered from a pit that was encircled by a group of soldiers, most of whom had their backs turned to the camp: something big was burning there.

Hans Bios and his comrades approached, casting greetings at their brothers in arms, and then let their silence and gazes direct them towards the smouldering ruins. The smell and heat intensified as they drew closer. Through the thick smoke they caught a glimpse of human legs, arms and heads, naked trunks.

A mass grave appeared before them, crammed with bodies, five layers of corpses and crackling flames that gave off an unbearable heat. They couldn't come closer to the grave without covering their faces. The bodies were little more than skin and bone, and pops were heard occasionally in the bonfire, like the bursting of twigs in a fireplace. Bladders or boils, someone explained, with the voice of an experienced traveller through hell. What was going on? Were these German prisoners of war?

'No, people from the camps,' said a black-browed Cossack, clenching a clumsily rolled snow-white cigarette between his red lips. 'Who were over there,' he added, pointing at the ruins of a building, west of the grave.

'Treblinka.'

Dad looked around at the faces of Russian soldiers and their inscrutable expressions. Young boys and fully grown men stood there, entranced, staring into the open heart of the war, the black hole of humanity. My father's gaze fell on the figure of a pregnant woman on the top layer. The skin on her abdomen was smooth and taut in contrast with the shrivelled and scrawny bodies all around it. He stood dead still, staring at her belly, as if he'd lost all self-awareness. It was as if life had abandoned him and death poured into him. His life had reached mid-course and he was therefore now being granted a ten-minute break. He didn't snap out of it until the pregnant bulge succumbed to the heat and burst with the most abhorrent sound.

Through the opening of the gaping womb a fully formed foetus appeared and lived for a blazing red moment before the heat blackened it like a piece of grilled meat.

Dad turned and walked away from the grave, as if in a trance. But couldn't get away from it. The smell haunted him for the rest of his life, and he always associated it with those pines.

'*It was so strange, but I felt an urge to look up at the horizon beyond the green treetops, and all of a sudden I felt guilt towards those trees. We men had left a black stain on the history of the earth and we had defiled those good trees, with this smell and these evil deeds, which no one should ever have laid eyes upon. It was so peculiar, but I was overwhelmed with guilt towards nature.*'

In 1979, Dad was sentenced by the District Court of Reykjavík for chopping down two tall spruce trees on the edge of his garden and forced to pay half a million kronur in damages. Iceland's version of the Nuremberg trials.

113

Every Man for Himself

1945

I sometimes stared at my feet with great interest, astounded by their stamina and perseverance. They seemed to belong to some other inexhaustible person. I called them Nonni and Manni, after the characters in the children's book. Those brothers always stuck together, never letting anything come between them except the mud.

No matter how far we walked, the war always resounded with equal loudness behind us. We'd thought we were fleeing, but now we seemed to be towing the war behind us like a heavy black-smoke-spewing locomotive. The Oder River seemed to have been no obstacle. The signposts promised Berlin on the other side of the next woods, next hill. We slept in barns and abandoned farmhouses. Occasionally we found potatoes in a drawer, a crust of rye bread on a counter, but more often than not we nourished ourselves on tales of lucky fugitives who had stumbled on mansions full of food. On a woman's corpse on the side of the road I found a piece of butter, which I stored inside my clothes; it lasted me a whole week.

The snow melted and the roads were filled with even more refugees: Prussians, Poles and Germans, even Volga Germans and other nationalities. Thousands of people trudged down the muddy paths, passing abandoned tanks and bomb craters full of water, like mute, weary figures out of the Old Testament, the only difference being that no god was observing them from the clouds on high.

Occasionally, trees appeared on the side of the road, standing in long rows, watching us march past towards the sunsets, which were sometimes beautiful but always sad. One morning a single file of Russian children paraded past us, with expressions that seemed to have already viewed their lives from beginning to end. The next day, dozens of Soviet women streamed by, heading east, and we had to step aside and wait for the flow to end. They were on foot, most of them around thirty or older, trudging by with sullen expressions as in a silent film. One of them spat at a German man in our group. Was the war over? Some were pregnant and now carried their German fruit towards their Belarus; ultimately these babies would be the only triumphant invaders of the eastern front, if they weren't drowned at birth.

Greybeard offered me a place on his carriage; I was allowed to dangle my legs from it for a whole two days, until his horse was stolen one night. We found its head in a ditch the next day. Even though he had lost all his family, Greybeard took the animal's death very much to heart and soon lagged behind. I looked over my shoulder and saw him vanish into a group of women enveloped in veils and shawls, his tiny, red-nosed face and greyish-white beard under the immense, sooty sky.

That's how people perish: they get sucked away with their red noses and grey beards into the grey sky.

I joined a group of Poles that day. Villages loitered like beggars by the roadside in the hope of some help. Every house and church seemed to be begging to be uprooted and taken to a better life. But where was there a better life? Someone said that we were all headed for the Führer's bunker, where he awaited us with boiled cabbage and schnapps.

One night we took over an old guesthouse in a deserted village. In the biggest bedroom, there was an immense bed; the heat from a steel stove warmed up the exhausted travellers. I ended up talking to a man who, of all things, turned out to be a Swedish oboe player. His cheeks and nose were sprinkled with sizable warts. He told me his strange story, how he had ended up in this historical context; but he was also willing to help, he said. Then he pulled out some cigarettes and offered me one, lit it for me, and taught me how to smoke. I threw up after the first, coughed through the second, but managed to tolerate the third. A few weeks later I tied the knot with Mr Nicotine, and we've been an item ever since and celebrated our diamond anniversary in the spring of 2005.

'The war is over,' said the warty Swede. 'It'll be finished in a month. The Yanks are crossing the Rhine. They'll meet in Berlin, Stalin and Roosevelt. I know a man there who can help you. He goes under a German name, but he's American, Bill Skewinson. You should look him up. He lives at Bühlstraße 14. If he can't get you to Iceland, no one can.'

Then he led me up to the second floor and lay me on the bed. I soon fell asleep but woke up with his hand under my jumper. 'I can help you,' he whispered in German with a Swedish accent, and then he shouted after me the name of the street in Berlin as I rushed out of the room.

I stuck to a group of women after that. We were all on our own. *Jeder für sich, und Gott gegen alle* – Every man for himself, and God against everyone. The war brought people together to then break them apart. Each day was an entire lifetime. Finally I shook off my fatigue and entered into a trance. The road turned into a conveyor belt, and I felt the forest, houses and signposts were moving towards me and not I towards them.

One day the following happened: Some officers beeped through the crowd, and people stood aside to make way for three uniformed SS men in an open convertible. They stiffly stared into the distance, as if sculpted in stone, until a puny woman threw a dead rat into their back seat; two of them turned, firing their revolvers: two women who had been standing beside the rat woman collapsed on the road, and the car vanished. Two screaming boys pushed the old woman into a ditch and trampled on her until she was swallowed by the mud. We silently passed the bodies. An elderly woman stood by them, staring into the leafless forest with vacant blue eyes. Why was I alive and they not? Why hadn't I been mowed down by some invisible machine gun? Why hadn't I had a sip of wine with the lads seven nights ago? They had found a wine cask in a shed that was full of poison and were now all dead. Was it all pure chance or was there some will behind it?

Nonni and Manni seemed to know the answer, because they pushed me along the path without hesitation. To my left a farm was burning in a blaze of flames and smoke, and through the trees the first birds of spring could be heard.

114

Broken Bridge

1945

They were ferried across the river on a military barge. The past few days were lost in a mist. Dad had crossed half of Poland in his sleep and remained awake at night, staring into the black sky and grey woods, numbed by war and consumed by thousands of burning corpses. He had accidentally plummeted into hell, and finding his way out wouldn't be easy.

We had all been living through years of war and accumulated many atrocities, but these men had actually peeped *below the war* and seen that mankind had written its history out of the books and into the fire, to a place where the beginning and the end resided and the only inhabitants were the devil and God. And man had appalled both. The history of mankind had been made void, and Dad, of all people, had been unlucky enough to stare into that great void. It had been opened to him with the cracking of a bulging womb. He had peered into *the horror*.

But now he was slowly recovering his senses. Now he was beginning to recognise his surroundings. The boat carried them over the tranquil river, a hundred Russian soldiers. He stood watching the bridge, contemplating the ruins, bare pillars and shattered floors, and remembered passing it three years earlier as a 'young' soldier on his way to the east, heading for the highest echelons of the Nordic Studies faculty of the University of Moscow. There were just a few details that had to be dealt with first. And now he was on his way back to Germany on a slow boat marked with a red star. He had ploughed through bloody fields, shot into the eye of war, lost one friend after another, and seen the fire inside Hitler's soul, smelled its stench, the stench of Hitler's ideals and his own, but it wasn't until this moment that he saw the total futility of war.

The World War had achieved nothing, brought nothing. Nothing had been won, nothing gained. Germany was still Germany, and Russia Russia. Between them lay Poland. Tanks had pushed borders to the east and west, but soon everything would fall back into their original positions. Because within a few weeks it would all be over. After years of clashes with guns and steel, everything was to be the same again. All that had happened was that the bridge had broken. The river was the same, the trees the same, the sky the same. Nothing had changed but the bridge. It was broken.

Yes, of course, 50 million lives had been lost. Or was it 70? What's 20 million between friends? Yes, that's 160 Icelands.

Now they were inside Hitler's Germany, and Dad had stopped talking. He said nothing else. His brothers in arms, however, cursed every field and every tree and spat on every stone. On the first night they stayed on a wealthy-looking estate, which the owners hadn't had time to burn, except for the bread in the oven. All the cupboards were full here, the buildings dry, and all the furniture palatially luxurious. Even the stables were more elegant than the hovels back home. All that Teutonic order deeply irritated the Russian soldiers. They stomped through the rooms with their guns in a rage, ripping paintings off the walls and kicking furniture. Their fury reached its peak in the pantry: one of the comrades stormed back into the kitchen, flour white, yelling, 'Why the fuck did they have to invade Russia!? They had everything here!'

He then grabbed a four-pound loaf of rye bread and started beating it against the wall, cursing until the loaf broke and he himself burst into tears, falling on his knees on the red tiles, invoking his mother, wife and daughter.

'*Mamushka, mamushka . . . Dashenka, Dashenka . . .*'

Three hours later they were all full and dead drunk. They congregated in the toilet while Dad sat in the kitchen. They had never seen a water closet, and one of them washed his face in it. How about that! Dad stared into his glass, wondering where his daughter was now. No, she was safe with her mother in Lübeck. They'd had luck on their side. Hadn't the town been liberated? Oh, Massa, oh, Massa. Come to me with your great thighs.

At midnight, two privates appeared, a tall and a short one, clasping two German girls with quivering lips and weeping eyes. They were dragged into the living room and thrown on the table. It all started with the shrieks and cries of the girls but ended in their total silence. Dad didn't know which was worse, but sat through it all staring at his fingers, five and five. His intellectual hands had turned into those of a gladiator. Was he perhaps the first Icelander in eight centuries to have turned into such a . . . murderer? Had he killed a man? Yes, probably in the battle alongside the Dniester, the first one. Suddenly a soldier reentered the kitchen, buttoning up his trousers before he collapsed on a chair by the table full of glasses, shaking his head and muttering to himself.

'*Ne mogu, nikak ne mogu* . . . I can't . . . fuck, I can't . . . that . . . fucking hell . . .' Then he looked at Dad and held out a glass. 'But I can drink! I can drink their fucking schnapps even if I can't screw their women! Fucking, fucking Germany! May it be damned for eternity! *Vypjem!*'

Dad raised his glass.

'You don't say anything, Hans. Have you lost your tongue?'

'What tongue?'

115

Bühlstraße 14

1945

It can undoubtedly be considered a privilege to have been able to walk into Berlin in the spring of 1945 and experience the beauty of its annihilation. And the freedom of despair.

What appeared was the skeleton of a city. Empty eye-sockets, gaping ribs and broken bones. The sun shone through the stone walls that still stood. Entire neighbourhoods had been transformed into heaps of rubble, and the streets were little more than hollow tracks between them. But in the public parks, God continued his tasteless comedy routine by allowing the trees to bloom and flowers to sprout out of the earth and filling them all with chirping birds.

Black-clad creatures scuttled across the streets like rats. We were all in the same boat: searching for food. Dark jets of smoke billowed in the distance, and somewhere the war still hissed like a wounded dragon trapped down a blind alley. On the corner a soldier lay face-down in a fancy uniform, and up against a wall sat a sleeping woman beset with flies. On the third floor a fire waved through a window.

Occasionally one could hear the sound of a collapsing building or an air-raid siren, but no one paid any heed. And somewhere, someone was playing an accordion, that resilient instrument that resounds on the most momentous occasions of European history.

A tank appeared at the corner and crawled down the road like some prehistoric beast, but no one tried to distinguish whether it bore a Nazi cross or a star. An arm protruded from the caterpillar track on its right side and followed the circular tread, up off the street and down again, like a tragicomic flag. We were all, like the city itself, on our last legs, numbed by the carelessness that takes over when prolonged fatigue is drawing to an end. When you've had to struggle to survive every day of your life for so many years and victory is finally in sight, you're suddenly overwhelmed by indifference.

I clambered over crumbled walls, having lost track of those two thousand people I'd encountered on my journey across Poland. And I didn't have a door to knock on, because there were no doors left. But I had more than many others: a plan and travelling funds; the name of an American man; and a rare pearl in my pocket. Maybe I was the richest girl in Berlin.

I asked for directions, slowly approaching the street. The neighbourhood was a mound of debris. A hunched woman was rummaging through the ruins for food and looked up when I asked her. With a cleft lip she answered, 'I think Bühlstraße was there where that building stands,' pointing out over the cluster of stones: a distant flat-roofed house stood in the wreckage like a summerhouse in the countryside. The spring sun shone on this entire tragedy like a housewife who switches on the light in the middle of a late-night party, making it shine with evil intensity on a mayhem of vomit and broken glass: although I welcomed the good weather after the long winter, it irritated me just as much as the darned birdsong. I scrambled towards the building as if I were crossing an Icelandic lava field. It was a classical two-storey building with damaged walls and two pillars in front of the door. In front of its four steps stood a guard in a long coat.

He was a tall German soldier, but obviously one of those dimwits who had been left at home, like that oaf Hans at the Hamburg station. He was sweating out his last days in the war there under the sun; drops trickled down from the shadow cast by his helmet. I asked him whether this was Bühlstraße and he answered yes. Then whether a certain Hauptmann lived here and he said no. The warty Swede had said that the American's code name was Gerhard Hauptmann.

'Does a man called Gerhard Hauptmann live here?'

'No.'

I pondered a moment.

'But an American called Skewinson?'

'No.'

But I could tell the guard was lying, and after some thought I finally dug into my pocket and took out the travelling funds that were supposed to buy my passage to Iceland on the next American ship *home*. Right, I wasn't just some destitute orphan but a girl who was perfectly capable of taking care of herself and paying full fare. I stretched out my open palm and showed the tall soldier the precious Italian pearl from the days of Casanova. Rainbows glistened under the sun; its value remained unchanged. He snatched the pearl out of my hand and slipped it into his mouth, tried to chew it, but then swallowed.

116

A Fresh Beauty

1945

I spent the night on a nearby heap of rubble. My hunt for food yielded nothing to chew on except the guard's stupidity. Should I have treated him to the grenade? No, no doubt he would have gulped it down as effortlessly as the precious pearl – there's no weapon against trollish imbecility of that kind.

I just cried in the dark and twice muttered 'Mum' with quivering lips, out loud. It gave me some comfort to hear someone say that word. The distance answered me with two flashes in the eastern sky, immediately followed by rumbles. I assumed them to be bombs, but it was obviously thunder because it was now starting to rain.

I crawled under a crumbled facade that leaned against the fragment of a wall that was firmly planted in the ground, thus creating a tiny cubbyhole padded with the smell of damp and dust. It was obviously risky to lie under this rubble, the whole thing could still collapse, but out of two bad options it was still better to die than to get drenched. I lay on my side – felt all my bones, how exhausted they were, lying on the stone like overused tools, probably the first premonition of death – and, famished, I stared into the rain-perforated darkness like some obscure animal dressed in a coat. The drops hollowed the stone relentlessly.

Finally, I fell asleep and, to tell the truth, slept remarkably well, so well that I woke up in amazement. When I wriggled out of my hole, only slightly damp on one side, I couldn't immediately remember where I was and experienced a brief moment of bliss before redis-covering that I was registered as a resident in the Second World War. It couldn't have been more than five or six, because the eastern sky was only starting to dawn red, the war was still sleeping, and there wasn't a single bird about.

I leaned on a broken wall to contemplate myself from the distance of a whole lifetime, and behold, there I was, in a dirty coat and dusty 'shoes,' with a tattered red scarf around my neck: a girl in the flower of her youth, four months shy of turning fifteen, with a fickle gaze and lips ripe for life – beautiful and perfectly free, perfectly hungry, perfectly hopeless.

I held one leg straight and the other flexed over a rock; I placed a hand on my knee. It was a classical pose. Like an ancient Greek statue of some beautiful young goddess, except that I was alive and everything around me was made of marble, dead: crumbled houses, mounds of bricks, stone fragments. Even the leaves of the hedges that still protruded from the ashes had turned to rock, and the fly that sat on the broken iron had been carved in stone. Everything was dead and everything was silent. The world was empty and the emptiness was with me. I was a European adolescent at the vernal dawn of life. And so very lucky because this had been the worst spring in history. The legacy of generations had been razed to the ground. Everything that mankind had achieved, built up, and aspired to for a thousand years, *everything that had delivered me into this world*, had been wiped out.

Now everything was open, everything was possible – but fate offered me only one option: I felt that scar in the atmosphere, a scratch in that red dawn that lay between me and what was to be, a long scratch my life *had to* follow, like water that always seeks the next course down. Yes. All of a sudden I was overcome by the deep certainty that this beautiful marble day would lead to my ruin.

I walked back to the building that still stood on Bühlstraße and saw that there was no guard standing there now. I tried the hall door but it was locked. Then I walked around the building and finally sat on some stone, waiting for the sun to bring out its shadow. After about an hour a woman staggered across the ruins and leaned against the steps. The guard violently pushed her away as he appeared out of the building and resumed his position.

I waited another two to three hours, but the giant idiot didn't budge to so much as take a piss. Finally hunger yelled so desperately inside me that I started walking towards 'the city,' to a place where buildings were still standing. In a dilapidated courtyard I spotted several women sitting over a pot. I stared at the group until they signalled me over to chew on some of the strange meat, and I didn't ask whether it was from a dog or a rat.

I thanked them and roamed down a narrow street. Both sides were lined with windowless facades like stage flats. On a dark porch two children were squabbling over a loaf of bread, a struggle that ended when one vomited on the other. Further down the street was a bookstore. The covers and spines of the books were covered in stone dust, making them look like a continuous body of work in a thousand tomes. I grabbed one of them and hid deep in the shop, falling asleep and waking up in a work by Schiller, while tanks rolled down the street.

It was growing dark and my stomach started howling again. But once more, luck was on my side; by some happy accident I stumbled on a rare find in some other ruins: the darkness revealed a glistening white egg to me, unbroken and hard boiled – how was that possible? I ate it in its shell in three bites. Then I spotted a grisly woman crouched over a crumbled fireplace, grinning at me with yellow teeth.

'Are you homeless? Follow me.'

Stepping through the back door, we entered a reasonably intact six-storey building. Most of the other houses on the street were roofless, and one of them was missing some floors. Soldiers sat on the steps outside, smoking in silence, but yelled something at us when they saw us vanish around the corner of the house. Russians, as far as I could make out. In the backyard lay the body of a young boy. Birds had flown away with his eyes. Black smoke bloomed in the next garden, like a beautiful war flower. The woman's name was Birgitte and she was having trouble climbing the stairs, taking just one step at a time and apologising with a snorting smile: 'Russian pain.'

In the corner of a landing, a piece of human excrement collected flies, exuding a stink. We stepped straight into an old yellow kitchen on the third floor, where her mother sat drinking and rejoiced at my arrival. '*Frische Schönheit!* A fresh beauty!' And poured her tufty-haired self a strong one. There was a tooth missing in her grin and no glass in the window frame. The mother and daughter were from Stettin and had once been major pavement beauties over there, but now the older one had virtually turned into a man and the younger one into a boy. They snapped at each other in a dialect I couldn't understand. But then smiled at me and pronounced a toast. I sipped on the firewater and held it down until the meal arrived, the first since I had been hosted by a friendly family in the town of Poznán sometime in that long winter. I threw it all up out of a skylight on the sixth floor. The moonlight illuminated the vomit. I looked out at the dark ruins of the city and listened to its sighs. There was no getting away from it, it was blatantly obvious: the city was breathing its last. No planes could be heard in the sky, and the air was pregnant with a deafening buzz, like the epilogue to some great commotion. In the distance I could hear the faint sound of a church tower collapsing, and someone shouted out a window: '*Der Führer ist tot!* The Führer is dead!' Later that night and the morning after, the Red Army streamed in with shouts of victory and Cossack songs.

I rushed down with bottles and cheese. The mother and daughter had used the apartment on the top floor as a larder and there was no shortage of food or wine. When I came back down to the third floor, some Russians were sitting with the two women and broke into howling when they saw me and the bottles. One of them, a young one with a big nose, pushed me into a corner and exhaled a stench that reminded me of both the nozzle of a cannon and the spout of a bottle. His black hands groped my breasts, and the small wounds on his face started to simmer. Then he said something in Russian and turned to his comrades, who burst into a triumphant, lustful laugh.

The tufty-haired woman filled the glasses and they sat and drank, toasting in all languages and cackling as buildings burned out in the night. I was sent back up to fetch more wine. In the staircase I came across a black-haired woman in a knee-length caftan, standing there as pale as a ghost with half-eaten fingers, asking me with a shattered gaze: 'Have you seen Johan? You haven't seen Johan, have you? He lived here, Johan.' She tried to follow me into the kitchen, but Birgitte's mother pushed her out and slammed the door.

'She's a nutcase. Nobody wants her.'

The eldest in the group was the leader, a slightly plump man with thin lips and thin hair who had obviously claimed Birgitte for himself. She seemed to be fully satisfied with his hand on her thigh. The old woman relished the males' attention, reborn to her former glory and pumping up her cleavage. I was surrounded by wanton eyes. I realised I had been led into a trap. If I had gone to the toilet, one of the men would have followed me.

For men the war was over, but for us women it was only just beginning.

117

Not the Right Face

1945

After I tried to escape, I was locked in the room day and night, with a bucket in the corner, like a caged animal. Two big windows looked onto the street. Occasionally I could hear tanks or troops marching by, or shouts and cries, sometimes a round of gunfire with clatters and gasps.

It was a pretty depressing form of entertainment, and I mostly kept to my bed. Birgitte pushed my ration of food along the floor with the tip of her smallest toe and then locked the door, which connected directly to the landing, on the other side of which was the Stettin ladies' kitchen, the Red Army's community centre. The partying started after noon and stretched into the night. When I was lucky, no one would show up until dinnertime, although there were seldom fewer than three before dawn, sometimes more. The first week was one long night of panting beasts, smelly sons of Volga and older groaning warlords blowing their load on a fifteen-year-old girl. It was all one big inferno, and no one was better than anyone else. I was numbed by the horror and paralysed with fear. I barely slept, and my dreams were a blaze of infernal flames, although I tried to believe in God during the daytime.

I sometimes heard the finger-eaten woman out on the landing. She either called out for her Johan as before or delivered long monologues on the psychology of women that could have been written by Samuel Beckett.

It was better in the dark because at least I couldn't see them. The door opened with a flood of light, and *Der Nächste* would be standing on the threshold, a drunken silhouette who would then close the door and turn into a puffing lump with hands and a hard piece of flesh, uttering the occasional word – '*Dashenka, Dashenka*' – groping his way into me, and finishing it off in a few minutes. If I was lucky he would die on the pillow and sleep a good while, during which time nobody else would come.

One of them fell asleep before even getting his trousers off. His comrades had pushed him in and he came crawling to the bed. He was an elderly bearded man with little hair and he snored like a horse. I tried to make the most of it and snatched his cigarettes. Where did all these men come from? Russia was like an overturned anthill. There were at least ten of them for every German girl. Some of them tried to be friendly and stroked me like a kitten, trying to convince themselves that they were lovers and not rapists, but they turned out to be the worst pigs of them all when it came to the crunch. But this one was too tired to do anything. He woke up later, though, and started to grope and pant in the dark. A curtain fell over my life, and there was a ten-minute intermission. When the curtain rose again and my heart resumed beating, he had gone back to his snoring. I lay with my back against his, curled up like a foetus, and thought of Mum. Mum, Mum, Mum. I remember your trying on those shoes at the embassy in Kalvebod Brygge, Copenhagen, and the time we fell asleep in bed together, listening to the BBC. I sniffed three times but there were no tears left. In its own way, the man's snoring had a soothing effect. There were no more noises from the kitchen, and the building had plunged into a kind of silence. The shift was over for the night.

I finally managed to fall asleep and dreamed of hay in the Svefneyjar islands, sunshine, and rolled-up sleeves.

The Russian soldier stirred in his sleep the next morning. Steel-grey light filtered through the two windows, illuminating the few hairs on the man's shoulders. I felt a strange urge to lightly blow on them, as I lay on the pillow staring at them. The hairs of varying length flickered in the breeze like Icelandic shrubs. Oh, would I ever see anything like that again, see my country again, see ... He turned over on his back and I saw his face.

It wasn't the right face, not the right face at all.

He gave a start, we looked each other in the eye, and our faces assumed the same expression; no father and daughter had ever looked so alike since the beginning of time.

In an instant my life arranged itself into chapters, immovable, cemented chapters, my entire future, like rooms off a giant stairwell. The only thing left to me now was to follow those steps all the way into this garage.

The madwoman could be heard howling. But outside, the birds were singing. The war was over and so was my life.

118

Milk and Champagne

1945

Polished black shoes glisten under the straight hem of equally black trousers. The soles press into the carpet. Are they Grandad's shoes? No, they're that fellow's with the hair. The prime minister, Grandma says. 'Grandad talks to him and then he talks and talks.' The prime minister is one of the Thors brothers from my dad's youth, the very ones who tried to drag him away from my mother and thus prevent me from being conceived. I'm wearing a flared white dress with a fine yellow-and-green floral pattern, and I waddle between the auks that stand in clusters of three in the living room of Bessastadir, as the sun is about to set, toasting together and laughing, with black tails and white breasts, Icelandic post-war males. Some have their wives standing beside them, with their hair done up, wearing gloves and long dresses, many of them trailing trains. The women's faces are powdered white and their lips and eyes are heavily painted. They all look like marble statues because none of them says a word, none of them move their lips towards a word or a smile.

But there is one exception: out by the window stands the famous Lone Bang in a simple black dress with her hair done up and high cheekbones, chiselled features and looking swell, with a radiant smile, surrounded by admirers and nodding. 'No, in London,' I

hear her say in Icelandic. 'Yes, for the entire war. I couldn't travel anywhere!' Her accent is both polished and pronounced.

The head of protocol bangs on a glass and opens the door to the dining room. Grandma and Grandad, the president and First Lady of Iceland, greet their guests at the threshold. The summer light shining through the French windows glistens on Grandad's glasses. Behind them stands a long dining table with standing napkins, set for thirty people. Every plate carries a name-tag written in ornate letters. I find 'Miss Herbjörg María Björnsson' between the names of two gentlemen close to one end of the table, the one closest to the kitchen. There is a glass of milk beside the plate, the only one on the table.

A tall man with an elongated face appears to my left, greets me with an amiable smile, and positions himself behind his chair. I misread his name on the plate: 'Mr Jóhann Fortuneson, wholesaler.' His wife, a tawny figure with film-star looks, stands opposite him with blazing red lips and a fur scarf draped over her shoulders and nods. A thin-haired, portly man takes his place opposite me, one of those jovial, country types whom Iceland never seems to run short of, and who all bear the name of Gudmundur. He's blazing crimson in the face, as if his collar were strangling him, with his puffed-up chest, as if a decade-old belch were trapped inside him. Trembling to his right is a pale lady wearing a traditional Icelandic costume. Her grizzled husband, with a bulging drawer-shaped chin, stands to the right: Mr Pétur Knudsen, permanent secretary of state.

As soon as Grandad and Grandma sit down at the table, everyone takes a seat and the chatter begins. Silence falls again when the prime minister stands.

'It is a great honour for us to be here in Bessastadir this evening. Through their cordiality and hospitality, the president and his wife have demonstrated to us . . .' As he continues his speech, I stare at the red-hued star on the other side of the table. Her skin is incredibly pure, thick and white, and bulges slightly in places as a result of the tight, stiff dress. Her face radiates health and good care. I've never seen a woman like this before. For some reason the term *geothermal water heating* springs to mind, words I learned only last week. Then I look down the table. Faces stare solemnly into space during the speech, with slightly downcast expressions, as if they could see beyond this silk-laced moment into the fate of our small nation. Grandma sits five plates away from me and bats her eyelids to the words of the orator standing beside her, who delivers his speech without any notes, with radiant dignity, with one thumb dug into the sleeve of his waistcoat, which makes him look like a vigorous alpinist, standing freshly awoken in front of a mountain cabin, adjusting the chest straps on his backpack. A snow-white tuft of hair stands upright on his head, conveying the impression that men of this kind are either geniuses or lunatics. 'We Icelanders have the deepest respect for the office of the president because it is the greatest honour we can bestow . . .' Grandad takes the praise with a suffering air.

At the end of the speech, Elín, the soft-cheeked but heartless maid, storms into the room with three colleagues with the starter: smoked trout on northern flatbread. I'm still unused to cutlery and grab the whole slice with my hand, bite into it, and then take a big sip of milk. The film star closes her eyes and offers me a forbearing smile. The chatter starts again and Mr Fortuneson talks over my head.

'Pétur, have you heard anything more from Dawson?'

I turn to the permanent secretary of state and have another sip of milk as I watch the answer flow out of his drawer.

'Yes, as a matter of fact. It's all looking pretty good.'

I feel the blood beginning to boil in my neighbour's veins, and his good wife's teeth sparkle as she smiles. She joins in with some flatbread on her fork.

'Oh, Mr Knudsen. You and your wife really must come visit us at our summerhouse east in Thingvellir before the autumn sets in. You're very welcome!'

Mrs Knudsen stretches out her chin and nods slightly with the hint of a mute smile. The Gudmundur across from me breaks into the conversation: 'Yes, were you applying for a licence, an import licence?'

'Yes, for American cars. *Chèvre au lait*,' says Mrs Fortuneson ecstatically, making the American car maker sound like a fancy French hors d'oeuvre.

'Yes, not just Chevrolets, but also Chryslers and Fords,' Mr Fortuneson explains. 'Soon we'll be able to start importing American cars on a proper scale.'

'Just imagine,' says the wife.

'Yes, it's a whole new country that lies ahead of us,' says Mrs Knudsen with a nodding head and northern accent. 'Who would have thought the war would bring us so much prosperity?'

'Yes, this was the best war,' says the thin-haired countryman, raising his glass. 'Let's toast to that. Cheers to the war!'

The Knudsens and the Fortunesons laugh at this joke, which seems far from a joke, however, and they raise their glasses. I notice that my glass has also been filled by accident, and I grab it without a second thought, clinking it against theirs and swallowing a giant gulp. I haven't tasted a fizzy drink since Miss Denmark offered me Coke at the beginning of the war, and I feel a headache developing within seconds.

'Pity the war didn't last longer. We could have made even more money!' the Gudmundur adds, triggering a chorus of polite laughter.

The ginger lady puts down her glass and stares at it with bewilderment as she asks, 'What's this white wine called? It's a bit different from the wines one knows, don't you find?'

The permanent secretary's wife puffs up her lips and leans over with some fine wrinkles around her mouth and nose to say, 'It's champagne.'

It doesn't seem to mix well with milk.

The main course comes in coated with sauce: mountain leg of lamb with garden potatoes, rhubarb jam, and red cabbage. The adults are given red wine. I have no appetite and think of Dad, who is still hidden on the top floor, locked in a room, like a freak in a cage. Down here it's all rustling silk and clanging silver, the old lady asks where one can get nylon stockings, and the tawny one answers 'my Jóhann' knows a man at 'the base.' All of a sudden I remember the finger-eaten woman on the staircase in Berlin. I accidentally have another sip of champagne and now feel queasy. Grandma stands up, puts down her big white napkin, and says a few words in Icelandic.

'Thank you all for being with us this evening. This food has travelled a long way, and many have helped to make it good for us. And then there's Icelandic skyr for desert.'

The old woman smiles slightly at her last line, generating mild laughter from the guests. Then she adds chirpily, 'But please let the girls know if you want more. There's plenty more in the kitchen!'

'No, there's nothing left,' Elín shouts from the centre of the room, holding a silver tray up to her waist.

Someone titters, and the Gudmundur has a coughing fit, growing even redder in the face, almost purple, his eyes bulging as he sticks two fingers into his collar.

'Thank you for that, Elín,' Grandma answers with a glare. The wholesaler beside me pulls out a silver cigarette case and offers people beautiful white Lucky Strikes. I look at them with longing eyes, but only his wife accepts. He lights her cigarette and then his own, while the thickset man opposite me lifts his glass of red wine and starts a new conversation.

'Where do you think the old man got his hands on all this red wine?'

'He obviously got it in his years as governor.'

'Yes, this vintage must be from 'thirty-nine, 'forty, because someone said this was French wine.'

'Did all wine production stop during the war?'

'It wasn't that bad, but exports virtually stopped from Europe.'

'Were things that bad on the Continent?'

436

Their words fuse with the shiny silk and chiffon, flickering candles and long gloves, resounding song and clinking plates, tobacco smoke and agitated waiters, paintings in golden frames, champagne milk in my stomach. The nausea is unbearable now. Suddenly the wholesaler turns to me and asks me in a smoke-spewing voice: 'And what about you, young lady, where were you during the war?'

'I? I . . . was . . . in . . . in Denmark and Germany.'

'Yes, that's right, isn't it?' a woman said.

'Yes,' I say, staring at the red mark her lips have left on the yellow filter. For some inexplicable reason it disgusts me.

'And how . . . how was the war there?'

Now I erupt like Haukadalur's Geysir. The jet gushes out of me in one big burst of vomit. The cascade lands on the table, toppling an empty glass and ending close to the film star's plate. A tiny drop ends up on her empty dish. Thirty heads are silenced and turn towards me. The last thing I see is the light brown spew surrounding the crystal foot of the champagne glass that rises from the sludge like a brave statue. At its base the bubbles effortlessly climb the stem like balloons released to the heavens at an outdoor celebration. I observe it as if I were a bird, from the height of the sky. From a distance this celebration looks quite minuscule.

119

8 December

2009

It doesn't look as if I'll make it to the fourteenth. How pathetic is that? The elves are constantly demanding new bottles. They demand bottles and continue their jumping around the cliffs, doing endless somersaults in their grassy green shoes. Oh, what could the country ask for, now that everything is lost? But give me my drugs, Lóa, dear, I'll take them with me to the other side. Where is my egg, my Führer's Fabergé egg? A picture of him hung on the kitchen wall in Amrum. Frau Baum was her name, the brooming bitch. Is this my last day on earth?

'Do you mean this here?'

'Yes, bring it over. Do you know what this is? That's a hand grenade. Maybe you could get my departure announced on the radio. Oh, you better ring my Magnús all the same.'

'He's here. He's here beside you.'

'Yes? And the little woman as well?'

'Yes, Sana is here, too, and . . .'

'Shouldn't we take that . . . that *hand grenade* from her?'

'Oh, my fortune. Grandma did fourteen fishing seasons . . .'

'Does it still work?'

'Mum?'

'Or was it seventeen? Seventeen probably.'

'She's just . . . this happens sometimes. But then she generally drifts back, you know.'

'But I had thirteen lives. Thirteen lives and one existence.'

Bob insisted on seeing Michelangelo's grave, so we went to Santa Croce, he's buried there with Galileo and Machiavelli, in these sumptuous tombs, and then he wanted to go to his house, oh, sweet thing. Where are you now, Bobby, dear? And always so cheerful . . . cheerful and cheerful, fine and fine . . . Darkness, darkness, now you're descending on me, and the funnel draws closer and closer, or is the boat being rowed? I hear the oars. But the sun followed us down the road like in a de Chirico painting. Yes, miserable century, you were . . . is that the funnel? Rusty, like a . . . like a Polish shipyard. We ran down Via dei Pepi like two silly tourists, what a sight, and turned the corner but didn't make it, the house closed at five on the dot, we reached the locked door, number 70, I think . . . Is that Dóra? The lovely Dóra? My hotel manager, bless her soul.

'A thousand four hundred liras a night, she says.'

'Huh?'

'A thousand four hundred liras, with made beds and a sink.'

'Mum . . .'

Oh, he gave me a ring on the landing that night, bought on the Old Bridge, the Ponte Vecchio, where Leonardo used to buy birds, oh, help me up, I want to piss, I need to piss, I want to end this life with a piss, I definitely want TO PISS.

'Up, up, I'm bursting.'

'Here, let me help you.'

'Via, Via Dolorosa . . . where is the light and where is mimosa? When does it close?'

'Huh? What did you say? Here, that's it, yes.'

'When do they close? We have to get there before five. Before five.'

'It's seven thirty now.'

'When does the toilet close?'

439

'The toilet? Ha-ha. That's always open.'

'He lives in Via Ghibellina, number seventy.'

'Huh? Who?'

'It says "Buonarroti" on the bell. I need to piss.'

'Yes, I'll help you.'

'Is that the line?'

'No, no, they . . . they don't need to go . . . These are your people.'

'All those people? To watch me pee? I'm no Ava Gardner.'

'Magnús is here, and Sana and Dóra, too, and then your son Haraldur and Thórdís Alva. And their daughter, Gudrún Marsibil, she just arrived . . .'

'Hi, Gran.'

'Hi, Mum.'

'Yes, he's certainly popular.'

'Huh? Who?'

'Death. A real crowd puller. And sold out every time it . . . No, keep it open.'

'No, shouldn't I close it?'

'No, keep it open. Let people see. Since they've come all this way. Did you get their numbers?'

'Sorry?'

'Get their numbers, ah, that's good . . . Yeah, get their numbers and invite them for the cream . . . cremation.'

'How are you feeling, Mum?'

'I'm peeing.'

'Shouldn't we let her pee in peace?'

'Did you say Gudrún Marsibil?'

'Yes, she's here.'

'Blessed sweetheart. Didn't you go off swim training to . . . where was it? Brisbane?'

'Yes! Hi, Granny. Good to see you. You . . .'

'Isn't that on the eastern coast?'

'Yes!'

'On the Pacific?'

'Yes.'

'Those were nice pics of you on . . . that New Zealand trip.'

'Huh? Did you see them?'

'Aren't they a little bit too big on you, your breasts, for swimming?'

'Huh?'

'He wasn't at home when we got there.'

'Who?'

'He lives in Via Ghibellina, number seventy. It says "Buonarroti" on the be . . . Lóa, remember to collect my ashes from the crematorium. It all has to be destroyed, everything thrown away. I don't want anything . . . to remain, not a single grain of dust. I really like the Philip guy.'

'Phi . . . you mean?'

'Is he from Brisbane? He reminds me of my Bob. He knew Michelangelo. They were at school together. Lóa, dear, help me up.'

'Yes, sorry.'

'If she hadn't spoken, she wouldn't have died.'

'Huh?'

'If she hadn't spoken, my little one wouldn't have died. But I know nothing about the Crocodile, what became of him.'

'What are you talking about, Mum?'

'She wouldn't have died, Blómey, my flower. Maybe you could put some flowers on her grave, Lóa.'

'Huh?'

'Maybe you could put some flowers on her grave. She's in the Chacarita Cemetery.'

Oh, now I'm staggering back to my bed before a throng of fans. No pictures, please! And isn't my Gudjón here, too? They look like his feet but I can't turn my head because of the pain in my chest. And the funnel approaches, looking so terribly rusty in the shadows, like a Polish shipyard. Polish shipyard. I hear the gurgle of oars.

'Why have you all come here?'

'Because we thought . . .'

'That I was about to die? Right, then, I'll give it a try. Try to do that for you.'

'No, Mum, no, I meant . . .'

'But I wasn't supposed to go until the fourteenth, what date is it today?'

'The eighth. Eighth of December.'

'Yes? It's Peace-Jón's day. Where's the egg? I need the egg. I have to take it with me.'

Oh, how awful it is to be alive. I allow her to fold me and put me under the quilt and then my sight grows misty. It'll be good to die. To finally be free of these lungs. Is that the laptop? No, I'll leave that behind, but the egg I'll take with me, and the drugs, the drugs. Yes, if she hadn't spoken, that blasted Evita, the streets wouldn't have emptied and my little sweetheart would still be alive. I've always carried the presidential curse. I was a presidential slut, Bæring was right. But I hope he isn't waiting for me on the other side in his blue jumper with rum and roses. One should be allowed to enjoy some peace after death, after presenting one's death certificate. I'd rather have Bob and all his plans. With him I could get an audience with the devil right away tomorrow morning. We'd walk along the carpet and kneel together like two tiny children of hell. And the Master raises his blazing finger and says, '*Velbekomme*,' in Danish. Yes, yes. Satan speaks Danish. But obviously has an interpreter. He has an interpreter. And then I want to carry it with me, my father's heart, locked between my clasped hands, they try to free it. Our Father who art in Heaven . . .

'I don't like the look of that.'

'Is that a real grenade? Is it live?'

'I don't know. Can't we take it from her? Try again.'

'I can't remove it. It's totally stuck.'

'Mum! You have to . . .'

'I don't like the look of this.'

'She's clutching it so tight.'

'Haraldur, let's go.'

'Has she had this for long?'

'Her whole life, she says. But I never realised that it was . . .'

'Maybe I'll meet the Half Hitler . . . in the Lord's court . . .'

'Herra, dear? Herra?'

'Maybe he's a court jester, whole and handsome again?'

'She's gone.'

'God Almighty.'

'Can you get me a certificate?'

'Huh?'

'Lóa, dear, a death certificate. Can you get me a death certificate?'

'But maybe it's okay, then, since she's had it for so long?'

'I don't know. It could still explode. See how she's clutching it.'

Oh, oh, hold your sailor tight and then go to the ball, my dear island girl.

'Mum, dearest, goodbye. Can I kiss you goodbye?'

Rain is pouring out of his eyes, wetting my old cheeks. I never knew his soul, and he never got any affection from me either. Life is too late, too late, now the abyss has opened and my son's tears trickle down his mother's weary path and how risible it is, but metal is good, to feel the metal of war is good, oh, his royal shyness, I live and now I die, I die like any other Arctic tern, no, look, now I'm sailing into the giant funnel of time, and look, there's a sign saying SORTIE in French . . . They're standing there with torches, the German soldiers, their flames reflected in the sewage . . .

'Mum. Mummy, dear.'

. . . yes, and Eysteinn and Lína sit there happily, stroking their beards and smiling at the candle, they are mine, I had a weekly father and a monthly mother, and oh, a good old folk song echoes behind them, sung down a long dark corridor, it's 'Blessed Be My Countryside,' and down there is twilight in a cup, with a coat of mould on it and whey in the window, streams in my chest, ooze with trickle, trickle with ooze, yes, wait, my dear mother, with the good barrel, God's barrel with Satan's whale meat, I slip into the bench and I look at the mainland mountains through the island windows and I mourn Iceland, because I never had anything but that, but the word, never the land, we all live on islands, yes, and nothing between us but the sea, that cursed sea, now the current of the funnel sucks my boat, I'm going swiftly now and what . . . it's raining more now and the troll of tears sends me a kiss from the dark heavens and a shower of tears floods my cheeks and lips, tasting of salt, yes, tasting of salt, my salty son, now I'm sucked in, *à dieu* . . .

120

Clasped Hands

2009

My eyes remained open even though they had been closed. Through my eyelids I could see everything that was to be seen and more. I had become all-seeing and all-knowing.

They sat around me and kissed my cooling cheeks, each in turn, and drew a cross over my body like slightly daft children, until Dóra invited them all into the house and put some coffee on. Then they called a priest and a doctor, who both discharged me in their own ways.

'Her taxi is here,' said Dóra on the kitchen threshold at midnight, slipping into her shoes, as the ambulance pulled into the driveway. Two members of Reykjavík's emergency response team tried to pry the Hitler egg out of my clasped hands without success and then saw the scar etched on my right arm. This didn't look good. An old woman is found dead in a garage, clutching a German hand grenade from World War II and sporting a swastika mark on her arm. It was like the opening to some third-rate crime novel.

They carried my body out into the blizzard and travelled cautiously down the deserted streets. They drove slowly over glistening-wet speed bumps, which I'd never noticed before but which are now to be found at every crossroads. It was a short distance to the morgue in Fossvogur. There my remains were put aside pending further examination.

Lóa kept her promise and demanded a cremation. And the reservation proved useful, Monday, 14 December at 1:30. In the morning an emergency team was summoned from the National University Hospital: a man and woman with a saw. Thus, I slid into a thousand degrees minus my hands and burned there for about half an hour. My phantom wrists still ache.

The clasped hands were handed over to the Coast Guards' explosives division. A few days later, in a pre-Christmas mist, my father's heart was blown up with dynamite in a sand ditch by Lake Raudavatn and thus delivered to God by my own two hands.

ACKNOWLEDGEMENTS

First and foremost, I thank the god of events, the one who brought Oddný Sturludóttir into my life and led her to politics, so that I would aid her in her 2006 election campaign: Here I was handed a list of phone numbers of all the residents of one random street in Reykjavík and told to call them and ask them to vote for the Social Democratic Party. The third person I phoned turned out to be an old lady living in a garage, Brynhildur Georgía Björnsson, and it was she who would become my great inspiration for this novel. I never met her in person (sadly she passed away a year later), but her brainy wit kept me on the phone for an astonishing forty minutes. After hanging up, I honestly asked myself why this woman was not a household name in Iceland.

I thank her, this woman at 1000 feet, in the sky above, and hope she is not too angry about all these words she inspired. (Although I did get a call from the south coast of Iceland, shortly after the book's Icelandic publication, in which a rough-sounding sailor told me that the old lady had appeared to him in a session with a medium, and that she was 'not amused.')

I thank my Icelandic editor, Guðrún Sigfúsdóttir, for her good influence. Her point of view, quite often being very different from mine, was crucial to this story, and her hardest punches usually resulted in good chapters. I also thank my Icelandic publisher, Jóhann Páll Valdimarsson, for his belief and faith – and relentless optimism.

As Guðrún and Jóhann Páll happen to be a couple, I also thank their union, for they were the ones who early in 2009, when I – broken and beaten by my sudden divorce from the politician, and angry and confused by the political collapse of Iceland (all this happened in the same week) – invited me out to their summer house, cooked me dinner and put me to bed, only to wake me up with a wonderful walk and a yet more wonderful question: What will be your next book? I told them about the two ideas I was considering and they voted for the latter one, the story about the old lady in the garage.

I also thank my oldest friend, editor and publisher Páll Valsson, who has read all my books before publication. Valsson is every writer's dream, an editor who always knows better than the author himself what he's up to.

My dearest Agla also gets her share of acknowledgement, the woman of all my degrees, the one I met, so to speak, on the first page of the book, and became a part of the whole project, reading versions, asking questions, and helping with details from a female perspective.

I am grateful to my good translator, Brian Fitzgibbon of Dublin, Ireland, who for decades has lived in Iceland and is always open to my suggestions.

For the long-fought publication of my novel in English I first thank my French publisher, Frederique Polet, at Presses de la Cité. It was her enthusiasm that brought the book to the attention of agent Molly Friedrich in New York. Soon after, on a cold and dark night in November 2014, when I was standing in front of the parliament building in Reykjavík, part of yet another protest, my phone rang and this bright and energetic American voice said 'Hi!' It even managed to cut through all the heavy drumming and shouting, as every agent's voice should do.

Many e-mails later, which all started with that same upbeat and very American 'Hi!', and with the crucial cooperation of Andrew Nurnberg, we found ourselves in the arms of Algonquin Books in the US and Oneworld Publications in the UK. I cannot thank dearest Molly Friedrich and Andrew Nurnberg enough, nor their people, Nichole LeFebvre and Ellen Gomory in NYC, and Eleonoora Kirk and Charlotte Seymour in London. All their reading, understanding and bottomless belief has proved to be priceless. I also thank master translator David McDuff for his contribution. Early on he translated the sample chapters of the book but was unable to carry on for health-related reasons.

I also thank my agent in London, Andrew Nurnberg, and all his people, who have managed to bring this book from a Reykjavík garage to territories as diverse as Albania and Argentina.

For the English version the story was re-edited, and here my *Woman at 1,000 Degrees* was lucky to land in the hands of a clever Scottish woman in Brooklyn, the wonderful Helen Rogan. Her deep insights were combined with the most sensitive touch. Like with the best of surgeons, her cuts required no anaesthesia for the trembling author, and all her subtle suggestions for clarifications and improvements proved to be spot on.

I am grateful to Juliet Mabey and Alyson Coombes at Oneworld for the cooperation and for betting on my strange book. Vimbai Shire also gets her share of thanks, for the final reading of the text.

Last but not least I thank you, dear reader, for coming this far. Without your support the writer is just a tree falling in the forest.

Oneworld, Many Voices

Bringing you exceptional writing
from around the world

The Unit by Ninni Holmqvist (Swedish)
Translated by Marlaine Delargy

Twice Born by Margaret Mazzantini (Italian)
Translated by Ann Gagliardi

Things We Left Unsaid by Zoya Pirzad (Persian)
Translated by Franklin Lewis

The Space Between Us by Zoya Pirzad (Persian)
Translated by Amy Motlagh

The Hen Who Dreamed She Could Fly by Sun-mi Hwang
(Korean) Translated by Chi-Young Kim

The Hilltop by Assaf Gavron (Hebrew)
Translated by Steven Cohen

Morning Sea by Margaret Mazzantini (Italian)
Translated by Ann Gagliardi

A Perfect Crime by A Yi (Chinese)
Translated by Anna Holmwood

The Meursault Investigation by Kamel Daoud (French)
Translated by John Cullen

Minus Me by Ingelin Røssland (YA) (Norwegian)
Translated by Deborah Dawkin

Laurus by Eugene Vodolazkin (Russian)
Translated by Lisa C. Hayden

Masha Regina by Vadim Levental (Russian)
Translated by Lisa C. Hayden
